Ruthless Vows

Also by Rebecca Ross

LETTERS OF ENCHANTMENT

Divine Rivals

THE QUEEN'S RISING DUOLOGY

The Queen's Rising

The Queen's Resistance

Sisters of Sword & Song

Dreams Lie Beneath

ELEMENTS OF CADENCE DUOLOGY

A River Enchanted

A Fire Endless

Ruthless Vows

A Novel

Rebecca Ross

W

WEDNESDAY BOOKS

NEW YORK

First published in the United States by Wednesday Books,
an imprint of St. Martin's Publishing Group

RUTHLESS VOWS. Copyright © 2023 by Rebecca Ross LLC. All rights reserved.
Printed in the United States of America. For information, address
St. Martin's Publishing Group, 120 Broadway, New York, NY 10271.

www.wednesdaybooks.com

Library of Congress Cataloging-in-Publication Data

Names: Ross, Rebecca (Rebecca J.), author. | Ross, Rebecca (Rebecca J.)
    Divine rivals.
Title: Ruthless vows : a novel / Rebecca Ross.
Description: First edition. | New York : Wednesday Books, 2023. | Series: Letters of
    enchantment ; 2 | Audience: Ages 13–18.
Identifiers: LCCN 2023040788 | ISBN 9781250857453 (hardcover)
    ISBN 9781250857460 (ebook)
Subjects: CYAC: Fantasy. | Letter writing—Fiction. | War—Fiction. | Magic—
    Fiction. | LCGFT: Fantasy fiction. | Novels.
Classification: LCC PZ7.1.R728 Ru 2023 | DDC [Fic]—dc23
LC record available at https://lccn.loc.gov/2023040788

Our books may be purchased in bulk for promotional, educational, or business use.
Please contact your local bookseller or the Macmillan Corporate and
Premium Sales Department at 1-800-221-7945, extension 5442,
or by email at MacmillanSpecialMarkets@macmillan.com.

First Edition: 2023

10 9 8 7 6 5 4 3 2 1

For anyone who sought a different realm through a wardrobe door,
Who wrote a letter and is still waiting for a reply,
Or who dreams of stories and bleeds words

Contents

PART THREE: *Wings in a Cage*

PART FOUR: *A Crescendo for Dreams*

Past the near meadows, over the still stream,
Up the hill-side; and now 'tis buried deep
In the next valley-glades:
Was it a vision, or a waking dream?
Fled is that music:—Do I wake or sleep?

—John Keats, "Ode to a Nightingale"

ENVA

There was never any doubt in her mind, even after all these dust-streaked mortal years, that Dacre would one day come for her. Enva knew her music would only hold him in his grave for so long. It didn't matter how much she had sacrificed to sing it; the twisted spell she had sung over him would eventually fade in power.

She had strummed the lullaby for the entire turning of a year, from spring to summer, when gray storms turned the world green and soft. And then from summer to autumn, when the trees turned umber and gold, and rime cast a cloak over the dying grass. From autumn to winter, when mountains grew fangs of ice and the air was brittle, and then to spring once again.

It was enough to hold her former lover beneath the loam for centuries by mortal reckoning, and she had reassured the human king at the time. As for the other three divines . . . Alva, Mir, and Luz . . . Enva had never been worried about their waking.

But all good things eventually came to an end. And all songs had a final verse.

Dacre would wake, and she would be waiting for him.

Enva curled her long fingers into a fist at her side, feeling the ache in her swollen knuckles. She had known her spell would end, but what she *hadn't* anticipated was the cost of swallowing so much power.

Momentarily lost to the past, Enva stood in a shadow on Broad Street, watching people hurry along their way, oblivious to her presence. But she was often overlooked, as was her preference. She could melt into a crowd of mortals like she had been born among them, with flesh doomed to bleed and decay, with a spirit that was like a candle flame, flickering and incandescent. Burning brilliant in the darkness.

She waited a few more moments for the sun to set. Only then did she step forward into the dusk and cross the street, her eyes on a particular café. She was almost certain she had been here before, long, long ago. Before this city had risen from a crosshatching of cobblestones. Before the buildings had been made of tall, steel skeletons.

She could *almost* remember this place if she let her memories fall back in time. If she dared to relive the era when she had dwelled with Dacre below. When she could have drowned in such lonely shadows, waking in his bed, longing for the sky.

He had put her in a gilded cage, but she had slipped away from his grasping hands.

Enva reached the café's threshold. It was closed for the night, but locks had never stopped her before, and she stepped into the building and studied her surroundings. Yes, she had been here once, but this place had been vastly different then. She had the strange feeling that while everything around her had changed and evolved like the seasons, she had not. She was the same as she had been centuries ago, drawn from very old wind and cold constellations.

But she was not here to fall prey to what had been.

Enva narrowed her sight and stepped forward, searching for the door.

PART ONE

The Magic Still Gathers

1

A Grave Encounter

Spring had at last found the city of Oath, but even the flood of sunshine couldn't melt the frost in Iris Winnow's bones. She knew someone was following her as she walked through the bustle of Broad Street, over tram tracks and scuffed cobblestones. She resisted the temptation to glance behind, instead forcing her hands into the pockets of her trench coat as she stepped over a row of weeds blooming from the pavement cracks.

The coat was only three days old and still smelled like the store Iris had bought it from—a hint of rose perfume and complimentary black tea and polished leather brogues—and the days were becoming too warm to truly need it on her walks to and from work. But she found that she liked to have the coat belted at her waist, as if it were armor.

She shivered as she wove through a crowd gathered at a bakery door, hoping the person on her trail would lose sight of her in the tumult of people purchasing their morning buns. She wondered if it was Forest following her. The image instantly made her feel better, and then profoundly worse. He had done such a thing before, back in Avalon Bluff. In fact, he had been watching her for *days*, waiting for the right moment to appear, and it still made her feel ill to remember.

Iris couldn't resist a moment longer. She cast a glance over her shoulder, the wind pulling a few tendrils of hair across her face.

There was no sight of her older brother, but then again he was no longer the swift-laughing, affectionate person he had been before he enlisted for Enva's cause. No, the war had left its marks on him, had taught him how to maneuver in the trenches and fire a gun and sneak across dead man's zone into enemy territory. The war had deeply wounded him. And if Forest was following her this morning, then it meant he still doubted her.

He continued to believe she would run, leaving him and Oath behind without a word of farewell.

I want you to trust me, Forest.

Iris swallowed and hurried on her way. She passed the building she had once worked in, where the *Oath Gazette* sat alight on the fifth floor, the place where she had first met Roman and thought him an arrogant upper-class snob. The place where her words had first found their place in the newspaper, where she had discovered the thrill of reporting.

Iris walked past those heavy glass doors, tracing the ring on her fourth finger. She turned onto a quieter side street, listening for the sound of footfalls behind her. There was too much din from the tram bells and the hawkers on street corners, though, and she dared to take a shortcut through an alley.

It was a strange, haphazard path that most vehicles couldn't navigate without knocking a side mirror loose. A cobbled street where magic could still be felt when passing over certain thresholds or glancing at the shine of windows or stepping through a shadow that never faded, no matter how brilliant the sun burned overhead.

But Iris paused when she saw words painted in bold red paint on a white brick wall.

Gods belong in their graves.

It wasn't the first time she had come across that statement. Last week, she had seen it painted on the side of a cathedral and on the library doors. The words were always in red, bright as blood, and often followed by a single name: *Enva.*

No one had seen the goddess in weeks. She no longer sang people to war, inspiring them to enlist and fight. Sometimes Iris wondered if Enva was even in the city, although others claimed they spotted the goddess from time to time. As for who was painting this sinister phrase all throughout town . . . Iris could only wonder, but it seemed to be a group of people in Oath who wanted no living divines in Cambria. Including Dacre.

With a shiver, Iris continued on her way. She was almost to the *Inkridden Tribune* when she allowed herself a final glance behind.

There was indeed someone farther up the street. But they spun and slipped into a shadowy doorway, and Iris couldn't discern their build, let alone their face.

She sighed, rubbing the gooseflesh on her arms. She had reached her destination, and if it *was* Forest on her heels, then she would speak to him later, when she returned to their flat. It was a talk that had been brewing for an entire week now, the two of them both too hesitant to broach it.

Iris slipped past the wooden door, her boots clicking over the black-and-white-tiled floor of the lobby. She took the staircase down, feeling the temperature shift as the lightbulbs emitted a faint ring above her. Yet another reason to wear her trench coat year-round.

The *Inkridden Tribune* was rooted in the basement of an ancient building, where it often felt like eternal autumn, with oaken desks piled high with paper, a ceiling veined with copper pipes, exposed brick walls with drafty fissures, and the light of brass desk lamps limning the dance of cigarette smoke and the glint of typewriter keys. It was a dark yet cozy place, and Iris stepped into it with a soft exhale.

Attie was already sitting at the table they shared, staring absently at her typewriter. Her slender brown hands cradled a chipped cup of tea, and her brow was heavy, lost in deep thought.

Iris shed her trench coat, draping it over the back of her chair. She still wore the laced-up ankle boots that had been provided for the front lines, which were much easier to walk in than the heels she had once worn at the *Gazette*. The boots didn't match the plaid skirt and white blouse she wore, but Helena Hammond didn't seem to mind her mismatched outfit, so long as Iris wrote good pieces for the paper.

"Morning," Attie greeted her.

"Morning," Iris echoed as she took her seat. "Weather's nice today."

"Which means it'll be storming by the time we leave," Attie countered wryly, taking a sip of tea. But then her voice gentled as she whispered, "Any news?"

Iris knew what Attie was referring to. She was asking about Roman. If Iris had somehow scrounged up any news on his whereabouts and status.

"No," Iris replied, her throat narrow. She had sent out multiple telegrams since she had returned to Oath. Shots in the dark to railroad stations that were still operational despite how close they were to the war front.

MISSING PERSON ALERT STOP ROMAN C KITT STOP BLACK HAIR BLUE EYES WAR CORRESPONDENT STOP LAST SEEN IN AVALON BLUFF STOP CONTACT I WINNOW VIA OATH TELEGRAM OFFICE STOP

Iris had received no answers yet, but then again, what had she expected? Countless soldiers and civilians were unaccounted for these days, and she distracted herself with readying her typewriter, which truly wasn't *hers* but a spare one that the *Tribune* was lending her. It was an old instrument; the space bar was worn down from countless thumbs and it possessed a few keys that liked to stick, creating plenty of errors. Iris was still trying to get used to it, longing for the magical one her nan had once given her. The typewriter that had connected her to Roman. The Third Alouette.

Iris fed a fresh sheet of paper into the roller, but she thought of her typewriter, wondering where it was. The last time she had seen it had been in her room at Marisol's bed and breakfast. And while the B and B had miraculously survived the bombing, there was no telling what Dacre and his forces had done to the town once they had overtaken it. Perhaps the Third Alouette was still there in her old room, untouched and coated in ash. Perhaps one of Dacre's soldiers had stolen it, using it for nefarious correspondence, or maybe had smashed it to glimmering pieces on the street.

"You all right, kid?" Helena Hammond's voice suddenly broke the moment, and Iris glanced up to see her boss standing beside the table. "You're looking a bit pale."

"Yes, just . . . thinking," Iris replied with a faint smile. "Sorry."

"No apologies needed. I didn't mean to interrupt your contemplations, but I have a letter for you." A smile broke Helena's stern countenance as she withdrew a crinkled envelope from her trouser pocket. "Someone I think you'll be happy to hear from."

Iris yanked the letter from Helena's hand, unable to hide her eagerness. It had to be news about Roman, and her stomach twisted with hope and terror as she ripped opened the envelope. Iris was first taken aback by how long the message was—too lengthy to be a telegram—and she exhaled, her breath tremulous as she read:

Dearest Iris,

I cannot even begin to describe how relieved I was (and still am!) to learn that you had returned safely to Oath! I'm sure Attie has already told you of what happened in Avalon Bluff that terrible day, but we waited for you and Roman at the lorry as long as we could. Even then, it felt like my heart had broken when we drove away without the two of you, and all I could do was pray that you were safe and that we would all find a way to reunite.

Helena wrote to me and shared that Roman is still unaccounted for. I am so sorry, my dear friend. I wish there was something I could do to ease the worry you must feel. Know that you are always welcome here at my sister's house in River Down. We are only a day trip away from you in Oath, and there is a room here for both you and Attie should you wish to visit.

Until then, my heart is with you. I miss you!

Your friend,
Marisol

Iris blinked away her tears, slipping the letter back into the envelope. It had only been two weeks since Iris had last seen Marisol. Two weeks since they had all been together at the B and B. Two weeks since she had married Roman C. Kitt in the garden.

A fortnight wasn't much time at all; Iris still had faint bruises and scabs on her knees and arms, from when she had crawled through the rubble and clouds of gas. She could still hear the thunder of the bombs exploding, sense the shudder of the earth beneath her feet. She could still feel Roman's breath in her hair as he held her, as if nothing would ever come between them.

Two weeks felt like a gasp of time—it could have been yesterday for how raw Iris's inner wounds were—and yet here in Oath, surrounded by people who were living life as normal, as if war didn't rage kilometers to the west . . . it made those days at Avalon Bluff feel like a fever dream. Or like they had happened *years* ago, and Iris's memory had retraced those moments so many times they had turned sepia with age and wear.

"Marisol is good, I take it?" Helena asked.

Iris nodded, tucking the envelope beneath a book on the table. "Yes. She invited me and Attie to visit her and her sister."

"We should go soon," Attie said.

Of course, Iris thought. Attie had already been in River Down. She had driven Marisol (as well as a mewling cat named Lilac) there to fulfill her promise to Keegan. And Keegan, a captain in Enva's forces, was another person whom Iris was worried about. She didn't know if Marisol's wife had survived the battle at Avalon Bluff.

Iris was just about to respond when a hush crept over the office. One of the lamps flickered as if imparting a warning, and the steady clack of typewriter keys faded until it seemed like the heart of the *Tribune* had ceased beating, suspended in silence. Helena frowned and turned to the door, and Iris followed her gaze, fixating on the man who stood beneath the brick lintel.

He was tall and thin, dressed in a three-piece navy suit with a red handkerchief tucked in the breast pocket. It was difficult to guess his age, but his pale face was creased with wrinkles. A mustache hovered above his pursed lips, and his beady eyes gleamed like obsidian in the low light. Beneath his bowler hat, his graying hair was slicked back with pomade.

Iris didn't recognize him at first. She wondered if he had been the one to trail her that morning, until she saw he had two security guards standing behind him in the hallway, their burly arms locked behind their backs.

"Chancellor Verlice," Helena said in a careful tone. "What brings you to the *Inkridden Tribune?*"

"A private matter," the chancellor replied. "May I have a word with you?"

"Yes. Right this way." Helena wove through the tables to her office.

Iris watched as Chancellor Verlice followed, his eyes sweeping over the editors and columnists he passed. It almost seemed like he was looking *through* them, or perhaps looking *for* someone, and her heart faltered when he glanced over and met her stare from across the room.

His inscrutable eyes held hers for a long moment before they shifted to look at Attie. By then, he had finally reached Helena's office, and he had no choice but to drop his gaze, stepping over the threshold. Helena shut the door behind him; the two security guards remained as sentries in the hallway, barring anyone from coming or going.

Slowly, the *Inkridden Tribune* resumed its hum of activity. Editors returned to editing piles of paper with their red fountain pens, columnists resumed their typing, assistants rushed from the tea sideboard and the phone, carrying steaming cups and scrawled messages to various desks.

"What's that all about, do you think?" Attie whispered, angling her head to Helena's office door.

Iris stifled a shiver. She slipped her trench coat back on, belting it tight at her waist.

"I don't know," she whispered in return. "But it can't be anything good."

Ten minutes later, the office door swung open.

Iris kept her attention on her paper and the words she was inking across it, falling into the rhythm of her typewriter, but she could see the chancellor from the corner of her eye. He took his time walking through the room, and she could feel his gaze again as if he were measuring her, measuring Attie.

Iris gritted her teeth, tilting her chin down so her hair would cascade around her face, coming between her and the chancellor's stare like a shield.

She was grateful when Verlice and his two guards disappeared up the stairwell, but the pungent cloud of his cologne lingered like fog. Iris was just about to rise and pour herself a cup of tea, to hopefully wash the bad taste from her mouth, when she saw Helena wave to her.

"Iris, Attie. I need to speak with both of you."

Attie stopped typing, rising without a word as if she had been waiting for it. But she chewed on her lip, and Iris knew her friend was just as anxious as she was. Whatever the chancellor had come here to say must have been about them. Iris followed Attie to Helena's office.

"Have a seat, you two," Helena said as she settled behind her desk.

Iris shut the door, moving to sit on a worn leather sofa directly to Attie's left. She resisted the urge to crack her knuckles, waiting for Helena to break the quiet.

"Do you have any idea why the chancellor paid us a visit?" Helena finally spoke, and her voice was strangely calm and cool. Like water beneath a sheet of ice.

Attie glanced sidelong at Iris. She had come to the same conclusion. Iris could see it in her eyes. The annoyance, the worry, the gleam of anger.

"He didn't like our articles," Iris said. "The ones you just published about Clover Hill and Avalon Bluff being evacuated, bombed, and gassed."

Helena reached for a cigarette and then sighed, tossing it onto a pile of paper. "No, he didn't. I knew he wouldn't, and I still published them."

"Well, he doesn't really have to *like* them, does he?" Attie said, raising a hand in frustration. "Because Iris and I both wrote the truth."

"He doesn't see it that way." Helena's auburn hair was limp on her brow. There were faint purple smudges beneath her eyes, as if she hadn't slept. Her freckles were vivid against her pale complexion, as was the scar on her face.

"What does he see it as, then?" Iris asked, rotating the wedding band on her finger.

"He sees it as fearmongering and propaganda. He thinks I'm trying to drive up my sales with such headlines."

"That's rubbish!" Attie cried. "Iris and I were *eyewitnesses* to the attack on the bluff. We're doing our jobs as reporters. If the chancellor has a problem with this, then he's obviously a Dacre sympathizer."

"I know," Helena said gently. "Believe me, kid. I know it. You wrote the truth. You wrote what you experienced, bravely and honestly, just as I needed you to. And yes, the chancellor seems to have strings attached to Dacre, willing to dance at the god's bidding. Which leads me to my next point: Verlice thinks I'm trying to stir up trouble by making people panic and angry. He blames us for the most recent *gods belong in their graves* vandalism, which was, in fact, painted on his driveway in big bold letters this morning."

Iris flexed her hand. She remembered seeing that fearless slogan on her morning walk. "People are allowed to have their own opinions and beliefs on divinity, whether they worship them or not. We can't control that."

"The very words I said to Verlice," Helena said. "Which he doesn't agree with."

"What does this mean for us, then? Do you want us to stop writing about the war? Should we act as if the gods don't exist?"

"Course not," Helena responded with a snort. But her defiance waned as she continued. "And I don't want to ask this of you two, because you've been through more than any of us here can fathom. You've only just returned. But if Dacre is making a hard drive to the east like both of you saw at the bluff . . . then we need to know, especially if our good chancellor is in bed with him. We need to know how much time we have before the god reaches Oath, and what we can do to prepare for it."

Iris's heart quickened. She had felt hollow since returning to Oath. She slept but she didn't dream. She swallowed but she couldn't taste. She wrote three sentences and deleted two, as if she didn't know how to move forward.

"You need us to return to the front," she stated, breathless.

Helena's brow furrowed. "Yes, Iris. But not exactly as you did before, since Marisol is no longer in Avalon Bluff."

"How, then?" Attie asked.

"I'm still working on those details, so I can't quite tell you at the moment." Helena raked a hand through her hair, leaving it more limp and mussed than before. "And I don't want answers from you right now. In fact, I want you to take the rest of the day off. I want you to truly *think* about this and what it means for you, and not just give me the answer you assume I *want* to hear. Do you understand?"

Iris nodded, her thoughts instantly drifting to Forest. Her brother wouldn't want her to leave, and dread welled in her throat when she imagined breaking that news to him.

She glanced at Attie, uncertain what her friend would do.

Because the truth was that Attie had five younger siblings and parents who loved her. She had been enrolled in prestigious classes at Oath University. She had many threads to keep her tethered here, whereas Iris only had one. But Attie was also a musician who kept her violin hidden in the basement, defying the chancellor's law to surrender all stringed instruments. She had gifted her stuffy old professor a subscription to the *Inkridden Tribune,* since he had once believed her writing wouldn't amount to anything.

Attie had never been one to let people like Chancellor Verlice or narrow-minded professors have the final say.

And, Iris was swiftly coming to learn, neither was she.

Dark clouds were billowing across the sky by the time Iris reached the riverside park. She had parted ways with Attie at a corner café, the two of them having eaten a late breakfast together before taking Helena's advice to heart. Attie wanted to walk the courtyard of the university again before heading home to her parents' town house, and Iris wanted to visit the park she and Forest had haunted when they were younger.

Iris stopped on a mossy rock, typewriter case in one hand weighing her down. She gazed into the shallow rapids.

Willow and birch trees grew crooked along the winding banks, and the air tasted damp and sweet. It was strange how this place felt far removed from the city, how the tram bells and sputter of vehicles and many voices seemed to fade away. For a moment, Iris could imagine she was kilometers from Oath, tucked into the idyllic countryside, and she knelt to gather a few river stones, the water a cold shock to her fingers.

Years ago, Forest had found a snail among the rocks and had given him to Iris. *Morgie,* she had called him, proudly taking him home as a pet.

She smiled, but the memory was sharp, cutting her lungs like glass.

If you see me too much, you're bound to tire of my sad snail stories, she had once typed to Roman.

Impossible, he had replied.

Iris let the stones fall from her hands, watching them splash into the water. Thunder grumbled overhead as wind rustled the tree boughs. The first raindrops plopped onto Iris's shoulders, rolling down her trench coat like tears.

She began the brisk walk home, the rain falling in earnest. Her hair was drenched by the time she made it to her apartment building, but her typewriter case was thankfully waterproof. She didn't normally tote the instrument home in the evening after work, but she had discovered that she didn't like to be without it. Just in case inspiration stuck at midnight.

Iris hurried up the outer stairwell to the second floor, boots clanging on the steel steps, but she came to an abrupt halt when she saw her flat door was ajar. When she had left that morning, Forest had still been home, sitting on the couch and polishing his old pair of shoes. He had seemed reluctant to leave their apartment, and Iris could only wonder if he was worried someone might recognize him, believing he had deserted his post. It was far more complicated than that, but most people in Oath didn't truly understand what was happening at the war front.

"Forest?" Iris called, stepping closer to the door. She nudged it open farther, listening to it creak on its hinges. "Forest, is that you?"

There was no reply, but Iris could see the lamplight, warm and hazy, within. Someone was inside her home, and a chill traced her spine.

"Forest?" she called again, but there was no reply. Only a curl of spicy smoke, and the sound of someone moving.

Iris passed over the threshold.

A tall, older man dressed in a calfskin jacket and dark suit stood in the living room, a few paces away. It was a man she had never seen before, but she knew who he was the moment their gazes crossed, and that chill spread further, making her blood feel like ice.

He took one last draw from his cigar as if he was preparing for a fight, the rolled tobacco smoldering as he lowered it from his mouth.

"Hello, Miss Winnow," the man said in a deep voice. "Where is my son?"

2

Words Bewitched

This was not the way Iris had envisioned meeting Roman's father for the first time.

In fact, this was the *last* thing she had expected. It wasn't supposed to happen in her sad little flat, with the stained wallpaper and tattered furniture and scuffed floors. A stark reminder that Iris was of the working class, while the Kitts were not. It wasn't supposed to happen with her disheveled and drenched from the rain, heartsick and alone.

No, in her mind, she would be wearing her finest clothes, with her hair curled and pinned with pearl barrettes, and her fingers woven with Roman's. It would take place at the Kitts' sprawling estate on the northern end of town, perhaps outside in the sunny gardens, and Roman's shrewd nan and gentlehearted mother would be serving tea and sandwiches cut into triangles.

How utterly sobering it was, then, to realize how seldom daydreams like that aligned with reality. How impossible the scene Iris had painted in her mind was. But she set her posture like iron, refusing to let her gaze break first.

"Hello, Mr. Kitt," she said. "I wasn't expecting you."

"Forgive me for dropping in unannounced," he replied, although Iris could tell he was not at all remorseful. "As you must know by now . . . my son isn't the best at keeping me informed of his whereabouts, and I need him to come home."

Home.

The word landed like a dart, and Iris took a moment to breathe, to set down her typewriter case and to remove her trench coat, draping it over the back of the nearest chair. Thank gods she had the electricity back on, and that Forest had busied himself with cleaning the flat since their return. It wasn't littered with wine bottles anymore. The cobwebs had been knocked down and the floors swept. There was food in the kitchen, and running water in the lavatory, though the place still felt strange without her mother.

Iris shook those thoughts away. She had a dilemma on her hands, one that she wasn't prepared for. She didn't know what to tell Mr. Kitt about Roman, or how much the man already knew. She didn't know what was safe to say, and what she should withhold.

She tried to think of what Roman would prefer but was met by a spasm of pain in her chest.

"Can I make you a cup of tea, Mr. Kitt?" she asked.

"No. Didn't you hear my question, girl?"

"Of course I did. You don't know where your son is, but you think I do."

Mr. Kitt was quiet for several tense seconds. He stared at her, and Iris forced herself to hold his gaze. She wouldn't give him power here; she wouldn't cower and glance away as if he had won this ground.

She could see the similarities between the two of them—Roman and his father. They were both tall and broad-shouldered with thick black hair and eyes blue as cornflowers. They had sharp cut jaws and chiseled cheekbones, and their skin was prone to flushing. Iris remembered how she could always tell when Roman was embarrassed or uncomfortable or angry, because his face would inevitably redden, and how endearing that was on him. In Mr. Kitt's case, however, his cheeks looked ruddy from years of smoking and drinking.

He took another puff from his cigar, the smoke swirling. Perhaps he didn't like how she was scrutinizing him, or perhaps he hadn't expected her to be so stubborn. Iris didn't really care, but she couldn't help but stiffen when Mr. Kitt reached into his jacket.

"I didn't understand it at first," he began, and the tension eased from Iris's bones when she realized he was only withdrawing a folded newspaper from the shadows of his coat. But then he tossed it to the floor between them, and Iris glanced down to see it was the *Inkridden Tribune*. She read the front-page headline, and her heart lurched in familiarity, as if she had just caught a reflection of her face in a mirror.

DACRE BOMBS AVALON BLUFF, GASSES CITIZENS & SOLDIERS IN THE STREETS by INKRIDDEN IRIS

"I didn't understand," Mr. Kitt continued, "why my son would give up everything to go work for a dingy, sensationalizing newspaper on the war front. Why he would give up his position at the *Oath Gazette*. Why he would break his engagement to a beautiful, smart young lady. Why he would disobey me and shatter his mother's heart for a second time. It was unfathomable to me, until I read your first article in the *Tribune*, and then it all made sense."

Iris didn't move, didn't breathe. Her bravery dwindled when she sensed that Mr. Kitt was setting a well-laid snare for her, and her mouth went dry as she waited for him to elaborate.

He smiled down at the paper, at the headline that was hers. The inked words that she had written. The horror she had lived through, surviving by the skin of her teeth. But when Mr. Kitt's gaze flashed up to meet hers again, she saw the barely concealed fury and resentment in his eyes.

"You see, Miss Winnow . . . Roman has always been drawn to stories and words. Ever since he was a lad, sneaking into my library to steal books off the shelves. It's why my mother-in-law gave him a typewriter for his tenth birthday, because he had dreams of being a 'novelist.' Of writing something that mattered to others. It's why he wanted to go to university and spend his hours doing nothing more than analyzing other people's thoughts and trying to pen his own."

Iris felt the heat rise in her skin. "What are you trying to say to me, Mr. Kitt?"

"I'm saying that your words have bewitched him. And I need you to let him go."

She had to smother the burst of laughter that wanted to escape her. Because as silence rang in the room, she saw that Mr. Kitt was deadly serious.

"If my words have bewitched your son, then know that his possess the same magic for me," she said, reflexively touching her wedding band again.

The memories surged, threatening to drown her.

Iris had relived them a hundred times, as if they were anchored to the ring. The moment Roman had slipped it onto her finger. How the stars had started to burn overhead, the flowers sweetening the dusk around them. How he had smiled at her through his tears. How he had whispered her name in the dark.

Her restless motion drew Mr. Kitt's attention to her hand. Iris saw him note the shine of the ring, the finger it claimed. A terrible expression stole across his face. One that made the breath freeze in her chest.

"I see" was all he said, but the words were drawn out, deliberate. He cleared his throat. "Are you with child, then?"

Iris startled as if he had slapped her. "*What?*"

"For I can grasp no other reason as to why my son would legally fasten himself to one such as you, a lowborn, freckle-faced girl who wants to drain him of his inheritance. Of course, Roman has his honor, although he often misplaces it—"

"You followed me to work this morning," Iris interrupted, beginning to list his offenses on her left hand, just so he could continue to see the gleam of her wedding ring. "You broke into my flat. You no doubt looked through all my personal belongings. You have now insulted me in such a way that I have nothing more to say to you." She motioned to the front door, which still sat open, the rain falling hard and cool beyond the threshold. "Now *leave,* before I call the authorities to escort you out."

Mr. Kitt snickered, but her words must have held weight, because he began to walk to the door. He stepped on the newspaper, marring Iris's headline, and she had to swallow the chain of curses she wanted to hurl at him.

But he paused when he reached her side. Mr. Kitt stared down at her again. Blue, bloodshot eyes. Smoke on his breath.

Mere moments ago, Iris had seen the physical similarities between Roman and his father. But as she stared back now, she was painfully relieved to acknowledge that Roman Carver Kitt was nothing like the man he had come from.

"He can't hide behind your skirts for much longer, Miss Winnow," he said, as if he would refuse to ever acknowledge her as a Kitt. "When you see him tonight, tell him I need a word with him. That his mother and I want him to come home. That I forgive him for what he's done."

Iris had two seconds to decide on her parting words. Two seconds, and while she wanted to keep Mr. Kitt completely in the dark, she also knew this man was powerful and keen to have Roman back home.

"He's not here," she said.

"Where is he staying?"

"He's not in Oath."

Mr. Kitt arched a brow, but then Iris's unspoken words seemed to hit him. "Some love you must have for him, then, Miss Winnow. To leave him behind in Avalon Bluff while you saved yourself."

He stepped past her, finally quitting the flat.

Iris, pale and trembling, watched until he melted into the storm, his cologne and cigar smoke lingering behind to choke her. Tears burned her eyes. Tears and anger and remorse that felt like a knife, slicing her open to the bone.

She waited until she had closed and locked the door before she slowly sank to her knees.

3

Two Sides to Every Story

Dear Kitt,

I'm becoming a girl made of regrets.

Every morning, I wake from my gray, dreamless sleep and I think of you. I wonder where you are. If you are hurt or hungry or afraid. I wonder if you are above or below ground, if Dacre has chained you to the heart of the earth, so far down in his domain that I have no chance of ever finding you.

I wish that I had never let go of your hand that day. I should have stayed at your side when we were trying to help the soldiers on the hill. I should have refused to let the gas come between us. I should have known my brother wasn't you. If I had done even one of these things, then you and I would still be together.

The front door opened.

Iris stopped typing, holding her breath. But she recognized the sound of Forest's steps, and she quickly rose from her place on the floor, emerging from her bedroom to greet him.

He was knocking rain from his coat and boots. It was nearly evening, and

Iris hadn't known where he was. She hated how it tore the scab off a half-healed wound within her—all those hours her mother had come home late, and all the moments Iris had been worried about her but had done nothing about it.

Yet another thing Iris regretted.

Forest sniffed and froze. He glanced up, rain shining on his face, to meet Iris's gaze from across the room.

"Were you smoking a cigar?" he asked, unable to hide his shock.

Iris winced. She should have done a better job of airing out the flat. "No."

"Someone was here, then. Who? Did they hurt you?"

"*No.* I mean, yes," she said, rubbing her brow. How much to say to Forest? "My father-in-law dropped in for a visit. He was asking me about Roman. Asking me where he is."

Forest heaved a sigh. He bolted the door behind him and walked to the kitchen table to set down a paper bag. Dinner, by the smell of it.

"And what did you tell him?" he asked in a careful tone.

"That Roman isn't in Oath. I didn't say anything about Dacre."

Forest set out two sandwiches, wrapped in newspaper. But Iris could see his jaw working, as if he were debating what he should say.

"Here, sit and eat," he finally said, drawing out one of the kitchen chairs. "I got your favorite."

Iris sat across the table from her brother, unwrapping her sandwich. It was indeed her favorite—turkey on rye with an extra slice of red onion—and her heart warmed until she saw there was a pickle resting on the bread. She had to swallow the lump in her throat. Swallow down the vivid memories of Roman again, that day she had sat beside him on a park bench, seeing who he truly was for the first time.

They ate in silence. Iris was coming to learn that Forest was very quiet these days. They both were, often finding themselves drawn inward. She was surprised when her brother gruffly broke the awkwardness.

"I'm sorry I wasn't here when you got home from work today." He paused, wiping the crumbs from his shirt. "I've been interviewing, trying to find a job."

Iris's brows rose. "Oh? That's great news, Forest. Are you thinking to re-turn to the horologist's shop?"

Forest shook his head. "No. Too many questions if I go back there. They knew I enlisted and I don't want to have to explain what happened."

Iris understood. But she also didn't want her brother to feel like he had to keep to the shadows and completely restart his life, all because Dacre had set his claws in him, manipulating him like a puppet.

She opened her mouth to say this, but then caught the words.

Forest glanced up. "What is it?"

"Nothing. It's just . . . I'm proud of you."

Her brother's face creased. He suddenly looked like he was battling tears, and Iris rushed to add, in a lighter voice, "And it would be nice if you left a note for me, so I know you're out but will be back. So I don't worry. I actually got off work early today. Helena gave me and Attie the day off, and—"

"Why did she give you the day off?" Forest interjected, like he sensed the brewing storm.

Iris curled her tongue behind her teeth. *Well,* she thought, *there's no sense in delaying the inevitable.*

"Iris?"

"Helena has asked me and Attie to return to the front."

"Of course she has." Forest tossed down the remainder of his sandwich. "You've only been back *two* weeks and she's ready to send you off again!"

"It's my job, Forest."

"And you're my *sister*! My little sister who I should have been protecting." He dragged his hand through his damp hair, his lips pressing into a thin line. "I should have never left you and Mum. I should have stayed here, and none of *this* would have happened."

This.

Forest being wounded and healed by Dacre, fighting for the enemy. Their mum succumbing to the bottle, being struck by a tram on a drunken walk home. Iris going to the front lines to report on the war, nearly blown to pieces by a grenade during the barrage.

It all felt hopelessly tangled, one thread entwined with the next.

"Why did you go?" Iris asked, so softly she wondered if Forest would ignore it.

She already knew part of the answer: her brother had enlisted because he had heard Enva playing her harp one evening on his walk home from work. And that song had pierced his heart with the truth about the war. For a complete stanza, Forest had seen the trenches as if he had been there. The wake of devastation Dacre's forces left behind in small rural towns. Smoke and blood and ash that fell like snow.

"Do you mean what was I fighting *for*?" he countered.

Iris nodded.

Forest was quiet, picking a hangnail, but then he said, "I was fighting for us. I was fighting for your future. For mine. For the people in the west who needed aid. It wasn't for Enva. Not really. She never once appeared at the front. She never once guided our forces after getting us to enlist."

"And I write for the same reasons," Iris said. "Knowing that . . . will you still keep me from going?"

Forest sighed, but he looked haggard. He placed a hand over his waist, and Iris knew he was touching one of his scars.

She wondered if the old wounds were hurting him. Three bullet holes had torn through his body, two hitting vital organs. *He should be dead,* Iris thought with an icy shiver. *He should be dead, and I don't know if I should be thankful to Dacre for saving him, or furious that my brother now lives with such painful scars.*

"Your wounds, Forest," she said, making to rise from the table. She wanted to ease the anguish he still felt but was at an utter loss when it came to helping him. Honestly, Forest didn't like her to acknowledge his injuries at all.

"I'm fine," he said, picking up his sandwich. He took a bite, but his face was pallid. "Sit down and eat, Iris."

"Have you thought about visiting the doctor?" she asked. "I think it would be good to go."

"I don't need a doctor."

She lowered herself back to the chair. The past fortnight, she had respected Forest's desire for privacy, and she had held most of her questions captive.

But now she was about to leave, whether Forest gave his blessing or not. She was about to move toward Dacre again—toward *Roman*—and she needed to know more.

"Do your scars hurt you all the time?" she said.

"No. Don't worry about me."

She didn't believe him. She could tell he didn't feel well on most days, and the thought was painful to her. "What if I went with you to the doctor, Forest?"

"And what are we going to tell them? How am I to explain how I lived with such mortal wounds? How I was healed when I should be dead?"

Iris glanced away, to hide the sheen in her eyes.

Forest fell silent, his face flushing as if he felt guilty for his short temper. Softly, he whispered, "Look at me, Little Flower."

She did, biting the inside of her cheek.

"I know you're thinking about Roman," he said, changing the topic so abruptly that it startled her. "I know you're worried about him. But chances are that Dacre has him very close right now. Healing his wounds, stripping away all connections he once had. Connections like Roman's family, his life in Oath, the things he once dreamt of. *You,* even. Anything that would interfere with his service and entice him to escape like I did."

Iris blinked. A tear trickled down her cheek, and she quickly wiped it away, looking at Forest's neck. He still wore their mother's golden locket. The tangible thing that had given him the strength to slip from Dacre's clutches.

"Are you saying that Kitt won't remember me?"

"Yes."

Iris felt her stomach wind into a knot. It hurt to breathe, and she rubbed her collarbone. "I don't think he would forget."

"Listen to me," Forest said, leaning across the table. "I know more than you about this. I know—"

"So you like to remind me!" she cried, unable to stop herself. "You tell me you *know more,* and yet you hardly tell me a thing. You give me bits and pieces, and if you would just be forthright with me—if you would tell me the entire story—then maybe I could understand!"

Her brother was silent, but he held her gaze. Iris's anger was like a flare, short-lived and bright for only a second. She hated this; she hated being at odds with him. She sank back into her chair as if the wind had been knocked from her.

"I don't want you to return to the front," Forest finally said. "It's too dangerous. And there's nothing you can do for Roman but remain safe yourself, as he would want. He won't remember you, at least not for a good long while." He crumpled the newspaper around the scraps of his sandwich. The conversation was over, and he rose to toss his dinner in the dustbin.

Iris watched as he retreated to their mother's old room, which he had taken for his own since they had returned home. He didn't slam the door, but the sound of it closing jarred her.

She wrapped up the remainder of her sandwich and set it in the icebox before returning to her room. She looked at the typewriter sitting on the floor, just as she had left it, with paper curling from the platen. A half-inked letter addressed to Roman in its clutches.

Iris didn't know why she was writing to him. This typewriter was ordinary; the magical link between her and Roman was broken. But she pulled the paper free and folded it. She slipped it under her wardrobe door and waited a few breaths.

When she opened the closet, it was just as she expected. Her letter was still there, sitting on the shadowed floor.

Sometime deep into the night, Iris was woken by the sound of music.

She sat up in bed with a shiver, listening. The song was faint but incandescent, a crescendo of notes played on a lone violin. Light flickered beneath her bedroom door, eating at the darkness, and there was the faint scent of smoke. It all felt strangely familiar, like she had lived this moment before, and she slipped from her bed, coaxed from her room by the music and that hint of comfort.

To her shock, she found her mother in the living room.

Aster sat on the couch wrapped in her favorite purple coat, her bare feet propped on the coffee table. A cigarette burned between her fingers and her head was angled back, eyes closed. Her lashes were dark against her pale face, but she looked at peace as she listened.

Iris swallowed hard. Her voice was ragged when she spoke.

"Mum?"

Aster's eyes fluttered open. Through the curl of smoke, she met Iris's gaze and smiled.

"Hi, sweetheart. Do you want to join me?"

Iris nodded and sat beside her mother on the couch, her mind full of fog and confusion. There was something she needed to remember, but she couldn't quite grasp it. She must have been frowning, because Aster took her hand.

"Don't think too hard, Iris," she said. "Just listen to the instrument."

The tension clinging to Iris's shoulders eased; she let the music trickle through her, and she didn't realize how parched she was for the notes, how daily life had become a drought without the sound of strings to refresh the hours.

"Isn't this against the chancellor's law?" she asked her mother. "To listen to music like this?"

Aster took a long draw on her cigarette, but her eyes gleamed like embers in the dim light. "Do you think something so lovely could ever be illegal, Iris?"

"No, Mum. But I thought . . ."

"Just *listen*," Aster whispered again. "Listen to the notes, darling."

Iris glanced across the room and noticed Nan's radio on the sideboard. The music poured from the small speaker, clear as if the violinist stood in their presence, and Iris was so pleased to see the radio that she rose and crossed the room.

"I thought it was lost," she said, reaching out to trace its dial.

Her fingers passed through the radio. She watched, astounded, as it melted into a puddle of silver and brown and gold. The music suddenly became dissonant, a screech of a bow on too-tight strings, and Iris whirled, eyes widening as Aster began to fade.

"Mum, wait!" Iris lunged across the room. "*Mum!*"

Aster was nothing more than a smudge of violet paint, woven with smoke and smeared with ash, and Iris screamed again as she tried to hold her mother.

"Don't go! Don't leave me like this!"

A sob cracked her voice. It felt like she held the ocean in her chest, her lungs drowning in salty water, and she gasped as a warm hand on her shoulder became a sudden anchor, pulling her up to the surface.

"Iris, wake up," said a deep voice. "It's only a dream."

Iris startled awake. She blinked against a wash of gray light to see Forest sitting on the edge of her bed.

"It was just a dream," he repeated, although he looked just as shaken as her. "It's all right."

Iris made a strangled noise. Her heartbeat was rapid, but she nodded, gradually returning to her body. The vision of Aster clung to her, though, as if burned behind her eyes. She realized it was the first time she had dreamt in weeks.

"Forest? What time is it?"

"Half past eight."

"*Shit!*" Iris lurched upright. "I'm late to work."

"Take it easy," Forest said, his hand falling from her shoulder. "And since when do you curse?"

Since you left, Iris thought but didn't say, because while part of that was true, part of it wasn't. She couldn't blame her brother for the words that came out of her mouth these days.

"Dress for rain." Forest rose from the bed but gave her a pointed look. "It's storming."

Iris glanced at the window. She could see the rain streaking down the glass and realized the dour light of the storm had made her oversleep. Quickly, she drew on a linen dress with buttons down the front and laced up her wartime boots. She had no time to fix her hair, and she combed her fingers through the long tangles as she flew out of the bedroom, gathering her small purse, her trench coat, and her typewriter, locked firmly in its black case.

Forest was standing by the front door, a cup of tea in one hand and a treacle biscuit in the other.

"Should I walk with you?" he asked.

"No need. I'll take the tram today," she said, surprised when he extended both the tea and the biscuit to her.

"Something to hold you over, then."

His way of apologizing for last night.

She smiled. It almost felt like old times, and she accepted the lukewarm tea, draining it in one long gulp. She gave the cup back to him in exchange for the biscuit, and he opened the door for her.

"I should be home by five thirty," she said, stepping into the damp morning air.

Forest nodded, but he stayed in the doorway wearing a concerned expression. Iris could feel him watching her as she descended the slick stairs.

She ate the biscuit before the rain could ruin it, dashing to the tram stop. It was a crowded, jostling ride, most people seeking shelter from the storm on their commutes. Iris stood toward the back, and she slowly became aware of how quiet it was. No one was conversing or laughing, as they normally did on the tram. The mood felt strange, off-balance. She thought it must be the weather, but the feeling followed her all the way to the *Inkridden Tribune*'s building.

She stopped on the pavement when she saw the words painted over the lobby doors. Bright as fresh blood and dripping down the bricks.

Where are you, Enva?

Iris shuddered as she entered the building, but she felt the weight of that phrase as she ducked beneath the lintel. Someone must have painted it hours ago during the night, because it hadn't been there yesterday. She wondered who they were, and if they truly wanted to put Enva back into a grave, dead or sleeping. Were they someone who had lost a loved one in the war? Someone who was weary of fighting for the gods?

Iris couldn't blame them; she was conflicted daily when she thought about what had happened to her brother, all because Dacre had woken and Enva had strummed the truth of the war. It made her angry, sad, proud. *Devastated.*

Despite it all, she also wondered where the Skyward goddess was. Why was Enva hiding? Was she truly intimidated by the mortals who were eager to see her gone?

Where are you, Enva?

While Iris was disquieted by the blood-red taunt, she still expected the

Tribune to be humming like a hive. She expected to see the editors typing and the phone ringing and assistants hustling around desks with messages. She expected to see Attie, already three cups deep in tea, typing out her next article.

Iris was greeted by a solemn, still office.

No one was moving, as if they had been charmed into statues. Smoke was the only thing that cut through the shadows, rising from cigarettes and ashtrays. Iris stepped into the quiet, her breath skipping in alarm. She could see Helena standing in the center of the room, reading a newspaper. Attie was beside her, hand covering her mouth.

"What is it?" Iris asked. "Has something happened?"

She felt countless eyes turn to her, gleaming in the lamplight. Some with pity, compassion. Others with wariness. But she kept her gaze on Helena, who lowered the paper to meet her stare.

"I'm sorry, kid," Helena said.

Sorry for what? Iris wanted to ask, but the words stuck in her throat when Helena extended the newspaper to her.

Iris set down her typewriter. She reached for the paper. Helena had been reading something on the front page.

It was the *Oath Gazette*. Iris's old place of employment. How strange to hold this paper now, in the basement of the *Inkridden Tribune*. It almost felt like Iris was dreaming again until she finally saw what Helena had been transfixed by.

A headline raced across the page in bold, black ink. A headline that Iris never expected to see.

DACRE SAVES HUNDREDS OF WOUNDED IN AVALON BLUFF
by ROMAN C. KITT

Iris stared at his name, printed on the paper. His name, which she had never thought to see bound to a headline again.

Kitt is alive.

The relief ebbed, leaving her cold and shaky as she began to read Roman's words. Iris could feel her skin prickling, her face heating. She had to read the same string of sentences multiple times, trying to make sense of them.

There are two sides to every story. You may be familiar with one, told through the lens of a goddess who has drawn many of your innocent children into a bloody war. But perhaps you would like to hear the other? One that would see your children not wounded but healed. One that would see this land mended. A story not just confined to a museum or a history tome that many of us will never touch, but a story that is in the process of being written. Written now as you hold this paper, reading my words.

For I am here at the front, safe among Dacre's forces. And I can tell you what you long to know from the other side.

"No," Iris whispered. She could feel bile rising, burning through her chest like fire.

"I'm sorry, Iris," Helena said again, the light vanishing from her eyes. "Roman has turned on us."

4

Spider Silk and Ice

R oman stared at the typewriter and its blank page. He was sitting at a desk before a window that overlooked a golden field, and the afternoon was waning. Soon it would be night; the stars would pierce the sky like nails, and he would light the candles and write by fire because the words came easier in the darkness.

This was always the hardest part for him. Beginning the articles. It hurt to write, and it hurt *not* to write.

The frustration felt familiar. Roman must have spent hours of his past staring at a blank page, deciding what words to strike across it. But despite the days that had passed since he woke, he still couldn't remember those old moments in detail. He flexed his hand when he thought about what Dacre had told him.

Only trust what you can see.

The god didn't have to worry about Roman's memories. It was hard for Roman to remember what had happened before he had stirred below, like mountains had grown through the mist of his mind, blocking off years of his life.

"It'll take time," Dacre had said, "but you'll remember what's important. And you'll find your place here."

When he had first woken below, Roman had gasped as if he were taking his first breath. He had opened his eyes to the flicking firelight, had seen the white marble walls around him, had felt the hard slab of rock beneath him, and he had known he was somewhere *else*. A magical place he had never encountered.

He was also naked.

With a groan, he sat forward, taking in the strange room.

It was an oddly sized chamber, hewn entirely from rock. It had nine walls, all of them white and veined with blue, gleaming like the facets of a diamond. The ceiling glittered with tiny flecks of gold, and it was reminiscent of the night sky if Roman squinted his eyes. Four torches burned from iron brackets, and the fire was the only source of light.

With a shudder, Roman slid from the hard table he had been resting on. The rock beneath his bare feet was smooth, and he began to walk before the walls, seeking a door. He could find none, and he swallowed his panic, walking a second time around, his fingers rushing over the planes of the stone.

"Hello?" he called, his voice still thick from sleep. "Is anyone here?"

There was no response. Only the sound of his own breath, rising and falling.

He couldn't remember being brought into this chamber. He didn't know how long he had been confined in this place, and he shivered, eventually coming to a halt.

He glanced down at his body, pale in the firelight, as if he might find answers on his skin.

To his shock, he found something.

Roman frowned as he leaned over, studying the array of scars on his right leg. There were many of them, some long and jagged, others small and smooth, and Roman traced them as if they were routes on a map. Eventually, he pressed hard against their soft marks, hoping pain would help him remember.

There was no pain, but he saw something flash at the corner of his eye. His head snapped up, but he realized what he'd seen wasn't something in the room but a snippet in his mind. Sunlight and smoke, the boom of artillery. The ground was shaking; the wind smelled like hot metal and blood. A lance of pain so sharp it had stolen his breath and made him crumple on the ground.

But he hadn't been alone. Someone had been with him, holding his hand.

Roman's fingertips fell away from his scars. He brought his palms close to his face and noticed there was an indention on his left pinkie. He must have been wearing a ring at some point, and he touched the slight mark it had left behind.

There was nothing to remember. No other flash of brilliancy or piece of his past to claim.

He flexed his hand until his knuckles bloomed white.

Am I dead?

As if in reply, pain suddenly surged. Roman's head began to ache so violently that he lowered himself to the stone floor. He cried out, curling his knees to his chest. There was a blade in his mind, sawing back and forth. A blade flaying him open from within.

The pain was so sharp he lost consciousness.

Sometime later, he woke again with bleary eyes.

A delivery had been made. On the floor sat a tray of food: a bowl of steaming stew, a hunk of dark bread, a pitcher of water and a small wooden cup. And beside it, a pile of garments and a pair of leather boots.

Roman crawled to the offering. He was so hungry, so *empty,* that he didn't think twice about eating the food or drinking the water. But when he reached for the garment, letting it unfold in his hands, he paused.

It was a jumpsuit. Again, that sense of familiarity washed over him. The garment was a dark red color, and he studied the white badge stitched over the left breast pocket: UNDERLING CORRESPONDENT.

Roman eased into the jumpsuit, ignoring the surge of uneasiness in his blood.

The moment he finished hooking the final button, the cold fled from his body. He felt warmth radiate from his ribs like he had swallowed sunlight, and he quickly donned the pair of socks and boots waiting for him.

A few heartbeats later, a sound broke the ringing silence.

Roman turned as a fissure opened in the wall. The door he had been seeking earlier and failed to find.

A young man in a tan-colored uniform stepped into the chamber. He looked to be around Roman's age, perhaps a few years older, and was fair-skinned with short blond hair. His brows were heavy, and his mouth was pressed into a thin line, as if he didn't smile often.

"Who are you?" Roman rasped.

"I'm Lieutenant Gregory Shane. And your name is?"

Roman froze. His name? He couldn't remember, and his mind reeled.

His panic must have bled through his expression, because the lieutenant said, "Don't worry. It'll come back to you. Don't force it."

"How long have I been here?"

"A couple of days. You were healing."

"From what?"

"He'll want to tell you. Now follow me." Shane began to walk away, and Roman had no choice but to follow before the door found its seamless lintel again.

The corridors were wide enough for two people to pass, shoulder to shoulder, and tall enough to give someone of Roman's height ease of passage. The walls were just like the ones in his previous chamber: smooth, cold, and white with glimmering blue veins. Torches lit the way every ten steps, and it was unnaturally quiet until they passed a branching tunnel, and Roman heard distant pounding.

He slowed, squinting into the shadows of the right corridor. It sounded like a forge. A hammer hitting an anvil, laced with shouts and clinks of machinery. There was a sudden waft of warm, metallic air.

"Keep moving," the lieutenant said sharply.

Roman resumed his pace. But he was keen to know where he was, and why he had been brought below. He noticed they passed two other corridors, one of which smelled foul like it held something rotten and dying. The other was choked with debris and cobwebs, as if the ceiling had collapsed decades ago.

Shane must have taken note of how observant Roman was being, how his strides slowed every time they passed branching pathways. The lieutenant stopped and yanked a blindfold from his pocket, fastening it around Roman's eyes.

"Just a precaution," he said, taking hold of Roman's elbow. "Follow my lead."

Roman bit down on his lip, but worry hung in his chest, turning his breath shallow. It felt like they took two more turns. His palms were clammy by the time Shane told him to reach out and touch the wall.

"We're at the foot of a stairwell," he said. "There are twenty-five steps in all, and they are steep. Mind yourself."

Roman slowly followed. His legs were burning by the time he sensed the shift of temperature. He heard a door click open.

He was greeted by a flood of sunlight seeping through his blindfold. A wash of fresh air, tinged in spring warmth. It must have just rained, because Roman could taste the petrichor as he fully stepped into the upper world. The floor was wooden beneath his boots, creaking like an old house. He nearly tripped on the edge of a rug, his arms flinging out to catch his balance.

"Wait here," Shane said, closing the door. "Don't move."

Roman only nodded, his mouth parched. He listened as Shane's heavy footsteps withdrew, but he sensed the room he stood in was full of furniture. There were no lonely echoes, only the steady tick of a clock somewhere to Roman's left.

He could hear someone speaking, the sound muffled through the walls. It was Shane's droning cadence, and Roman dared to take a few steps forward, trying to catch the words.

"He's awake, my lord. I've brought him here with me. He's waiting in the other room if you'd like to see him."

Silence. The voice that spoke next was one Roman had never heard before, but it was a deep baritone. Languid and rich, it sent a shiver up his spine.

"I thought I told you not to bring him here, Lieutenant."

"It's his memory, sir. He can't even recall his name. I thought it would help . . ."

"If he saw this place?"

"Yes, my lord. I know we are short on time, and we could use his——"

"Very well. Bring him to me."

Roman eased a step back, heart thundering in his ears. He was tempted to tear the blindfold from his face and *run,* somewhere far from here, but his hesitation cost him. He heard Shane return to the room, and winced when the lieutenant removed the fabric bound across his eyes.

Roman took in his surroundings. He had been waiting in a small but inviting room; an oil painting hung over a stone hearth, and cherrywood furniture with green velvet cushions held down a plush rug. Floral curtains framed tall windows, which were cracked open to welcome fresh air. A parlor of sorts, he realized, glancing at the door they had first stepped through.

It was a very unassuming door. Carved from wood, with white chipped paint and a brass doorknob with a rusted keyhole. A wardrobe for coats, Roman imagined. Only they had emerged from the underground instead.

"The Lord Commander Dacre will see you now," said Shane. "Come with me."

"Dacre?" Roman whispered. The name rose like fire in his throat, scalding his tongue. He saw himself dressed in leather braces and perfectly pressed trousers and a button-down shirt, standing on a street corner as he read a newspaper with that name printed in the headline.

"Come," Shane repeated.

Roman stepped into a foyer and immediately saw that there were two armed soldiers stationed at the front door. Their gazes were cold and pointed, their faces like statues. Roman averted his eyes and moved down the hallway, Shane on his heels.

The floor felt unlevel in places. There were also large cracks in the walls, racing down the wallpaper like veins, as if this house had suffered a terrible storm. But it wasn't until Roman stepped into the wide kitchen and saw the table, the rafters overhead strung with herbs and copper pots, and the twin doors with cracked glass, that he felt pain well in his chest.

He had been here before. He was certain of it.

And yet all he could do was stare at the two typewriters, resting side by side on the table. They were nearly identical, their keys gleaming in the sunlight.

"I take it one of these typewriters looks familiar to you?"

Roman glanced to his left. A tall, broad-shouldered man was standing at the end of the table, his long blond hair brushing the collar of his pristine tan uniform. Strange how Roman hadn't noticed him until he spoke and, now that he had, how Roman couldn't seem to look away.

The stranger appeared to be older, although it was difficult to measure his age. There indeed seemed to be something timeless about him—his presence held weight in the room, but there was no silver in his hair, or wrinkles at the corners of his eyes. His face was angular, sharply cut, and his eyes were a vivid blue.

Roman had never seen this man before, but he couldn't deny there was a sense of familiarity about him. Just like the house and the typewriters, as if Roman had walked this place in his dreams. But perhaps that was only because this stranger was looking at Roman as if he knew him, and the acknowledgment was uncomfortable, like running his fingers over a woolen scarf before touching a light switch. Static and metal, and a jolt to his bones.

He had never thought he would stand face-to-face with a god. The divines were defeated. Sleeping, buried powers. They were never supposed to rise and walk among mortals again, and Roman inwardly winced as threads of his memory began to return to him. A sigh, a whisper.

A shiver.

Dacre smiled, as if he could read Roman's thoughts.

The god extended his elegant hand, indicating the typewriters again.

Roman blinked, remembering the question. "Yes, sir. They feel familiar to me."

"Which one is yours, then?"

Roman stepped closer to the table. He studied the typewriters, but sight alone was not enough for him to fully know. Both seemed to hold gravity for him, and it was perplexing.

"You can touch them," Dacre said gently. "I find that helps with remembering after healing."

Roman stretched out his hand, fingers trembling. A blush nipped his cheeks. He was ashamed that he appeared so weak and fragile before the god. He couldn't even remember his own name, but then he touched the space bar of the typewriter waiting to his left, and the frantic beat of his pulse calmed.

This one, he thought. *This one was mine.*

A flash of light teased his peripheral vision. This time he knew it was only his mind, a memory falling back into place. He remembered sitting at a desk in his bedroom, writing on this typewriter. He would work by lamplight, late into the night, books and cups of cold coffee scattered around him. Sometimes his father would knock on his door and tell him to *go to sleep, Roman! The words will still be there in the morning.*

Roman let his fingertips slide away from the space bar, his name echoing through him. He glanced to the typewriter waiting on his right, curious. He traced its keys, waiting for another memory to stir.

There was no light, no images to grasp. At first, there seemed to be nothing at all but a cool, deep quiet. Ripples expanding outward on the surface of a dark lake. But then Roman felt the *tug.* It came from deep within him, an invisible cord hidden between his ribs, and he could not see but he *felt.*

The emotions stirred his blood.

He could smell a faint hint of lavender. A rush of warm skin against his own. Pleasure and worry and bone-aching desire and fear all snarled together.

He had to grit his teeth, struggling to hold everything in. But his heart was pounding and hungry when his hand slipped away.

"Which one is yours, correspondent?" Dacre asked again, but his voice had shifted. It was not as friendly as before; Roman could hear the hint of an edge within the words. This must be a test. There was a right and wrong answer, and Roman hesitated, torn between the typewriter that had reminded him of his name and the one that reminded him that he was alive.

"This one," he said, pointing to the typewriter on the left. The one steeped in his past. "I believe it is mine."

Dacre nodded to someone behind Roman. Shane moved forward, approaching the table. Roman had forgotten about the lieutenant's presence.

"Take the appropriate typewriter up to our correspondent's room," Dacre said. "Have the other destroyed."

"Yes, my lord," Shane said with a bow of his head.

Roman startled. A protest began to climb up his throat—he didn't want to see the other one destroyed—but he couldn't find his courage, or the correct words, to convince Dacre otherwise. His mind still felt like a sheet of ice, capable of fragmenting into a hundred directions, and the god must have known.

"Come with me, correspondent," Dacre said. "There's something I'd like to show you."

Roman followed Dacre out the back doors and through a weedy garden. The soil was damp, and rain puddles shone between the rows of sprouting vegetables. But it was blue sky and sunshine overhead, and the clouds were smeared thin as wind blew from the west.

They passed through an iron gate and crossed a road with broken cobblestones, venturing into a field.

Dacre cut through the long grass with ease, his shadow rippling over the golden stalks. With every step he took, there was the very faint sound of a chime. Or pieces of metal, clinking together.

Roman followed closely, but his heart quickened. There was something about this place. It made him shiver in the broad daylight. Sweat gleamed on his skin.

"Here," Dacre said. "This is where I found you."

Roman came to a reluctant stop. He gazed at the ground, noticing some of the grass was bent and stained. It looked like old blood, dried like dark wine.

"You had only moments left before you died. Your lungs were brimming with blood. You were crawling through the grass, as if you were searching for someone." Dacre paused. The breeze tousled his flaxen hair when he met Roman's gaze. "Do you remember?"

"No." Roman's head was starting to throb again, and he frowned at the smattering of blood and the crimped grass. He tried to envision himself almost dying in such a place and felt nothing but gratitude that a god would want to save him.

"Mortal bodies are such fragile things to mend, as are your minds," Dacre said with a hint of amusement. "Like spider silk, like ice in spring. In order for my magic to heal your physical wounds, I had to build walls in your mind to protect you when you woke again. Given that, it's best if your memories return gradually."

Roman was quiet for a beat. He was still staring at the bloodstained ground when he said, "Why did you save me?"

"You're going to be a vital part of this war," Dacre said. "And I'd like for you to write my side of the story."

That evening, Roman stood in the room that had been assigned to him. A room on the upper floor of the house he almost remembered.

The curtains were a forest green. There was a makeshift pallet with folded blankets along one wall. The windows were webbed with cracks, the glass flaming iridescent as the sun set. The door struggled to latch, as if the building's foundation had shifted, and despite the privacy Roman now had with a personal room, he knew it was an illusion. There was no lock, and Shane was standing guard in the hallway.

But Roman's sole attention was on the desk aligned with one of the windows. On the typewriter that sat in the waning light, waiting for him.

Exhaustion made his bones feel heavy, but duty was a well-worn shape in his existence, and he approached the desk. He sat in the chair and stared at the typewriter. He didn't know what he would write yet; he didn't even know if there were words to be found within him.

There was a stack of fresh paper on the desk. A notepad and pencils. A host of candles as well as a lamp with a yellow-hued lightbulb, so he could write through the night. Dacre had thought of everything, it seemed, and Roman carefully fed a sheet into the typewriter. He sighed, raking his hand through his dark hair. He needed a shower. He wanted to sleep, to not have to think about anything for a little while. But when he at last set his fingers onto the keys, he was met by a surprise.

This wasn't the typewriter he had told Dacre was his. This wasn't the one he had grown up typing on, the one that had shown him a fleeting glimpse of his past self.

Roman closed his eyes, breath hitching.

He felt the tug again, the medley of emotions. He tried to imagine who had once touched these keys, time and time again. He tried to envision who had once written on this typewriter.

Who are you?

There was no answer. There was nothing for him to see, but he felt it again. A small yet unmistakable taunting. That invisible cord, knotted between his ribs.

He resisted the pull toward the unknown.

5

The First Alouette

I don't think he's *turned*," Iris said. "Roman is trying to stay alive."

Helena arched a brow. "That very well could be. But that also means he's unreliable and compromised. I can't trust him anymore, and now he's going to cause conflict for us by writing for our competitor."

Iris returned her gaze to the *Oath Gazette*, still in hand. Her mind was spinning, but she focused on Roman's article. She could almost hear him reading it to her, his cadence sharp, cold. Almost unfamiliar. Until her eyes caught on one word, easily overlooked in his sixth sentence: *A story not just confined to a museum or a history tome that many of us will never touch, but a story that is in the process of being written.*

"Museum," Iris whispered.

"What's that?" Helena asked.

Iris blinked. Her heart was suddenly racing. "Nothing. Just a thought."

Helena sighed, hands on her hips. "Is this going to interfere with your ability to report, kid?"

"No. On the contrary," Iris said, striding to the telephone. "I'm going to get to the bottom of this." She held up the *Oath Gazette* and gave the newspaper a good shake, just to appease Helena and the editors who were still watching her. Then she picked up the earpiece and dialed for the operator.

A male voice crackled over the line. "How may I direct your call?"

"The *Oath Gazette,* please," Iris said.

"Please hold."

She waited, tapping her foot. She could hear the static on the line, the sound of switches being flipped, and then a steady ringing in her ear. She knew the *Oath Gazette* had multiple telephones. There was no telling which one her call had been directed to, and she counted in her mind, waiting, hoping, praying . . .

"Hello, this is Prindle speaking for the *Oath Gazette.*"

A smile broke across Iris's face. It was just as she had hoped, and it took her a breath to gather her words.

"Hello?" Sarah Prindle said again, a touch impatient.

"Prindle." Iris spoke in a low voice. "I have some important news for you. It must be delivered in person. Meet me at Gould's Café in twenty."

"Meet at——" Sarah sounded indignant but cut herself off. Her voice softened with a small gasp. "Wait a minute . . . Winnow, is this you? I recognize your voice."

"Yes, it's me."

"But Autry . . . I don't have off until my lunch break."

"I know, but I need to see you as soon as possible. Can you slip away?"

It was quiet for a minute. Iris could nearly see Sarah in her mind's eye, glancing furtively across the hustle of the *Oath Gazette.* No doubt Zeb Autry was in his office, pouring whiskey over ice with a stack of papers on his desk.

"Yes, I think I can," she finally said, her voice tinged with excitement. "Twenty minutes, you say? At Gould's?"

"Yes," Iris replied. "I'll be waiting for you."

"Then I'll see you in a bit."

Iris hung up the receiver and turned. The *Tribune* was still watching her, wide-eyed with interest.

She tucked the *Gazette* under her trench coat, to protect the paper from the rain. With Roman's traitorous words pressed to her heart, Iris departed the *Tribune*. She walked through the swirling gray mist to Gould's Café.

Sarah Prindle was a few minutes late, but Iris didn't mind. She had chosen a small round table in the corner of the café, between a bookshelf and a potted lemon tree. A perfect place for a surreptitious conversation, and Iris had just hung up her trench coat and ordered a pot of tea when she heard the bell ring above the café door.

Sarah looked just as Iris remembered. Although truth be told, it had only been a matter of months since they had worked together at the *Gazette*. But since then, the weeks had been full of strange, darkened days, and Iris's breath snagged when she acknowledged that it truly felt like years had passed.

"Winnow!" Sarah whisper-cried in excitement, hurrying to the corner.

Iris rose with a smile. "It's good to see you, Prindle."

They embraced so tightly that Iris felt her spine pop, and she got a good mouthful of Sarah's fine blond hair.

"Please, sit," Iris said, easing back into her chair. "I just ordered us a pot of tea."

"Which never gets cold. A nice perk of an enchanted building." Sarah leaned her umbrella against the wall before she sat.

A waiter delivered a steaming pot of tea—it was true; it never got cold at Gould's—along with a pitcher of creamer and honey and a plate of butter-glazed scones. The girls were quiet as they prepared their cups. But then Sarah must have felt the worry that had followed Iris into the café. She glanced up and said, "I take it you saw Kitt's article this morning."

"Yes." Iris reached down to where she had the paper waiting on the floor, setting it on the tabletop. Roman's headline continued to draw her in, like an eddy in the ocean. "And I have some questions."

"As do I," Sarah said, removing her glasses to wipe the fog and speckled rain from them. "I've had questions ever since you left the *Gazette,* such as why did Kitt resign only a few weeks after you left? It all seems serendipitous, until I look at it closer." She placed her glasses back on her nose, her eyes flaring wide. "And oh my gods, I just noticed you have a ring on your hand! Is that . . . did the two of you . . . ?"

"Shh," Iris said, noticing they had drawn a few glances. "And yes. Kitt and I are married."

"*When* did this happen?"

"At the front."

"Oh, you have *so* much explaining to do, Winnow. Or should I also call you Kitt now?"

"Winnow is fine," Iris said, taking a sip of tea. "But it's a long story and it'll have to be shared later, I'm afraid. Right now, I need to know how Kitt's words arrived at the *Gazette*. Did they come by letter? Was it addressed to Autry? Was it handwritten or was his article already typed?"

Sarah frowned. "You know, it *was* very odd. But two days ago, I was sitting in Autry's office, taking down his lunch order, when a man knocked on the door."

"Who was this man?" Iris demanded. "What did he look like? What was his name?"

"I . . . I don't know who he was," Sarah replied. "I honestly couldn't see his face. He was tall, I remember. He wore a cloak, and the hood was up. His voice was rough and had a strange, almost languid lilt. Not unpleasant, but it made me feel cold when I heard it."

Iris sat back in her chair, cracking her knuckles. This man must have been one of Dacre's associates. One of Dacre's most trusted servants had been *in* Oath, standing not far from where Iris and Sarah sat now, sharing tea in a café. How had the man moved so seamlessly, without detection? Had he taken the train to Oath? Had he walked from the war front to the city? Ridden in a vehicle?

It made the hair rise on Iris's arms. The war was much closer to the city than she had once believed.

"So this man *hand* delivered Kitt's article to Autry," Iris surmised.

"He did. And he said it was something Autry would surely want for a price."

"And what was the price?"

Sarah fiddled with the dainty handle of her teacup. "That Autry could have

it, but only if he agreed to continue publishing *all* the articles that were delivered to him. He couldn't pick and choose from that moment onward."

"So more will be coming?"

Sarah nodded. "Autry was very pleased with it all. He sent me away from
his office so he could open the delivery in private. Not two minutes later,
he called me back in, and told me to carry the article to Benton's desk, for
proofing. So I did, and I got a glance at it, shocked to see it was Kitt's writing."

"His handwriting?" Iris asked.

"No. It was typed," Sarah answered. "I only meant that I was taken aback
to see his *words* again, and that he was to publish with the *Gazette* once more,
especially after he quit and caused such a stir with Autry."

Roman's article had been typed, which meant he had access to a typewriter. *Hopefully one of the Alouettes,* Iris thought.

"Is Kitt . . . is he in trouble, Winnow?" Sarah asked.

"I believe he is," Iris said. "And I'm about to ask you to do something very
illegal and very dangerous."

"Illegal?"

"Yes. And I wouldn't put you in this position if I didn't desperately need
you to pull it off."

Sarah's mouth quirked to the side. She set down her teacup and laced her
fingers together, leaning closer to Iris with a conspiratorial air. "I'm listening,
then."

"You're still very familiar with the museum, aren't you?"

"Well, yes. I go there every weekend with my dad."

Iris chewed on her lip, knowing this was the moment of no return. And
yet there was no other option. She was consumed by the thought of writing
to Roman again. Of taking that magical connection into her hands once more,
letting it slip over thresholds and cross war-torn kilometers.

"I need you to help me break into the museum, Prindle."

Sarah, to her credit, only blinked. "All right. And why would we do that?"

"Because I need to steal a typewriter."

6

We Like Our Middle Names Best

By all rights, I should be dead. I shouldn't be sitting at my desk, writing these words for you to read. I shouldn't be drawing air—inhale, exhale, inhale—and staring at the stars, feeling how ~~immense beautiful~~ cold the world is now that I've evaded death, like a house guest who has overstayed their welcome. I don't know what else fuels me to keep rising at dawn and continuing forward other than this: there is ~~a song~~ a story hiding in my scars. One that whispers to me, even though I have yet to fully capture the words.

"You should be buried in a grave," the world says, so loudly it drowns out all other sound.

And yet I press my fingers to the scars in my skin—soft, tender, warm as the blood beneath—and I hear, "~~There is a divine....~~There is someone who has kept you here, breathing, moving, living."

Roman's hands slid from the typewriter keys. What he *should* have been doing was writing his next article for Dacre, except when he sat down to work, different words had emerged.

Night had just fallen, and the house was quiet. But if Roman focused, he could catch the faint rumble of Dacre's voice, speaking on the floor below. He could hear the hardwood creak beneath walking boots, the rattle of the front door opening and closing.

Every day was like this, full of mysterious meetings and comings and goings. Roman remained out of sight on the upper floor, taking his meals in his room and transcribing for Dacre when the god visited with ideas for articles. Roman would have felt like a prisoner if he hadn't experienced the terror of being locked in a chamber below ground.

He thought of the door in the parlor, opening into another realm.

Dacre wanted the next article ready to go by tomorrow, and Roman sighed, staring at his sad words. His head was aching, as if he had pushed his mind too far that day, trying to remember the years that remained lost to him. He rubbed his eyes and resigned himself to the fact that the words simply weren't there to harvest that night.

He stood, shoulder blades twinging after hours of sitting. He extinguished the candles until he stood in the dark, breathing in shadows and wisps of smoke. Slowly, he felt his way to his pallet and lay down on the cold blankets, still wearing his jumpsuit and boots.

He must have been far more exhausted than he realized.

Roman felt asleep within moments.

There was a girl. A small, dainty child with two braided pigtails, her hair the color of a raven's feathers. The same shade as his. Her cheeks were rosy from the summer heat, and she was smiling, tugging on his hand.

"This way, Carver!" she cried.

Roman only laughed, letting her draw him across the grass. They were barefoot and wearing daisy crowns, which they could only do when their father was away. The garden unspooled before them with ivy-laden arbors and perfectly trimmed hedges. The roses had bloomed; bees and damselflies droned through the sultry afternoon light.

"Where are you taking me, Del?" he asked as his sister continued to drag him along.

"To a secret place," Del said with a giggle.

They strayed toward the back end of the garden, into a thicket and out of sight from the grand house. Blackberries grew wild among the thorns, and Roman and Del ate handfuls of them, their fingers stained violet by the time they heard their mother calling for them.

"Roman? Georgiana? It's time for supper."

I remember now, Roman thought with a jolt. *We like our middle names best.*

More memories flared, melting into each other. Days Roman had lived that had once seemed dull and insignificant—the same routine, over and over—but were now comforting, spellbinding to rediscover. He hadn't been alone in that vast, sprawling house. He had his sister Del, and she was light and courage and whimsy.

He saw the day she was born. The first time he carefully held her, the rain pouring beyond the windows. And then he saw the day she died. The pond reflecting the storm clouds overhead, her body floating face down—*I just closed my eyes for a moment*—and the ripples on the water as he flung himself toward her.

"Breathe, Del!" he cried, pumping her chest. Her lips were blue, her eyes open and glassy. "Wake up! *Wake up!*"

Roman startled awake.

He stared wide-eyed into the darkness as the dream settled like silt. His pulse throbbed in his ears and blood rushed hot beneath his skin.

It was only a dream.

But Roman could still taste that pond water, feel it drip from his hair. He could smell the damp earth of the shore, like it had only been yesterday when the water had stolen Del away.

He didn't remember having a sister. But the dream had been so vivid, he couldn't help but wonder if his mind was trying to help him recall those lost pieces of his past.

If this wasn't just a dream, then it's my fault that my sister is dead.

He covered his face with his hands, trying to swallow the tears. But the sobs racked him like a storm tide. Roman eventually curled on his side and let them shudder through his bones. He lay there until his weeping subsided. His throat was raw, his stomach ached.

If he remained here any longer, the pallet would feel like a grave.

He forced himself to rise.

Flushed and bleary-eyed, he moved to the door. It opened, swinging crookedly on its offset hinges. To Roman's surprise, Shane wasn't posted in the hallway as guard. In fact, the corridor was empty and quiet, full of night's deepest shadows.

Roman stepped into the hallway. He let his feet take him to the staircase and quietly descended, pausing only when the two guards at the front door met his gaze with brows arched in suspicion.

"I'm going to the kitchen," Roman whispered hoarsely. "For a glass of milk."

One of the soldiers gave him a slight nod. Roman continued on his way, drawn by the warmth and flickering firelight of the kitchen.

He expected it would be empty and was once again shocked when he saw that Dacre was sitting at the table, staring at a spread of maps. He cradled a glass of dark red ale in his large hands, and the sight was so domestic that it could have fooled Roman into believing that the gods were cut from the same cloth as mortals. That they were not so terrifying and omnipotent as human-kind was bred to believe.

"Roman," Dacre greeted him, his deep-timbred voice rising with surprise. "What has you up at such an hour?"

"I could ask the same of you, sir," Roman replied, his gaze coasting over the maps. "Don't divines need sleep?"

Dacre smiled and stood. He put his ale down and began to gather up the paper. "Perhaps we do, from time to time. But you're a welcome sight and a reminder that I should take a break."

A welcome sight, Roman's mind echoed as Dacre set aside the stack of caramel-edged illustrations. *And he doesn't want me to see those maps.*

"Here, sit," Dacre said, drawing out one of the chairs. "Would you like a dram?"

"I didn't mean to disturb you," Roman replied. "I came for a cup of milk, actually. I used to drink it when I couldn't sleep."

A line furrowed Dacre's brow. In the candlelight, he suddenly looked older, almost haggard. His eyes narrowed, gleaming like gemstones. "The typewriter is helping you remember?"

Roman nodded, but his tongue curled behind his teeth. He still wasn't sure why Dacre had asked him to identify his old typewriter and then secretly given him the other.

Unless he doesn't want me to remember.

The thought nearly struck Roman off-balance and he sank into the chair. He watched as Dacre opened the fridge and withdrew a bottle of milk.

"We're fortunate the people of this town left their livestock behind," Dacre said as he poured a tall glass. "A thoughtful offering, or else my forces would be hungry. As would you, correspondent."

"Yes," Roman whispered, his thoughts preoccupied with the account Dacre had given him of Avalon Bluff, days ago.

They had walked the streets together, observing the damage. Some houses sat in heaps of rubble, charred from fire. Others had escaped the bombs' destruction, but still held evidence of the terror with shattered windows and crooked doorways and pieces of shrapnel glittering in the yard. Roman had written it down in his notepad, but he had also transcribed what Dacre had said. In many ways, that account didn't feel like Roman's words at all.

"Whatever happened to that first article I wrote for you?" he asked. "The one detailing how you saved Avalon Bluff?"

Dacre set the milk in front of Roman before returning to his chair at the head of the table. Again, there was that faint metallic clink when he moved.

"Would you like to see it?"

Roman frowned. "What do you mean, sir?"

Wordlessly, Dacre pulled a folded newspaper from the stack near his elbow. He set it down with a plop, and Roman leaned forward, reading the dark-inked headline.

DACRE SAVES HUNDREDS OF WOUNDED IN AVALON BLUFF
by ROMAN C. KITT

Roman's heart slowed to a heavy beat. As if responding to a siren's call, he reached out and took the newspaper in his hands, if only to read his words again in such fine print. To feel the ink rub off on his fingertips.

"The *Oath Gazette*," he read aloud, admiring the paper's calligraphic header. And there, deep in his chest, was a spark. "How far is Oath from here?"

"Six hundred kilometers to the east."

"Is that where you're heading, sir? To the city?"

"Yes. To reunite with *Enva*."

The goddess's name made Roman freeze. It felt familiar; Roman knew he had spoken it before.

"My wife," Dacre supplied with a sharp smile. "She lived in the realm below with me, and while I loved her and gave her my vow . . . she was a trickster, biding her time and scheming to betray me."

"I'm sorry." Roman was uncertain how else to reply. "Is that what this war is about? A broken vow between you and her?"

"It is about far more than that, but I don't expect you to understand, given that you are mortal and unmarried. You've never uttered a vow, or felt it settle in your bones like magic. You've never sworn yourself to another."

Roman wanted to protest. His cheeks warmed, but he didn't understand why. He forced himself to remain silent, listening as Dacre continued.

"I hoped that she would meet me halfway after I woke from my grave. That she would come to me; but she has chosen a coward's path, remaining in Oath. It is now up to me to save this realm from her deceptions."

More questions bloomed in Roman's mind, but they withered when he hung on the word *save*. He saw Del again—her gaze vacant, her mouth full of water, her heart unresponsive beneath his frantically pumping hands. Roman hadn't been able to save her in the dream, and he still felt bruised from that horrible mistake. A mistake that should never have happened. If it had happened at all.

"You're thinking of someone," said Dacre. "Or perhaps remembering them?"

Roman inwardly shook himself. Yet another foolish thing, to let his mind wander when he was alone with a god. "Yes. I had a dream."

"You *dreamt* of someone you loved?" There was a sharpness in Dacre's tone. "Someone from your past?"

Roman hesitated. "I dreamt that I had a little sister. Delaney." He wasn't sure how much to tell Dacre, but once he started speaking, the account flowed from him. It was strange how tasting the dream with his voice only made it more solid.

This really happened. His heart pounded the assurance through him. *I had a sister, and I lost her.*

Dacre was silent for a few moments, as if weighing the dream. But when he spoke, his words were the last thing Roman expected.

"Did you know I also have a sister? She is one of the remaining Underlings in this realm, sung to sleep in a grave south of here."

"Alva?" Roman said, reflexively. He had a faint recollection of a schoolroom, a map of Cambria pinned on the wall, a teacher droning on about the five divine graves in the realm. *The gods we championed and buried—Enva Skyward, Dacre Underling, Alva Underling, Mir Underling, and Luz Skyward. The gods who will be captive to eternal sleep.*

"Yes, Alva," Dacre replied, his voice softening on her name. "We shared the same mother, hence why the two of us were bound for everlasting trouble, even though our powers, compared to others of our kin, were quite harmless."

"Your powers?"

"Did they fail to teach you about the full breadth of divinity in that school of yours?" But Dacre didn't give Roman a chance to respond. "Of course they did. Mortals are often afraid of the things they don't understand."

"I know that you heal, sir," Roman said, tracing the scars around his knee. "But what was your sister's power?"

"You mean what *is* her power. She only sleeps, as I once did. She's not dead."

"Y-yes, of course. Forgive me, I only meant—"

"Alva is the goddess of dreams," Dacre interrupted. "Of nightmares."

Roman stiffened. He could still feel his own nightmare shadowing him, and he drank a sip of milk, trying to chase away that hint of pond water and anguish.

"When we were young, our powers seemed harmless amongst our own kind and we never worried about them being stolen from us," Dacre continued. "For gods rarely need sleep, and our bodies can heal themselves. What good are healing and dreams amongst divinity? But it was a much different story when it came to mortal kind. You bleed and break. You crave sleep, even as it makes you vulnerable. You dream to make sense of the world you are in."

"Is that all it was, then?" Roman asked. "My dream of Del?"

Dacre sighed and leaned closer. "I will tell you what Alva told me long ago. For she has walked many mortal dreams. Sometimes your kind dreams of things you wish had happened. The images are wrapped up in your present emotions, or the troubles you are currently facing. Your envisioning of a little sister is a simple expression of how much you long for family, to be known. But that's all it is: just a dream."

Roman swallowed. The god's words, although kindly spoken, landed like darts.

"You disagree?" Dacre said.

"The dream," Roman said, but his voice was faint. "It *felt* real. I saw the house I grew up in. I saw my father, my mother. Heard their voices. Walked through my old room. All the details . . . I just don't see how I could make them up."

"Do you *want* it to be real?" Dacre countered. "Would it make you feel better about yourself to know you had a sister, but that it was your fault she drowned?"

Roman couldn't speak. The lump returned to his throat; it tasted sour like guilt, catching his breaths.

"Roman?"

"I'm not sure," he whispered, clenching his eyes closed.

"Perhaps I should ask you this. Even if the dream was real, which I believe it *wasn't,* do we live by our past, or do we live by what is to come? Do we choose to waste time looking behind to things that have already happened and cannot be changed, or do we keep our sight forward on what we can see?"

Roman's eyes opened. He focused on the candlelight, the glass of milk before him. The shadow of a god, cast over the table. "Forward, sir."

"Good lad." Dacre reached for a piece of paper in the stack at his elbow. It looked like a typed missive, crinkled and bloodstained. It took Roman a second to realize that he was being dismissed. "If you have any other dreams, I'd like to hear them, Roman."

"Yes. Of course, sir." Roman stood and finished his milk, setting the glass in the sink. But he stopped at the table once more, reaching for the newspaper. "May I keep this?"

"If you want it, it is yours. But I do hope your next article will be ready in the morning?"

Roman tucked the *Oath Gazette* beneath his arm. "I'm afraid I might need a little more time."

Dacre was quiet. The firelight flickered across his face, turning his hair a dark shade of gold. "Tomorrow, then. Have it ready for me to review by sundown."

"Thank you, sir." Roman began to leave but paused on the kitchen threshold to glance behind him. A god sitting at a table, sipping ale, reading a blood-splattered page. This honestly felt more like a dream than the one about Del.

Dacre felt the draw of Roman's stare and glanced up. "Is there something else?"

"No." Roman gave a hint of a smile. "Thank you for the milk, sir."

It didn't hit Roman until a few minutes later, when he was back in the safety of his room. He lit a candle and sat at his desk again, studying his headline in the *Oath Gazette*.

Roman C. Kitt.

He had remembered his first and last name days ago, but his middle initial? He hadn't included it in his typed article. He hadn't known his middle name at the time. Someone else had added that *C.* to his byline, whether it was Dacre or a newspaper employee. Someone else. Roman felt tension coil in his stomach until he heard Del's sweet voice echo through him.

This way, Carver.

Slowly, his hands found their place on the typewriter keys.

Once more, he tried to type for Dacre. The article he wanted Roman to spin about his healing mercies and powers. And once again, different words flowed out.

My name is Roman Carver Kitt, and this is a dead man's story.

7

Every Lost Letter

I ris crouched in the boughs of an oak tree, waiting for Attie. It was one in the morning, and a cool mist spun through the night, turning the lamp-lights below into hazy rings of amber. The city felt strangely quiet, although if Iris held her breath, she could hear faint conversation spilling from a pub a few streets over, and the occasional clop of horses' hooves as constables rode their sleepy rounds.

She carefully shifted her weight to keep her feet from going numb, mindful of the leather bag she carried on her back. The tree bark was slick from the mist, and Iris had just discovered she wasn't keen on heights, or scaling trees in the dark. But this was the only way to gain access to the museum without setting off the alarm. Or so Sarah Prindle had said, and she had taken two full days to come up with a watertight plan.

Iris frowned and felt the mask stick to her face. She resisted the temptation to scratch her nose through the damp fabric and sighed.

She had been waiting in this oak tree, staring at the back wall of the museum and its third story window, for what felt like an hour now. Sarah and Attie had been waiting for much longer within, entering the museum as unassuming visitors and then concealing themselves in the lavatory before the doors magically locked at dusk. There they would hide until midnight, when the two of them would catch the night guard by surprise on his security rounds. Only then would Attie be able to open the window for Iris to climb through.

"The museum is an enchanted building," Sarah had said at breakfast that morning, when the three girls had gathered to solidify their plan. "Once the doors are locked and bolted at nightfall, there is no opening them without setting off a horrendous alarm."

"So how do we do this?" Iris set down her toast, stomach churning. "Is it even possible?"

"It's possible, thanks to a window that was added to the third floor a few decades ago," Sarah explained. "One of the museum's best-kept secrets is that that window isn't enchanted like the original windows and doors are. As long as we don't trigger the alarm, it will be our way out."

"How did you discover this, Prindle?" Attie asked.

"My father knows one of the guards," Sarah replied with a shrug. "They've been friends since childhood. And men like to talk when they get drunk."

"Is this particular guard going to be on watch tonight?" Iris said.

"No." Sarah smiled, wrapping her fingers around her teacup. "Grantford is on duty tonight, and he's renowned for his laziness. It'll be perfect."

There was no question of the thievery taking place that night, Grantford or not. Iris and Attie were supposed to head west to River Down the next morning.

Iris now stared at the window until it blended into the darkness. She could just discern the gleam of glass panes and she continued to wait, relieved when she finally heard a squeak.

The window was lifting.

Stage one of the heist had been successful.

Iris released a deep breath, tasting salt on her lips. She began to move along the branch until she could see Attie within the narrow window frame, whistling a mourning dove's song.

Iris returned the sound and prepared herself, one hand holding fast to the bough above her, the other outstretched. Dimly, she saw Attie hurl the rope her way, its thick body like a snake striking the night. The end of the rope hit somewhere to Iris's left, and just a few feet shy as it tore through the leaves. While Attie reeled it back in, preparing for a second attempt, Iris's nerves sang.

She could sense the distance beneath her. If she fell, the ground would break her into pieces.

Three more tosses, and Iris finally grasped hold of the rope.

She was trembling as she walked it back to the trunk of the oak. Two deep inhales to calm her mind, and then she deftly began to knot the rope to the tree. Iris and Attie had practiced tying this particular knot endless times that day, because if they did it wrong, they would be plunging to their deaths. Yet one more number to add to the failed museum heists.

But once the rope was secured, Iris hesitated, feeling the tingling draw of the fall.

There was a courtyard below. Plots of wildflowers and a small reflection pond. The oak's gnarled branches shaded half of a cobbled patio where museum employees and guests could sit and enjoy a cup of afternoon tea.

Another whistle of birdsong.

Iris glanced up, measuring the distance between herself and Attie. It felt as vast as the ocean, although it was just over ten meters. Her friend was still waiting, a shadow in the frame. Waiting to take hold of Iris's hand and haul her in through the window.

She just needed to take that first step into midair.

Carefully, Iris did, letting herself hang from the rope. It held firm overhead, but five arm-lengths down the line, her hands began to sting, her grip inevitably weakening. Her gloves were slick; she clenched her jaw and welded her focus to the task.

She was halfway to the window when she heard a clatter beneath her.

She paused, glancing down at the courtyard.

Far beneath her dangling feet, the world seemed to spin in the mist until she saw four figures walking over the cobblestoned patio. They were dressed in dark garments, their faces concealed behind masks.

Iris bit her lip, heart thrumming in alarm. Was this another heist in progress? Surely not, but she didn't dare move as the figures strode directly beneath her. If one of them happened to glance up and see her, it would all be over.

Her shoulders burned as she held still, the cords of her neck tense. The seconds felt like years, but to Iris's relief, the figures continued on their way, crossing the street before they melted into the night.

She continued to move along the rope, grinding her teeth when she reached the brick wall.

"Take my hand," Attie urgently whispered.

Iris pried her right hand off the rope. She could scarcely feel her fingers as Attie's firm grip came around them, hauling her upward and in through the window.

"Did you see them?" Iris asked, struggling to catch her breath. She reached out to lean on a battered chair, realizing they were standing in a storage room. It was overcome with crates and busted frames; the clutter made Iris feel even more anxious.

"Yes," Attie replied. "I counted four of them. All wearing masks. Thought another heist was about to happen."

"So did I. Who do you think they were?"

"Gods only know. Thieves with a different destination, maybe?"

Iris removed one of her gloves to wipe the sweat from her eyes. "You don't think they saw me, do you?"

"No." Attie's attention darted back out the window, as if she didn't quite believe it. "But in case I'm wrong . . . let's not waste any time here."

Iris followed Attie down two flights of stairs to the ground floor. At night, the museum felt like a different place, full of dangerous gleams and moving shadows. Or perhaps it was only a play of the low-lit lamps and the darkness in between? Iris wasn't certain, but she shuddered when she thought she saw one of the marble busts move on its pedestal.

"Where's Prindle?" she whispered.

"In the main office, guarding Grantford," Attie replied in a low tone. "He didn't put up much of a fight. He's gagged and blindfolded."

Iris nodded, turning down one of the wide hallways. The air felt cold and thick when she at last arrived at the chamber of mismatched, odd things. A pair of pointed leather shoes worn by one of the dead gods, a pocket watch that was rumored to provoke rainstorms every time it struck midnight, a sword named Draven that had once seen battle against the divines centuries ago, a small inkwell that brimmed with glimmering liquid, and a magic-forged typewriter. All enclosed in glass and set on display.

Iris eased the bag from her shoulders as she approached the First Alouette. Her fingers felt slow and numb as she unbuckled the pack, withdrawing the baseball bat.

This feels wrong, she thought with a prick of guilt. But she studied the glass case that held the First Alouette and a collection of old letters, and she added, *I didn't come all this way to turn around empty-handed.*

She envisioned Roman in the west, trapped within Dacre's cloying hold.

Iris swung.

The bat collided with the display case, shattering the glass. The pieces scattered across the floor, gathering like crystals between the typewriter's keys. One of the letters fluttered down and rested amid the glittering carnage like a white flag of surrender.

Iris set the bat aside and stepped over the glass, feeling it crunch beneath the soles of her boots. She picked up the typewriter and turned it over to check the underside. A few more pieces of glass rained down as the strike bars shifted, but Iris found what she sought. The silver plaque was bolted to the inside of the frame, engraved with THE FIRST ALOUETTE, MADE ESPECIALLY FOR A.V.S.

This was what she needed. What she *wanted.*

She was holding magic in her hands, and she carefully set the typewriter into the black case she had brought, buckling the lid closed. Attie helped her slip the case into the pack, along with the bat. The thievery was over and done within heartbeats, but Iris couldn't shake the eerie feeling that someone was watching them.

"I'll go get Prindle," Attie said. "We'll meet you at the foot of the stairs?"

Iris nodded, hefting the pack onto her shoulders. She crouched to pick up the letter that had fluttered to the floor, a letter Alouette Stone had written decades ago, gently setting it on the glass-strewn pedestal. But her eyes caught on a line of typed words.

> The magic still gathers, and the past is gilded; I see the beauty in what has been but only because I have tasted both sorrow and joy in equal measures.

Iris turned away, heading to the stairs. But she blinked back tears and thought, *As have I, Alouette.*

A light rain was falling, and the night felt ancient by the time Iris reached her flat. She had parted ways with Sarah and Attie at the museum once the three of them had made it safely out the window and back onto solid ground. They had been breathless and giddy and a touch paranoid from the fact that they had just pulled off a successful heist.

They would revel in this secret later, at a nice restaurant. When the war was over. Iris would treat her friends to a fine dinner. And then she would return the First Alouette to the museum. Anonymously, of course.

Despite those promises and the aches in her hands, none of this felt real. Iris could have convinced herself she was dreaming until she was safe in her room and had shed the bag from her shoulders. Her mask and dark clothes, her gloves and her boots. She drew on a nightgown and pinned up her damp hair. Carefully, she retrieved the typewriter and sat on the floor in the very place where she had once typed letter after letter to her brother, then to Roman.

She set the First Alouette before her crossed knees, feeding a fresh page into the roller.

The minutes began to pass; the night crept to its coldest hour. The rain started falling in earnest beyond her window, and Iris stared at the blank page, wondering what she should say to Roman. She didn't know where he was. She didn't know if he was safe, if he was imprisoned. If he even had his typewriter with him.

There were too many unknowns and communicating with him could put him in danger.

The silence broke when paper began to whisper over the floor. Iris watched, astounded, as page after folded page appeared from the shadows of her wardrobe door. So many they were creating a pile. She lunged toward them, heart frantic, and quickly unfolded one.

Do you ever feel as if you wear armor, day after day? That when people look at you, they see only the shine of steel that you've so carefully encased yourself in?

Iris lowered the page, bewildered.

This was an old letter. One Roman had written to her when she had known him only as C.

She reached for another and was shocked to discover it was one of hers. Iris went through them all until she realized she was familiar with every single letter. She had either authored them or read them so many times the words had become imprinted on her mind.

Iris exhaled a shaky breath, sitting back down on the rug. She had thought her correspondence with Roman had been lost at Marisol's. But the First Alouette hadn't forgotten its magic, even when it had been confined in the museum. This typewriter had been holding the letters, waiting for the moment it could deliver them by a wardrobe door.

Iris reread her favorite ones until it felt like her chest had cracked. Roman's words echoed in her bones, waking a fierce ache in her.

She set down the letters, resolved. She would be shrewd and careful, although a part of her believed her letters wouldn't be able to find him.

He won't remember you.

Forest's words haunted her.

Iris felt bruised by the memory. She chewed on a hangnail, wondering if Forest had spoken truth or if he was only trying to wound her. To keep her home and safe. To keep her from reaching out into the darkness again.

Be mindful, she told herself, her fingertips finding their place on the keys. *Make sure it's him before you reveal yourself or say anything important.*

Iris typed a brief message. Her hands trembled as she drew the paper from the roller and folded it. It felt like no time had passed as she slid the page beneath her wardrobe door. No time at all, and yet it also felt like seasons bloomed and molted in a single unsteady breath. How odd that magic could be two different things at once. Young and old. New and familiar. Worry and comfort.

She didn't know what she was expecting, whether it was for the wardrobe to return her letter unopened or for Roman to write her back within seconds. To her shock, neither happened.

Iris paced, bleary-eyed and exhausted, realizing . . . *nothing had happened.*

Her letter was gone, magically delivered elsewhere, but Roman hadn't replied.

Defeated, she sank onto the bed. She fell asleep to the rain, but her dreams were nothing more than a gray, empty expanse.

8

The Name of a Pet Snail

Roman woke to sunlight dancing across his face.

He didn't know where he was for a moment. His breaths shuddered through him and his mind was foggy from a dream he couldn't remember. But he began to piece together his surroundings.

He was looking at his typewriter. A nearby candlestick had burned down to a wax puddle on the wood. His cheek was pressed to the hard surface of his desk, and a loose sheet of paper stuck to his skin as he lifted his head.

I'm in the room they assigned me. I'm safe.

He must have fallen asleep at his desk last night, and he rubbed the crick in his neck before standing with a groan.

That was when he noticed it.

A piece of paper rested on the floor, just before the wardrobe.

Roman frowned. He had no memory of putting it there, and he approached the closet, sweeping the page up with his hands. Shocked, he read:

1. What was the name of my pet snail?
2. What is my middle name?

3. Which season is my favorite and why?

He stared at the words until the type seemed to bleed together.

"What is this?" he whispered, reaching for the wardrobe door. He opened it, prepared to find anything. To both his disappointment and relief, the closet was empty save for the trio of hanging coats and the folded quilt, musty on a shelf.

There was absolutely nothing magical about it.

Roman shut the door, reading the message again. He could feel a faint tug in his chest. One that made him wary as well as ravenous.

Should I know these answers? he thought, staring at the words.

How could he mourn something that he couldn't remember? Roman wondered if there was a word to describe such a feeling, for the way it gathered on his shoulders like snow. Cold and soft and infinite, melting as soon as he touched it.

He was still grappling with his emotions and the three riddles when he heard a heavy tread beyond the walls. Someone was approaching his room. Roman shoved the paper in his pocket, the corner of it jabbing his palm just as the door blew open.

"Pack your things," Lieutenant Shane said. "We're finally leaving this shithole. You have five minutes to meet me downstairs."

As abruptly as he had arrived, the lieutenant left, leaving the door cracked.

Roman exhaled, but he felt stiff with unease. He could hear Dacre conversing with someone a floor below. Boots were clomping on the hardwood. Out on the streets, there was a chorus of rumbles as lorries were cranked.

They were leaving this sad town, and Roman could only dread where they would go next.

He packed his belongings. He didn't have much, but as he was locking his typewriter in its case, he drew out the strange message again and studied it. Was it a code? Who would ever have a pet snail?

He dropped the letter into the rubbish bin and walked to the door. But something within him stretched tight, like skin about to split. Roman went back to the bin and withdrew the note. It returned to his pocket as he made his way down the stairs, thinking Dacre might be interested in the message.

The front door was open; the foyer was sunlit, smelling of lorry exhaust, cigarette smoke, and burned bacon from the kitchen. Shane stood on the threshold, hands linked behind his back as he gave orders to a private on the porch. Roman took that moment to study the adjacent parlor.

The door he had once passed through, the one that connected the world above to the realm below, was wide open.

He was still staring at the shadowed passageway, gooseflesh creeping over his skin, when Dacre emerged from it. The god shut the door behind him and took hold of a key that hung from a long chain around his neck. Roman had never noticed it in their previous meetings, but Dacre must have always worn the necklace, concealing it beneath his uniform.

He locked the door and let the key slide back beneath his clothes, turning when he sensed Roman's attention.

Their gazes aligned and held, like predator and prey.

Dacre began to close the distance between them. Roman had the sudden urge to back away, but he forced himself to remain upright and unmoving.

"I would like you to ride with me," Dacre said when he reached the foyer.

"Yes, sir," Roman replied. "May I ask where we're heading?"

Dacre smiled. The sunlight flashed on his teeth as he said, "We're going east."

Iris stepped out of her bedroom, surprised to find Forest sitting at the table with a cup of tea. Her brother looked disheveled and glum, his eyes bloodshot, his chestnut hair tangled across his forehead. Had he heard her sneaking in and out last night? Had he heard her typing, pacing?

If he had, he would say something, Iris thought. She imagined Forest hearing about how the First Alouette had been stolen from the museum. It was only a few more hours until that news would break but Attie and Iris would be long gone by then. Her brother didn't know about the magic of the Alouettes like she did, so he might not connect the crime to her. Yet the thought of shaming him with her thievery, or realizing he was disappointed in her, made her feel small, breathless.

For a tense moment, their gazes held. Neither of them spoke, but Iris watched as Forest noticed her jumpsuit with the INKRIDDEN TRIBUNE PRESS badge stitched over the heart. She also wore her boots with new, sturdy laces, and held her typewriter case in one hand and a leather duffel bag in the other.

"You're leaving," he said in a flat tone.

"I told you I was."

Another twinge of silence. Forest sighed, glancing away from her.

"I don't approve of this." His voice was rough but soft, as if it hurt to speak the words.

"I didn't want you to leave either," Iris said. "When you left to fight for Enva months ago. And yet I understood why you did. I knew I couldn't stand in the way of it."

When Forest remained quiet, Iris thought that was it. He wasn't going to say another word to her, and she bit the inside of her cheek as she headed to the door.

"Wait, Iris."

She paused, shoulders stiff. But she waited, listening as Forest rose from the chair. She felt him draw close to her. He smelled faintly of motor oil and petrol, from his new job at the mechanic shop down the road. No matter how much he washed his hands in the evenings, his nails remained stained with grease. Sometimes he scrubbed his knuckles so hard the skin broke.

"You'll write to me?" he said, taking hold of her elbow. "You'll keep me updated?"

"I promise."

"If you don't, then you can expect me to raise hell at the *Tribune*."

That drew a small smile from her. "I'd like to see that."

Forest snorted. "No, you wouldn't." It seemed like he wanted to say more but couldn't. Instead, he reached for the golden locket hanging from his neck. The locket that had belonged to their mother.

"Wear this at all times," he whispered, draping it over Iris's head. "Promise me."

"Forest, I can't take this—"

"*Promise* me."

Iris flinched at his harsh tone. But when she met his gaze, she saw only fear, burning like embers in his eyes.

Her fingers closed over the locket, holding to it like an anchor. She remembered what Forest had once told her: when he had found this locket in the trenches, his strength and determination had rekindled. He had rallied and slipped away from Dacre's hold, remembering who he was and where he had come from. It was only when he held something tangible of home—a memory strung on a long chain—that he was able to break the god's power over him.

"I won't take it off," she whispered. "At least, not until I return home and can give it back to you."

Forest nodded, worry etched on his brow. His last words to Iris made her shiver.

"You're going to need it, Little Flower."

Roman gazed out the lorry window, catching a final glimpse of Avalon Bluff.

It was a landscape made of rubble and ghosts. A town spun with small testaments to the people who had once lived on this hill. They had left behind trampled gardens, crumbling stone fences, shadowed doorways, and walls that held abandoned belongings. Debris, burnt thatch, and glittering shards of glass. Roman wondered who had once lived in the homes they passed. He wondered where they were now. If they were safe.

That was what he wanted to write about. And he lowered his eyes when he realized he had lost his chance.

Dacre sat beside him on the bench, newspaper in his pale, elegant hands. The sight of the paper roused Roman's curiosity.

"Sir?" he dared to ask. "How did you know my middle initial?"

Dacre shot a curious glance at him. "What do you mean?"

"My byline in the *Gazette*. You submitted it as 'Roman C. Kitt.'"

"I only submitted what you gave me."

"Then who—"

"In your life before your healing, you worked at the *Oath Gazette*. Your articles were published several times a month. You were striving to become a columnist."

Roman's mind wheeled, desperate to grasp hold of a memory. "I don't remember."

"Of course you don't remember. Not *yet*. Your former employer was the one to resurrect your old byline."

"I see."

Dacre tilted his head to the side. "Do you, Roman?"

"You knew me before you found me dying in the field."

"I knew *of* you," Dacre corrected before his attention returned to his newspaper. Roman could see it wasn't the *Gazette* but a paper called the *Inkridden Tribune*. "You have a prestigious family name. One that has been a great support to me and my efforts. And I will not forget those who have faithfully served me."

Roman was frozen, silent. But his heart ached, desperate for home. For *family*.

He couldn't deny that he wanted to feel like he belonged somewhere. He wanted to trust what he was seeing. To fight for something.

"Sir?" he said. "There's something I'd like to show you."

Dacre was quiet, but interest lit his eyes.

Roman began to reach for the paper in his pocket, to pull out the strange note. But something tugged within his chest, sharp as a fishing line cast out to sea.

Wait.

He flexed his hand, hesitant.

Who wrote this? What sort of magic delivered it to me? Will I ever truly know the answers if I give it to him?

"You wanted to show me something?" Dacre prompted.

"Yes." Roman reached down to open his typewriter case instead, withdrawing his half-written article. "What I was last working on."

"Save it for this evening when we reach camp," Dacre said, his focus returning to the *Inkridden Tribune*.

Roman felt stung at first by Dacre's lack of interest. But then he realized the *Tribune* must be dictating what Dacre wrote for the *Gazette*. It was like a game of chess. Roman tucked his article in the case.

He sat back in the seat and watched Avalon Bluff fade away as if it had never been, that strange letter heavy as iron in his pocket.

9

Roadster Post

Iris was almost to the *Inkridden Tribune* when she sensed someone following her again. She could feel their gaze, boring into her.

She stopped and glanced behind, her arms tired from hauling her typewriter and duffel bag.

It was half past seven in the morning, and the shadows were still long and blue between buildings. But she could see the man who was trailing her, a dark trench coat belted at his waist and a hat tilted on his head, shielding his face.

"Mr. Kitt?" Iris called to him, trying to quell her fear. But her voice held a slight ring of alarm, even as she lifted her chin in defiance. "Why are you following me?"

The man said nothing but continued to walk toward her. His brogues clicked on the cobblestones, and his hands remained tucked away in his coat pockets. As the distance closed between them, Iris swallowed. This man was not as tall and trim as Mr. Kitt. He was broader, shorter. The trench coat couldn't hide his brawn. When he finally glanced up to meet her gaze, she saw that his nose was crooked. One of his ears looked permanently swollen, and there was a prominent scar on his jaw.

A boxer, or a fighter. Someone who dealt blows for a living.

Iris's first piercing thought was *He knows. He knows I stole the typewriter and he's come to take it back.*

She whirled on her heel, blood coursing hot in her veins as she prepared to flee.

"Miss Winnow," he called to her. "I've an important message for you. From Mr. Kitt."

That stopped her, as if her ankles had sunk into a bog.

Slowly, Iris turned around to face the man. He stood two paces away, regarding her with an amused gleam in his eyes. His expression seemed to say *you can run, but you won't get very far.*

"What is the message?" she asked. "And why didn't you mention it sooner, rather than follow me?"

"Did I frighten you? My apologies, miss," he said, laying a beefy hand over his heart.

She couldn't tell if he was being sincere or mocking her, and she frowned, resisting the temptation to step back. The *Tribune* was only a block away. Five minutes from where she stood. If she hurled her duffel bag at the man, she might be able to outrun him . . .

He withdrew something from his pocket. An envelope with her name scrawled over the front. Quietly, he extended it to her.

"What is that?" she asked.

"Take it and you'll see."

She hesitated, staring at the envelope.

"Go on, little miss," he said. "It's something you want."

I sincerely doubt that, Iris thought, but then she imagined what it might be. It was possible Mr. Kitt had begun his own inquiries into Roman's whereabouts, ever since he realized his son wasn't in Oath. As one of the richest men in the city, he might have gained some valuable insight.

Iris set down her bag and typewriter and took the envelope, surprised by how thick and heavy it was. She broke the seal only to realize it was brimming with money. Bill after bill after bill. She had never held so much money in her hands before, and she shivered, gaping down at it.

"Mr. Kitt has requested that you sign this agreement here, annulling your marriage to his son." The man reached into his coat and pulled out a legal document and a fountain pen. "It also states that you will relinquish whatever hold or claims you have on Mr. Roman Kitt, and that you will not interfere with his current work at the *Gazette*. The money should provide a comfortable living for the next few years and—"

Iris hurled the money to the ground. The bills spilled from the envelope, spreading like a green fan on the cobblestones.

"My father-in-law can keep his money," she said. "And I will not sign that document. Tell him to save his efforts because my answer will never change."

She picked up her luggage and strode away, relieved when the man didn't follow. But she could feel him staring at her.

Iris's hands were like ice as she turned the corner.

She could see the old building that held the *Inkridden Tribune* ahead, the upper windows reflecting the rising sun. But her attention was promptly snagged by a smart-looking motorcar, parked at the curb. Attie was standing beside it, as were Helena and a young man Iris had never seen before.

She quickened her pace, heart in her throat. Returning to the front almost felt like a dream. It didn't feel real yet, and Iris wondered when it would. She could scarcely believe she was doing this again.

"Helena?" Iris said, finally reaching the group. "Sorry I'm late."

Helena turned, left brow arched. Her auburn hair was slicked back, and she held an unlit cigarette. It was evident she was trying to kick the habit. "You're not late, we're simply ahead of schedule for once."

Before Iris could reply, the young man stepped forward. He was dressed in gray trousers, knee-high boots, leather braces, and a white shirt, the buttons undone at the collar. His skin was a rich brown, his face freshly shaved. His eyes were dark and mirthful, framed by long lashes. A bowler hat with a feather tucked within its band sat on his head, and a pair of goggles hung from his neck.

"I'll take your bags, miss," he offered.

"Oh, thank you," Iris said, surprised, as he took her things and stowed them in the trunk of what she assumed was his motorcar. "We're not going by train?"

"No," Helena replied, finally lighting her cigarette with a defeated sigh. She drew in a few puffs, the smoke curling in the air. "The train has become unreliable and untrustworthy. It's also too slow for our present needs."

Iris could hear the words she didn't utter. The Kitts had chartered the railroad. The Kitts held immense power over most of the transportation in Oath, and now that Iris was refusing to do what Mr. Kitt wanted, she could only assume matters would get worse when it came to crossing paths with her father-in-law.

"We're going by *roadster*," Attie said in a low, excited voice. She was also wearing her correspondent jumpsuit with a leather belt fastened at her waist. Her favorite binoculars hung from her neck, as did a set of goggles, just like the driver's.

Iris studied the motorcar again. It was built of sleek black metal with gold-rimmed headlights and wooden running boards. The tires gleamed with white spoked wheels, and there were two doors: one for the driver, and one for the back seat, which was upholstered in red leather. There was a windshield but no cover for the cab.

"I've never ridden in a roadster," Iris said.

"Well, there's a first time for everything. Make sure you wear these when you're out on the open road going full speed." Helena handed her a pair of goggles. "This is Tobias Bexley. He's one of the most prestigious post runners in Cambria, and he'll be driving you to each town. When you have your articles drafted and ready, he'll transport them back to me while you wait for him to return. Then he'll drive you to the next stop. I told him to take you as far as Winthrop in Central Borough. It's as close to the front as I feel comfortable allowing you both to be, but even so, things can change overnight, so be alert."

Iris nodded, slipping the goggles over her head. They clinked against the locket and she couldn't help but picture Forest. Grease on his hands, scabs on his knuckles, sitting in their flat as the shadows crept across the floor in the evenings. A stab of worry made her stomach clench. She wished her brother wasn't alone. She wished there was someone she could send to be with him while she was away.

"Are you listening, Iris?" Helena said wryly.

"Yes, ma'am." Iris tucked a few threads of hair behind her ear. "Where is our first stop?"

"River Down, with Marisol. From there, you'll go to my next contact, Lonnie Fielding in Bitteryne. After that, you'll have to find places to lodge on your own with the funds I've provided, but most of all, if Bexley says you need to retreat, you jump into his roadster without question and let him drive you back to Oath. Understood?"

"Understood," Attie echoed. "Anything you want us to report on in particular?"

"Whatever you find," Helena replied, dropping the half-smoked cigarette to the pavement. She crushed it beneath her heel. "Dacre's plans, his movements, what he's doing to the land, to civilians. Updates, stories from eyewitnesses, things you observe."

"The chancellor . . ." Iris's voice trailed off.

Helena gave her a knowing look. "He won't like it, but I've a mind to publish the truth, consequences be damned. Now, get along, the two of you. I expect your first article by tomorrow evening."

Iris took a step forward but then paused, turning to look at Helena again. "I was thinking."

"About what?"

"About my byline. I think I want to change it."

"You *think*?"

"I do. I want it to be Iris E. Winnow."

A pensive expression stole over Helena's freckled face. But then she nodded. "Very well. But what's the E stand for?"

"Elizabeth," Iris replied. "It was also my nan's middle name."

"An homage to her, then?"

Yes, Iris thought, but Roman also haunted her in that moment. She remembered how much it had once irritated her that she didn't know what the C stood for in his byline.

Tobias opened the passenger door. Attie climbed aboard first, followed by Iris. The leather seat was cold, and she made herself lean back. She told herself to relax, *breathe,* and set her mind on what was coming, because looking behind would only slow her down.

And yet she couldn't resist glancing over her shoulder as Tobias began to drive them down the street.

Helena stood on the curb, twirling a new cigarette. But she wasn't the only one watching their departure. Iris saw a man leaning against the wall a few paces back, hands shoved into his pockets and a smile cutting across his shadowed face.

Mr. Kitt's associate.

Oath melted like rime in the sun as they took to the open road.

Iris watched the city fade as the roadster devoured kilometers, defying her own orders to keep her eyes ahead. She watched until the cathedral steeples, the shiny high rises, and the old castle towers were nothing but a haze in the distance, and she thought how odd it was. To see something that felt strong and vast slowly become small and quiet. A mere ink blot on the horizon.

"What's a post runner, exactly?" Attie asked over the hum of the motor.

Iris turned her attention back to Tobias Bexley, who hadn't said a word since he cranked the motor.

"It's exactly how it sounds," he replied. "I drive people's post and deliveries to and from Oath."

Attie leaned forward, resting her arms on the driver's seat. "And how does one get into such a business?"

"I suppose it's similar to how you got into reporting."

"To prove a point to a narrow-minded professor?"

Tobias was quiet for a beat. "Then no. I became a runner because I liked racing fast motorcars and needed income to pay for my hobby. Might as well do what I love for a living."

"You *race* motorcars?" Iris asked.

"I do," he said. "My mum is always relieved when I take time off for post assignments, although she and my father never miss a race of mine. Granted, these days even the post is dangerous and unpredictable."

"How many races have you won?" Attie said, settling in for a nice, long story.

Tobias countered, "You assume I've won?"

"Well . . . yes," she said with a wave of her hand, indicating the pastures that bordered the road. The landscape continued to roll by them with an ex-hilarating speed. "You're quite fast, in case you didn't notice."

He laughed. "That's what your boss is paying me to do. I'm to transport you as well as your articles from one place to the next, as quickly and safely as possible."

"I didn't even know roadsters could go so fast," said Iris, squinting against the wind. She had yet to put her goggles on, waiting for Tobias to tell her when to do so. But she loved the sting of fresh air on her face. The way the breeze drew through her hair like fingers.

"They normally can't accommodate this gear," Tobias said.

"Then you're saying this is no *normal* motorcar," Attie was swift to surmise.

"I might be saying that."

"Why the vague answers, Bexley?" Attie nudged him in the shoulder. "Are you worried we'll write an article about you and your magical roadster?"

"I worry about one thing only," he answered.

Iris and Attie both waited, hanging upon the suspense. When the silence continued, filled only with the roar of the wind and the comforting purr of the engine, Attie leaned even closer to him.

"I imagine you worry about flat tires, or running out of petrol, or getting lost."

"I worry about *rain*," he said, but he finally turned his head, meeting Attie's gaze for a split second. "Rain makes the roads muddy and treacherous."

Iris looked up at the clouds. They were white and fluffy, but a few on the western horizon were building into tall thunderheads.

"You know what they say about springtime in Cambria," Attie drawled, also taking note of the clouds.

"I know it better than most." Tobias pushed the clutch and moved the gear-stick. It was such a smooth transition Iris hardly felt the car shift. "Which means we only have a few hours to get to River Down before that storm breaks. Goggles will come in handy right about now. Secure anything you don't want to fly away." He removed his hat, tucking it safely in a glove compartment. "Also, there's rope attached to the seat in front of you, in case you need to hold on to something."

Iris and Attie dutifully donned their goggles. As the roadster drove even faster, all hopes of conversation died in the howling air and speed. But Iris could *feel* the thrill of it through the soles of her boots. She could feel it hum in her bones, and she reveled in watching the land blur as they raced westward.

The clouds hung low and dark by the time Tobias drove them into River Down.

It was a small, sleepy town, tucked away in the rolling hills of the countryside. A babbling, shallow river cut through its heart, and a stone bridge connected the two halves of town: the east side that was a patchwork of markets, a library, a communal garden, a school, a small church with stained glass windows; and the west side, which brimmed with thatched cottages laced together with winding, cobbled roads.

Iris removed her goggles, taking it in. A few people were walking the streets with baskets, and they watched with bright curiosity as Tobias drove carefully down one road, then another.

"Are we almost there?" Iris asked, breathless.

"Yes, that's it up ahead on the left, with the yellow door," Attie said.

Iris spotted it—a two-story cottage with a stone chimney and blue shutters, nearly devoured by ivy—and as Tobias shifted the roadster down to a crawl, she noticed someone was waiting for them in the front yard. Someone with long black hair and a smile that crinkled her eyes, her red dress striking against her light brown skin.

"*Marisol!*" Iris cried, standing up in the cab to wave.

Marisol waved back and threw open the yard gate, standing in the street with a grin. As soon as Tobias cut the engine, Iris launched herself from the car. She raced the short distance to Marisol's welcoming embrace. It almost felt like everything—the sky, the ground, the daily routine—was about to crumble again, and Iris needed something steady to hold on to.

The last time I saw you, the world was burning, Iris thought, clenching her eyes shut as an unexpected wave of emotion struck her chest. She hadn't cried much the past few weeks. Indeed, she thought she had recovered from most of the trauma she had experienced, letting it hollow her out. But perhaps it had only been buried. Perhaps she had shoved it down to dark forgotten places and it had grown roots while she had been sleeping.

It was alarming to Iris at first, to feel it blister again.

She began to pull away but Marisol only held her tighter. Attie joined them, and the three wrapped their arms around each other. Iris sniffed and lifted her head, trying to hide her emotion until she saw that Marisol also had tears shining in her eyes.

"My girls, it's so good to see you both! And you know what this calls for? Hot cocoa and a biscuit."

"I've only dreamt of such since arriving back in Oath," Attie said. "No other café comes close to your hot cocoa, Marisol. Or your biscuits."

"Is that so?" Marisol sounded shocked as she led the girls to the front yard. She paused two steps later to call out, "And it's nice to see you again, Tobias! We would love for you to join us for a cup of cocoa."

Tobias was busy unloading the trunk. But he glanced up and nodded, a corner of his mouth curling in a half smile. "I would be happy to, Mrs. Torres. As soon as I tend to the car. The storm is not far off."

"Of course," Marisol said. The air smelled like distant rain; the wind was beginning to whistle through the narrow streets. It lifted tendrils of sable hair from her brow. "The front door will be open, and we'll have a seat ready at the table for you."

"Oh!" Iris's voice finally worked its way free. "My luggage."

"Don't worry, Miss Winnow," said Tobias, his eyes focused on his task as he withdrew an oilcloth from the trunk. "I'll bring it in for you. As well as for Miss Attwood."

"Thank you," Attie said. "But in case you didn't notice . . . I go by Attie."

Tobias latched the trunk door, but his eyes flickered upward. "Very well then, *Attie*."

As he returned to his task of covering the cab with the oilcloth, Marisol guided Attie and Iris along a brick path.

"Come," Marisol said, her gaze alight with excitement. "Come meet my sister, Lucy."

10

Laundry for Old Souls

Iris stood in the laundry room of Lucy's house, typewriter case in hand. It was a small chamber with one window, but it held a large wooden tub and a well spigot. Rope was strung from one wall to the other, with clothes hanging from it, and jars of wash granules sat on a shelf. But most of all, there was a wardrobe. Tall and made of oak, and quite unassuming.

It was the only wardrobe in the house, which meant this would be where Iris would work.

She sat on the herringbone brick floor and opened the case. Drawing on her old rituals, she set the typewriter before her knees and the wardrobe door, and she waited.

Once more, nothing happened.

No letter arrived. No letter was returned.

Maybe this was all for nothing. Maybe the magic between us has broken.

Iris shivered as she reached for paper, tucked away in the case. She fed the blank sheet to the typewriter, her fingers touching the keys.

Dear Kitt

She watched those familiar words strike across the page but then stopped herself. *He won't remember you.* Forest's words echoed through her. She wrote in defiance of them:

Are you safe? Are you well? I can't stop thinking about you. I can't stop worrying about you.

 Please write to me, whenever you can.

Iris stared at her words for a long moment before she tore them from the typewriter.

I can't send this, she thought, biting her lip until the pain swelled. *I can't put him at risk.*

She rubbed the ache in her chest before she crumpled the paper and tossed it into the dustbin.

Roman stood in the upstairs room of a farmhouse, gazing out the window as evening spilled across the sky like ink. This was their stop for the night, a stone-walled house with a thatched roof and crooked floors, with a barn and sheds scattered around the muddy yard. A halfway point to their next destination, and a place abandoned not so long ago by its tenants.

One of the platoons had found preserves and smoked meat in the cellar. The soldiers had filed through the kitchen, jubilant and hungry for pickled beets and onions and pork links, and now they were camped in the farmyard with makeshift tents and campfires. Even Roman had devoured the food dished onto his plate; it had been a while since he had fully calmed the gnawing ache in his stomach.

He turned away from the window, studying the room Dacre had given him for the night. It must have belonged to the farmer's daughter. The walls were covered in floral wallpaper, and there was a vast collection of poetry books on the fireplace mantel. The wardrobe was brimming with pastel dresses and blouses, and Roman studied the garments, unable to describe the twinge of sadness he felt.

What had happened to these people? Where had they gone?

He thought about the letter, tucked away in his pocket like a secret.

Roman read the three odd questions again before he set the paper down on the bedroom desk. His typewriter was waiting on the wood, the keys glinting in the candlelight. When the first stars burned through dusk, he began to type.

It felt good to write to someone, even if they were nameless. And he wanted answers. It would be wiser if he gathered useful information for Dacre before sharing the mysterious letter with him, and Roman was glad he had trusted his intuition to *wait* earlier.

Finished, he pulled the paper free and felt a tingling shock down his arm. This felt like a memory. Something he had done, time and time again. It was comforting, and he let himself follow those old movements.

Before he could think better of it, Roman folded the paper and slipped his letter beneath the wardrobe door.

Dinner at Lucy's was a singular affair. The kitchen tapers were lit, and golden light danced over the mismatched china and green glass stemware. Faint music flowed from a radio on the counter, the notes occasionally smudged by static. Marisol cut fresh roses from the garden, the first blooms of the season, and set them in old metal tins along the table spine. Bowls of food were passed around, and Iris filled her plate with fried fillet, green beans that had been canned the previous summer, pickled peaches and figs, roasted potatoes with generous heaps of butter, and sourdough bread.

Lucy, who Iris had come to learn was the direct opposite of Marisol, poured milk into everyone's goblets before she settled at the head of the table. She was tall, fair-headed, with freckled skin and shrewd gray eyes. She seemed to wear a perpetual frown, but Marisol had warned Iris that her sister was reserved and wary to trust strangers. To earn a cup of tea from her was a sign that one had earned her friendship and respect.

"I love this song," Attie said, tilting her head toward the radio.

It was a melancholy score, made even more so because parts of it were missing. Iris knew only because she had heard this song before. The strings were culled from it, all due to the recent ban in the city. The law had been the chancellor's way of curbing Enva's magical abilities with her harp, but Iris considered it a restriction built on fear. Fear of losing control and power. Fear of watching the truth about the war and what was to come spread across Oath.

"G. W. Winters," Lucy said, snapping wrinkles from her napkin. "One of the greatest composers of our time."

"You know of her?" Attie asked.

"I do. I attended a few of her concerts back in the day when I lived in Oath. Marisol accompanied me once."

"*That* was a night to remember," Marisol said. "Everything that could have gone wrong did."

"Save for the music," Lucy countered.

"We're lucky to be alive."

"A touch dramatic, wouldn't you say, little sister?"

Marisol glared, but she couldn't maintain the facade for long. Her lips betrayed her with a smile, and then she laughed.

"I think this is a story that should be shared," Iris said, glancing between the sisters.

"Only if I can tell it." Lucy held up her goblet of milk.

"Fine," Marisol sighed, but she sounded amused. "I get two interjections, though."

"Deal."

Their banter was interrupted by a startling trio of beeps on the radio.

Iris turned to look at it, a chilled silence settling over the table.

"*We interrupt tonight's broadcast to share an important message from Chancellor Verlice,*" a monotone voice said through the box. "*All visitors to Oath must register their presence in the city, as well as that of their family members, with the Commonwealth Ministry. Please bring a form of identification as well as all pertaining relatives to be photographed for our records. Thank you for your attention and cooperation, and tonight's broadcast will now continue.*"

The music resumed—woodwinds and brass and percussion—but no one moved. Iris released a shaky exhale, her appetite gone. She glanced around the table, noticing the deep furrow in Lucy's brow, the tense posture of Marisol's shoulders. Attie looked troubled, and Tobias was scowling.

"By visitors they mean refugees," Marisol said. "People fleeing to escape the war."

"Have there been many refugees coming to River Down?" Iris asked.

"We've had a few families arrive over the past week," Lucy replied. "But I imagine that number will only increase when Dacre begins to march. We're prepared to help house and feed as many people as we can."

"Last we heard, Dacre was sitting on Avalon Bluff," Attie said. "Like a hen on a nest. Biding his time for reasons we can only dread."

"Keegan wrote to me not long ago," Marisol said. "She said Enva's forces have retreated to Hawk Shire but she expects they'll be marching farther east soon. Scouts have reported that Dacre has recovered enough soldiers now to make his next assault. She told me to prepare for things to turn quickly, even here, deep in the east. I don't think you should mention this in your articles, Iris and Attie, and I don't want to scare you, but Keegan said she doesn't think her forces can hold Dacre off again if he makes a hard press for Oath. His army has grown considerably, and he's been able to take these small towns of the boroughs with terrible ease."

Iris was quiet as she met Attie's gaze.

"How far does Helena have you three traveling?" Lucy asked.

When the girls hesitated, Tobias replied, "She asked me to drive them no further than Winthrop."

"*Winthrop!*" Marisol cried. "That's far too close to the front, especially if something happens overnight. Winthrop is just a stone's throw from Hawk Shire."

"Mari," Lucy said.

"No, Luce! I have some *choice* words for Helena, and I'm not going to sit back and swallow them this time. Like I've done all the times before!"

Marisol rose and stormed from the kitchen, to Iris's great shock. It felt like a rock was in her stomach, weighing her down, when she heard Marisol weeping down the hall.

"Should I . . . should we . . . ?" Iris could hardly find the words through the pain in her chest.

Lucy shook her head. "My sister loves you both. It's hard for her to acknowledge that you'll be driving toward the fray."

"And she's worried about Keegan's safety," Attie said.

"She is *very* worried about her wife." Lucy left the kitchen, seeking to comfort Marisol.

Iris fiddled with the edge of her napkin but eventually looked up when Attie stood and turned the radio off.

"Do you want me to take you both home?" Tobias asked. "If you do, just say the word."

Iris looked at him, but his mahogany brown eyes were focused on Attie.

"That's kind of you to offer, Bexley," Attie said, leaning against the counter. "But I want to keep going, just as I said I would."

"As do I," Iris said.

Tobias nodded, but his expression was grave. "Then we need to discuss our plans."

"Plans?" Attie frowned. "What do you mean?"

"If something should happen to me while I'm away delivering your articles, you'll be stranded in town. And you need to stay put unless there's an emergency evacuation. If so, take the first ride you can find back to Oath."

"What could happen to you on the road?" Attie asked.

"Anything, really. A flat tire. An overheated engine. Impassable roads."

"I thought you don't worry about those sorts of things."

"I don't," he said. "But I'll be worried about *you*. What I'm trying to say is . . . don't panic if I fail to return on time. It's extremely unlikely because not much comes between me and assignments. But I don't want the two of you waiting on me if a situation arises that calls for you to immediately evacuate. It's been an easy trip so far, but beyond River Down, I don't know what to expect. Do you both agree to that?"

"Yes," Iris said, even as her heart pounded at the thought of evacuating without Tobias.

The furrow in Tobias's brow eased until he realized Attie had yet to respond.

"Miss Attwood?" he prompted.

Attie was gazing out the window, watching the rain trickle down the glass panes. "Of course I agree," she said, meeting his gaze. "But let us hope it never comes to that."

11

R.

I ris left Attie and Tobias in the kitchen with a pot of fresh-brewed coffee, drawn back to the laundry room. She was prepared to work for most of the night and was surprised to discover a cushion had been set on the floor beside her typewriter, as well as a soft blanket. There were also three candles and a matchbook, so she could work by firelight rather than by the exposed lightbulb in the ceiling.

Marisol must have thought of it, and Iris smiled as she lowered herself down to the cushion. She struck a match and lit the candles. That was when she finally saw it.

There, on the floor before the wardrobe, was a folded sheet of paper.

Someone had finally written her back.

Iris stared at it until her sight blurred. She blew out her match and crawled to the wardrobe. She felt dizzy as she took the paper in her hand, returning to sit on the cushion.

She stared at the folded page. There were most certainly words on it, even though they looked sparse. Iris could see them, a dark chain of thought.

This could change nothing, or it could change everything.

She swallowed and opened the letter.

Who are you? What magic is this?

Iris closed her eyes, the terseness striking her like a fist. If this was Roman, then he didn't remember her. The mere thought made her breath catch. But before she did anything else, she needed to be certain it was him. She needed to be clever.

Iris wrote and sent:

Your typewriter. There should be a silver plaque bolted to the inside of the underframe. Can you tell me what it says?

She paced while she waited for the reply, careful not to disturb the hanging laundry. Perhaps he wouldn't write her back, but if she knew anything about Roman . . . he liked a challenge. He also had a curious mind.

His reply came a minute later:

THE THIRD ALOUETTE / MADE ESPECIALLY FOR D.E.W.
Should I assume you are D.E.W.? For I'm certainly not.

P.S. You have yet to answer my questions.

Iris traced the bow of her lips as she read his letter. *Odd that he has my typewriter,* she thought, but a comforting warmth spread through her chest. She had worried that her nan's typewriter had been lost, and that had grieved her. The Third Alouette was a piece of her childhood, a thread of her legacy. She had written so many words with those strike bars and keys.

But to imagine Roman typing on it now, keeping something of her close, made her hope rekindle.

"You always were fond of postscripts, weren't you, Kitt?" she whispered. And then it hit her.

This was Roman, and he didn't remember her.

The realization was like a knife, plunging into her side, and she let herself melt to the floor, her cheek pressed to the bricks. Roman's letter remained clutched in her fingers, crinkling beneath her body.

Forest was right.

Iris let herself feel the gravity of that statement; she let herself feel the pain and the anguish rather than bury them for another day. It was okay to feel sorrow, anger. It was okay for her to weep, in sadness, in relief. When she was able to push herself back up, Iris read Roman's letter again.

He didn't remember her yet, but he would. Soon. The memories would return to him, just as Forest's had resurfaced.

Most important, Roman was writing to her again. She had a way to communicate with him.

Dacre believed he had the upper hand, grooming Roman to be his dutiful correspondent. But little did the god know that he was not the only source of magic.

"You will regret ever taking him from me," she whispered through her teeth, feeding paper into her typewriter.

Fingertips on the keys, she thought she was ready to write Roman back but hesitated.

As much as she longed to, she couldn't come out directly and say who she was to him. She couldn't risk him panicking or overwhelming him to the point that he would cease writing or, even worse, that Dacre would interfere. She also needed to protect her own identity.

It needed to be a gradual experience. She needed to go slowly.

She wrote:

I'm not D.E.W., nor am I a goddess who possesses the enchantment of sending letters to someone who doesn't want to read them. I must give credit to the wardrobe doors for that. But I know the history you touch, and the Third Alouette was crafted with magic, connected to two other typewriters. One was the First, which is now mine, and one was the Second, which I assume is now lost.

As long as you have a wardrobe door nearby and the Third

Alouette in your possession, your letters will be able to reach me, even over great distances. Although I imagine you are busy, swept away by war efforts, most likely. And who has time to write letters to a stranger these days?

P.S. I seem to recall that <u>you</u> have yet to answer my three questions!

Iris sent the letter. She impatiently waited, the minutes passing as the night unfurled. She could suddenly feel her exhaustion, and she heaved a sigh, preparing to work on her article. But then paper whispered over the floor.

Roman replied with:

I realize I've come across as rude. Forgive me. One can't be too careful these days when it comes to knowing who to trust, and your letter this morning jarred me.

I unfortunately don't have the answers to your three questions, so I must have failed a test in your mind. Or simply made you realize that you are not writing to the person you hoped you had been, because the Third Alouette just came into my possession, and I don't know who took care of her before me. For that, I'm sorry, but I will guard her carefully now.

All of this to say, thank you for sharing your insight about the typewriters. You may not be a goddess, but nor am I a god. Despite our mundane lives, perhaps we make our own magic with words.

Also, I never said I didn't want to read your letters, now, did I?

—R.

P.S. If you and I are to keep corresponding, perhaps you could tell me how I should address you?

Iris stood, giving herself a moment. She chewed on a hangnail, trying to sort through the tumble of emotions, words, thoughts. Eventually, she couldn't wait a moment longer and settled back down on her cushion. A flash of lightning lit up the chamber; thunder rumbled, shaking the walls.

Would it be too much to give her name? Even though she longed to?

What if her letters were confiscated? Would she be putting herself at risk if she typed out *Iris*? It was only four letters, and yet they felt far too dangerous to surrender.

Be cautious. Go slowly.

Iris sent a reply before she could doubt herself.

Dear R.,

    Rest assured, you didn't fail a test. I'm also careful when it comes to trust. But I must remind myself that sometimes we write for ourselves and sometimes we write for others. And sometimes those lines blur when we least expect them to. Whenever such happened in my past...I remember that I have only been strengthened by it.

    P.S. You can call me Elizabeth.

PART TWO

Drawn to the Flame

12

A Captive Nightingale

The sun was shining and last night's rain glimmered in shallow puddles when Tobias drove away from River Down. He carried Iris's and Attie's articles for Helena, as well as post from the town to be delivered in Oath.

"I'll be back in a few hours," he had said at the yard gate, his roadster shined and ready for the haul. "We'll leave for Bitteryne first thing tomorrow."

Iris nodded.

Attie only said, "The muddy roads won't slow you down? It poured yesterday, in case you forgot."

"I don't forget anything," he replied, opening the driver's door. "And no, the roads won't slow me down."

The girls watched him depart, the familiar sound of the motor fading in the morning haze.

Iris glanced sidelong at Attie. "You're worried he'll get stranded?"

"No. I'm worried *we'll* be stranded if he doesn't make it back." But Attie continued to stare down the street, her fingers gripping the iron scrollwork of the gate. "I'm going for a walk."

Iris stood in the yard, until Attie was out of sight. Only then did she turn to the house, seeking Marisol. She found her in the backyard, kneeling in the garden with a pocket-sized book open on her lap.

"This is a lovely garden," Iris said.

Marisol glanced up with a smile. But her eyes were bloodshot, as if she hadn't slept the night before. Her dark hair was caught in a braided crown, and she was wearing a pair of work coveralls, stained with dirt.

"Yes, Lucy is an avid gardener. She inherited our aunt's green thumb." Marisol returned her attention to the book, her fingertips tracing the illustration of a bird on the page. "But I'm trying to identify this singer in the bushes. Do you hear him?"

Iris lowered herself down to her knees, listening. Over the clatter of a wagon on the neighboring street, and children calling to one another, she could hear a bird's song. It was rich and melodic, full of trills and gurgles.

"He's just there, in the thicket," said Marisol.

Iris found him a moment later. A small bird with soft brown feathers was perched in the shrubbery at the back of the garden.

"I've never heard a bird sing like that." Iris was spellbound, watching him warble again. "What is he?"

"A nightingale," Marisol replied. "It's been so long since I've seen or heard one, but when I was younger, I remember they would appear every spring in Avalon Bluff. I would often sleep with the windows open at night so I could hear their songs. I fell asleep to their tunes, dreamt of them sometimes." She gently closed the book, as if lost in memory. But then she added, "Years ago, a study was done on nightingales, and quite a number were caught and put into captivity."

"Why?" Iris asked.

"They wanted to trade the birds, as well as study their songs. Most of the nightingales died, but the ones who lived until autumn . . . they eventually killed themselves trying to escape, bashing their wings and their bodies against the cages that held them. They felt the need to migrate, and they couldn't."

Iris studied the nightingale in the bush. The bird had fallen silent, cocking his head to the side, as if he were also listening to Marisol's doomed story. But then he gathered his wings and flew away; the garden felt quiet and wistful without his song.

"I'm sorry," Marisol said, to Iris's surprise. "About how I acted last night. We only have such a brief amount of time together and I feel like I ruined it."

"*Marisol,*" Iris whispered, her throat narrow. She reached out to gently touch her arm.

"But then I woke up this morning and heard that nightingale sing in the garden, and it reminded me of my aunt's story of the captive birds," Marisol continued. "It reminded me that I cannot hold those I love in a cage, even if it feels like protecting them."

She exhaled, as if a weight had fallen from her shoulders. And then she extended the book to Iris. It was small, the pages tinged caramel with age. A bird was embossed on the green cover.

"I'd like to give this to you, Iris."

"I can't take this," Iris began to protest, but Marisol set it firmly in her hands.

"I want you to have it," she insisted. "As you travel west once more and encounter new towns and stories, perhaps you will still have moments of rest when you can sit and watch the birds. When you do, think of me, and know that I will be praying for you and Attie and Tobias and Roman every morning and every evening."

Iris blinked back tears. It was only a book, but it felt far more than leather and paper and ink. It felt like something to tether her in the coming days, something to protect her as well as encourage her to *keep going,* and she traced the bird on the cover before glancing up to meet Marisol's gaze.

"I will. Thank you."

Marisol smiled again. "Good. Now, why don't you come help me pack a few welcome baskets for our new guests in River Down. I'd like for you to meet them."

Iris nodded and rose, brushing the damp soil from her knees. But she felt a shadow flicker over her, and she paused, watching as two vultures settled on the rooftop next door. They spread their wings, dark feathers gleaming in the sun.

With a shiver, she held the book close to her heart and followed Marisol inside.

Dear Elizabeth,

Tonight, I can't sleep, and so I find myself writing to you again. You can't see me, but I'm sitting at a desk before a window, gazing into the darkness, and I'm trying to envision you.

I have no idea what you look like, or where you reside, or what your voice sounds like. I don't know your age, or your history. I don't know the events you have lived through, moments that have shaped you into who you are now. I don't know which side of the war you fall beneath.

I don't have to know these things, I realize. Perhaps you shouldn't tell me. But I think I would like to know something about you that no one else does.

—R.

Dear R.,

I fear I'm not much to see at the moment, but to give you a glimpse: I'm sitting on the floor of a laundry room as I type, with hanging shirts and dresses for company. My hair is long and braided and quite messy, and there is a book about Cambria's many birds beside me.

Today I learned that vultures mate for life. Did you know that? I honestly haven't paid much attention to birds in the past, but maybe that's because I grew up on the brick and pavement of a city. I also learned that a nightingale can sing over a thousand different songs, and an albatross can sleep while flying, and male sparrows are responsible for building the nest.

Here is something no one else knows about me, because it just happened today:

I would like to one day be adept enough to simply hear a song and know which bird it belongs to.

I've cracked the window tonight, hoping I might hear something familiar, or even unexpected. A song that will remind me that even when I feel lost, the birds still sing, the moon still waxes and wanes, and the seasons still cycle.

—Elizabeth

P.S. A fact most people know: I'm eighteen, but I've always had an old soul.

P.P.S. Tell me a fact about you. It could be something everyone knows or something no one knows.

Roman didn't write Elizabeth back.

What could he tell her? That he couldn't remember his past?

Irritated, he shoved his bedroom window open. They were still camped at the abandoned farmhouse, which made him feel uneasy. But the moment he breathed in the cool night air, damp from spring rain, the tension in his body eased.

With a sigh, he unlaced his boots and lay down on his bed. He blew out the candle and as the night embraced him, he listened.

Beyond the open window, he could hear crickets chirping and leaves rustling in the wind. There were the distant voices of soldiers drifting from their tents. But beneath all those sounds was the haunting song of an owl.

Roman drifted off to sleep.

His dreams were stark, vivid.

He sat at a desk with a typewriter. Dictionaries and thesauruses were aligned before him. A tin of pencils, a notepad, and a stack of obituaries rested at his elbow. The vast room smelled like cigarette smoke and strong black tea, and the air was metallic with the sound of keys and strike bars and ringing typewriters as new paragraphs were born.

He was at the *Oath Gazette*. And it nearly felt like home to him, more than the mansion on the hill he still dreamt of.

"Kitt? In my office, now," Zeb Autry said as he walked past Roman's desk.

Roman gathered his notepad and followed his boss. He shut the door behind him and anxiously sat across from Zeb.

"Sir?"

"I wanted to give you a heads-up," Zeb said, reaching for the decanter of whiskey on his desk. It sparkled in the slant of morning sunshine. "I have a new hire coming in. She'll split the obituaries, classifieds, and advertisements with you."

"*She?*" Roman echoed.

"Don't sound so surprised. I read an essay of hers and couldn't let her slip by me. I'd like to see what she could do here."

"Does this mean I'm no longer getting the columnist position you offered me, sir?"

Zeb was quiet for a moment, mouth puckering. "It means the two of you both have a fair shot at it. A little competition will be good for you, Kitt."

Roman took that as *everything has been handed to you.* He felt his face flush, irritation catch in his throat. But he nodded, jaw clenched.

"Don't look so glum!" Zeb said with a chuckle. "She didn't even graduate Windy Grove School. Chances are the promotion will still go to you."

If she had attended Windy Grove School, then she came from a part of town where Roman rarely ventured. He didn't know whether that should comfort or worry him. Whoever she was, she was going to have a different viewpoint on things. Her writing could be either atrocious or exquisite, but most of all, Roman didn't feel like competing for something that he needed.

"When is her first day?" he asked.

"Today. She'll be here soon."

Wonderful, Roman thought drolly. Although perhaps it was for the best. To get this torture over with as soon as possible.

For the next few hours, he kept his attention divided between the obituaries and the glass doors of the *Gazette,* waiting for this enigma who could potentially ruin everything to appear. At noon sharp, she did, as if by spell.

She was petite and pale with a heart-shaped face. Freckles spilled across her nose; her eyes were wide as she took in her new surroundings. Her chestnut brown hair was slicked back in a tidy bun, but she wore a tattered trench coat that seemed to swallow her, belted tightly at her waist. She was cracking her knuckles when Sarah Prindle pounced on her with a lively welcome.

"Here, let me introduce you to everyone!" Sarah was saying, linking their arms as she walked Roman's worst nightmare around the *Gazette*.

He got up from his desk and moved to the sideboard, to pour a cup of tea and continue watching as the new girl met the editors, the assistants, Zeb. The only person whose hand she had left to shake was his.

He couldn't avoid it forever. Sarah had shot him a few pointed glances as she settled the girl in at her new desk—only two away from his own—and Roman stifled a groan.

He set down the teacup and walked the aisle to meet her.

She was tracing her typewriter keys, still wearing that drab coat, although her high heels gave her an air of command. She must have sensed him coming, like a storm building on the horizon. Or perhaps she felt his cold gaze. She glanced up to meet it, giving him a bold assessment before she smiled.

"I'm Iris," she said in a bright tone, extending her hand. "Iris Winnow."

What sort of name is that? he inwardly grumbled, already picturing it as a byline. It was a good name. One that he was tempted to taste, but he refrained.

"I'm Roman Kitt," he said gruffly. "Welcome to the *Gazette*."

Her hand was still between them, waiting for his. It would be rude for him to ignore it. In fact, it already was rude that he had left it hanging for so long. He reluctantly let his hand meet hers and was promptly surprised by how firm her grip was. How touching her sent a shock up his arm.

Roman gasped awake.

13

You've Seen Worse than This

Y ou've been unusually quiet," Dacre said.

Roman drew his attention away from the lorry's dirty window. The troops had finally departed the melancholy farm, pressing eastward along a winding road. "Sorry, sir. I've been enjoying the change of scenery."

Dacre was sitting on the bench beside him, regarding him with shrewd eyes. "Are your old wounds hurting?"

The inquiry was so unexpected that Roman gaped for a moment. Hadn't Dacre healed those broken pieces of him? Why would the pain return?

"No," Roman said, but his fingertips traced the scars around his knee, hidden beneath the jumpsuit. "I feel perfectly well, sir."

"You can tell me if they do. Sometimes wounds run deeper than I first realized, and I have no choice but to heal them again." Dacre paused, as if lost in thought, before asking, "Did you have a dream last night? It's been a while since you shared one with me."

"If I did, I don't remember." The lie flowed smoothly, but Roman felt his throat constrict. He kept seeing Iris Winnow, smiling up at him. Why did the gravity seem to gather around her, even hours after he had dreamt of her?

He traced his palm with his thumb—he could still feel her touch—and he sensed that Iris was more than a dream.

"If you could have any magic of the gods," Dacre said, "what power would you choose?"

Roman was once again surprised by Dacre's question. "I'm not sure. I've never thought about it, sir."

"When I was younger, I wanted my cousin's power. Mir's." Dacre's voice was deep and warm as he remembered an era of his past with apparent fondness. "Mir was much older than me, and far more ruthless. He was born with the power of illusions and could come and go as a mere shadow, stealing from one place to another unnoticed. He gathered up family secrets like jewels in a coffer, and then wandered above to glean what he could from the Skywards. I remember when he returned below one day, looking vibrant and hale, like he had swallowed all the stars from the sky. He told me that he had acquired another power. One that enabled him to read minds should he touch someone. From then onward, I avoided him, fearful of what he might find in my own thoughts even though I had only ever envied him."

Roman studied Dacre's sharp profile. The sunlight limned his strange beauty.

"You can acquire more power? I thought you were born with your magic, and that is what sets you apart from us," Roman said.

"We are born with our appointed magic, yes," Dacre answered. "But that never stopped us from wanting more and finding ways of taking it."

Roman wiped his palms on his thighs. He wanted to ask further questions, but the words wouldn't come, and he thought of Mir instead. Another divine who was sleeping in a northern grave.

A few hours of stilted silence passed, Roman dozing in and out of dreamless sleep. He was relieved when they reached their destination.

The town of Merrow was similar to the Bluff but smaller, comprising thatched cottages with brightly painted shutters and overgrown gardens. A main thoroughfare was the only cobbled road. Apple orchards dotted the landscape, their white blossoms drifting from the branches when the wind blew.

As soon as the lorry came to a halt, Roman gathered his typewriter and opened the door. He stepped down carefully, minding the long line of trucks rumbling into town behind him, and he gazed up at the nearest cottage.

The windows were full of shadows, laced with gossamer. No smoke rose from the chimneys; no children raced along the streets. The market was boarded up. Even some of the doors looked to be barricaded and difficult to reach.

"Where is everyone?" he asked, not expecting an answer. But Dacre heard, as did the soldier who had been driving their lorry.

"Evacuated to the east, thanks to Enva's forces," Dacre replied, looking to the captain who stood at attention nearby. "Set up a watch at the perimeter. Have your company choose the best place to lodge for tonight and see what we can recover from the cellars for a meal."

"Yes, sir." The captain saluted and began to call out orders.

The town buzzed like a hive as the soldiers carried out their tasks, and Roman was considering wandering on his own for a moment, drawn to the quiet peace of the orchard, when gunshots cracked the air.

Not three paces ahead of him, a private went down with a scream.

Roman felt the blood splatter on his face and he froze, heart thundering in his chest. Another trio of shots—earsplitting, bone-jarring. A second and third soldier went down, and through the panicked scuffle and shouts, Roman realized the bullets were coming from a second-story window.

"*Move*," Dacre hissed, grasping Roman's arm.

A shower of bullets followed them, whizzing over their heads, nipping at their heels.

The shots were aimed at Dacre, but he dodged the assault effortlessly.

Roman tripped before he found his footing. He let Dacre propel him to the safety of a lintel, out of sight of the sniper. But his blood was coursing hot in his veins. He trembled, studying the upper windows across the street. Every shadow now felt ominous, a veil for someone to hide behind.

"How many, Commander?" It was the captain again, shadowed by Lieutenant Shane. Blood speckled their faces and uniforms, but both seemed unharmed as they crouched beside Dacre and Roman, guns in hand.

"I believe there's only one," Dacre replied. He sounded strangely calm, almost amused. "Upper floor of this building. Do not kill them. Wound and then bring them to me."

The captain stood and motioned to the soldiers taking shelter behind a yard fence across the road. They returned fire at the sniper, but it seemed to only be a distraction that enabled the captain and Shane to covertly find a way into the lower level of the cottage.

Roman cowered but Dacre took hold of his arm again, keeping him upright.

"Come with me," he said. "We need to find the door."

Through the chaos, this seemed like a perfectly reasonable thing to say. Roman nodded, pulse hammering in his throat as he fought the urge to run and hide. He followed Dacre through the dirt-packed roads.

They eventually stopped at a house on a street corner. Lichen was growing through the roof, and the yard was larger than most, with lilac blooming on a trellis.

"Yes, it should be here," Dacre mused, but he glanced up as if measuring the horizon.

"What should, sir?" Roman asked, his voice breaking when another volley of gunfire sounded. He glanced over his shoulder, but he couldn't see the cottage with the sniper. He could only discern Dacre's soldiers taking cover behind stone walls, slipping in and out of darkened houses, guns in hand.

An explosion rocked the town. Roman saw a flash of light, felt the ground quake beneath his boots. Smoke rose from a neighboring street, provoking a cascade of yells, screams.

The sound nearly drove him to his knees. He could taste blood in his mouth. Blood and salt and dirt, but when he touched his lips, he was dry as parchment. He wondered if he was remembering a fragment of his past, but the tension in the air left him no time to examine it.

"Sir?" he said. "Should we go back and help them?"

Dacre didn't answer. He opened the yard gate and strode to the front door. It opened with a creak, exposing a dim interior.

"*Commander?*" The word wrenched from Roman's chest. He was struck by the fact that he had never called Dacre by this title before. "Shouldn't we wait? What if there's another sniper, or a trap?"

Dacre paused on the threshold to look at him. "It will take more than a few poorly shot bullets to kill me."

"Yes, and you are immortal. I am not."

"But aren't you? In case you forgot, you were a minute from death when I found you. With me, you're safe."

Dacre ducked inside.

Roman hesitated until the sounds of gunfire faded. The quiet that followed was eerie. It crept into his bones like winter ice, making him feel slow and clumsy, and Roman shivered as he hurried to follow Dacre into the cottage.

"Look for a room with a hearth." Dacre's voice came from the shadows.

"What?" Roman panted, standing in the foyer.

"My doorways like to be close to fire and stone. They swallow up ashes and embers and all the unseen magic of a hearth. Ah, here it is. The parlor."

Roman stepped into the room. There was a rug on the floor, a dusty settee, and bookshelves built around a fireplace. But Dacre was standing before a tall wardrobe door, waiting for Roman to join him.

"I want you to open this door," Dacre said. "Tell me what you find."

Roman merely stared at the door, his voice like a splinter in his throat. But his palms were damp. He felt the weight of his typewriter like it was a millstone.

Did Dacre know he was exchanging letters through closets?

Roman bit the inside of his cheek as he opened the wardrobe door. "There are only coats inside, sir," he said, seeing the outline of winter jackets. "And parcels."

"Good. Now close it."

Roman let the door latch, preparing to step away, but Dacre had retrieved the key from around his neck. There were two chains hanging beneath his uniform, one for the key, and one for something that looked like a small silver flute. Roman realized they were the cause of the clinks he sometimes heard when Dacre walked.

He watched as the god brought the key to the wardrobe's brass handle, slipping it into a keyhole that hadn't been there before. This time when the door swung open, there were no coats or boxes. There was only a stone staircase, leading down into the under realm.

"I don't understand," Roman said, catching the waft of cold, dank air.

"I learned a hard lesson years ago," Dacre began. "One that made me vow that I would make it harder for those who would seek to harm me or my family again. I forged five keys in the hottest fire of my realm, and only those who I trust can carry them. Those keys can unlock the thresholds between our worlds."

"Why five?"

"It is a sacred number. For you mortals, there are five days of the week, five boroughs, five chancellors, five remaining divines. For us gods, it is a blessing and a warning. When it comes to trusting others, pay heed to the magic of five. Having four confidants is one too few, and six is one too many."

Before Roman could raise another question, the lights flickered on overhead. It was the captain, bloodstained and grim, his soldiers dragging in a young man dressed in coveralls. One of his legs appeared broken, and his abdomen shone with bright red blood.

"The sniper, Commander," the captain said. "Wounded, as you requested."

Roman studied the stranger. His hair was a dark shade of auburn, his face starkly pale, and his brown eyes glistened in agony until he caught sight of Dacre. Then his expression electrified with hatred. He spat at Dacre's feet.

Dacre politely smiled. "I see you were left behind."

"By my choice," the young man rasped. Blood continued to run down his clothes, gathering in a pool beneath him. "And I will not fight for you."

"You would rather perish?"

"Yes. Give me a clean shot and leave me here, to die where I was born."

Dacre was quiet, but he studied the man. "You think I want to be merciful when you have harmed my soldiers?"

The sniper was silent. He looked kissed by death now. The edges of his lips were turning blue as his breaths labored.

"I will not fight for you," he said again. "And you will not win this war. No matter how many of us you turn . . . we'll abandon you, eventually. When we remember."

Dacre held up his hand. He drew the air from the young man's lungs with an unspoken spell that made the temperature in the room plunge and the lightbulbs flicker. Roman thought Dacre had honored the sniper's request and killed him until Dacre said, "Take him below to one of the holding cells. Keep him stable until I can tend to his wounds."

Roman watched as the soldiers hauled the unconscious sniper through the enchanted doorway to the world below, leaving a trail of blood behind.

"Two other privates were also wounded, sir," the captain said. "Grenade blast. They're four doors down, waiting for you."

Roman was silent, but a numb feeling crept over him. He watched as Dacre followed the captain and the others out of the house, leaving him alone in the parlor.

Am I supposed to follow them? he wondered, but his thoughts slid like fog through his mind. *Is this a test?*

His stomach churned.

Roman strode for the front door, but he didn't follow Dacre and the others. He hurried to the edge of town, his eyes on the orchard. The apple trees drew him in, as did the soft grass and the sunshine, spangling the ground.

He dropped his typewriter, fell to his knees, and vomited. There wasn't much to give, but he heaved until he felt empty, his hands clinging to the roots in the ground.

He felt a tiny bit of relief and tilted his head back, blinking the tears from his eyes. That was when he realized he wasn't alone. Lieutenant Shane was leaning against a nearby apple tree, smoking a cigarette and watching him.

"I needed a moment," Roman said.

"Then take one," Shane replied with a halfhearted shrug. "Although you've seen worse than this before, correspondent."

The remark blistered like skin over fire. Roman was irritated by the gaps in his mind. By trying to weave together all the pieces of himself, only to find endless fragments were still lost.

"You say that as if you were there," Roman said. "As if you know what happened to me."

Shane was quiet as he smoked, his eyes set absently on the distance. A few of the apple blossoms drifted from above, settling like snow on his broad shoulders.

"In a manner of speaking, I was," he finally replied. "But I can't tell you what happened. You'll have to remember for yourself."

"How much longer until I do?"

"Can't help you there either."

"And why is that?" Roman asked, impatient. "You've never been wounded one time in this war? You've never been healed by Dacre?"

Shane stared at him. "You think everyone who is healed with his power forgets who they were?" He flicked his cigarette to the grass and crushed it beneath his boot before he turned away. "That's the furthest thing from the truth, correspondent."

14

Hunger

Dear R.,

I made it safely to my next destination, and I can only wonder about your own.

Let me confess now by candlelight, in the embrace of a new town, that I look forward to your letters. And just for one moonrise, let us act as if there are no burdens weighing us down. No responsibilities or tomorrows. No gods and no war.

I want

Iris stopped typing.

She was sitting on the floor of her new room, a small chamber on the main level of Bitteryne's B and B. Iris had chosen this room because there was a wardrobe and a small brick hearth and a rug on the floor, which would suit her just fine for writing. But *because* she was sitting on the floor, she felt something odd.

Her hands drifted from her typewriter, resting on the threadbare rug. Perhaps she had only imagined it, but for a few moments, it had almost seemed as if something was clinking far below her. A slight rumble, deep in the earth.

She waited, palms to the rug. Just before she pulled them away, she felt it again. There was a rhythm of vibrations, as if a pick was striking stone. Was there a mine beneath Bitteryne? Her breath snagged when she remembered the myth Roman had once shared with her. The one that told how Dacre had left his realm below to capture Enva. The tunnels, the underground hall, the realm made of limestone and blue-veined rock.

Something isn't right, Iris thought, waiting to see if she felt it again. The clinking seemed to grow stronger, then fainter. *Perhaps I'm only tired and imagining it.*

She let her fingertips find their places on the keys again, staring at her half-written letter.

> Never mind. I am too full of wants and it has made me heady and bold.
>
> I shouldn't send this letter to you. I shouldn't, but only because I fear what you may think. And in the same breath...I fear that it will never reach you.
>
> And that is why I am surrendering it. To prove myself wrong and to prove myself right.
>
> —E.

Roman wanted nothing more than to close himself up into his new room and peel away his jumpsuit. To scrub his skin until it felt raw. To unlace his boots and lie on the bed. To reread Elizabeth's letters until he lost himself in her words.

He wanted to forget—just for an evening—what had transpired that day.

No matter how many of us you turn . . . we'll abandon you, eventually. When we remember.

The sniper's words continued to echo through him. Roman wondered if the man was fully healed now, somewhere far below. If he would remember what had transpired when he woke. How he had dared to assassinate a god.

"Roman?" Dacre's voice suddenly boomed from the floor below. "Bring your typewriter down to the parlor."

Roman froze with a grimace. He glanced around the room he had chosen for the night—a small but cozy chamber, with a slice of a wardrobe door—and he decided a letter to Elizabeth would have to wait. He still hadn't heard from her, and he tried to tamp down his worries as he gathered up his typewriter. Down the stairs he went, returning to the parlor where the sniper's blood still stained the floor and the doorway still led to the underground.

Dacre had turned the parlor into a makeshift office, pushing away the settee and dragging in the kitchen table. A fire now roared in the hearth, although family photographs remained on the mantel, their brass frames gleaming in the light.

"Sit down," Dacre said. "I need you to type out missives for me."

Roman found a bare spot on the table to set his typewriter. But he took note of the papers that were scattered around him—maps, letters, documents—as was a plate of half-eaten dinner, a bottle of wine, and an earthenware cup.

"What would you like me to write, sir?" Roman asked as he drew out his chair.

Dacre was quiet, his eyes on the map spread before him. It was a drawing of Cambria and its five boroughs. Every town and city. Every river and forest. The roads that connected them all like veins.

As Dacre began to speak, Roman listened and typed:

Captain Hoffman,

In six days' time, your forces need to join us at Hawk Shire. If you have not succeeded in your northern mission, you will have to resume it after the battle. My brigade will begin the assault from within by utilizing my doorways, as previously discussed, and your troops should be prepared to assist in the undertaking if the sacking takes longer than I expect. I am also low on supplies; prepare to bring whatever food rations and canteens you have.

Dacre Underling
Lord Commander of Cambria

Roman drew the paper free and handed it to Dacre. As the god signed his name and pressed a wax seal to the letter, Roman's gaze coasted over the map.

He located Hawk Shire, a large town not far from where they were currently camped in Merrow. It had a figurine of a woman set upon it. A representation of Enva's forces, Roman knew. But then his attention drifted to another map, tucked beneath the one of Cambria. He could only see the edges of it, but it looked like a drawing of gnarled tree roots. Winding, slithering passages. Some were marked in blue, others in green.

It was a map of the underworld.

He forced his eyes to shift before Dacre noticed.

"Now ready another," Dacre said, and Roman dutifully rolled a new page into the typewriter.

Mr. Ronald Kitt

Roman stopped typing, staring at the words Dacre had just uttered. The words he had just inked on paper.

"You're writing to my father?" he asked.

"Did I not mention that he has been a faithful servant?" Dacre countered. "Don't worry. Your family is fine. Your father knows you're safe. He's proud of you, in fact."

Roman didn't know what to make of that statement. It seemed to glance off him, as if he was enclosed in steel.

"What message do you want to send to my father, sir?"

Dacre continued:

I'm writing to remind you of our agreement. I'm still awaiting the next shipment you promised me, and, as the railroad has faced some difficulties lately, I wonder if we can devise an alternative for the deliveries to be made. I know you were previously concerned with Enva's forces intercepting, but the worst of your worries should be

They were interrupted by a soldier, the same captain Roman had seen earlier that day. He abruptly entered the house through the front door. A waft of cool evening air swirled around him as he paused on the parlor threshold.

"Forgive my interruption, Commander," the captain said, bowing his head. As he did so, an iron key slipped from beneath his collar, hanging on a chain. Roman stared at it, realizing it was one of the five keys Dacre had mentioned. "But I've urgent requests that need your immediate attention."

Dacre sighed but raised his hand. "What do you want, Captain Landis?"

"The first concerns the hounds. They haven't been fed in weeks, and they're hungry. They mauled two different handlers this afternoon, and their constant baying is upsetting the workers. Forward progress, as a result, has been slower than we need."

Roman's fingers slid from the typewriter. His gaze inevitably went to the parlor's wardrobe door, as if the hounds might burst through it at any moment. But all imaginings of Dacre's deadly pets dissolved when Roman saw what was resting on the bloodstained floor.

A folded piece of paper.

"Do I have your permission to set the hounds free?" Captain Landis continued. "They can roam tonight and feed."

"No," Dacre replied. "My messengers are delivering time-sensitive missives, and I cannot have my hounds interfering with their routes."

"Then what is to be done, my lord?"

Roman forced his gaze away from the paper on the floor. But his blood had gone cold. He could hardly hear the captain and Dacre over the roar of his pulse.

Elizabeth's letter was lying before the door to the underworld, in plain sight of Dacre. Just four paces away from where Roman sat, frozen at the table.

If he sees it . . . Roman's thoughts spun. *If he reads her words . . .*

It would be over. This strange correspondence would end, and there was no telling how far Dacre would go to ensure it never happened again.

Roman stood from the table, pretending like he was stretching. Dacre's attention fixated on him, an irritated line in his brow, but he had more important things on his mind. The god looked to the captain and said, "Take the weakest of the workers and feed them to the hounds for now. That'll hold them over."

Those words should have chilled Roman, but his bones already felt coated in ice. He ambled to the wall, pretending to study the hanging portraits.

"I'll personally see it done, Commander. As for the next matter . . . it has to do with the sniper you healed earlier today."

"Yes, what of him?"

"He's already woken. And his mind . . ."

Roman could sense Landis glancing at him. He acted like he hadn't heard the captain's comment, running his fingers along the portrait frames, catching up the dust. He noticed how white his knuckles were. The blue tinge of his nails.

"He's not ready, then," Dacre drawled.

"No, Commander. He's currently trying to harm himself."

"Then restrain him!"

"My lord, most of your forces are above, preparing for the assault. The others are kept busy overseeing the workers. I think if you could descend and put him back into a deep sleep . . ."

A loud screech of a chair sliding across the floor. The captain left his sentence hanging as Dacre stood, and Roman used that moment to approach the wardrobe, quickly covering Elizabeth's letter with his boot. He drew it back with him a step, glancing down to make sure it was completely hidden. Only a corner of it shone, stark against the dirty floor. Carefully, he adjusted his stance.

"Roman?"

"Sir?" Roman glanced up to meet Dacre's heavy stare.

"I'm needed elsewhere at the moment, but we'll resume this when I return."

"Yes, Commander."

He held his breath as Dacre and Captain Landis strode past where he stood awkwardly against the wall. But he felt that cold, stone-moss air hit his face the moment the wardrobe door creaked open.

He waited until they were gone, the door closed in their wake.

Alone, Roman let his guard drop. He gasped, a shudder wracking his spine. It was ridiculous that he didn't realize how much something meant to him until it was nearly taken. He remembered how, just the other day, he had been willing to give Dacre her first letter, and now he was desperate to hide them.

He could hardly explain it. But perhaps he didn't need words.

Roman lifted his boot and picked Elizabeth's letter up off the floor.

Dear Elizabeth,

(Or should I call you E. now?)

Your letter was almost discovered tonight by someone who would seek to come between us. I haven't mentioned this yet, but you are my secret. I have kept you to myself; no one knows of you but me. No one knows of our connection and I want to keep it that way.

We must be careful.

—R.

Dear R.,

You're right. I'm terribly sorry for putting you at risk. Perhaps we might establish a routine? Should you write to me first when you are safe to do so? And should we send a test message first?

—E.

P.S. Yes, maybe do call me "E." from now on. It seems to suit me better.

Dear E.,

The problem is...I want to hear from you at all hours. I want to read your words. I am greedy for them. I am <u>hungry</u> for them.

You say you are moving locations day by day. Don't answer if you don't feel like it's safe or right to do so. But I cannot help but ask...which direction are you heading?

Yours,

R.

Dear R.,

Let me be **your** secret, then. Tuck my words into **your** pocket. Let them be **your** armor.

I am heading westward.

Love,

E.

Roman held Elizabeth's letter in his hands, staring at the one word that made him ache. *Westward.*

She must be fighting for the other side. For Enva.

She was moving toward danger.

Toward *him*.

15

Strike Bars E and R

Do you think I should send it to Helena?" Iris asked the next morning. She and Attie were sitting at Lonnie Fielding's kitchen table, waiting for breakfast to be served. Tobias was outside, cranking the roadster's engine. He was about to leave for Oath, and Iris had spent most of the night preparing articles for the *Inkridden Tribune*.

Attie set the papers down. Her lips were pursed, her left brow cocked. Iris knew that meant she was deep in thought.

"I think you should, Iris," Attie finally said, pouring herself a second cup of tea. Steam rose in the air, fragranced with bergamot and lavender. "At the very least, Helena will want to see it, even if she doesn't publish it in the paper."

Iris nodded, staring at her pages. It was nothing like the original myth Roman had once found and sent to her, but it was close enough. The doomed love story of Dacre and Enva. How he used his hounds and his eithrals to terrify mortals above until Enva had agreed to live below with him.

"The only thing I wonder . . ." Iris trailed off, grimacing. "Should I include the second half when Enva sang him to weep, then laugh, then sleep?"

"Why wouldn't you?" Attie asked.

"I don't know. But I have this *feeling*."

"What feeling?"

"A warning, maybe. Like this knowledge shouldn't be broadcast in the paper."

"That Enva's music controlled him when she played underground?" Attie reached for the pitcher of milk. "But what if it *was* widely known? Maybe people's opinions on music wouldn't be so severe."

"Or maybe they would only worsen," Iris said. "Maybe people like the chancellor already know of this myth, and that is why he outlawed stringed instruments. *That* is why this story has been torn away from all the tomes about divinities and why it was never taught to us in school. Because it's dangerous."

Attie didn't have a chance to reply. The back door opened and Tobias stepped into the kitchen, his trench coat beaded with mist.

"Are your articles ready?" he asked them.

"Good morning to you, too," Attie said wryly. "Shouldn't you eat breakfast before you depart?"

"No. A storm's blowing in from the west. I need to outrun it."

"Can we have Mr. Fielding pack you a lunch, at least?" Iris said. "He's cooking right now."

Tobias granted her a smile, a dimple marking his cheek. "I appreciate the offer, but I'll be fine."

Attie already had their articles packed in a folder, ready for transport. She slid it across the table; Tobias seamlessly picked it up.

"When will you be back?" she asked.

"Tomorrow evening," he replied. "I need to have the roadster serviced in Oath, which will delay me. You both remember our agreement?"

Iris was quiet, but she recalled Tobias's request from the other night. It was hard for her to think about something happening to him on the road when their surroundings felt so normal and familiar, as if the three of them had been here before. Indeed, Lonnie Fielding was whistling as he cooked in the adjacent kitchen. Bacon was sizzling in a pan and a kettle was hissing. The dining room was a cluttered space with a timber-beamed ceiling and books piled up in the corners. Iris felt *safe* here, but she knew Tobias was right. Things could escalate quickly, just like they had in the Bluff. Their group needed to be prepared for the worst.

She shuddered, pulling the sleeves of her jumpsuit over her hands as she crossed her arms.

"Don't worry, Bexley." Attie finally broke the silence. "We won't wait on you if people begin evacuating."

Tobias held her stare for a moment before nodding. Then he turned and was out the door before Iris could so much as blink. She realized her typed myth was still on the table, and in that split second, she decided she wanted to send it.

She followed Tobias out the door, running along the stone path through the garden to the road. He was just about to drive away, his hand on the gearstick, when Iris caught his attention.

"Wait! I have one more article," she panted, holding up the papers.

Tobias didn't seem shocked. He only snorted as he handed the folder to Iris.

"You'll be careful?" she said as she hurried to tuck her papers inside.

"Of course," he replied. "I'll see you and Attie tomorrow night."

Iris nodded and stepped back. The mist swirled as Tobias drove away, but Iris remained standing on the cobbled street, soaking in the morning.

She had never been to Bitteryne before, but it felt like Avalon Bluff and River Down. Cottages, winding streets, idyllic pasture views. *When the war is over,* she thought, *I'd like to live in a place like this one.*

The peace was broken when Iris felt a rumble beneath her feet. She stared at the cobblestones in disbelief before glancing up the road, wondering if a line of lorries was driving into town. But there were no signs of life on the streets.

The rumbling faded, although Iris could still feel an echo of it in her bones.

She remembered the night before—the clinking beneath the floor. Like axes hitting stone, deep in the earth. Swallowing, Iris turned and hurried back inside.

Lonnie was setting breakfast down on the table. He looked up expectantly and said, "Oh, there you are, Miss Winnow. Glad to see you look well rested. Is Mr. Bexley with you?"

"Did you feel that?" Iris breathed. "That rumbling in the ground?"

Both Lonnie and Attie froze. The seconds stretched on, tense and silent, but there was nothing odd about them. The floor did not shake again, nor did the pattern of clinks return.

"I'm sorry," Iris said, pinching the bridge of her nose. "I must have imagined it. I stayed up late last night writing, and—"

"No," Attie gently interrupted her. "I sensed something peculiar last night too. It was faint, but the floor was shuddering."

The girls looked at Lonnie. He was an older farmer, one who had lived his entire life in Bitteryne. His wife had died years before, and his two grown sons and their three daughters were all fighting in the war for Enva's cause. Iris and Attie were currently staying in his granddaughters' rooms because Lonnie had decided the best thing to do with a suddenly empty house was to rent the rooms and help the cause as much as he could.

"You didn't imagine it," he said. "For the past week now, we've felt the rumblings throughout the town."

"What could be causing them?" Iris asked.

Lonnie sighed. "None of us know. This is a peaceful valley. We've never encountered anything like ground shakes before. Honestly, it's very noticeable some days, and others not so much. But don't you two worry about it! I'm sure it's nothing to fret about. Here, help yourself to the bacon and scones. I'm sorry to say I don't have any eggs today. I sent them west to Hawk Shire, for the army."

"Thank you, Mr. Fielding," Attie said. "This is more than enough for us."

"Yes, thank you." Iris smiled, but her stomach churned as she sat down. She met Attie's gaze from across the table. She was thinking about the myth she had just sent with Tobias. A myth full of winding tunnels, deep in the ground.

This is a test to ensure the strike bars E and R are in good working condition.

ERERERERER EEEEEE RRRRRRRRRRRRR
RERERERERERE REEEEEEE?

. . .

Test confirmed and easily passed. (Although I thought we had agreed that I was to write first, Elizabeth.) Regardless, you are quite lucky that you found me in a quiet moment. This rain has delayed the move to our next destination.

—R.

Dear R.,

I'm writing to gain your insight on a strange matter. Last night, I sensed something odd. There was a clinking in the floor beneath me, followed by rumbles, like thunder. My host says that this has been happening in town for a week now, and none of them can explain it. But I sense that it may be something sinister, and I don't even know why I'm telling you all of this save for my fervent hope that you may have an answer or advice?

Yours,

E.

Dear E.,

I'm afraid I don't have an answer at the ready but give me a day. I may be able to find one for you.

In the meantime, remain on guard.

I'll write soon.

Yours,

R.

The rain continued to fall hard the following day, turning Bitteryne's streets into creek beds. Iris and Attie spent the afternoon going door-to-door, gathering reports and stories from the townspeople. But there wasn't much new information to glean. Rumors swirled that Dacre had finally left Avalon Bluff and was now stationed in a town called Merrow. Why was he taking his time moving eastward? What was he waiting for?

Iris didn't know, although she sensed Roman might. She was anxious, waiting for his reply, but as the afternoon waned into a stormy eventide, he had yet to write.

She decided to sit in the dining room with Attie and work after dinner. They spread their notes out on the table, sharing a pitcher of chilled cider while a fire crackled in the stone hearth. Iris was halfway through with her article when she realized that Attie had gone still, her gaze fixated on the back door.

"What is it?" Iris asked. "Is it the ground again?"

"No, it's Bexley," Attie replied. "He said he would be back by now."

Iris was quiet, listening as the rain continued to pour through the night.

"I'm sure it's just the storm slowing him down," she said, but she was anxious about Tobias driving through such weather. "And it's only evening. He may still arrive tonight."

Attie sighed and resumed her typing, but her words seemed to come slower. Her eyes continued to dart to the back door, as if she expected it to swing open any moment.

The hours melted. The storm only grew stronger.

The electricity flickered and eventually went out. Iris and Attie worked by firelight, bidding Lonnie Fielding goodnight when he ensured they had everything they needed.

But when midnight struck, the girls finally packed up their typewriters and notes, returning to their rooms.

Tobias Bexley had failed to return.

16

Nine Lives

Iris woke to a clap of thunder.

She opened her eyes to the darkness, uncertain where she was. Her heart was pounding as she sat forward, lightning illuminating her surroundings with an impatient flash.

You're in Bitteryne, she told herself. *Everything is fine. It was just the storm that woke you.*

She waited for the next clap of thunder, but it never came. The lightning was bright but silent, and Iris could hear the *clink, clink, clink* below the foundation followed by a startling boom in the house, just down the hallway. It sounded like the back door had blown open.

Iris threw off the blankets, rising in a breathless rush.

Remain on guard, Roman had told her.

She grappled in the dark, remembering the electricity was out. Slowly, she opened her door and peered into the hallway. It was pitch black, but she could hear someone walking through the house. The floor creaked beneath their steps.

"Mr. Fielding?" Iris said, her voice thin.

"*Iris.*"

She turned, sensing Attie's presence to her right.

"Did you hear that noise?" Attie whispered.

"Yes. I think someone's in the house."

They stood shoulder to shoulder and listened. A clatter, like a bowl had overturned. A deep-pitched curse. A chair scratching along the floor.

Attie began to stride down the hall, fearless. Iris hurried after her.

"Attie? Attie, *wait*."

All Iris could think was that something had come from the ground. A hole had opened in the garden. One of Dacre's creatures had slithered through it and was now in the house, hungry for blood.

The girls reached the dining room. The hearth still glowed with dying embers, but the rest of the room was stained in darkness. Iris saw a tall shadow walk in front of the mullioned windows.

"Who are you?" Attie said sharply. "What do you want?"

The shadow ceased moving, but Iris could feel someone gazing in their direction. The hair rose on her arms as her heart quickened. She curled her fingers into a fist, preparing for a fight.

A deep, mirthful voice broke the silence. "Attie? It's only me."

Attie drew a sharp breath. "Bexley?"

"Yes, who else?"

"Who the bloody else? We thought you were a burglar!"

"I *did* tell you I'd return tonight."

"Yes, and in case you lost track of time, it's *three* in the morning. When midnight struck, we realized you were running late."

"Wait up on me, did you?" Tobias said.

"We were *working*," Attie amended, but she had stepped deeper into the room, heading in the direction of his voice.

Tobias was silent, but his breaths were heavy. Iris began to edge along the wall toward the hearth mantel, where she knew Lonnie kept a matchbook and candle tapers.

"Are you hurt?" Attie asked.

"No. And don't . . . don't touch me. At least not yet."

Iris lit a candlestick. The firelight cast a ring into the darkness, and she could at last see Tobias clearly.

His clothes were plastered to him, drenched from the rain, and his arms and face were splattered with mud. He looked exhausted, but his eyes gleamed, feverishly, as if he had just won a race.

He glanced at Iris, reading her expression.

"Do I look *that* bad, Miss Winnow?"

"You look like you just drove all night through a storm," Iris replied, awe-struck.

"I told you not much comes between me and assignments," he said, his attention returning to Attie. "Not even impassable roads."

Attie crossed her arms, jaw set. "What if you had wrecked your car?"

"Always a possibility." He set his valise down on the floor. "But I didn't. Not this time, at least. And I have letters for you both."

Iris stepped closer, watching as Tobias carefully removed his drenched gloves and opened the valise, handing them each a letter. Hers was from Forest; she recognized her brother's handwriting and it warmed her from within to see it.

"Your brother actually helped service the roadster this time," Tobias said. "At my mechanic's shop."

Iris glanced up, surprised. "Oh? I'm glad to hear it."

"He did a good job," Tobias said. "And I promised him tickets to the next race. He mentioned he would like to take you, when the war is over."

Iris smiled, but she felt a sudden twinge of homesickness. She glanced down at the letter in her hand, thankful for the faint light as she blinked back her tears.

"Do you need a cup of tea? A sandwich?" Attie asked Tobias. "The electricity is out, but I can set a kettle over the hearth."

Tobias sighed. "Thank you, but no. I've been up for a while. I'd only fall asleep before you could get the water to boil."

"Then let me at least fetch you a towel."

"That would be quite helpful."

Iris lit a second candlestick to take back with her to her room. She bid the two of them goodnight but paused in the hallway to glance over her shoulder. Attie was wiping the mud from Tobias's face; he was smiling and she was scowling as they spoke in hushed tones. But their voices still carried, enough for Iris to catch the words.

"I told you not to worry about me," he said.

"I wasn't worried."

"And it's nine, by the way."

"Nine what? Nine lives?"

"I've won nine *races*. If that will help ease your mind next time."

Iris didn't wait to hear Attie's reply. She pressed a smile to her lips as she slipped into her room.

Roman stole down the stairs quietly. The cottage felt empty, full of nothing more than long, dusty shadows. No one was in the foyer, guarding the front door, and no one was in the parlor. Not even Dacre. A fire had burned down in the hearth, but golden light continued to flicker along the walls.

Roman approached the war table.

He stared down at the map of Cambria, studying the places he knew—Oath, Avalon Bluff, Merrow, the chain of railroad tracks that his father controlled— and the multitude of places and landmarks that were still unfamiliar. The divine graves were marked in red ink, Alva's in particular drawing his gaze south and Mir's to the north until his attention snagged on Hawk Shire.

He dared to lean closer, touching the map with his hand. To his shock, lines bloomed along the paper. Some were dark, others brilliant. They moved like lightning, like tree roots. Quite a few of them fed into the towns closest to Roman. Places in Central and Western Borough. Places the war had already devoured. But his attention was soon captivated by glimmers of pale blue light. A cluster of towns pulsed with it like small cerulean hearts, including Merrow and Hawk Shire, while others remained unlit.

The map beneath, he remembered, carefully removing his hand.

The routes vanished, as if they had never been. But Roman could still see them when he closed his eyes—tangles of light and darkness—and he carefully lifted the edge of Cambria's map, beholding the illustration of the underworld, resting beneath. Nearly forgotten and easily overlooked by those who only saw the surface of things.

Roman studied what he could see, mesmerized by the twisting of passages. The cities and hubs of life they fed into. A world he had touched, but only briefly.

"I take it another dream has kept you up?"

Dacre's voice broke the silence. Roman released the map, letting it flutter down to the table. His pulse spiked but he kept his face calm, collected, as he straightened, glancing toward the foyer.

Dacre stood beneath the lintel, watching him. He had arrived soundlessly, as if he had materialized from the darkness.

"On the contrary, sir," Roman said, lacing his fingers behind his back. "I can't sleep these days. I want to know what awaits us."

"If it's death you fear, I have already told you once." Dacre stepped into the parlor. He seemed taller, broader, but maybe it was only the shadows, playing a trick on Roman's senses. "Remain at my side, faithful to me, and you shall never die. You shall never feel pain."

Roman held the god's steady, blue-cut gaze. But he could feel a bead of sweat begin to trickle down his spine. "And will I be at your side in Hawk Shire?"

"Why are you so concerned about Hawk Shire, Roman?"

"It sounds like an important battle."

"And do you see yourself as one of my soldiers, ready and willing to fight? To take back what was mine?"

Roman studied the map of Cambria again. "I'm not a soldier, sir. I've never been trained how to shoot a gun, or to handle a grenade, or to move like a shadow. At least, not that I remember. But what I do have are my words." He paused, surprised by how his voice trembled. As if he were surrendering a piece of himself. "I don't want to fight with half a heart, but all of it."

Dacre was silent for a long, torturous moment. But then he took hold of Cambria's map and let it fold over itself, revealing the world beneath.

"Tell me, Roman," he said as the under routes illuminated again. "What do you see?"

"I see paths. Roads."

"Is that all?"

Roman studied it closer. He was drawn to the dim, pulsing lights. He wondered if they marked enchanted thresholds. "I see cities. Towns. Doorways."

"Yes," Dacre said. "My domain. My ley lines. A realm of magic that most of your kind will never see or know or taste, even though our two worlds are connected."

"Are you rebuilding it, sir?" Roman asked. "The roads below?"

Dacre was quiet. Roman wondered if he had been too blunt, and he swallowed.

"I've noticed that there are still portions of the map that are darkened, as if they are waiting for you to return," he explained.

"A canny observation," the god replied. "And yes. While I slept, my domain fell into disarray. Ruin. Many of the roads became full of debris, my doorways forgotten and cloaked in cobwebs. My people are now currently working to repair them."

Roman stared at the map again, his gaze drawn to Hawk Shire. "Is that how my articles reach the *Oath Gazette*? By your underground roads?"

"Concerned about your articles reaching their destination?"

"I only thought—"

"Yes, Roman," Dacre cut him off. "Val uses the underground to deliver your articles to the city."

"Who is Val?"

"One of my favored advisors. Who else would I entrust such a task to?"

Roman wondered if that meant Val also possessed one of the five keys Dacre had mentioned. Keys forged over enchanted flames, capable of unlocking endless doorways. Roman's eyes drifted to Oath on the map. There was still a portion of work to be done to clear the eastern passages, although there was one fragile, tiny thread that had lit its way to the vast city.

One pathway cleared. One doorway active in Oath. Val's door.

The city's markings on the map were too minuscule for him to note the exact location of the door, and he didn't want to draw Dacre's suspicions. Roman returned his attention to the god, who was carefully observing him.

"Will you use your roads to take back what is yours, lord?" he dared to ask next. "To end the war?"

"Does it not make sense to do so, if my realm gives me an advantage?" Dacre covered the under map once more, the illuminated routes and cities fading until they were only blurs when Roman blinked. "I can end this war swiftly, mercifully, once my realm has healed and remembered itself. When the cities below gleam with firelight and laughter, and the roads connect one place to another, and my doorways spill magic into the mundane. Once I have Hawk Shire, we will be one step closer to peace. To victory."

"Will you find your sister's grave, sir?" Roman asked. "To wake her so she may join your cause?"

Dacre's eyes narrowed. "Why would you think that?"

"The map," Roman replied, indicating it. "Alva's grave is marked in the Southern Borough. Not far from here. I remember how you once spoke fondly of her, and I assumed . . ."

"What good would Alva's powers be to me when all of us live daily in a nightmare?" Dacre's voice held a cold edge, but it melted as he smiled. "But you are right about one thing, Roman. It is time to prove your heart steady. Tomorrow at dawn. Meet me here in the parlor. Bring your typewriter."

Roman nodded, sensing the dismissal.

Whatever was coming at daybreak, he wasn't sure if he was prepared for it. But he could feel his heart beating in his throat as he ascended the stairs. And he knew what he needed to do.

17

Burn My Words

Dear E.,

I write this to you in the dark, with only a sliver of moonlight on my desk. I haven't eaten in a while, and yet the shadows and my hunger are good. They sharpen me; they make me feel my own limitations. I'm not immortal, even if I once thought I could be. Most of all, they make me desperate and so I must ask one thing of you:

After you read this letter, I need you to burn it.

What I'm about to relay to you is time sensitive, and dangerous—for you and for me and this connection we have forged—if it falls into the wrong hands. I've asked myself multiple times why I'm surrendering this to you, as I sense you are fighting for Enva's cause while I am not, and it comes down to two simple truths:

1. A loss of life and freedom is imminent, and I cannot bear to stand aside and let it happen.
2. I care about you. The last thing I would ever want is for you to find yourself caught up in what is about to occur.

But to answer your previous query about the strange clinks and rumbles in the earth. Dacre is restoring the pathways of his realm that have fallen into disarray over the past few centuries. He plans to reach Oath below ground before he arrives above. I imagine the sounds you hear are his workers, clearing the rubble from the ley lines.

As to the most pressing matter at hand...he is preparing to take Hawk Shire. In three days' time, he will storm the town, attacking from within by utilizing his magical doorways while his remaining forces surround the town. If you are in Hawk Shire, I beg you to retreat. Get out while you can; head south or north. Anywhere but Oath, where he plans to attack after Hawk Shire falls.

Please don't reply to this letter. I won't be able to respond for a span of days and I don't know where I'll be after Hawk Shire. Burn my words. Keep yourself safe. If fate will have it, I'll write to you again soon.

Yours,

R.

I can't burn this.

Iris stared at Roman's letter. It was midmorning, and she had overslept, waking to a blissful stream of sunshine on her face and to Roman's words on the floor. She didn't know what she had been expecting, but it wasn't what he gave her. *Repairing the ley lines.* She felt chilled at the thought of Dacre's workers somewhere beneath her, cutting through rubble. The idea of Hawk Shire being attacked made her stomach clench.

She stood in the silence of her bedroom and read it again. Again and again, until she felt both icy and hot, until the air cut her lungs and she strode from the chamber, seeking Attie.

She found her outside on the curb, helping Tobias clean the roadster. They were laughing together as the last of the mud was washed away from the tires, and Iris almost stopped herself. She didn't want to ruin this moment for them, and she slowed on the brick path, hiding Roman's letter behind her back.

Burn my words. Keep yourself safe.

"Miss Winnow?" Tobias stood with a rag in his hands, the brightness in his eyes dimming when he saw how pale she was. "Is everything all right?"

"You can call me Iris. And if I asked you to drive me to Hawk Shire . . . would you do it, Tobias?"

Attie dropped the bristle brush she had been wielding and rose, brow furrowed with concern.

Tobias was silent for a beat. But when he spoke, his voice was firm. "Ms. Hammond gave me strict orders not to drive you beyond Winthrop."

"Then do you know how far Hawk Shire is from Winthrop?" Iris asked. "If it's not too much distance, I can walk there or hitch another ride. But I need you to take me to Winthrop today. It's very urgent."

"What's happened?" Attie closed the distance between them.

Iris bit her lip before surrendering Roman's letter. She watched as Attie read it, her brown eyes going wide in shock before meeting her gaze.

"Marisol said Keegan is in Hawk Shire, didn't she?" Attie whispered.

Iris only nodded. It felt like a splinter was in her throat. Her eyes were burning and she rubbed them for a moment, a stray eyelash clinging to her fingertip.

"Why do you need to go to Hawk Shire?" Tobias asked, stepping closer.

Attie only stared at Iris. When Iris tilted her chin, acquiescing, Attie handed the letter to him.

And this was what Roman meant, Iris thought. His letter had been intended for her eyes only, but to prevent the devastation planned for Hawk Shire, she would have to show it to others. She would have to then reveal *how* she had received the letter. Those secrets she had been holding like jewels in her hand would be exposed, and it made her feel vulnerable.

Tobias exhaled, slow and deep, as he finished reading the letter. "How did you get this? Who is R.?"

"It's a long story," Iris said, a blush creeping over her.

Tobias was pensive, his expression almost stern. But he handed the letter back to her. "Then you'll have plenty of time to tell me on the ride there. Go pack your bags. I'll drive you to Hawk Shire."

18

Nothing More than Mist
and Memory

R oman followed Dacre over the parlor threshold and down the hewn
stairwell, leaving the morning sunlight of Merrow behind. He carried his typewriter and Elizabeth's letters, folded and hidden in his
inner pocket. He had known Dacre would be taking him to the realm below at
dawn, and yet he hadn't been able to destroy her letters before slipping from
the privacy of his room.

He was relieved when they reached a narrow corridor, lit by torches. From
there, they walked for a while in silence with nothing but the clip of their
boots and the rush of their breath for company. But Roman sensed the floor
tilting, ever so slightly, as if they were traversing further and further downward. Without any warning, the corridor suddenly ended, ushering them into
a massive chamber. *Although perhaps* chamber *is the wrong word for it*, Roman
thought as he came to a slow halt, craning his neck to take it all in.

This place was vast and lively, like a courtyard in a market square, with
windows and doors and balconies carved high up into the white stone walls.
It was another *world,* truly, and Roman was surprised to find so many people
within it. Mainly soldiers, who were swiftly identified by their uniforms. Some

were gathered around a forge, where sparks danced in the air and a wash of heat could be felt, while others were in line for food, bowls in hand. Another company looked to be in the midst of a drill, their boots stomping the stone floor in perfect rhythm, their rifles catching the firelight.

It all felt strangely normal save for the lack of sky and sunlight, until Roman noticed other things.

There was a creek babbling nearby, cutting a serpentine path through the rock. The small stones in its bed looked to be silver coins, and smoke was rising from the currents. And then a woman walked by with a basket of freshly laundered uniforms on her hip. Upon first glance, she looked human, until Roman blinked and saw a flash of the otherworldly in her—talons curling from her fingertips, silver hair with bloodstains on the ends, and long canines protruding from her mouth. She was wearing a glamour of some sort to make her appear human, a camouflage, and Roman shivered, watching her melt into the crowd. Lastly, a dog was trotting about, looking for scraps. A dog and yet not, for it had two limp wings on its back, and three eyes in its face.

"Welcome to Lorindella," Dacre said. He sounded amused, and Roman realized the god had been watching his reaction. "Are you hungry?"

Roman nodded, feeling the hollow ache of his stomach. He was ravenous. For food, for warmth, for home. For safety.

He shifted his typewriter to his other hand and followed Dacre to the food line. The air became delicious to breathe, overwhelmed with the aromas of chargrilled meat. Roman didn't realize he was shaking until a bowl of what looked to be chicken, bread, and some sort of thick red sauce was given to him.

"Go rest and take your fill," Dacre said, indicating the heart of the square, where soldiers were sitting while they ate. "I'll come for you when it's time to move."

"Yes, sir," Roman said, but his voice was hardly above a whisper.

He found a place to sit and devoured the food. He could have eaten three more bowls, but he distracted himself from the lingering pangs by studying the city again. *Lorindella,* Dacre had called it. Roman tried to imagine it on the under map he had seen earlier. He closed his eyes and remembered all the illuminated passages he had seen, flowing like rivers, tangling like tree roots.

When he opened his eyes again, he saw Lieutenant Shane standing a few paces away, speaking to Dacre.

Roman glanced down at his hands, but a few moments later, two shined boots came to a stop before him.

"You'll be marching with my platoon, correspondent," Shane said. "Here's your pack." He dropped a bedroll strapped down with a water canteen, a small iron griddle, and a leather pouch of food. "You're responsible for carrying it from now on. You have ten more minutes before we depart. Take care of any other business you may have before then."

Roman stared at it, numb with shock, before looking up at Shane. "Why am I in your platoon? I didn't think I would be fighting."

"Dacre thought it best you remain under my instruction since we come from the same place."

"What are you talking about?"

"You didn't know I'm from Oath?" Shane said with a smirk. But before Roman could scrounge up a reply, the lieutenant had turned and walked away.

It was nearly impossible to tell how much time had passed, but Roman had blisters on his heels and an empty, growling stomach by the time Shane brought his platoon to a halt. They had been marching along an eastern route, one that had led them to another vast chamber, although this one was empty and dim, laced with fog. There was no forge or market, nor were there windows or balconies hewn from the walls. It felt quiet and reverent as a forest, although no trees grew here. Only straggly plants blossomed from cracks in the rock.

Roman felt dried out, like a stone that had cracked in two. He rushed to untether the canteen and drank a few sips, the water so cold it made his teeth ache.

The privates around him were beginning to bed down for the night. Roman followed suit, keeping his typewriter close—the only weapon that he possessed. The bedroll was two woolen blankets, scratchy but warm, and Roman lay down with a sigh, his arms crossed, his palms resting on his chest, just above Elizabeth's letters. He couldn't resist pressing down until he felt the paper crinkle.

He fell asleep with a shiver.

He dreamt of Iris Winnow again.

But of course he would, and he tasted the irony like he had set a coin in his mouth. She seemed to haunt his dreams at the direst of times. When the waking world felt the most uncertain and bruised.

This time, they sat on a park bench side by side, eating sandwiches. It was cold and the trees were bare overhead. Iris was telling him about her brother, Forest. He was missing in action.

Then he dreamt of home again. He was in his room; it was late, and he was typing on his typewriter. He was writing about Del's drowning and the guilt that still haunted him like a shadow he could never escape. When he was done, he folded the paper and slipped it beneath his wardrobe door. After that, he sat on his bed and reread the letters that Iris had written to him.

He saw Iris again at the *Gazette*. Their battleground. She was leaving. She was *quitting,* and Roman didn't know what to do, what to say to convince her to stay or why this truly mattered to him. He only knew that he felt most alive when she was near, and he stood before the doors and watched her walk to him. He sought to read every line of her expression, every thought flickering through her mind, as if she were a story on a page. He was desperate to know what she was thinking, what he could say to convince her to stay.

Stay, Iris. Stay here with me.

"Roman."

Dacre's voice woke him. The deep timbre moved like shockwaves in Roman's mind, trespassing into the dream. Iris Winnow melted into iridescent rain at the sound. Roman surprised himself by reaching out to touch her. But she was nothing more than mist and memory. She slipped through his fingers, leaving behind the taste of tart citrus in black, sugared tea.

"Wake, Roman," Dacre was saying, his grip hard on his shoulder. "The hour has come."

"Sir?" Roman said reflexively, his voice rusted. He opened his eyes to the blurred sight of a god staring down at him.

But even under the heavy watch of immortality, all Roman could think was *this*: he had been writing to Iris the same way he was writing to Elizabeth now. He had been slipping typed letters under doorways for a while. Long before he had ever become entangled with the war. It made his blood quicken, his skin warm like gold heated over fire.

"Get up," Dacre said. "It's time for us to take Hawk Shire."

19

A Brigadier Made of Stars

Hawk Shire wasn't what Iris was expecting. Although to be honest, she wasn't sure *what* she had thought it would be like.

All through the night ride, she had leaned back and let the motorcar hum through her bones, her eyes on the sky. The stars had glimmered overhead like devoted guardians, the western constellations guiding them onward like an arrow set to a bowstring. Iris, too electrified to sleep, had tried to envision what was to come. To prepare her statement and set a plan of action, Roman's letter tucked away in her pocket alongside Marisol's bird volume. A few times, she had let her fingertip trace the sharp corner of the folded paper, Roman's words a brilliant seam in the darkness.

I don't know how to prepare for this, Mum, Iris caught herself thinking, studying the stars. They continued to gleam, cold pinpricks of fire. *I don't know what I'm doing.*

The sun was rising like a bloody yolk on the horizon when Tobias geared down the roadster. Hawk Shire came into view through a veil of fog, a town spun from tall shadows in the distance. There was a patrol on the road with a crudely made barricade. Tobias brought the motorcar to a stop when a soldier lifted his hand.

"This town is closed to civilians," the soldier said in a curt tone, studying the three of them with a suspicious eye. "You should return to where you came from."

Iris sat up straighter, removing her goggles. Gods only knew what she looked like, wind-snarled hair, cheeks and shoulders freckled with mud. A desperate gleam in her eyes.

"I have an important message for Captain Keegan Torres," she said. "It's very urgent. Please let us pass."

The soldier merely stared at her, but his gaze dropped to the white badge on her jumpsuit, stitched over her heart. INKRIDDEN TRIBUNE PRESS.

"If you're here to report, I'm sorry to say that's prohibited. This is an active war zone, closed to civilians, and you—"

"We aren't here to report," Iris interrupted, her voice sharper than she intended. She made herself draw a deep breath, made her shoulders relax. "Like I said, I am carrying an extremely important message for Captain—"

"Yes, you mentioned that. What is the message?"

Iris hesitated. She could feel both Attie and Tobias watching her, waiting. The air suddenly felt tense. Many things had crossed her mind in the dark, but not once had she thought that they would be barred from Hawk Shire.

"It must be hand-delivered to the captain," she replied firmly. "By me."

A second soldier joined the first, drawn to the motorcar. Iris watched as the two of them spoke in low tones, glancing their way with arched brows. Sweat prickled along Iris's palms as she waited; she was tempted to touch Roman's letter but resisted, tracing her wedding band instead. She inhaled draughts of air, tasting the exhaust from the car, the redolent mist, the smoke from a campfire. The sun continued to rise; the fog was melting quickly now, like snow in spring. Hawk Shire looked dark and dismal, a chain of circular stone buildings reminiscent of the points of a crown.

"All right," said the private who had first spoken to them. "Only one of you can come. I'll escort you now."

Iris's heart leapt into her throat. But she looked at Attie, who nodded solemnly in encouragement, and then Tobias, who cut the engine.

"We'll wait here for you," he said, and by the tone of his voice Iris knew nothing would make him break his word.

It gave her the confidence to step out of the roadster, chin lifted high. Her legs felt weak from hours of sitting, but she followed the private around the barricade and up the road. They passed a sea of linen tents. Rings of soldiers sitting around campfires as they fried links of sausage and eggs in cast iron skillets. A line of parked lorries splattered with mud, the sunrise limning their cracked windshields and bullet-sprayed fenders. The air was solemn and silent and still, as if Enva's forces had been defeated, and it made the hair stand up on Iris's arms.

Wordlessly, she followed the private into town, gazing up at the buildings of Hawk Shire. One in the center of town caught her eye. It was very tall and wide—four stories high with several sets of chimneys—and built from red brick and shining glass windows. A factory, Iris realized, with modest houses strung around it like dew on a cobweb.

The private led her through a wide city market, and Iris stopped abruptly. Over the cobblestones, cots and makeshifts beds were set up in rows, wounded soldiers lying on tattered blankets. The soldiers far outnumbered the doctors and nurses, who seemed to be in constant motion, moving from cot to cot, carrying bedpans, bloodied bandages, and cups of water. Not even the gray-tinged sunshine could hide the exhaustion and concern etched onto their faces.

The staggering number of wounded stole Iris's breath; it made her think of Forest. Of Roman. She forced herself to continue following the private into the factory, although her thoughts bent to one horrible question: how would Enva's forces evacuate all the wounded before Dacre arrived?

The private led her up flights of metal stairs to the uppermost level, passing a few long-faced soldiers along the way. Again, Iris was surprised by how quiet it was, as if no one had the heart to speak. As if they were simply holding their breath and waiting for Dacre to come and crush them, one last time.

"In here," the private said, opening a squeaky door. "The brigadier will meet with you soon."

Iris stepped into the room, jolted by his words. "The *brigadier*? I asked to speak with Captain Keegan Torres."

The private only sighed and shook his head. He closed the door, leaving her alone in the chamber, which Iris turned to take in. It was a long and narrow room, with a threadbare rug along the hardwood floor, a stained walnut desk covered in papers and wax-dribbled candelabras, and one wall full of windows. It was to these windows that Iris was drawn, realizing the glass afforded her a bird's-eye view of Hawk Shire, as well as the deep blue horizon of the west.

She watched as the fog continued to recoil. She could see the market square once more, her heart aching as she studied the rows of wounded soldiers. A doctor strode from one building to another, blood on her clothes. Nurses carried a stretcher, the body draped in a white sheet.

Iris's eyes eventually settled on a pair of vultures, perched on a nearby roof.

She stared at the birds as they sunned their wings, wondering if they had followed her from River Down. With an anxious twitch of her hands, Iris reached into her pocket and retrieved Marisol's book. She sifted through the worn pages, admiring the intricate illustrations, until she came to the page devoted to nightingales. There her eyes remained, reading through the fine-print description:

A small and secretive bird that is rather plain to behold, the Nightingale is difficult to spot. They keep to thick cover, and while their feathers might be unexciting, they have a repertoire of more than two hundred different phrases that they can sing.

The door creaked open.

Iris closed the book, her mouth suddenly dry. All the words seemed to scatter from her thoughts as she turned away from the windows, preparing to ask for Keegan again. But Iris stopped short, her breath catching.

It *was* Keegan. Marisol's wife stood tall and proud in her green uniform, three golden stars pinned over her breast. Her blond hair was slicked back and her jaw was set, as if she too had come to this meeting with preconceptions. Her dark eyes were keen but red-rimmed, as if she hadn't slept a full night in weeks, and her expression was inscrutable. Her mouth was set in a line that looked chiseled from stone.

"Cap—Brigadier Torres," Iris said. "I know you probably don't remember me, but I'm—"

"Iris Winnow," Keegan said, shutting the door behind her. "Of course I remember you. Didn't I oversee your vows in the garden? My wife is very fond of you and Attie, as well as your Kitt. But what in all the gods' names are you doing here?"

Iris drew a deep breath. "I have a message I think you should see."

"A message?"

"Yes. I . . ." How much to say? Iris reached into her pocket again, withdrawing Roman's letter. "Please read this."

She gave the letter to Keegan, watching as the brigadier read Roman's words. Keegan's expression didn't change; indeed, Iris was beginning to believe that the brigadier might doubt it all, and Iris didn't know what she would do if that happened. But then Keegan exhaled sharply and met Iris's gaze. Her eyes glittered as if she had just been shaken from a dream.

"How did you get this, Iris?"

"I have a magical connection to Roman through our typewriters," Iris began. She shared everything with Keegan, from the beginning in Oath when they were mere rivals at the paper to where she stood now, writing to her husband even though he was Dacre's prisoner and couldn't even remember her name.

"I know it sounds impossible, but Roman wouldn't lie to me," she finished, surprised by the hoarseness in her tone. She swallowed the lump in her throat, but it only wedged in her chest, and she knew it was the grief she hadn't allowed herself to process. Grief over Roman being a captive, his mind scrambled by Dacre's magic. Grief that whatever they once had might not ever be recovered.

She was very good at burying things like that, her anguish and her sorrow and sometimes even the reality of what she faced. But she didn't quite know how to let them go without losing vital pieces of herself.

Keegan was silent, staring down at Roman's typed words again. "When did you receive this letter?"

"Yesterday morning. I came as soon as I read it. We drove all night from Bitteryne."

"Which means we only have another day or so before Dacre attacks, if what Roman says is true." Keegan rolled her lips together but then glanced at Iris. "Who is *we*? You said you drove here with someone?"

"Attie and Tobias Bexley."

"Where are they now?"

"At the barricade in the motorcar, waiting for me to return."

"Then the three of you must be exhausted and hungry. I'll send breakfast for you, as well as find you all a quiet room to rest." Keegan strode to the door and opened it, murmuring to a soldier waiting in the hallway.

Iris hesitated, her eyes drifting to Roman's letter, still in Keegan's hand.

"Go with Private Shepherd. He's going to take you to a room on the lower floor to rest and eat," Keegan said, glancing back at Iris. But she must have seen the stricken light in Iris's eyes. The brigadier softened her tone, adding, "Don't worry. I need to speak to my officers, but I'll come find you in a little bit, after you've rested."

"Of course," Iris whispered with a half smile. "Thank you, Brigadier Torres."

But despite her relief at having delivered the news in time, Iris still found it hard to quit the room, to follow another stranger, leaving Roman's letter—*burn my words*—behind to an unknown fate.

None of them planned to sleep for more than an hour, but after a warm fare of eggs and buttered toast, accompanied by watered-down chicory with no sugar and only a splash of cream, Iris, Attie, and Tobias fell into a deep slumber on the cots Keegan had provided. They had been given an inner room in the factory, one with no windows, and the darkness felt like a balm until Iris was woken by the distant sound of a violin.

It was playing a poignant, lovely song, one that filled Iris with nostalgia, and she rose from her cot and followed the music out of the dark room.

She walked down the hallway, the violin's melody growing louder, as if she was on the cusp of finding it. She turned a corner and nearly ran into her mother.

Aster was leaning against the wall, wrapped in her purple coat with a cigarette smoldering in her fingers.

"There you are, darling," she said brightly. "Have you come to enjoy the music with me?"

Iris frowned, unsettled. "Who is playing the violin?"

"Does it matter? Listen, Iris. Listen to the notes. Tell me if you know them."

Iris fell quiet. She listened to the violin, and while the music curled through her like sun-warmed vines, there was no recognition. She had never heard this song before.

"I don't know it, Mum," she confessed, watching a furrow form in Aster's brow. "And why are you here?"

Aster opened her mouth, but her voice was robbed as the colors began to melt together. Iris felt a prick of fear, watching the features of her mother's face begin to smudge, until she raised her own hands and saw they were also fading, breaking into hundreds of stars.

"This is a dream," she panted. "Why do you keep appearing to me, Mum?"

The floor shook and cracked beneath her boots. Iris was about to fall through the widening crevice when she gasped and sat forward, blinking into the peaceful dark. It took her a moment to gain her bearings, but she remembered where she was. She could hear Attie, her breathing heavy with dreams, in the cot next to her, and Tobias's soft snores on the other side of the room. There was no way to tell the time, and Iris ran her fingers through her tangled hair as she set her feet on the floor. There, she felt it again. A steady rumbling.

Iris slipped from the room and moved down the hallway, searching for someone to tell her what was happening, but she soon found the answer herself when she passed a set of windows. She paused, watching the doctor she had seen earlier help load a line of wounded patients into the back of a lorry. Another truck was passing by on the road, brimming with soldiers.

It was Keegan's forces, Iris realized. They must be retreating from Hawk Shire.

They believed Roman's words.

Iris rushed down the long hallway, through amber squares of sunlight. It looked to be midafternoon, and every minute suddenly felt dire. She slipped out the door and approached one of the nurses in the market square.

"What can I do?" Iris asked.

The nurse glanced her over, sweat beading on her face. "If you want, you can help us load the wounded into that lorry."

Iris nodded and hurried to the closest cot, where a young man with bandages on his face was struggling to sit forward.

"Here," Iris said. "Take my hand." She eased him to his feet and offered him balance, walking him toward the truck. The lorry was nearly full, the wounded packed in close together. As Iris helped the soldier up the ramp and into the back, worry flooded her lungs.

They couldn't leave any of the wounded behind. Not with Dacre's imminent arrival. He would heal these soldiers only to use them for his own gains.

"Iris!"

She turned to see Attie and Tobias hurrying through the chaos. Iris wove her way to them, heart drumming in her ears.

"They believed Roman's warning?" Attie said in a low but hopeful tone.

"Yes." Iris tucked a tangle of hair behind her ear. She realized there was blood on her hands. "They're loading all the wounded, but I'm not sure where—" She cut herself off when she caught sight of Keegan approaching them. "Brigadier Torres."

"I was just coming to wake you," Keegan said. "Evacuations have commenced, and the three of you should depart as swiftly as you arrived."

"Where are you evacuating to?" Attie asked.

"To Oath," Keegan replied. "We are the last of Enva's forces. And we will make our final stand in the city."

Those words went through Iris as a shiver. She studied Keegan's face. "You are the last?"

"Our battalions holding the southern front have fallen. Dacre has killed and taken a great number of our soldiers. And I will not let him capture and turn this final brigade."

"Then let us help you with the wounded," Tobias offered. "We can stay and get them safely loaded."

Keegan shook her head. "You should leave immediately. I couldn't bear it should something happen to you three."

"But nor can we leave you and the wounded behind," Iris insisted. "*Please,* Brigadier."

Keegan hesitated but held Iris's gaze. Maybe she saw it in Iris's eyes: a glimmer of the past. That fateful day in the bluff when Keegan had delivered a letter to Iris. Words that had conveyed that Forest wasn't *dead* but *wounded.* And how that message had strengthened Iris's resolve to stay behind rather than evacuate with the rest of the town residents.

"If I let you stay and help," Keegan began, "then you'll be at the back of a slow line of lorries. You'll be in a very vulnerable position if Dacre decides to pursue us."

"I know a shortcut," Tobias countered. "From my early post-running days. Your troops will be taking the high road to Oath, Brigadier?"

"Yes. Why?"

"We're in my roadster, and I can drive us down the narrow but faster Hawthorne Route, which will have us meeting up with your brigade in River Down in no time."

Iris held her breath as she waited for Keegan's response. Her fingers instinctively went to the locket hanging from her neck.

"All right," Keegan relented. "The three of you can stay and assist. But when I say it's time for you to go, you take Hawthorne Route and you don't look back. Agreed?"

"Yes," Iris answered in unison with Tobias and Attie.

The brigadier withdrew a crinkled sheet of paper from her pocket. Roman's letter, Iris realized, and a sigh escaped her when Keegan gave it back to her.

"Thank you for delivering this message," Keegan said. "For driving through the night to reach us in time. I will always be indebted to you three."

Iris's throat went narrow. She only nodded, tucking the paper into her pocket. But as she began to guide soldiers to the lorry, she couldn't help but think of Roman, deep in the earth. Walking ever closer through those tangled ley lines, somewhere just beneath her feet.

20

A House That Knows
What You Need

The afternoon slipped away beneath a bright blue sky. Iris, Attie, and Tobias didn't stop until every wounded soldier was safely evacuated and Keegan gave them the signal to depart.

It was much later than they had anticipated leaving, with the sun sinking toward the western horizon and spring's chill blooming into shadows. But a strange energy stirred Iris's blood; it cut through her exhaustion and held her fear at bay as she followed Attie and Tobias to the roadster. It felt triumphant to slip into the car's familiar leather seat.

The three of them had warned Keegan's brigade in time. They had seen the wounded safely loaded and driven to the east, troops that Dacre wouldn't capture and turn. It was a sweet victory, and Iris leaned back with a smile as Tobias cranked the car.

"We make a good team," he said, as if he also felt the same thrill in his blood.

"I can already see tomorrow's headline." Attie propped her elbows on the back of Tobias's seat. "It's sure to sell a thousand papers in Oath."

"*Two brave reporters save Enva's last brigade?*" Tobias guessed as he drove through the streets. The roadster's engine purred a familiar *tick-tick-tick* as they followed the army's trail.

"I think you're forgetting someone, Bexley," Attie drawled. "He has nine lives, if you recall."

Tobias laughed, but Iris didn't hear how he replied. Her attention was snagged by a few privates who lingered behind, boarding up lintels, garages, and windows of buildings on the outskirts of town. Iris turned to watch them, hair tangling across her face. Cold dread began to seep through her bones.

She wondered if this was a last-minute order of Keegan's, to make it more difficult for Dacre's forces when they arrived by inner doorways. But Iris couldn't deny that it felt more like the town was bracing for a windstorm. Something that would level every building into rubble.

The roadster passed the last barricade, reaching the open high road. Up ahead was the line of lorries, fading into the distance as they drove eastward. The motorcar followed for half a kilometer before the road branched.

"Hawthorne Route is notorious for its bends," Tobias said as he turned the car, taking the shortcut. "You might need to hold on."

"*Might?*" Attie said dryly as she slid across the seat, bumping into Iris. "I thought I was promised a smooth ride."

"And I have a retort to that statement," Tobias said, meeting Attie's gaze in the rearview mirror. "But gods know I shouldn't say it."

Attie took hold of the rope handle in front of her, drawing closer to him. "Is that a challenge, Bexley?"

Iris, who had been watching them with an amused smile, suddenly felt like she needed to glance away. She did, looking through the mud-speckled windshield at the serpentine road they raced along. Her eyes widened when she realized the shadow up ahead was something else entirely.

"*Tobias!*" Iris cried just as they hit the pothole.

Tobias jerked the wheel. The roadster spun with a stomach-churning lurch. Both girls scrambled to hold on as Tobias recovered control.

"Again, a smooth ride," Attie teased, attempting to lighten the mood. But Tobias's posture had gone rigid. Iris felt him gear the car down, the engine whining.

"Is everything all right?" she asked.

Tobias didn't answer as he brought the roadster to a sudden halt in the middle of the road.

He vaulted over the door, frowning as he studied the left side of the car. Iris didn't have to see for herself; she felt how the roadster listed, and she held her breath as Tobias knelt.

"A flat tire," he announced in a clipped tone. "I shouldn't have hit that pothole."

"I'm sorry," Attie breathed. She chewed on her lip as she slipped out the door, standing beside him to survey the damage. "I shouldn't have distracted you."

Tobias stood, brushing his hands on his trousers. "It's not a problem. I have a spare in the boot, but it'll take me a moment to fix."

"Let me help."

As Tobias and Attie began to pull everything out of the trunk to find the spare and the jack, Iris set their luggage off to the side, feeling the tension brew in the air. Night was fast approaching. The first stars had broken the dusk when Tobias let out a curse.

"I can't find my tire iron," he said, racing a hand over his black, crew-cut hair. "Iris, will you light that lantern for me?"

Iris reached for the glass lantern and matchbox she had set beside the luggage, items that Tobias always carried in case of a night emergency. Which was unfolding at the moment, making Iris's heart pound. Her fingers felt numb as she struck the flame and lit the wick, holding the lantern up so Tobias could see.

But his eyes weren't on the car. They were fixed upon Attie, who was wringing her hands and rambling off another apology.

"I'm terribly sorry, this is all my fault, and I—"

Tobias reached out, gently taking her arm. "It's not your fault, Attie."

"It *is*. I took your attention off the road!"

An awkward silence welled between them. Iris rushed to say, "If you're missing a tire iron, maybe I can run back to town and find one? We passed a garage right before the barricade." In all honesty, she wanted to be back on their way as soon as possible but also give the two of them a moment alone.

"Run back to town?" Attie cried. "For gods' sake, Iris!"

"It's not far," Iris insisted. "I can still see the second-story windows of a few town houses from here. You two can get the car raised with the jack, and I'll return with the iron. Then we'll be back on our way as if this never happened."

Tobias was quiet, but he eventually nodded. "All right. But take the lantern. If there's any trouble, give us a signal by blowing out the flame from one of those upper windows."

"Of course. I'll return in a few minutes. Don't worry." She took two steps and then spun back around with a grimace. "Just one last question. What exactly does a tire iron look like?"

Hawk Shire was a different town in the evening with abandoned streets.

Iris's breath was ragged by the time she passed the barricade on the high road, her muscles burning as she eased to a stilted walk over the cobblestones. It was that eerie hour when night had almost swallowed the last threads of sunset, and shadows felt crooked and sinister. Iris startled herself a few times, searching for the garage she had seen earlier. She paused, wondering if a platoon of Enva's soldiers had been left behind, but it was nothing but a play of the darkness and the wind, whistling through the streets.

Iris stared at the quiet town, lantern in hand.

No, she was utterly alone here, and what triumph she had tasted earlier suddenly went sour on her tongue.

Find the tire iron and get out, she told herself, at last locating the garage.

It hadn't been boarded up like the nearby windows and doors, and she sorted through a cabinet of tools, her options sparse as she frantically examined them by firelight. None fully matched the description Tobias had given her. With a sigh of defeat, she retraced her steps down the thoroughfare until the outermost street caught her eye.

Iris decided to take it, seeking another garage.

She passed house after house, all which were boarded up, until she reached the place where the soldiers had abandoned their hammers and planks. A few homes beyond that was another garage, sitting open like a monster's maw. Iris was approaching when she heard a noise from within the shadows. A clink of metal, like something had fallen from a shelf.

"Hello?" she called, but her voice was fragile in the sudden gust of wind. She held her lantern out stiffly, letting the firelight guide her, and it wasn't until she was in the garage that she saw a wrench gleaming on the floor.

She studied it a moment before noting the shelves before her were empty, and there were no other tools save for this one. How odd that it had fallen the moment it did, as if desperate to catch her eye. Disquieted, Iris bent down and took the wrench in hand. It was heavy, speckled with rust. For some odd reason, it made her think of the grocer in Oath. How those enchanted shelves had known the amount of coin in her purse, easing the items she could afford to the forefront.

I'm standing on a ley line.

The realization shivered through her. A magical place to be, as well as a dangerous one. No sooner had that thought unfurled in her mind than she heard another noise. The door to her right creaked open, as if beckoning her into the adjacent house.

Iris flinched, fear coiling tight in her body. *Fight or run,* her heart pounded, the indecision burning through her chest. But as she continued to stare at the doorway, studying the moonlit interior of the empty house, she reached another acknowledgment.

This house is rooted in magic, and it knows what I need.

She decided to trust it, even as sweat gleamed on her skin. The magic of a quiet, abandoned house. She stepped inside, wrench gripped in one hand, lantern in the other.

The tiles beneath her feet were glazed blue, eventually transforming into scuffed hardwood. Stray leaves gathered in the corners of a parlor. A chandelier hung from the ceiling above, as if it had blossomed from a crack, its crystals glittering in the lantern light. But it was a stairwell with a fancy banister that drew Iris's attention. The steps led to a darkened second floor, and an idea occurred to her.

As Iris took the stairs up to a narrow hallway, she didn't know if the house had magically prompted her, or if it truly was a thought of her own. In the end, it didn't matter, as she entered a bedchamber at the back of the house. The room was reminiscent of her own, with a mattress against one wall, a desk piled high with books, and a wardrobe door that was open, revealing metal hangers. Most of all, there was a window that overlooked the way she had run to town. Iris held her lantern up to the glass panes as well as the wrench, waiting to see if she could get a signal from Attie and Tobias.

"Will this tool work?" she whispered, hoping Attie would use her binoculars to get a closer look.

A moment later, she spotted a firefly of light in the distance. Attie had struck a match in reply. When Iris squinted, she could even see the faint trace of the roadster, a dark shadow on the road.

Attie waved her small flame. Iris couldn't tell what that meant and was debating on what to do when she felt the floor tremble. She thought she had imagined it until the walls shuddered, making a nearby picture frame fall from its nail.

Breath suspended and feet rooted to the spot, Iris strained her ears against the roar of silence.

A door opened below. Boots began to tromp along the floor. Voices rose like smoke.

Run or fight.

The magic she stood upon now felt treacherous. A net that had caught her limbs. Her hands trembled as she opened the lantern. With her eyes still riveted to Attie's distant flame, Iris blew hers out.

21

Face-to-Face with a Dream

Roman couldn't breathe.

They had him in a line with the soldiers. His typewriter case banged against his knee every time he took a step, and the pack strapped to his back made him feel unbalanced and slow. There was no option but to move forward, as if he were in a river and its current was dragging him to a waterfall. Dragging him to his death. A battle was imminent, and he was going to be caught in the middle of it with nothing more than a typewriter in hand.

He tried to draw a deep breath to steady his heart, but stars danced at the corners of his eyes. The line slowed when they left the cavernous chamber, feeding into a winding corridor again that was studded with shards of emerald. Blue lightning flickered through the stone overhead, lighting the way. Roman could taste it, a weird medley of ozone and damp rock, and he briefly wondered if it was magic crackling on his tongue.

"Eyes forward, guns ready." Lieutenant Shane was passing by, walking against the flow of their progress. He repeated the phrase, again and again, his gaze moving over every soldier in line. The moment he brushed Roman's shoulder, Roman frantically reached out and snagged his sleeve.

"*Please*," Roman panted. "I don't think I'm supposed to be here."

Shane paused. "You're exactly where you need to be, correspondent."

"I have no weapon, no training. I . . . I don't even know what I'm supposed to be doing!"

"You're part of the press. No one will shoot you," the lieutenant said, indicating the badge on Roman's jumpsuit. The badge that proclaimed Roman was far from neutral but an UNDERLING CORRESPONDENT.

Before Roman could form a reply, Shane slipped from his grip and continued on his way repeating his phrase.

Eyes forward, guns ready.

Numb, Roman resumed walking. But then a whisper came in his ear, a hiss to get his attention.

"Pssst. You're with the greens," said the soldier behind him. "Don't worry, they have us entering the city on the outskirts, away from the worst of the battle. We'll be arriving through a door on the edge."

That revelation did nothing to ease Roman's fears, and he gritted his teeth together. He had once thought that he would want to be here. To be an eyewitness to fate unfolding. But now that he was seconds away from it, he couldn't help but feel how unprepared he was.

The floor was rising, forming into a stairwell. Roman began to ascend, step by step, feeling his muscles burn from the exertion. Cold sweat beaded along his skin. His stomach churned and he swallowed a surge of acid.

This is it, he thought, his eyes on the blue veins that shone in the rock around him, on the doorway that loomed in the distance, marked by a crown of emeralds. *I will die far from home, with words I wanted to say but never did.*

He finally reached the top of the stairs, sensing the air shift from the underworld's to that of the realm above. Fresh and cool with a hint of sweetness. He gasped mouthfuls of it, as if he had been underwater, drowning. His skin flushed. He was embarrassed by how weak he appeared, and he stumbled off to the side to gain his bearings.

He stretched out his hand, touching the wall. Soldiers continued to pour through the door behind him, but Roman studied his surroundings—the scuffed hardwood, the speckled mirror above the mantel, a hearth full of ashes.

He was standing in a parlor.

His knees went weak, and he was sliding to the floor when Lieutenant Shane appeared and took hold of his arm, hauling him back up.

"Breathe," Shane said briskly. "You're going to be fine, correspondent."

Roman nodded, but sweat had soaked through his clothes. He fought a wave of nausea.

"Look, take a moment to compose yourself," the lieutenant said. "And then I want you to search the upper floor of this house. Use this torch to see. Check under every bed and every wardrobe. Report back to me here when you're done." He handed Roman a small rectangular box with a lens and bulb. "Turn it on with this switch."

He demonstrated, and the torch emitted a soft beam of light, limning the parlor and the soldiers who had gathered within the room.

Roman stared at the incandescent box, shifting it so that the beam pointed downward. "What should I do if I find someone upstairs?"

"Take them captive."

How? Roman wanted to demand. His hands were occupied by a typewriter and a torch, but Shane had turned and was rattling off an order to another private. It occurred to Roman that the lieutenant had given him a harmless task. This house felt empty, abandoned. Shane was simply getting Roman—who had proven himself quite useless as a soldier—out of their way.

Roman cracked his neck before he stepped out of the parlor. He felt stiff and strange, as if his bones had become iron, weighing him down. Or maybe it was only his fear, which continued to spread like ice, making him feel cold and clumsy. But he reached the foot of the stairwell and stared into the shadows, the torch's light cutting through the darkness.

With a shiver, Roman took the first step upward.

Iris set the extinguished lantern and wrench on the floor.

She listened as Dacre's soldiers moved through the main story of the house, her eyes adjusting to the swell of darkness, her breaths rapid. The front door was now inaccessible; she would have to flee through the window, and she began to heave it upward. The frame opened a hand's width, welcoming in a current of cool night air, but then caught and stuck.

Iris clenched her teeth, straining to push it higher.

"Come on, you *bloody* window!" she whispered, adjusting her stance. She heaved again, feeling the taut cords of her muscles, and the window began to rise with shuddering resistance. It wasn't enough, though, and Iris remembered the wrench, wondering if she could use it as a lever.

Her palm was slick as she grabbed the tool, but she never had a chance to use it. From the corner of her eye, she saw a beam of light. Someone was in the corridor with a torch, coming her way. She could hear their footsteps draw near.

Within a span of breaths, the soldier would be at the threshold. Their light would pour into the room, exposing her.

Hide! Iris's mind railed.

It was either beneath the bed or into the wardrobe.

She darted across the room for the closet, thinking it would grant her the stronger position if she had to fight. Wrench still in hand, she slid into the wardrobe's small space, closing the door behind her. It didn't latch, stubbornly popping back open a sliver. Iris almost reached for the handle again but froze when the beam illuminated the room.

She held her position.

She could hear the intruder breathe, a pattern of unsteady breaths that mirrored her own. She could hear the floor creak beneath their feet as they moved toward the bed, searching beneath it.

It would come down to a fight, then, and Iris raised the wrench. She would strike as hard as she could. She would aim for their head, for their eyes. She needed to either render them unconscious or kill them, quiet and quick.

I've never killed someone, she thought.

Iris waited, watching as the beam moved across the room, touching the wardrobe. The light splintered around her, seeping through the cracks, but she kept to the shadows. The soldier's steps approached and then halted until there was only silence and a door between them.

Strike fast, Iris told herself, even as her arm shook. *Don't hesitate.*

She waited for the door to open.

Roman stood before the wardrobe, the hair rising on his arms. Static danced in his blood; he could scarcely understand why until he set down his typewriter and opened the door, the torch light melting the shadows.

He saw the shine of the wrench first, then the slender arm that held it. Even then, he was so shocked that he merely stared at her. In that tense moment, she could have bludgeoned him. She could have split him open to the bone and, by the fierce expression on her face, it seemed she *wanted* to. But she was just as frozen as he was.

He wondered if he was dreaming, if he was asleep, because it was *her.* She was here, gazing up at him with those bewitching hazel eyes, her lips parted, her long brown hair tangled around her shoulders.

The recognition tore through him like a bullet, and Roman knew he was awake and lucid, even as he stood face-to-face with a dream.

He was looking at Iris Winnow.

22

Evanesce into Smoke

I ris lowered the wrench.

Chills raced along her skin as she stared at Roman. She couldn't draw breath; she could only wonder if she was imagining him. If he would morph into a stranger when she closed her eyes. It felt like a cruel enchantment that Dacre would delight in, granting her a surge of hope before reality broke her.

Sweat trickled into her eyes, burning her vision.

Iris blinked, but Roman remained, just as solid and tangible as she remembered him. She let herself relax, and perhaps that was foolish. But she wanted to savor him, retrace every line and bend of his body.

To her shock, he looked older, thinner. There was a hollowness to his face that hadn't been there before, and a cold slant to his expression.

"*Kitt?*" she dared to whisper.

He didn't move, but Iris watched as he swallowed. His blue eyes smoldered as he studied her; she was jarred by it until she realized he was also taking in her every detail, from her neck down to her toes. Her skeins of hair, the freckles on her face. The longer he beheld her, the more his countenance softened, and she wondered if he was remembering her. If there was something about her that called to him. A mortal bond that was stronger than any divine magic.

"Kitt," she said again. "Kitt, I—"

Roman laid a finger to his mouth. The two of them fell silent, listening to a burst of angry voices on the floor below. As far as Iris could tell, Roman was the only one who had ascended the stairs. But by the way the house shuddered, others might not be far behind him.

His gaze never left hers as they waited for the commotion to calm below. Doors opened and closed. An order was barked, although the words were indecipherable.

Iris bit her lip until it stung. She wondered if she was about to be captured. If Roman would fall with her. The image sent a shiver down her bones.

"Do you have a place to go?" he whispered at last. "A way to escape?"

Iris glanced at the wrench in her hand. She slid it into her pocket, flexing her tingling fingers. "Yes. There's a car waiting for me. I was planning to crawl out the window."

Roman hesitated, a tendril of black hair cutting across his brow. "I think that's your best bet at the moment."

She nodded, suppressing the urge to throw herself into his arms. To breathe him in. It was tempting to surrender to the past as if they had never been separated, to let those old days pull her under like a tide. But his polite reserve doused that fire. His guarded expression and words . . .

He doesn't remember me.

Iris nearly bent over from the anguish. She twisted her wedding band on her finger instead, Roman's inscrutable gaze tracking the movement. Even so, there was no spark of recognition within him.

It felt like a stone had settled in her stomach as she watched Roman stride to the window. He hefted it fully open without struggle, and a flood of crisp night air stole into the chamber, beckoning Iris forward.

"There's a porch roof just beneath here," he said after examining the view. He glanced back at Iris, motioning for her to come closer. "You should be able to climb down easily if you're careful. It's clear if you go now."

Iris reached the window, the breeze stirring her hair. She stood so close to Roman she could feel the heat of his skin, and yet she didn't touch him.

"Why are you helping me?" she murmured.

Roman became very still, his eyes riveted to the nightscape beyond the window. For an excruciating moment, Iris thought he wasn't going to answer her. But perhaps she didn't need his words; she could see it in his face when he met her gaze. He *did* recognize her, although it seemed pieces were still missing.

"I've dreamt of you," he said. "I think you and I were friends before I left for the war cause."

"Friends?"

"Or enemies."

"You and I were never enemies, Kitt. Not exactly."

"Then were we something more?"

Iris was quiet. She could feel the ache in her throat, how it brimmed with words she yearned to say but should probably swallow. In the end, she spoke them—in a husky whisper that he leaned closer to hear.

"Yes. I'm your wife."

Roman reeled as if she had struck him. His eyes went wide and dark, a stark contrast to his pale face, and Iris couldn't bear to see his flicker of disbelief.

She turned and clambered out the window, hitting her shin on the frame. The pain was an echo as she prepared to drop to the porch roof, the world feeling off-kilter, the air too sharp in her lungs. She was about to fall when a hand grasped her arm.

The heat of his fingers seeped through her sleeve like sunlight. Iris reveled in the feel of his hand, holding her steady as if she straddled two worlds.

That hand had once caressed her in the darkness, the one and only night they had ever shared together. That hand had once worn a ring, a symbol of their vows, and had typed countless letters to her, words that had fed and comforted and strengthened her. That hand was terribly familiar; she would have known it was him touching her, even if her eyes had been closed.

Iris exhaled, tasting salt and the metallic zing of blood on her lips.

Slowly, her gaze drifted back to meet his.

Roman's eyes were still dark as he stared up at her, but there was no glint of doubt. No scathing disbelief. There was only the shine of hunger as if Iris had just roused him from a long slumber.

His fingers trailed down her arm, following the curve of her elbow until his hand found hers, his thumb touching her wedding band. He softly gasped as if in pain, but before Iris could respond, he tugged on her. While her face dipped down, his tilted upward, until their gazes aligned and there was nothing more than a breath between their mouths.

"*Iris,*" he said. "Iris, I—"

He was interrupted by gunshots, sounding off in the distance.

Iris startled and crouched lower on the windowsill. She envisioned Tobias and Attie, waiting for her on the side of the road. She needed to go, and yet it felt like she was about to tear her heart up by its roots.

"Come with me, Kitt," she whispered, tightening her hold on his hand. "*Come with me.*"

Roman glanced away. She could see the struggle within him. The perspiration that gleamed at his brow, as if his body was under tremendous strain.

"I can't," he said hoarsely. "I need to stay."

Iris nodded, a protest dissolving on her tongue. Tears pricked her eyes, turning the world into a blurry haze. She turned to flee but Roman held on in a white-knuckled grip, as if he would evanesce into smoke the moment he let her go.

"Look at me." His voice was pitched low. Confident and compelling. The way he had sounded before the war had come between them. "I'll find you again when the time is right. I swear it."

"You had better," she countered.

The corner of his mouth quirked. A smile, but it was fleeting. "And when I do, you can ask me for the favor I owe you."

Iris frowned. What favor? She didn't remember them ever speaking about this. Roman must have read her face; he began to say more but was interrupted by an unfamiliar voice. A sharp call that emerged from the stairwell.

"Correspondent? Report in."

"*Run,* Iris," Roman begged as he let her go.

Her palm felt bereft without his until she flexed her fingers. She saw her ring catch the light of the torch.

Iris had never removed it. The band had remained on her finger since Roman had first guided it there, gleaming at eventide in a garden. But she didn't hesitate now; she slid the ring off and gave it to him.

"Keep it," she said. "A token to remember me by."

Roman said nothing in reply. But his fingers curled around the ring, hiding it like a secret in his palm.

Iris turned away. She could feel his eyes on her, watching her every move as she let herself fall into the darkness.

23

Incandescent Hearts

Iris hit the porch roof with a clatter. Her right ankle smarted from the drop as she managed to tuck and roll, catching herself before she found the edge. The thatch cut her palm but the pain was like a flare, guiding her focus as she perched on the eaves.

She was tempted to glance up at the window. To look at Roman one last time.

Iris resisted, keeping her eyes forward instead. There was a field directly before her, tall grass bending to the sough of the wind. She could see the high road off to her left, a shadow in the moonlight, as well as Hawthorne Route, which cut through the meadow like a slithering snake.

It was a good distance away, but she was confident she could escape using the cover of the grass until she reached safety. Then she could sprint back to Tobias and Attie.

Iris scrunched her eyes shut for a second before letting herself fall over the roof's edge.

She landed on her feet, her ankle throbbing again from the impact, but it wasn't a long drop. Stumbling, she reached out to find her balance. Two rain barrels sat in the grass nearby, and she ducked down to hide between them, assessing her surroundings.

A minute passed. Then another. Iris made herself wait. She was worried there might be a patrol that she hadn't noticed yet, and no sooner did the thought cross her mind than a door opened behind her. She heard boots clipping on the stone pavers, heading in her direction.

Iris kept close to the barrels, using them as a shield to avoid being spotted. She watched from the corner of her eye as a tall shadow strode past her.

Again, she waited. The soldier returned, as if he had been assigned to watch this plot of ground.

Iris counted his steps the next time he passed, to see how long she had with his back turned toward her. Then she took a hard swallow and forced herself forward. She crept through the grass as quickly as she could manage, eyes trained ahead to where she knew the route lay. She made it all of ten steps before someone spotted her.

"*Halt!*"

Iris instinctively froze until she remembered Roman's voice. The last words he had said, whisper soft against her parted lips.

Run, Iris.

She broke into a sprint.

"I said HALT!"

It was too late to hide. Iris pushed herself faster, harder. The grass whisked against her legs; the night air was frigid against her damp skin. She felt like wings had unfurled from her shoulder blades, like nothing could stop her, until rapid gunfire chased her heels.

Iris tripped, her blood humming with fear.

Somehow, she managed to stay upright, dodging the shots. Bullets peppered the ground to her left, so close that she could smell the pierced loam. Panic coursed through her like a river breaking a dam.

She was almost to Hawthorne Route.

Another round of gunfire pierced the darkness, followed by shouts. Iris never looked back. When her boots hit the road, she knew she had reached the place where Tobias had once been parked. She knew, because she passed the pothole in the road, but the roadster was nowhere to be seen.

They're gone.

Iris laid her hand over her chest, relieved. Devastated. *Where do I go from here?* she thought, lungs heaving as she tried to calm her heart. She needed to forge a new plan, one that had her slipping from Dacre's soldiers, but her pace began to falter. Her thoughts scattered like broken glass.

Exhausted, she eased to a brisk walk on the road. Her surroundings felt murky until she heard the familiar roar of an engine. A beat later, two headlights cut through the night.

Tobias's roadster sped toward her, emerging from the wispy grass on the other side of the road. Iris sprinted forward to meet him, the bright sting of the headlights washing over her face. Behind her, Dacre's soldiers were screaming for her to *halt, halt!*

She didn't stop. Their orders melted into the darkness, like stars at dawn. When Tobias swung the roadster to the side, angling the back door in her direction, Iris leapt.

She slammed into the side of the car, her knees denting the metal door. Attie reached down and grasped hold of her arms, hauling her into the cab, and before Iris could so much as wince, Tobias had floored the accelerator. Tires squealed on the road, slinging mud as bullets plinked against the bumper.

The girls remained hunched on the floorboard as another medley of gunshots snapped in the distance. But the threat soon grew fainter, and the motor beneath them faster.

"Iris?" Attie said, helping her up to the seat. "Are you hurt? Did they . . . ?"

"I'm fine," Iris replied in a ragged tone. "Will they pursue us?"

"I don't know," said Tobias, shifting the roadster to the next gear. "Best if we act like they will, though."

Iris nodded and withdrew the wrench from her pocket, only to realize her hands were quivering. The adrenaline was dimming, leaving embers behind in her bones. She let the tool clatter to the floorboards and rubbed her palms against her sleeves, eager to feel something other than the dread that was stealing over her.

"Hold on," Tobias warned as he took a sharp curve.

Iris was glad to have something to distract her. She craved the wind's bite in her face, the fury of consumed kilometers beneath the wheels. Anything to remind her she was moving away from danger.

"I see you got the tire fixed," she said.

Tobias snorted, but Attie only groaned.

"The tire iron was in the boot the whole time," Attie said. "Under a blanket. I'm sorry, Iris. We shouldn't have sent you into town. I tried to signal you back with the match, but it was too late."

"It's all right," Iris said. "It was good that I went."

She didn't explain why, although Attie tilted her head to the side, curious. Later, Iris would tell her everything. When the sun rose, and Iris could convince herself that Roman hadn't been a phantom of her imagination. Because a part of her still felt softened from his hand and his words, like the entire encounter had only been a reverie.

Iris touched her finger, the groove that her wedding ring had left behind, and leaned her head back until her gaze was on the stars. She thought the constellations had never looked so close or so lovely.

"Do you see that? There's something flashing in my rearview mirror."

Tobias's soft but urgent words woke Iris.

She didn't know how long she had dozed—two minutes or maybe half an hour—and she sat forward, rubbing the crick in her neck. Her friends weren't looking ahead but behind, and she turned in the seat, squinting into the darkness.

"I see it," Attie said, just as Iris also discerned a pinprick of red-hued light in the distance. "But what is it?"

Another orb of light. And then a third, until they were in a line, growing steadily larger. *Hearts,* Iris realized. They were incandescent hearts, beating through pale, translucent skin.

"It's the hounds," she said, her stomach twisting into a knot. "Dacre's set the hounds on us."

Attie spun back around to lean closer to Tobias. "Erm, Bexley? Don't panic, but you need to drive a bit faster now."

"A *bit* faster?" Tobias cried over the steady roar of the engine. "I'm already in gear five."

"Please tell me there's a gear six, then. Or a seven."

Tobias looked over his shoulder, the moonlight dousing his face in silver.

Iris wondered if he knew the old myths and recognized the lights as unnatural hearts. Or maybe he saw the long legs and bared teeth, which were coming into sharp focus. Tobias turned back around and shifted the roadster into the next gear.

The motorcar gave a lurch of protest. Iris closed her eyes, hair tangling over her wind-burned face. All she could think was *Please, please don't break down. Not here, not now.*

"They're gaining on us, Bexley," said Attie. "God's bones, how are they so fast?"

"They were made for speed, but not stamina." Tobias shifted again. The engine revved in complaint before the car's speed began to markedly dwindle.

"Tobias, are we *slowing down?*" Attie asked, incredulous.

"Yes, I'm gearing down." He adjusted his rearview mirror. The hounds' hearts reflected in his eyes, but he seemed calm, collected. "I've stressed the engine enough as it is, and I need it to power up again."

"All right. We're going to let the hounds reach us, and then what?"

"Trust me," he said, so softly that the wind almost stole the words.

Attie opened her mouth, but she only sighed at his behest.

Iris took that tense but quiet moment to look behind again. She could see the hounds clearly now. Beasts the size of unnaturally large wolves, their mouths shining with caches of sharp teeth. Their eyes were like coals and their paws struck the ground like lightning.

"Tobias," Iris said. "I think . . ."

She couldn't finish the sentence.

Tobias was silent, but his eyes were trained on the hounds' reflection in the rearview mirror. As if he were counting their steps, the shrinking distance, the speed, the acceleration. The possibility of impact.

The roadster geared down again. It felt like they were crawling along the road.

"Listen to me," Tobias said, his voice vibrant in the dark. Confident, like he was no stranger to racing hounds on country back roads. "I'm going to outrun them, but you need to trust me and you need to remain low and safe in the cab. Take hold of the rope handle in front of you. Whatever happens, don't let go."

The girls grasped the handle, Tobias waiting for Attie to give him a nod. In the next breath, he hit the brakes. As the roadster came to a screeching halt, the hounds soared over them.

Iris could feel the frigid air that haunted their long legs, rushing a mere arm's length above her head. Their claws stirred her hair, and she could smell the dank, rotten scent of their flesh. She could nearly taste the under realm— shadows that were never touched by light, stone floors that were slick with blood—as time moved achingly slow. It felt like a year had come and gone with the hounds arcing overhead like three meteors, the roadster shuddering beneath her.

But when the hounds hit the ground before them, the world came back to alarming focus. Two of Dacre's creatures seemed confused, but one turned around quickly to double back.

Tobias was ready for it.

He smoothly shifted the engine into first gear, then second, the roadster leaping forward. At the last minute, he cut the motorcar sharply, and they spun in a tight circle.

The tension in Iris's chest was almost unbearable, as if gravity had been suspended. She was rising from the floorboard like she had been caught in a levitating spell, her mother's locket hovering before her face. A flash of gold that reminded her to *hold on, don't let go.*

The side of the roadster slammed into the returning hound's hind leg. There was a sickening crunch followed by a piercing keen.

Tobias kept the car going, the wheels churning over the divots in the road until they launched eastward once more. The roadster slipped between the other two hounds, who lost time turning around again to pursue. Their angry growls shook the ground like thunder.

Iris tentatively rose to her knees, one hand clinging to the handle, the other to Attie.

She dared to glance back.

Only two hounds were in pursuit now, the third left behind to flounder in the road. But the pair were gaining on them again, as if wide open spaces and straight paths fed their mythical speed.

This time, Iris didn't look away. She stared at the creatures as the distance waned once more. And she counted each time Tobias shifted, until she knew he was in the highest possible gear. The roadster was at its top speed; there was no power left for the engine to give them. They were all but flying over the road, and still the hounds came.

Iris stiffened when the hounds lunged forward with yawning, rotten maws. They surged like a tide only to ebb as Tobias drove through a sharp bend. Their pace at last faltered, and they slowed, slinging drool from their mouths along with snarls of defeat.

Still, she would not believe it. She could hardly trust her own eyes this night.

Iris kept her gaze on the road behind them, marked by tires, rutted by storms. She kept her gaze on the shrinking hounds until their hearts winked out, like candle flames being snuffed into darkness.

24

What Truly Happened in the Bluff and Beyond

Roman was sitting at a desk when the news arrived. He was in a room on the upper floor of the factory, watching as Dacre paced before a wall of windows. A few of the officers were standing in a group to the left, stoic and silent, and while Roman was waiting for Dacre's command, he couldn't deny that, in his mind, he was very far away.

He was in another small room, a cozy chamber in Marisol's B and B, and there was a host of candles burning, casting soft rings of light along the walls. There was a pallet of blankets on the floor, and a pile of crinkled letters that Roman had read more times than he could count. He wasn't alone, and he had never felt more alive, his blood singing when he looked at her, when he breathed in the lavender scent of her skin . . .

The door banged open.

Roman blinked, letting the memory shatter in his mind. He returned to his body where he sat dutifully at the table, kilometers from home, waiting for a god's command.

Dacre, the officers, and Roman all looked at Lieutenant Shane, who was panting on the threshold despite his perfectly composed salute.

"What news?" the god asked. His tone was impassive, but Roman wasn't fooled. He could tell Dacre was furious about the foiled attack in Hawk Shire. He was like a frozen lake, seemingly placid until one noticed the hairline cracks expanding across the ice. The dark, frigid water seeping through the gaps, hungry for a drowning.

"Lord Commander," Shane began hoarsely. "The hounds have returned. One of them is gravely injured. The other two show no signs of spoils."

"You mean that Enva's scout got away."

"It appears that they did, sir."

"*Appears.*" Dacre smiled, a cold crescent of a moon. "Tell me, Lieutenant, how does an entire army evacuate before we arrive? How does a mortal girl evade multiple rounds of bullets in a wide-open meadow? How does a motorcar outrace three of my finest hounds, injuring one in the process?"

For the short amount of time that Roman had known Shane, the lieutenant had never failed to appear stalwart and gallant. But at that moment his complexion was waxy and deathly pale; he seemed incredibly young and vulnerable.

"I . . . I don't know, sir," he stammered.

"Then let me tell you how," Dacre said. He turned and glanced at his officers, who were now standing in a perfect line. "It happened because someone here has betrayed me."

"If I may, my lord," Captain Landis said with a bow of his head. The key he wore around his neck shined with the movement. Roman had no doubt the captain displayed it to remind everyone of his status. That he was a member of Dacre's favored circle with the power to unlock doors. "All of us in this room are faithful to you. You know that we—"

Dacre lifted his hand. Captain Landis hushed, face flushing.

"Someone among my ranks has turned on me," Dacre said. "Since I woke, you have known me to be a god who heals your wounds and takes away your pains. A merciful and just god who is building a better world for you and your lovers, you and your children, you and your dreams. But betrayal is something I cannot forgive." He paused, and the words sat in the air like smoke. "All of you . . . leave me. *Now.*"

Lieutenant Shane backed away. Most of the officers—the wise ones—also made a beeline for the door while a few others tarried, red-faced and worried-looking, as if they were terrified Dacre suspected them.

Roman rose, keeping Dacre in his peripheral. Quickly, he packed up his typewriter as quietly and unobtrusively as he could manage. He wanted to be a shadow. Unnoticeable. A tiny moth on the wall.

He walked to the door, back ramrod straight and typewriter case in hand. He waited, stiff with dread, for Dacre to say his name and hold him back. For Dacre to pin him to the ground with those uncanny blue eyes and tear the truth from his throat. For him to smell the betrayal on his clothes.

But Dacre had turned, and his face was angled toward the windows and the night beyond the glass. His eyes were on the stars and moon and a city that was full of empty shadows.

Roman slipped away with the officers.

It was a good thing he had managed to leave when he did, Roman realized when he was halfway down the metal stairs. A twinge of pain shot down his right leg. At first he thought it was only the aftershocks of his fear and the effort of countless steps until he felt it in his chest next. Something was gnawing at him from within, making his lungs heavy.

He stifled a cough, hid his limp.

Roman finally made it to the main doors. He stepped outside and walked until he found a vacant side street. Only then did he stop to lean against the brick wall.

He covered his mouth with his palm and coughed. His temples throbbed in response and nausea crept up his throat. He didn't know why he felt so terrible, until he remembered the taste of the gas, weeks ago in Avalon Bluff. How it had stung his lungs. How it had spread through him, making his head ache, his stomach churn, his legs feel shaky.

He could feel his panic rising, connected to that memory. The terror he had felt when the gas surrounded him, when he had crawled through the field.

You survived that day, Roman told himself. *It's over, and you survived. You're safe now.*

He closed his eyes, drawing slow, deep breaths. The tension in his bones eased although the twinge of pain in his leg remained, as did his headache and nausea.

Roman laid his hand over his pocket, where Iris's wedding ring hid.

I pray that my days will be long at your side.

It had all started to come back to him the moment he had touched her.

Let me fill and satisfy every longing in your soul.

He remembered running to her through the golden field.

May your hand be in mine, by sun and by night.

He remembered exchanging vows with her in the garden.

Let our breaths twine and our blood become one, until our bones turn to dust.

He remembered how she had whispered his name in the sweetened darkness.

Even then, may I find your soul still sworn to mine.

A shiver coursed through him as he looked up at the moon and the stars.

He remembered everything.

PART THREE

Wings in a Cage

25

Outshine, Once Again

They rolled into River Down on fumes.

It was late afternoon and scathingly sunny. Not a cloud was in the sky, and Iris shielded her eyes as Tobias shifted the roadster to a low, rumbling gear. The town was teeming with soldiers and lorries, making it difficult to navigate the winding roads. Enva's brigade had arrived hours ago, it seemed, settling in wherever space could be found—street corners, backyards, the mossy riverbanks, the city square. The town's citizens were a stark contrast as they carried out hot meals and coffee and washed laundry, hanging it to dry on clotheslines.

Iris watched it all with vague interest. Her mind felt kilometers away, as if she had left it behind in that wardrobe. In that strange, torch-lit room with Roman.

When Tobias at last parked in front of Lucy's home, Iris snapped out of her daze. It had been a while since she had slept soundly or eaten a proper meal. None of them in the roadster had, letting their exhaustion and hunger grow long and sharp as fangs within them. There was no time to rest, hardly time to eat. Not with the hounds and an angry god behind them. Tobias had only stopped in Bitteryne to refill the petrol and to let Iris and Attie snag some sandwiches and a thermos of coffee from Lonnie Fielding before they were on the road again.

Attie opened the car's back door. Iris followed her out, wincing when her feet touched the cobblestones. She hadn't realized how sore and battered she was until she had stood and was moving again, forcing needlelike blood into her feet.

To Iris's shock, Lucy was standing on the front porch like a statue, gazing at them. No, it was more like a scowl, and Iris braced herself as Marisol's sister descended the steps and approached them. She was wearing a black blouse, dark brown trousers, and tightly laced boots that squeaked.

Iris waited, preparing herself for a scolding, but the lines in Lucy's brows gentled.

"You three all right?" she asked gruffly.

"We're alive," Attie said.

Lucy was silent, but her blue eyes rushed over them, as if searching for wounds. Her gaze lingered a bit too long on Iris's face, and Iris resisted the temptation to touch her tousled hair, her sunburned cheeks, her chapped lips. She knew she must look awful, and she was about to apologize for her appearance when Lucy spoke.

"Come inside," she said in a softer tone. "I have a pot of tea and some biscuits waiting for you."

Marisol and Keegan were truly what were waiting inside, sitting at the kitchen table. Their hands were laced together, their heads bent close to each other as they conversed.

Marisol must not have heard the roadster park on the curb like Lucy had, because she glanced up and gasped when she saw Tobias, Attie, and Iris step into the kitchen.

"Are you hurt?" she demanded, standing in a rush. "Keegan told me the three of you showed up in Hawk Shire, after you told me you wouldn't pass Winthrop!" But there was hardly any bite in her words, only relief as she embraced the three of them at once, gathering them as a hen does its chicks, warm beneath her wings.

"We're fine," Iris said, inadvertently meeting Keegan's sharp gaze over Marisol's shoulder.

The brigadier rose from the table but remained silent.

Marisol swung back around, fire in her eyes. "You told me they were in the procession, Keegan. You told me they were *safe*."

Lucy set the kettle on the stove, but her eyes darted back and forth, taking note of everything.

"We had an agreement," Keegan said calmly. If Marisol was fire, she was water. "What happened?"

"A flat tire," Tobias answered. "We were able to fix it in time but some of Dacre's soldiers saw us retreat." He glanced at Iris, as if uncertain what else to say.

Keegan noticed.

"Iris?" the brigadier said.

Iris cracked her knuckles. "Dacre set his hounds loose."

The kitchen fell deathly quiet. Not even the birds sang their melodies from the backyard.

Marisol laid her hand over her throat, as if hiding the erratic beat of her pulse, and finally said, "The hounds? The *hounds* chased you?"

"Bexley outran them in his roadster," Attie stated. Her shoulder was close to Tobias's; there was only a fraction of space between their fingers, hanging at their sides. "We have all the dents and mud to prove it."

"There shouldn't be *any* dents or mud to prove it," Marisol said, her cheeks flushing. "There shouldn't be any hounds, or eithrals, or bombs. You should get to be children, young people, adults who can dream and love and live your lives without all of this . . . *horrible* mess."

Once more, the kitchen fell silent. A breeze stirred the curtains from the open window, and it was a soft reminder of constancy. The sun would continue setting and rising, the moon would persist in waxing and waning, the seasons would bloom and molt, and the war would still rage until one god or both fell to their grave.

The tense lull finally broke when the kettle began to hiss. Lucy moved to tend to it.

"Mari," Keegan whispered gently.

Marisol sighed, but despair passed over her expression, as if she had been struck by an arrow and didn't know how to pull it free from her bones. Iris understood, because she felt it also—that heavy, terrible sorrow—but the words were thick, catching behind her teeth. She swallowed them back down and told herself she would type them all out later. When it was dark. When it was just her and the keys and a blank page, waiting for her to mark it with ink.

"Join us at the table," Marisol said. "I know I cannot keep you safe or protect you from the worst of this war. But for now, let me feed you. I know you must be hungry."

After Lucy's perfectly brewed tea and a ham-and-mustard sandwich from Marisol, Iris retreated with her typewriter to the laundry room.

It felt odd to be here again, the sunset staining the windowpanes, the laundry hanging like ghosts. The wardrobe waiting for her to kneel before it.

Iris set down the typewriter case. She lowered herself to her knees, feeling the sting of her bruises and scabs. Slowly, she unlocked the First Alouette. The keys gleamed in response, as if beckoning her to write. And yet Iris realized she didn't know where to begin. She was gripped by a sudden wave of grief and covered her face with her hands, tasting traces of dirt, metal, and rye on her palms.

Over the uneven rhythm of her breath, she heard a familiar sound.

Iris wiped her eyes and glanced up to see two different letters waiting for her at the wardrobe door. There was no way for her to know what she was about to read. Something wonderful or something that would shred her heart even further.

She steeled herself for anything, unfolding the closest page to read:

1. Morgie was the name of your pet snail. (I will never grow tired of hearing all your "sad snail stories," in case you were wondering.)
2. Your middle name is Elizabeth, in honor of your nan. (Hi, E.)
3. Your favorite season is autumn, because that is when you believe magic can be tasted in the air. (You have almost made me a convert.)

She paused in shock, staring at Roman's typed words. It was the answers to the three questions she had sent days ago.

A pang scraped along her ribs. She was ravenous for more and swiped the next letter, unfolding it in her hands. She read:

It would be remiss of me not to return the same unto you, so let me ask my questions, as if I am sowing three wishes into a field of gold, or conjuring a spell that requires three answers from you in order for it to be whole:

1. How do I take my tea?
2. What is my middle name?
3. What is my favorite season?

P.S. Apologies for stealing two of your questions. Quite unoriginal, I know, but I don't think you'll mind.

Iris smiled. She typed her reply effortlessly, and sent:

Three questions, three answers. Here is the second half of the spell you ask for:

1. You prefer coffee, not tea. Although I saw you drink it enough times at the <u>Gazette</u>, and you only put in a spoonful of honey or sugar. No milk.
2. Carver. (Or should I affectionately say "C."?)
3. Spring, because that is when baseball returns. (Confession: I know next to <u>nothing</u> about this sport. You will have to teach me.)

Iris hesitated. She wanted to say more but held back, still uncertain. How much did he remember? But she closed her eyes and imagined him sitting in that strange bedchamber far away, typing by firelight. Her wedding ring slipped onto his littlest finger, guiding him to regather all the moments Dacre wanted him to forget.

She sent her letter through the wardrobe and waited. Night had almost fallen and the house beyond the laundry room suddenly became alive with voices, footsteps, and the clink of dishes. The scent of mutton stew and rosemary bread wafted down the hallway, and Iris knew one of the platoons had arrived at Marisol and Lucy's to be fed that evening.

Iris remained on the floor, fingers drumming across her knees.

At last, Roman replied.

Dear Iris,

Should I be surprised that I was falling in love with you a second time? Should I be surprised that your words found me here, even in the darkness? That I've been carrying your E. letters close to my heart like they are a shield to protect me?

I know we are no longer rivals, but if we are keeping tally like the old days, you have far outshined' me with your wit and your courage. Which reminds me of one simple thing: how I love to lose to you. How I love to read your words and hear the thoughts that sharpen your mind. And how I would love to be on my knees before you now, surrendering to you and you alone.

For the past few weeks, I thought you were nothing more than a dream. A vision that my scrambled mind created to process the trauma I couldn't even remember. But the moment I touched you, I remembered <u>everything</u>. And now I see that all this time, every night when I dreamt, I was trying to bring all the pieces back together. I was trying to find my way back to you.

I don't know where you are now. I don't know how many kilometers have come between us again, and I don't know what awaits us in the days ahead, but I will give you as much information as I can so long as you promise me that you will be very careful. I know this is a strange thing to say—we are a country at war, and nowhere is safe. All of us must risk and sacrifice something dear to us—and yet I could not bear it if corresponding with me brings the end for you or gives you a burden that is too heavy to bear.

If you agree to this, write me back. If you don't agree, still write me back. I want to know your thoughts. I confess that I am hungry for your words.

Love,

Kitt

Dear Kitt,

Your words have moved me, deeply. I also hunger for them, for <u>you</u>, and feel as if I could devour tomes of your writing and never be satiated. These letters will hold me over until we meet again.

We aren't keeping tally, but your courage and your wit have kept you alive in a place where hearts have faltered and beat their last. You are the bravest person I know, Kitt.

And I do agree to what you ask, but only because you seem to have stolen the words from my mouth. You are in a precarious position— far more than me—and giving up Dacre's movements and tactics is something I dread to ask you to do, even as it feels inevitable. It seems like this is the road we were destined to travel, you and I, given our typewriters and where we are. But I want, more than anything, to keep you safe. To protect you as best I can from afar.

Whatever information you come across that you want to provide, you can send it to me if you promise to be careful in return. That you will destroy all my letters as soon as you read them, so they cannot be traced to you. Perhaps you and I can help shorten this war, or at least dare to change the course of the tides. Or maybe that is too much to hope for. But I find that I am leaning more on the side of impossibility these days. I am leaning toward the edge of magic.

Love,

Iris

P.S. I noticed there was an asterisk by the word "outshine" in your previous letter. A typo?

My Dear Iris,

  Agreed. Let us dare to change the tides. Write to me and fill my empty spaces.

Love,

Kitt

P.S. A typo? No, Winnow. I simply forgot to add a footnote, which should have read as:

'outshine: <u>transitive verb</u>
a. to shine brighter than
b. to excel in splendor or showiness

  You remember how you said that word to me in the infirmary, post-trenches? You believed I had come to the Bluff to outshine you. And I would speak this word back to you now, but only because I would love to see you burn with splendor.

  I would love to see your words catch fire with mine.

26

Tell Me of Iris E. Winnow

The pain and discomfort of Roman's wounds had fully returned with his memories.

He thought about what this meant when he was lying in bed, staring into the darkness and struggling to breathe. When he was nauseous at the dinner table, eating meals with the officers, forcing himself to swallow down the food. When he was at his desk, fighting a dull throb at his temples as he typed propaganda for Dacre. When he had a moment alone in the night, and he would sit at his typewriter and try to make sense of what he was experiencing.

Dacre claims he healed me that day in the Bluff. He claims that I could live forever at his side, if only I remain faithful to him. And yet my memories suggest otherwise, and what I'm feeling in my body is a testament that I'm not fully mended.

He healed me just enough to be of use to him, as if covering my wounds with a bandage, holding things together. To make me numb and to forget what brought me here. But now that I remember who I was before...it seems his magic has lost a few threads of its power.

He has deceived me, as well as so many others, by making us believe we are whole and mended when he has intentionally left pieces
of us broken so we remain close to his side. Submissive and obedient
to what he wants.

Roman would type his thoughts but wouldn't let them survive on the
paper. He yanked them from the typewriter and watched them catch fire with
a match.

But his new reality was often at the forefront of his mind.

He wondered what this meant for him in the days to come, the *years* to
come. If he survived this war, then how long would he truly have to live? How
much damage had the gas done to him, and was it something he could manage
with proper medical treatment?

Roman pushed those uncertainties aside as he ascended the metal stairs,
typewriter case in hand. He was almost to Dacre's office, ready to report for
the day's duty, and he could feel the shortness of breath again, the throb in his
temples. It typically happened when he had to climb the stairwell, and he took
his time, careful to hide his limp and give himself moments to take deep breaths.

At last, he reached the top floor. He wiped the perspiration from his brow
and stepped into the office.

Dacre was alone, staring out the windows. But Roman could instantly tell
something was *off*. His ears popped as he felt pressure in the air, like a storm
was brewing.

"I'm here to write the next article, sir," Roman said, pausing by the desk.
"Unless you'd like me to come back later?"

Dacre was quiet, as if he hadn't heard. Something beyond the windows
must have truly captured his attention. Roman was considering easing away
when the god finally spoke, his voice smooth and polished, like water rushing
over stones.

"Tell me of Iris E. Winnow."

Roman froze, his eyes widening. He was thankful that Dacre's back was
still angled to him; it gave him three beats to compose himself by the time
Dacre turned. Dust motes spun in the weak sunshine between them.

"I'm sorry, sir?"

"Iris E. Winnow," Dacre repeated, and Roman inwardly flinched. "Surely you remember her by now?"

Was this a trap? A test?

Did Dacre know of their letters? Their brief meeting in Hawk Shire? The wedding ring Roman continued to hide in his pocket?

Was this the beginning of the end?

Roman licked his lips. *Calm,* he told himself, even as his blood surged, hot with panic in his veins. *Stay calm.*

"Vaguely. She wasn't very memorable, but I believe she and I both worked at the *Oath Gazette* around the same time. Why do you ask of her, sir?"

"See for yourself." Dacre indicated the desk.

Roman stepped closer. He hadn't noticed the newspaper when he had first entered the room, but now that he looked down, he could see the bold headline of the *Inkridden Tribune.*

THE MUSIC BELOW: THE DOOMED LOVE STORY BETWEEN ENVA & DACRE by IRIS E. WINNOW

Roman read the first few lines, his pulse hammering.

He recognized this myth. He had typed it to Iris and sent it to her months ago, thinking it was harmless enough at the time. Something like bread to feed her imagination. But now here it was, brazenly printed in the paper, exposing Dacre's humiliation like split skin reveals the shine of bloodied bones.

Here was a testament that Dacre had a weakness. It was Enva. It was love he could never have. It was music played for him in his own realm. Here was the truth that a god was not as invincible and powerful as he wanted people to believe.

"I'm not familiar with this myth, sir," Roman lied, glancing up to meet Dacre's cold, level stare. "Is it really that important, though?"

It was the wrong thing to say. Or perhaps it was a brilliant thing. Fury rippled across Dacre's pale countenance, curling back his lips. His teeth looked sharp; his eyes glittered darkly. But as quick as the emotion came, it was gone, and his face fell into a neutral, almost bored expression.

"Is it important if people believe a lie to be the truth, Roman?"

"Yes, my lord." But Roman's mind whispered, *This truly happened then. This is not just a myth to entertain, like I once thought.*

"So tell me of her," Dacre said, taking a step closer. His shadow grew long and sinister on the floor. "Who is this journalist named Iris?"

"I truly don't remember much about her, other than the fact she was a low-class girl," Roman said with a shrug, even as the acid burned his throat. He sounded just like his father, and how he wanted to despise himself for it. "I don't think you should be threatened by her, sir."

"Oh, I am not threatened by *her*," Dacre said. "But this is a lie that must be answered. You will write it for me, of course. The *Gazette* will set things right. You are telling my side of the story, and I want the denizens of Oath to know the truth."

"Of course, sir."

"Then sit. Let's begin. We don't have much time before Val comes for the article."

Roman had still never seen Val, who was no more than a phantom in his mind, but he sat at the desk, unpacking his typewriter.

They weren't three sentences in when the door blew open, revealing a red-faced Lieutenant Shane.

"We found the grave, sir," he said, panting. "Captain Landis asked me to deliver the news to you at once."

"A grave?" Roman echoed in shock. "Whose?" But a breath later, it hit him, and he inhaled sharply.

"Luz Skyward's," Dacre answered, glancing sidelong at Roman as if measuring his reaction. "God of harvest and rain. Magic that seems quite useless, wouldn't you agree?"

Roman didn't reply. Mortal kind needed harvest and rain to survive.

Dacre seemed to be weighing a thought in his mind, but then he motioned for Roman to rise.

"Come, you should see this. Leave your typewriter. We'll resume the article when we return."

It went completely against the grain for Roman to leave the Third Alouette. But he stood, heart laden with dread. Without another word, he followed Lieutenant Shane and Dacre out the door.

27

Gods at Gravesides

A lorry was waiting for them in the courtyard, engine rumbling. Puffs of smoke rose from the tailpipe as Roman settled in the back with Lieutenant Shane. Dacre, thankfully, took the cab with another officer. It was a jostling ride, Roman catching glimpses of the land through the flapping canvas. When Hawk Shire faded from sight, he could take the stilted silence no more and he looked at Shane.

"You said something to me in Merrow that I haven't forgotten," Roman said. "Not all the soldiers Dacre heals lose their memories. I can only assume that people like you—the ones who enlisted to fight for him from the very beginning—can hold on to their pasts, while people like me cannot."

"A wise observation," the lieutenant drawled. "And one that you should keep in mind in the days to come."

"Why is that?"

Shane glanced at the lorry's grimy rearview window, as if paranoid Dacre might overhear him. "Has he asked to heal your wounds further?"

Roman frowned. "Yes. Once."

"He'll no doubt ask you again. It's his way of gauging how fast your mind is remembering. If there's a possibility you'll turn against him."

"I don't understand. I thought he healed my wounds. Why would that be—"

"There is always pain in healing," the lieutenant interrupted. "To fully avoid it is impossible."

Roman fell pensive, but apprehension trickled through his thoughts.

Shane must have sensed it. He said, "I've had a few privates in my platoon who were like you. When their memories fully returned, so did the pain in their wounds. And because they couldn't hide their disgust, the Lord Commander took them below once more and doled out another round of healing."

Roman swallowed. "You mean he wiped their memories again."

The lieutenant made no response, but his eyes narrowed.

The lorry hit a pothole, jostling them both. The sideways jar was good; it reminded Roman of his position. That even though Shane was speaking to him like an equal, they didn't stand on common ground.

"Is this why we haven't marched onward?" Roman asked, changing the topic. "Because he was looking for a grave?"

"If you must ask such a thing, then you don't deserve to know the answer."

That stung, and Roman curled his tongue. He had decided he wouldn't speak to Shane again when the lieutenant surprised him.

"Where did you go to school, correspondent?"

Roman glanced at him. "Why do you care to know?"

"I told you I'm from Oath. Thought I'd ask and see. Perhaps we ran in the same circles once."

Not likely, Roman thought with a sigh. "Devan Hall."

"The rich school, then. I should've known."

Roman braced himself, waiting for more jabs, but Shane only leaned closer, a shadow cutting across his face as the sunlight began to wane.

"Did they teach you about divinity at Devan Hall?" the lieutenant murmured.

"The basics," Roman replied. "Why?"

"Then I surmise you don't know what happens when a human kills a god, versus when a god kills one of their own?"

Roman's mind whirled. He thought back on the mythology books he had inherited from his grandfather. Even those old tomes were missing pages, just like the ones in the city library. Knowledge torn away and lost.

"When a human kills a god," Roman said, "they simply die. Their immortality comes to an end."

"As does their magic," Shane added. "It fades away into the ether. Their power leaves our realm altogether with their death."

No one had ever taught Roman such a thing. He mulled it over but didn't have a chance to counter before Shane continued in an urgent whisper.

"Why do you think the king of Cambria wanted the last five divines buried centuries ago, rather than killed? If he had killed them all, magic would have completely vanished from our realm. And he didn't want that. He had the gods enchanted into sleep and buried them instead, so their divine power would continue to trickle through the loam. So *we* could reap the benefits of it, while being free of meddling, violent gods altogether."

If that were truth, then it was a wise move save for one ugly inevitability: what sleeps will wake at some point, brimming with vengeance.

The lorry began to downshift. Roman could feel this moment slipping away.

"And what happens when a god kills a god?" he asked, even as his memory dredged up Dacre's words, spoken weeks ago. *We are born with our appointed magic . . . but that never stopped us from wanting more and finding ways of taking it.*

The lorry came to a squeaky halt. Shane's face resumed its cold indifference, but as he rose, he said, "You're a writer. I'm sure you can imagine it, correspondent."

From the parked lorry, it was a short walk to Luz's resting place. The grave was on a grassy knoll with nothing but hills, a crumbling medieval tower, and the blue haunt of northern mountains within view, and Roman shivered as a burst of wind gusted through their small party. A storm was gathering overhead; the clouds hung low and bruised, and Roman could taste rain.

Dark hair tangled over his eyes as he stood off to the side, watching Dacre speak to Captain Landis. He could hear snatches of their conversation, and he was able to glean that while the map had been slightly inaccurate, this small hill was undoubtedly where Luz rested. While he spoke, the captain wrapped his fingers around the key hanging from his neck, and it was only then that Roman realized that graves were doorways of their own.

Dacre nodded to the captain, who proceeded to take his key in hand and crouch down. Captain Landis began to draw a wide circle in the dirt with the tip of the iron. Roman could feel his bones hum, static rush over his skin. He couldn't explain why this felt familiar, this seemingly simple drawing in the dirt, but he recognized the crackle of magic in the air.

He took a step back but froze when the captain finished drawing the full circle. The grass was parting, the dirt peeling back like old skin. All of it revealed a door forming in the ground, similar to that of a cellar, only this one was covered with intricate carvings.

Captain Landis backed away as Dacre shifted forward.

No one moved as Dacre opened it. The door looked heavy, ancient. It settled on the ground with a resounding thud, golden dust drifting upward.

A stairwell led down into the grave. Dacre, wholly transfixed, seemed to forget about the two captains, the lieutenant, and the correspondent who were watching him. He alone descended into the darkness just as the rain began to fall.

Roman shifted his weight from foot to foot, aching with worry. He glanced across the distance at the lieutenant, but Shane was staring at the grave's doorway, a strange expression on his face.

We aren't prepared to have a third god wake, Roman thought, shoving his trembling hands into his pockets. *Why is Dacre doing this?*

But then it hit Roman like an arrow.

Dacre wasn't waking a third divine. He was killing Luz while he slept.

No sooner had this revelation stunned Roman than Dacre emerged. He hadn't been gone but a minute, and his face was starkly pale. His eyes gleamed in the storm light as he closed the grave's door, so roughly it made its own thunder.

"Lord Commander," Captain Landis said. "Was it a success?"

"Close the threshold," Dacre replied in a clipped tone.

Roman could see the fury mounting in the god's countenance, the way his hands curled into fists. How his tongue traced the edges of his teeth.

Captain Landis hurried to draw the circle in reverse. The dirt shifted; the grass wove back together. While the doorway faded, evidence of the circle remained, soft in the loam.

The rain fell in earnest as they strode back to the lorry, tense and silent. But Roman's thoughts were reeling. All he could think were two things: either Luz had already woken, or he had been killed by someone else.

28

When Home Doesn't Smell Familiar

The return to Oath was not a triumphant processional as Iris had imagined it would be.

It was a dreary gray afternoon, the sort of day that begged for an endless cup of warm black tea and a thick book by the hearth. A persistent soft rain fell, and soon the eastern roads were like swamps, iridescent with motor oil. A few of the lorries got stuck in the mud as a result. Platoons began to walk on foot, tromping through the damp grass on the side of the road. They had to stop at one point to let a flock of sheep pass by.

When they finally reached the outskirts of the city, Chancellor Verlice was waiting for them, standing in the back of a roadster, holding an open umbrella in his white, spindly hand.

"Is that who I think it is?" Attie growled as Tobias cut the engine.

Iris only sighed, watching as Keegan jumped down from the lorry at the front of the line, walking to meet him. Even though Tobias's roadster was only a few vehicles behind, they couldn't hear what the chancellor was saying. Before Iris could think better of it, she slipped out of the motorcar.

"Where are you going?" Attie asked.

"We're the press," Iris said, her boots sinking in the mud. "We need to hear what he's saying, right?" She began to hurry up the road, careful not to slip. A few seconds later, she could hear Attie close behind.

The girls stayed back a respectful distance but dared to draw close enough to gather what the chancellor had to say to Keegan and Enva's army.

"This road needs to remain clear and passable," Verlice was saying. "And Oath is still declared neutral ground. I cannot permit you and your forces to infiltrate the city."

Infiltrate? Iris nearly breathed fire at that word. She ground her teeth together as she stared up at the chancellor. He wasn't going to allow Enva's army to find shelter and provisions in the city. He wasn't going to allow the army to protect the people within the city walls.

Keegan was silent, as if she too was shocked by the chancellor barring their entrance. But she only said in a strong voice, "If that is what you have decided for Oath, then so be it. We will make camp here on the outskirts. All I ask is for my wounded to find care and shelter in the hospital."

The chancellor narrowed his eyes. It was apparent he wanted Keegan to return from where she had come, taking the trail of lorries and troops with her. But he only inclined his head and said, "Very well. As long as the road remains passable, and your troops cause no inconvenience for the citizens of Oath, remaining outside of the city limits, you may camp in this field."

"And my wounded?" Keegan pressed. "They have been traveling for days and need medical attention."

"I will take this up with my council," the chancellor replied. "In the meantime, the wounded will need to camp here with you until I gain approval for their admittance."

Iris set her jaw. She couldn't believe this was happening until the chancellor sensed her stare and glanced up to find her and Attie standing side by side, ankle-deep in mud. Irritation pulled his mouth into a thin line, made his brow slant heavy over his beady eyes. Iris could almost hear the trail of his thoughts. How annoying the journalists at the *Inkridden Tribune* were, writing about things he didn't want the people to know.

A wordless challenge was set down between them, and the chancellor took his seat in the back of the roadster. His driver stirred the engine to life and drove away, and Iris shivered as her damp clothes chafed against her skin.

The mist was growing thicker, transforming into a hushed rainfall. But she watched the chancellor disappear into Oath, and she knew exactly what article of hers would be in the paper tomorrow.

"Are you sure, Marisol?" Iris asked for the third time. "You and Lucy are more than welcome to stay with me and Forest."

Marisol smiled as she set down a crate. Her black hair shined in the rain, falling loose from her long braid. "I'll be fine here. I want to stay with Keegan, you know."

Iris nodded, although a knot of guilt and anger soured in her stomach at the thought of leaving Marisol and Keegan and all the soldiers behind to sleep in tents on wet ground. They didn't even have a way to stoke campfires and cook a warm meal or make a pot of coffee, and Iris wondered what she could do to help.

Marisol read her thoughts.

"You must remember that they've been through much worse than a little rain, Iris," she murmured as tents continued to rise from the ground like mushrooms. "A little foul weather won't hurt us. Perhaps the sun will be shining tomorrow."

Iris couldn't hide her grimace. The weather in Cambria was notorious for being ornery.

"Do you still have the bird book I gave you?" Marisol asked suddenly.

"Yes. It's in my coat pocket."

"Have you read the page on the albatross?"

"A few lines," Iris replied. "I remember that they can sleep while flying."

"As well as fly into the strong wind of a storm, rather than having to avoid it and head to the shore like other birds would do," Marisol said, snapping wrinkles from a blanket she found in the crate. "It's safer for them to fly toward the storm than away from it, as counterintuitive as that may seem to us. But they can soar for thousands of kilometers without ever touching land, and they know their strengths. They lean into them in times of trouble."

Iris fell quiet, mulling on those words.

"Are you suggesting I be *counterintuitive?*" she eventually asked.

Marisol smiled. "I want you to remember that you have already flown through a strong storm, as have most of us here. And a little rain from the chancellor won't unsettle us now."

"I hope you're right, Marisol."

"When have I ever been wrong?" She tapped Iris's chin affectionately before turning away, passing the blanket off to a soldier.

But Iris could see the stiffness in Marisol's shoulders, as if she were weary of holding herself upright. As if she knew the long flight was just beginning, and they were all soaring toward the boiling eye of the storm.

Tobias drove the girls into Oath. They left behind the sea of tents and mud-riddled roads for the brick and cobblestone of the city. It felt strange to return, and even stranger that Oath didn't truly *feel* like home anymore.

They reached Iris's flat first. She climbed from the roadster, glancing down at the dents in the door that her knees had made. She still had the bruises to prove it, to remind herself that chilling run from Hawk Shire had happened.

"*Inkridden Tribune* tomorrow?" Attie said.

"Tomorrow," Iris agreed, thinking how odd it would be to return to confined work in a building after they had been roaming the realm in a fast car, sleeping in unusual places, and dodging bloodthirsty hounds.

"Can I carry your luggage up?" Tobias asked, holding her typewriter case in one hand, her duffel bag in the other.

"Oh, no, I can handle it. But thank you, Tobias." Iris took the luggage from him. "I hope I see you again soon?"

"I'm sure you'll see me around," he said with a hint of a grin.

Iris glanced at Attie, who acted like she hadn't heard him. But Iris found herself smiling into the shadows as she hurried up the flight of stairs to her flat door. It wasn't fully dark, although the rain was ushering in an early dusk, and she imagined Forest wasn't home yet.

He would be surprised to see her. Iris found the hidden key, tucked behind a loose stone in the lintel. She unlocked the door, waving to Tobias and Attie to let them know she was good. The roadster drove away with a puff of exhaust, heading to Attie's town house near the university side of the city.

Iris stepped inside the dim flat.

She had been right. She was the first home and she knocked the rain from her boots and jacket and set down her luggage. As she turned on a few lamps, she was struck by how clean and tidy it felt. How the flat smelled *different*. Not in a bad way, but she stood for a moment in the center of the room and breathed it all in, wondering if home had always held this strange scent and she had simply grown accustomed to it in the past.

"Not that it matters," she whispered, hurrying to shed her damp clothes for a sweater and a pair of brown trousers, and to unpack her typewriter on the kitchen table.

But she noticed a vase of daisies, brightening the room, and two bottles of medicine on the sideboard, prescribed to Forest. She felt a wash of relief to know her brother had finally gone to the doctor.

Iris had set a kettle to boil and was beginning to type an equally heated article about the chancellor barring Enva's forces from the city when the front doorknob squeaked.

She paused.

It must be her brother, and she was both excited and anxious to see him again. Iris stood and reached for the locket, hiding beneath her sweater, and held on to it as the door swung open.

There was a shuffle, a low curse as someone tripped and dropped a baguette wrapped in bakery paper.

Iris stepped forward, eyes widening. This person was too short and slender to be Forest, and as they threw back the hood of their raincoat and struggled to keep the other parcels in hand, Iris took in their light-colored hair, frizzy from the rain, and the endearing flash of glasses on their nose.

Iris stopped upright.

It was truly the last person she expected to see stepping into her flat.

"Prindle?"

29

Fifth-Floor Signals

Sarah Prindle froze. Her mouth formed a perfect O before she cried, "Winnow? I'm glad you're back! We weren't expecting you home so soon!"

We? Iris thought with a shock down her spine, but she seamlessly hurried forward to take the packages from Sarah's arms. They were heavy and warm—a fragrant dinner—and Iris set them on the kitchen table beside the typewriter before turning back around to hang up Sarah's rain-dappled coat.

"Do you know when Forest will be home?" Iris tentatively asked, feeling uncertain of things, like she was a stranger in her own home.

Sarah picked up the fallen baguette before she removed her foggy glasses, wiping them on the edge of her skirt. "Should be home any minute. Usually he arrives before me, and—" She cut herself off with an awkward grimace. "I'm sorry, I know this must seem terribly odd."

"It's okay, Prindle," Iris said. "Truly. I take it you and my brother are an item now?"

Sarah flushed scarlet. "No! I mean to say . . . maybe. *If* he asked me. But no. I honestly didn't expect any of this to happen."

The kettle began to whistle from the kitchen.

"Why don't you sit and we can share a pot of tea," Iris said, striding to shut off the cooker. "And you can tell me what happened while I was gone?"

Sarah nodded, but she went pale, like she was worried about what Iris might think. Iris, honestly, also wasn't quite sure what she thought. But she was eager to hear what Sarah had to say as she carried over the tea tray, sitting down across from her.

"Erm," Sarah began, wringing her fingers. "I'm sorry to catch you by surprise like this, Winnow."

"You have *nothing* to apologize for," Iris rushed to say. "Truly. I'm simply . . . surprised, but only because my brother has been very guarded and closed off since returning from the war front."

"I know," Sarah said with a sigh. "But it all began when I came by one evening to see if he had an update about you. When I knocked on the door, I assumed no one was home, because it seemed very quiet and empty. But then he opened the door and he just seemed . . . so sad. I realized he had been sitting alone in the dark."

Iris felt a lump well in her throat. It *killed* her to imagine Forest like that, and guilt flooded her chest as if she had breathed in water. *I shouldn't have left him,* she thought, but then realized if she had stayed home, Hawk Shire would have fallen. She wouldn't have ever received Roman's message about the assault, and Keegan and the last of Enva's forces would have been pulverized.

Quietly, Iris poured the tea. She and Sarah added their cream and honey, and only then did Sarah clear her throat and continue.

"Forest didn't really want to talk to me. And he said that he didn't have any word from you yet. I decided I wouldn't bother your brother again. But then I couldn't stop thinking about him sitting alone in the dark, knowing he had been to war and back. I . . . well, I decided to take him dinner the next evening, to see again if he had an update on you. He thought you had set me up to do it, because he said, *You can tell Iris I'm fine.* But then he invited me inside—I think he felt a bit bad, for being so gruff—and we had dinner together. And I thought, *Well, this will be it.* But he said I could come by the next evening for an update about you, and that this time he would have dinner. To repay me, of course."

Sarah glanced up to meet Iris's gaze, her cheeks rosy.

"And that's how it began. I find it easy to talk with him. Mainly because he is such a good listener, but he remembers everything I say and no one has ever really done that before."

Iris couldn't help but smile. She was about to express how thankful she was for Sarah when gunfire popped in the distance.

"What was that?" she demanded, rising from the table.

"It's probably just a warning shot," Sarah said, but her shoulders were hunched close to her ears.

"A *warning* shot?" Iris echoed, incredulous. "Shot by whom?"

"The Graveyard."

"And who is that?"

"A guard for the city," Sarah explained, but her voice was almost a whisper, as if the walls could hear.

"Is this the chancellor's doing?"

"People say it is, but I honestly think that it's not. To me? It looks the chancellor is losing control over the city. The Graveyard claims allegiance to no god, and they instated a curfew, without the chancellor's approval. Only they can roam the streets at night as they hunt for Enva."

Iris's mind reeled with this new information. She had no idea something of this caliber had unfolded, and she wondered what else had changed while she had been away. And then it struck her: of course, Chancellor Verlice would keep Enva's army at bay if the city was truly being commandeered by another militant group. If he had allowed Keegan and the troops to enter, then there would have been armed conflict and potential bloodshed.

"Who are these people?" Iris asked. "And why are they firing warning shots?"

"Not many of us know who they truly are," Sarah said. "They keep their identities hidden. By day, they could be anyone. But by night, they patrol the streets with masks and rifles, and they fire warning shots when they find someone breaking curfew. They claim their watch is to keep us safe, but I think it's about power."

Masks and rifles.

Iris shuddered as those words evoked a memory. The night the girls had broken into the museum, and Iris had been dangling from the rope. Four people with masks had walked beneath her; she had thought another heist was about to unfold. She then remembered all the painted words on buildings—*gods belong in their graves*—and Iris realized this unrest had been brewing for some time.

She walked to the window, where darkness seeped through the curtains. Parting the drapes a sliver, Iris gazed out at the rain-smeared dusk. Not half a minute later, the front door blew open. It was Forest, drenched and panting, but his face was turned to the light. To the table, where Sarah stood.

"You're here," he said, closing the door behind him. "I heard a gunshot. I was worried . . ."

Iris stood frozen by the window. Relief softened her breath, to see that her brother was safely home. But it was eclipsed by the cold revelation that she was on the outside. A moon that had spun loose from its orbit.

"Don't worry, I'm fine," Sarah said, hands pressed to her chest. "And so is your sister."

Forest paused. But he must have sensed Iris's gaze, or maybe he heard her wavering breaths. He spun and saw her, still positioned by the window.

"*Hi,*" Iris whispered.

Forest gaped at her, his shock tangible as the rain. But then he crossed the distance and wrapped his arms around her, lifting her off the ground.

Iris couldn't understand why she wanted to weep until she felt the joy radiating from her brother, warm as a furnace on the coldest night. It almost felt like the old days, long before the war. He had those he loved dearest safe and close. And what Iris would give to feel the same.

They ate dinner together at the table, and Iris noticed how Forest looked at Sarah.

It was soft and frequent and very attentive.

It reminded Iris of how Roman had once looked at her, and she felt both happy and sad. A strange, bittersweet medley that brought tears to her eyes.

She blinked them away, but her thoughts then quickly gathered to the war again, and the distance that now stretched between her and Roman. The danger he was in.

When Forest carried the dishes to the sink, Iris held Sarah back, speaking to her in a low tone.

"Do you remember what you told me about the person who delivers Roman's articles to the *Gazette*?"

Sarah's eyes widened. She glanced at Forest, whose back was turned to them as he scrubbed the dishes.

"Yes. But why do you ask?"

Iris leaned closer. "When does he come next to the office? And what time?"

"He'll be arriving at nine sharp tomorrow morning," Sarah replied. "You're not thinking to confront him, are you? Please don't! There's something about him that feels very sinister."

Iris shook her head. "No, he won't see me. But do you think you could give me a signal?"

"A signal?"

"Yes." Iris noticed the blue handkerchief knotted at Sarah's neck. "Could you hold your handkerchief to the window as soon as he leaves the office tomorrow morning? So I can see it from the street below and know when he's about to exit the building."

"Yes, I can do that," said Sarah. She pulled a loose thread from her cardigan. "But what do you intend to do?"

Iris chewed on her lip. Forest must have sensed their conspiratorial whispering, and he glanced over his shoulder, granting them an arched-brow look.

Iris only smiled at her brother until he returned his focus on the dishes. But she whispered to Sarah, "I need to find a magical door."

At ten till nine the following morning, Iris found herself waiting in the shadow of the building she had once worked in, cutting her journalistic teeth on obituaries, classifieds, and advertisements. The place she had first met Roman. The *Oath Gazette* was on the fifth floor, and she knew the exact line of windows to watch.

She kept her attention on the shine of the glass now, waiting for Sarah's signal. The street before her was busy, cars and wagons and pedestrians flowing from one place to the next.

It was a place where one could strangely feel both lonely and satisfied, surrounded by people who might acknowledge you or might not. By people who didn't know your name or where you had come from but all the same shared the same air—the same moment in time—with you.

The clock struck nine.

Two minutes ticked by, two minutes that felt like years. But then Iris saw it. Sarah pressed her handkerchief to the windows.

Dacre's man had just left the *Gazette*.

Iris shifted her gaze to the glass doors of the building, which were tall and trimmed in brass, a constant glimmer as people entered and exited. It would have been easy to miss someone slipping out amongst the activity, but Iris knew how slow the lift in that building was, and she intuitively knew when he should be departing.

She spotted him, a lithe figure in a cloak, the hood drawn up.

He descended the marble steps with ease, heading northwest.

Iris began to trail him.

She kept a safe distance, but a few times she was worried she would lose track of him in the crowd, and she drew as close as she dared. She paused when he did, her heart quickening in dread, but he was only stopping to purchase two papers from a newsboy. The *Gazette* and the *Tribune*.

He continued on his way with a brisk pace. Iris followed.

Eventually, he wound deeper into the northern ridge of the city, over the river to what was known as "the Crown." This was the wealthier side of Oath, and Iris wasn't familiar with these streets. She pulled her trench coat tighter around her, shivering when it began to mist.

At last, he arrived at a large iron gate, its finials shining with bronze pearls. It opened for him before shutting once more, latching with a metallic rattle.

Iris hung back to make it seem like she was casually walking by. But she paused long enough to take in the long cobbled drive beyond the gate. It led up to a grand estate on a verdant hill with a manicured yard, veiled by swirling mist.

Iris froze, hands shoved deep in her coat pockets.

Her eyes cut to the gate again, to the brick pillars. There was a name carved in a smooth piece of stone, eye level on the right column. A name that made her breath catch.

THE KITT ESTATE.

30

Don't Let This Freedom Fool You

This is a test to check and see that the strike bars R & E are in working condition.

ERERRRRRRR EEEE RRRRR

R

E

E

??

.

Iris!

What's happened? Are you all right?

—Kitt

KITT!

There's a DOOR to the UNDERWORLD in your HOUSE. Did you
know this?!

P.S. I'm sorry, I didn't mean to startle you.

P.P.S. And yes, I know I just broke a rule by writing you first today. You can scold me later. (In person... preferably.)

Gods, Iris. My heart is still racing, thinking you were about to write and tell me something horrible had happened.

(Note: I promise to scold you later. In person... as you'd like.)

And no, I didn't know there was an active threshold in my parents' estate, but it should have crossed my mind. I can also say that gsrmyl—wait, sorry but I need to go. I hear them summoning me. Until I can write you again, stay safe and well.

Love,

Kitt

It was Lieutenant Shane, knocking on Roman's door.

"You've been summoned," he said tersely through the wood.

"I'll be right along," Roman replied, his fingers flying over the keys as he rushed to finish typing to Iris. He bit his lip as he tore the paper from the typewriter, sliding his letter beneath the wardrobe.

He packed up his typewriter and stepped into the hall, expecting to find Shane waiting for him. But the dimly lit corridor was empty, and Roman walked to the factory alone through the rain, teeming with the same curiosities and questions as he had the day before at Luz's graveside. He had wanted to speak to the lieutenant alone again but hadn't been afforded the chance, and as he now ascended the stairs to the top floor of the factory, he mulled it over for the hundredth time: the key in the soil, creating a threshold. Dacre's expression as he had emerged from the grave.

What did he see? Is Luz truly dead?

To Roman's shock, two soldiers were guarding Dacre's office, the door closed.

"The Lord Commander doesn't wish to be bothered at the moment," one of them said.

"I was just summoned by him," Roman replied, coming to an unsteady halt. "Should I return later?"

The soldiers exchanged a glance. It was apparent they feared Dacre's wrath in all its shades, whether that be by interrupting him or by sending away his pet of a correspondent.

"Go on, then," the other said, inclining his head to the door.

Roman nodded and passed between them, slipping into the office.

The first thing he noticed was how dark it was in the room. Even with the wall of rain-streaked windows, afternoon storm shadows gathered deep in the corners and around the furniture. Only a few candles were lit on the desk, their flames wavering as if there were a draft.

Roman stood, stiff with uncertainty, his eyes cutting through the darkness. Dacre wasn't here, and he wondered if the god had returned to Luz's grave alone. He was turning to leave when he heard someone breathing. Deep and heavy, the rhythm of dreams.

Swallowing, Roman edged to the center of the room, where he could see a shine of golden hair draped over the arm of a divan. There was Dacre, sleeping on the cushions, his hands laced over his chest, his eyes shut and his mouth slack.

Dacre had once told him gods needed little to no sleep, which made Roman wonder why was he making himself vulnerable now.

He stepped closer, his heart beginning to pound.

I could kill him, Roman thought, staring down at Dacre's placid face. *I could kill him and end everything here and now.*

The only weapon he held was his typewriter, enclosed in its case. Which made him swiftly realize that he didn't know the most effective way to kill a divine, even if he had been granted a blade or a gun or a match to burn their immortal body down to ash.

Despite that stark reality, Roman glanced around the room, wondering if there were any weapons hiding in the shadows. There were none to be found, but his gaze landed on the candlelit desk, where maps were spread across the wood.

He had been eager to study the map of the underworld again, waiting for a moment when he could be alone with the drawings.

Roman walked to the table and laid his hand over the detailed drawing of Cambria, watching as the map beneath was illuminated. He studied it, his gaze racing along the active routes, all the way to Oath. This time he knew what to look for, and even as the city remained mostly dormant and dim, due to the routes still being repaired, there was a single, brilliant vein that ran beneath the city, straight through its heart, up to the northern side.

The current active route.

It ended in a blue flickering circle, marking the Kitt estate. Just as Iris had suspected, and Roman wished he had thought of his father's potential involvement sooner. That he had recalled those magical quirks of the house he had grown up in, and how they might be connected to the under realm's doorways.

Where are the other thresholds?

He leaned closer so he could study the details of the city. He scrutinized the active route, noticing there were other circles that were not lit in blue. Other magical doors, then? And this didn't even account for the additional routes that he knew must run beneath Oath that still needed to be repaired. There could be hundreds of doorways, and Roman gave himself three more breaths to memorize the lit route and the circles before he lifted his hand and stepped away.

He walked to his appointed desk and drew a fresh sheet of paper from the pile. Closing his eyes, he saw the illuminated path again. It was burned into his vision, and he drew it as best he could on the page with a fountain pen.

The room suddenly felt colder.

Roman opened his eyes.

Dacre was beginning to stir on the divan. His breaths quickened as if he were in a nightmare, hands clenching into fists. Roman glanced at the door, measuring the distance. He wouldn't have time to slip away before Dacre woke, which meant he needed a reason to be here. He noticed the *Inkridden Tribune* was still on his desk, Iris's headline about Dacre's doomed love with Enva wrinkled as if it had been roughly handled.

Roman marked three potential doors on his crudely drawn map, identifying general buildings in Oath that might be hosting magical thresholds. Then he forced himself to fold the paper and tuck it into his pocket. He had begun to unpack his typewriter as if it were any other afternoon work session when Dacre's voice broke the silence, darkened by fury.

"*Enva.*"

The sound made Roman's blood turn to ice. He froze, watching as Dacre sat forward on the divan. The god's back was angled to him; Dacre still hadn't seen him, and he covered his face with his hands—such a human gesture that Roman felt a pang in his chest.

"My lord," Roman rasped, thinking he had better announce himself. "I'm here to finish our article."

Dacre didn't move. He could have been hewn from stone; there was no draw of breath, no reaction to Roman's presence.

"Are you all right, sir?"

"Get out," Dacre said in a low, sharp tone.

Roman didn't need to be told twice. With a shiver, he took his typewriter and fled.

A few hours later, just before dusk, Dacre sent for him.

Lieutenant Shane once more came to fetch Roman, his eyes hooded as if he were bored.

"A true summoning this time?" Roman asked, a touch sardonic.

Shane held his stare, impassive. "And what of it? Did you not write a new article for him, as is the norm every afternoon?"

Roman frowned. He was about to ask if Shane had known Dacre was sleeping, or had suspected it and wanted confirmation, when the lieutenant said, "Leave the typewriter. You won't need it."

Roman paused, his hand reaching for the case handle. If he didn't need his typewriter, then what did Dacre want with him? It couldn't be good, given the private moment Roman had witnessed earlier.

He followed Shane without another word, leaving the Third Alouette behind in his room. He was too preoccupied with his worries to speak as Shane kept a brisk pace, weaving them through the damp streets of Hawk Shire. All Roman carried was Iris's ring and the map he had drawn of Oath's ley line, both tucked deep into his pocket. He was beginning to feel uneasy, keeping such items on his person.

He didn't know what to expect, but sweat was trickling down his back and nausea was roiling through him by the time they reached the office.

Dacre wasn't alone. There was a tall, pale man standing at the god's side, a black cloak fastened at his collar. His face was angular, like the facets of cut rock, and his eyes were narrow and cold, glittering with judgment as he studied Roman.

"I've given some thought to the article we were planning to write, Roman," said Dacre. His voice was languid. There was no trace of the nightmare or its lingering fury in his visage, although Roman could still feel an echo of the goddess's name, hours after it had been spoken.

Enva.

Dacre had dreamt of her.

What did that mean for them, for the war? It felt like the tide had altered, and yet all Roman could feel was the sand shifting beneath him, uncertain of the new ebb and flow.

He laced his hands behind his back to hide how he trembled. "Which article, sir?"

"The one in response to Iris E. Winnow. To the article she wrote for the *Tribune,* championing Enva's cleverness and deceit and victory over me." Dacre took a few steps closer, the space between them shriking until his shadow touched Roman's feet.

"And what have you decided, sir?"

"I'm sending you to Oath," Dacre announced. "I would like you to meet with this Iris E. Winnow. You said that you once worked with her and have an acquaintance. Would she be willing to speak with you?"

"I . . . *yes,* I believe so, sir. But why—"

"Not only is she a skilled writer, but she has the ear of the *Tribune,* which is gaining more popularity by the day," Dacre cut him off. "She is also writing for Enva. I can see the touch of the goddess on her, claiming her words, twisting them against me. For this reason alone, I would like to steal her from my wife. I would like Iris E. Winnow writing for me. If you agree to go on my behalf, then you must take this and meet with her in a public place."

Dacre extended an envelope. It was a faint blue, like the color of a robin's egg, shimmering in the late-afternoon light. *Iris E. Winnow* was scrawled in elegant penmanship—the mere sight of her name made Roman's heart quicken—and he reached out to take the envelope.

He was about to go home.

He was about to see Iris again.

"When should I go, sir?" he asked, glancing up to meet Dacre's steady gaze.

"You'll go now."

"Now?"

"Val is here and can escort you to the city." Dacre indicated the strange, cloaked man in the room, who continued to watch Roman like a hawk does a mouse. "If you depart this evening, you'll reach Oath by sunrise."

Oath was still a good distance away, but here was the chance to see how Val was coming and going. Here was the opportunity to confirm where the door was in his family's estate, and for Roman to see the active route with his own eyes.

He only wished that he had his typewriter in hand. Iris wouldn't know he was coming. He would catch her by surprise and, as Dacre had said, their meeting would have to be in a public place. Most likely because Val would be watching them to ensure nothing suspicious occurred.

It felt risky, seeing her without warning. It felt liberating, as if Roman was being set loose from a gilded cage.

Don't let this freedom fool you. The warning shivered through him. At once, Roman sobered.

"I'm ready, my lord," he said. "But my clothes . . . should I go to the city like this?" He looked down at the dark red jumpsuit that boldly proclaimed he was an UNDERLING CORRESPONDENT.

"You'll have the chance to change your clothes upon arrival." Dacre cast a glance at Val, who only arched a brow in response. "And I want you to deliver a second message for me while you're in Oath."

"Of course, sir. What is it?"

Dacre extended another envelope, the same color as the first. The addressee was different but just as meaningful, and Roman merely stared at it for a beat.

Mr. Ronald M. Kitt.

"A letter for my father?" Roman asked in a wavering tone.

"Indeed," Dacre replied, amused. "You'll be seeing him."

Without another word, Roman took the envelope. He felt stiff, like he was covered in frost, when he imagined seeing his father. The last words they had shared had not been kind, gentle ones. Roman didn't like to remember them, to retrace the day he had left his father angry and his mother weeping. The day he had struck out to follow Iris westward. He had quit his job at the *Gazette*. He had broken his engagement to Elinor Little, whom his father had arranged for him to marry in order to keep the Kitts in Dacre's good graces as the war progressed.

Roman had left it all behind without a backward glance.

It felt strange that Dacre would now trust him blithely; the divine was sending him home, knowing the last of his memories would click into place. Something didn't quite feel right, and Roman wondered if this was a test. Dacre knew someone amongst his forces had betrayed him. Perhaps this was his way of proving Roman's innocence or, at the very worst, seeing if Roman was that treacherous link.

If so, then Roman couldn't afford to let the truth rise to the surface.

And yet he dared to look Dacre in the eye and make one final request. "May I spend a night with my family? It's been so long since I've seen my parents and I'd like to have more time with them before I return to you, sir."

Dacre was silent. It felt tenuous—the way air crackled before lightning struck. Roman inwardly braced himself, waiting for the lash.

"Yes," Dacre said at last with a smile. "I don't see why not. Spend a night with your family. Remember what is true, and what is false, and all that I have done for you. Val will be waiting the following sunrise to bring you back to me."

This was indeed a test, then. If he failed to convince Dacre of his dedication and allegiance, post memory repair, then Roman might find himself waking in another cold chamber below, unable to recall his name. Unable to remember Iris.

The thought was agonizing. A sting between his ribs.

"Thank you, sir," Roman managed to say.

He was ready to leave, even without his typewriter, but Dacre drew close to murmur, "It's always best to say less, to let others wonder where you've been and what you've seen and what you think. Let them imagine what *could* be. There's great power in a mystery. Don't spoil yours."

A sharp response gathered in Roman's lungs, but he only cleared his throat. *Be submissive. Convince him of your loyalty.* He felt the ache in his chest as he said, "Yes, my lord. I'll keep that in mind."

Dismissed, he followed Val past Lieutenant Shane, who stood quiet as a statue, taking account of everything with shrewd eyes. Roman left the office, descending the long, circling stairwell.

I'm going home, he thought, and the excitement carried him through the pain in his stride, the shortness of his breaths. *Iris, I'm coming to you.*

But just before he and Val slipped through a door to the under realm, the warning came again like a whisper.

Don't let this freedom fool you.

31

Gravity in a Different World

Roman followed Val through the under realm's passages.

They walked routes that led downward, as if they were descending into yet another world below. One that was darker and older. When they reached a door carved with runes, Val brought out a key, hung from a chain around his neck. Another one of the five magical keys, Roman thought, watching as the door unlocked.

They continued onward. The air felt heavy and thick, almost reverent, and soon carried hints of sulfur and rotting flesh.

Roman reached out to steady himself on the wall and felt briars growing along the stone. He swallowed his gorge and wondered if Dacre's permission had all been a ruse, and Val was taking Roman levels below to dispatch him.

Was it sweeter to kill someone after you had given them hope?

Roman shivered as the thorny passage at last opened to a wide, vast landscape. Yellow, gurgling pools emitted light from the stone floor, as well as releasing wisps of steam, and the ceiling was so high it was impossible to see. It almost felt as if Roman was standing beneath the night sky culled of stars, and he stared upward into those shadows, feeling small and homesick.

"Watch where you step," Val said as he began to weave around the yellow pools, stirring the steam with his long strides and the flap of his cloak.

Roman hurried to keep up. The putridness of the air finally coaxed him to cough into his sleeve. He began to breathe through his mouth, his stomach churning with fear and nausea.

He wanted clean air. A cup of scalding hot coffee. Something to smooth away the discomfort in his chest and throat.

"No sudden movements," Val said, his pace slowing.

"All right." Roman stifled another cough.

Half a minute later, he understood why. Through the curls of sulfurous steam, a huge shadow of a wyvern loomed on the ground, as if waiting for them. An eithral, Roman realized with a sharp intake of breath. Its pronged wings were outstretched and soaking in the heat from the pools, its white-scaled body shining with iridescence. Its maw was closed, but long, needlelike teeth still protruded and gleamed like ice, and its uncanny red eyes were the size of Roman's palm, one of them fixed upon him and his abrupt halt.

"Keep walking," Val said in a low voice. "Slow and steady. Follow my approach to its left side."

Approach? Roman wanted to protest, but he did as Val instructed. He eased into a walk and kept to Val's shadow, and that was when he saw the saddle buckled to the eithral, nestled on its horn-ridged back between its wings.

"Are you bloody serious?" Roman said, his teeth clicking together as a shudder rippled through him. "How will you control it? There's no bridle."

Val began to haul himself up into the saddle with practiced ease. "Do you want to walk to Oath, or do you want to fly?"

A protest melted on Roman's tongue. He didn't know if he had the strength to pull himself up, to sit on the back of the very creature that had played a part in his wounds. But his legs were trembling—*I can't walk to Oath*—and his heart was striking his chest like a hammer. He was both exhausted and electrified, and he finally thought of the poetic justice. That an eithral would carry him and his map to the city, where Dacre was destined to lose.

An eithral was about to fly him to Iris.

Roman followed Val's path, pulling himself up the eithral's side to the slope of the saddle. He settled on what felt like impossibility incarnate.

"Don't let go," Val said gruffly. "It's always a bumpy takeoff."

Roman grasped the edge of the leather saddle with a white-knuckled grip, pressing his knees inward until they ached. He felt in no way secure enough to be lifting *off* the ground astride one of Dacre's not-so-mythical creatures. A creature that had caused fathomless devastation and pain and death.

He clenched his eyes shut. He struggled to hold his last meal down. Cold sweat was breaking out over his skin, but then he firmly told himself, *Open your eyes.*

Roman did, taking in his surroundings again. He would have never believed he would be here, in this moment, months ago. *Weeks* ago, even. And he wanted to soak it all in. He would have never believed that he would be in the realm below, beneath layer after layer of earth, in a world made of starless night and languid smoke, about to ride an eithral.

In that moment before flight, when the air took on a hush of awe and expectation, Roman heard Iris's voice in his memory.

I find that I am leaning more on the side of impossibility these days. I am leaning toward the edge of magic.

Her words grounded him. He envisioned Iris typing by candlelight, as if she were his gravity.

Val withdrew a small flute, hanging on a chain, from beneath his shirt. He blew three long silver notes—they shimmered in the air like sunlight catching rain—and the eithral jerked its head up and began to flap its wings.

Of course. Roman nearly laughed. *They're controlled by an instrument. By music.*

The eithral was beholden to the flute's three notes, even after they had faded into shadows. Its wings spun up the steam and flashes of heat and golden light until it felt like Roman was lost in a windstorm, the sulfur stinging his eyes and making him cough again. But then the eithral took a lurch forward. One lumbering step after the other, expertly dodging the hissing pools.

They took flight as if they had done so a hundred times before.

It was a bumpy takeoff, but once the eithral was fully in the air, the ride was smooth.

Roman was initially surprised that they never left the under realm. He hadn't realized that this innermost world was so open and vast—an endless waste of landscape, pocketed with bubbling sulfur pools and veiled with steam. A few times, when Roman dared to look down, he saw something glittering through the haze. His eyes widened when he realized it was rusted chains and skeletons, the bones scattered across the rock paths. They looked like animal bones, until Roman undoubtedly spotted a human skull.

His throat burned as he glanced away. His mouth was parched and held a strange aftertaste, but he was relieved to discover that the warm, moist air eased his cough. Now that has panic had subsided, he could draw a deep breath here and not feel that awful pinch in his lungs.

Eventually, after what could have been half an hour of flying or three—time was impossible to measure without the sky and the sun and the moon—Roman noticed that in some places, the steam from the sulfur pools rose higher than others, as if there was a draft, drawing it upward. After the seventh instance of this, he began to surmise that those must be the places where the eithrals could emerge from the ground. More doorways, large enough to let the creatures pass from one realm to the next.

He wanted to ask Val, but Roman kept his questions captive. Val didn't seem like a very patient individual, and if Roman wanted to press his luck, he thought he should wait until they had landed. But the roaring silence didn't quell his imagination or his theories.

Val was obviously close with the eithrals. Perhaps he trained them, or was their caretaker? He also carried the flute beneath his clothes like Dacre did and knew all the melodies to play to control the creatures. What other commands did the eithrals know, and did they still obey musical orders when they flew in the world above?

Roman remembered his time on the front lines, how Lieutenant Lark of the Sycamore Platoon had said eithrals were rarely spotted flying over the trenches because the beasts couldn't differentiate between enemy and friendly forces. That if Dacre had let them loose with bombs in their talons, they would have just as easily dropped them on Dacre's soldiers as they would Enva's, and therefore the creatures were used to bomb civilian towns, a good distance from the front lines.

Dacre's tactics were to use the eithrals to not only strike fear into the hearts of people, but *bomb,* then *gas,* then *recover* wounded soldiers, so that he could heal them in what felt like complete measures before scrambling their memories to make them feel beholden and subservient to him. It was a terrible and ruthless way to build an army and a following, and Roman could feel heat rise beneath his skin.

But this thought remained at the forefront: surely the eithrals could still be commanded when they flew above. Surely Dacre wasn't surrendering complete control of his creatures. There had to be a way he could still harness them, as Avalon Bluff had revealed. The eithrals had made two rounds over the town, carrying different materials each time.

Val shifted in the saddle in front of him. The flute flashed in the mellow light as he raised it to his lips.

Roman tucked away the anger and the wonderings when he realized they were preparing to land.

Val blew the flute again, this time two long notes followed by three short ones. The music claimed the air, spawning rings of iridescence that grew so large they faded from sight, and the eithral screeched in response. The creature tossed its head as if resisting the order, but began to angle downward, wings flapping in short but powerful bursts.

Roman clung to the saddle, rigid with dread. But the landing wasn't as terrible as he expected, and before he could even catch his breath, the eithral had come to a halt—wings outstretched once more over the bubbling pools—and Val was dismounting.

"Let's go," Val said.

Roman half-slid, half-fell his way down, his right ankle hitting the stone floor with a painful jar. Val, thankfully, didn't notice, as he was already walking along the pathway that wound through the sulfur eddies.

Roman hesitated, glancing at the eithral. It was watching him again, eye sparkling like a ruby. With a pang in his stomach, Roman realized it was just as captive as he was.

He hurried after Val, stepping over pieces of a skeleton and a chain of iron that vanished into one of the boiling pools. Soon, veins of briars began to crosshatch over the floor, and Roman found that the plants guided them to where the doorway was, its arched lintel covered entirely in thick vines, clusters of amethysts, and bloodstained thorns.

"This way," Val said, his impatience ringing just like one of his musical notes. He stepped over the threshold and into the shadows, and Roman followed, his eyes struggling to adjust to the darkness.

He could feel the floor steadily rising beneath him. The incline turned his breath to fire, his temples throbbing in response. They passed through another door, returning to the main level of Dacre's realm, only this time it was deathly quiet. There was no city market to greet them, and the air tasted dusty and stale. A lonely echo reverberated through the darkness.

Val struck a match. Its meager light helped more than Roman would have thought possible, and they soon began to wend through a very narrow passage that broke into multiple new routes. Cobwebs were strung thick overhead; small bones were piled in corners. Amethysts grew from the wall in clusters, glittering like a thousand eyes in the firelight, and Roman had to duck and squeeze his way through, mesmerized by the haunting beauty of it.

"Are we beneath Oath?" he finally asked, trying to memorize the exact path they had taken.

"Yes. We are approaching the doorway."

"How did you know when to tell the eithral to land? There were no markers, no way of knowing where we were."

"There's always a way of knowing," Val answered. "If one pays attention."

Roman pondered over that a moment before he remembered the steam vents. Perhaps Val had counted them as they passed, knowing which number corresponded to Oath. It seemed the only plausible explanation, but Roman didn't have time to dwell on it as Val began speaking again.

"You'll recognize where you are the moment you pass through the door. It'll be dawn, and I'd advise you to change your clothes and then do what needs to be done with Iris Winnow *first* before speaking with your parents. Do you know where Gould's Café is located?"

"Yes," Roman said.

"That's where you should meet Miss Winnow. Keep your explanations brief and vague. Say nothing of the doorways or the eithrals. Most people who have never been below struggle to understand our ways here."

Roman waited for more, but when Val remained quiet, he said, "I'll keep this in mind. Thank you, sir."

Val came to an abrupt halt, his boots crunching a tiny skeleton. Roman dodged stepping into him but noticed that the amethysts grew into a glittering archway above one of the branching routes.

"Take this passage. It will lead you to the door," Val said. "I'll be waiting here for you at dawn tomorrow. Don't be late."

Roman nodded. He gazed up at the crystal archway, unable to fight his admiration of it. Darkly gleaming facets that would lead him home.

He began to walk, unsteady at first. He was surprised by how much he missed Val's light as he drew farther away from it, and how chilling it was to move through such dark passages alone. But then the air began to shift as one realm melted into the other.

Roman caught a draft.

It smelled like lemon polish on hardwood floors. Like bouquets of flowers that had bloomed in a glass house, and treacle biscuits, still warm from the oven. Like cigar smoke and his mother's rosewater perfume.

It smelled like *home,* and Roman ran toward it, his breath loud and jagged in the shadows.

The stairs were steep and rough-hewn, just barely discernable as if starlight limned them. Roman took two at a time until his legs almost buckled, and then he slowed down. He made himself swallow, *breathe,* step carefully. Higher and higher he ascended, until he felt the power of Dacre's domain shiver down his spine, stripping away like a shed coat.

Roman approached the door. He could see the handle flash in welcome, as if it sensed his heat.

He wondered how many times he had walked past this door before, completely unaware of what it could become with the turning of a key. He wondered how many mundane things hid magic, or perhaps it was better to think of it as how much magic liked being married to the ordinary. To simplicity and comfort and overlooked details.

Roman took hold of the handle and turned it. The door popped open; he was greeted by a slender shaft of light, tinged blue with dawn.

Heart in his throat, Roman passed over the threshold.

32

Static on the Line

I
t was the parlor.

Roman stood and soaked in the familiar blue-and-gold features: the ornate rug that muffled footsteps, the marble hearth on the wall, the floor-to-ceiling windows with the brocade drapes, the piano that sat quietly in the corner, the gilded wainscotting, and the framed oil paintings that had been in their family for generations.

Clothes, he thought just as the grandfather clock in the foyer struck the seventh hour. His father would already be up, smoking in the study with a hearty dose of brandy in his coffee. His nan was cloistered in the western wing of the estate with her dogs and her books, but his mother liked to rise after the sun, which meant she would be moving through the house soon. And she had always been more in tune with ghosts than his father. If anyone sensed his presence, it would be his mum.

Roman raked his fingers through his dark hair and quit the parlor.

Up the grand staircase and down the hallway, his boots hardly making noise on the plush runner. He slipped into his old bedroom, quietly locking the door behind him. Everything was just as he had left it. Everything but the vase of flowers on his desk.

Frowning, Roman walked to them, touching the small but fierce blue petals. Forget-me-nots. They grew in abundance in spring, brightening the garden and the woodlands on their property.

His mother had been here, then. How often did she come to his room?

He felt a welt of shame for how he had left things with his parents weeks ago. His father not so much, but his mother? Roman hated to think of causing her any more grief and anguish.

There will be time for this later, he thought, stepping away from the flowers. *Don't get distracted.*

He removed his map, Iris's wedding ring, the two letters from Dacre. That was all he had carried from below to above, and he quickly changed into a crisp white button-down and a pair of black trousers before clipping leather braces over his shoulders. His trench coat, because the morning looked like rain, and then a fresh set of socks that made him wiggle his toes in relief. Lastly, his favorite pair of brogues.

He returned all four items to his inner pocket, although he held on to Iris's ring for a moment, watching it gleam in the morning light.

Val had instructed him to meet her at Gould's Café. Roman had no doubt that Val would follow him up the stairs to watch him the entire time he was out in the open, moving from place to place. Above all, Dacre would want eyes on Roman.

The most important thing was to keep Iris as safe as possible. Which meant Val couldn't know that they were married or had any sort of affection for each other. They needed to fall back to their old patterns during the café meeting, just to be careful.

Roman sat at his desk. He wrote a quick message and then folded it into thirds, tucking it behind Dacre's envelope. Without his typewriter, there was no way to give her a warning. She was going to be blindsided, and he could only hope that she would know to play along.

Roman stood and glanced around his room a final time. He hid his Underling jumpsuit and worn boots in his wardrobe and then realized he needed one more thing before he headed downtown.

A telephone.

. . .

Iris hadn't heard from Roman in over a day.

This wasn't *exactly* unusual, but ever since that moment in Hawk Shire when his memories had come flooding back, he had written to her at night when he was safe in his room. She didn't want to let worry overcome her thoughts, but she also couldn't help but feel like fate had shifted, like a star falling from a constellation.

Something must have happened.

She paced her bedroom, glancing sidelong at the wardrobe door. It was always best if he wrote first, since he was mobile with his typewriter, spending hours in Dacre's presence. But there was still a way for her to initiate the contact. She had taken advantage of it multiple times before and didn't see why it couldn't be used now.

Part of her bid herself *patience*. But the other side, the one that was smoldering like coals, told her to *do something. Don't just sit back and wait.*

Iris sat on the floor and typed out:

This is a test to see if the strike bars E & R are in working condition.
EREEERRRRR
E

She kept it brief this time, sliding the paper under the wardrobe door. She waited, but as the minutes spread into a dark hour, she settled on the edge of her bed, her hands icy.

Iris slept very little that night. But when she woke in the morning, she didn't feel any better. Her heart felt bruised when she saw there was no letter on the floor for her to read.

There was no word from Roman, and it was time for her to go to work.

Iris washed her face and combed the tangles from her hair. She found a clean sweater in her wardrobe, a pale blush color that made her feel brave, and a brown plaid skirt. She drew on her knee-high stockings and boots and left for the *Inkridden Tribune*.

Forest was already at work, but he had left her a scrawled note on the kitchen table: *Sarah is coming for dinner tonight. Help me decide what to make? She doesn't like olives or mushrooms. Also, please don't be out past dark.*

It was the only bright spot in Iris's morning, making her worry dwindle during the tram ride. Imagining her brother cooking dinner for the woman he fancied was amusing. But by the time Iris stepped into the *Tribune*'s office, her fears had returned tenfold. It felt like a brick had settled in her stomach when she wondered where Roman was, and why he had gone silent.

Attie was already at their desk, looking over notes. She glanced up when Iris collapsed into her chair.

"You're here early," Attie remarked.

"So are you," Iris said, but before she could say another word, her attention was drawn to Helena, who strode from her office to pour a cup of tea from the sideboard.

Their boss looked haggard, as if she hadn't been sleeping. Her shoulders were stooped, her auburn hair lank and dull. Purple smudges marked her eyes as she took a sip of the scalding hot tea, but Helena didn't even wince. She returned to her office, not saying a word to anyone, and Iris exchanged a worried look with Attie.

"Two things," Attie whispered, leaning close. "The first? I hear Helena has finally given up smoking. The second? The Graveyard doesn't want her reporting on the war or the gods unless they approve."

"They can get in line, then," Iris said, but she shivered when she remembered that gunshot the other night. Sarah had to spend the night with them after dinner, because it was too risky for her to walk the streets at night. "What use is the press if we can't write about what we witness? If we can't share the local news?"

Attie sighed, taking her teacup in hand. "They didn't like our report on Enva's soldiers and wounded being barred from entering the city."

That article had just been printed yesterday morning. Iris gnawed on her lip. "How do you know this?"

"Here." Attie tossed an envelope across the table. "This was waiting on Helena's desk first thing this morning."

Iris slid a letter from the envelope, startled when flowers spilled free. Two anemones, one red and one white, pressed flat. "Flowers?"

"I think it's their leader's calling card," Attie replied. "A way to express the importance of an order, maybe? Although I have a theory."

"Which is?"

"The flowers represent Dacre and Enva, and how the Graveyard hopes to bury them both eternally."

Iris studied the anemones before she unfolded the letter and read:

To Ms. Hammond of the <u>Inkridden Tribune</u>,

    From this day forward, we ask that you run all articles pertaining to gods and soldiers by us first for approval. Failure to do so will result in undesirable consequences to your paper. Let us remind you that we have the good of the people in mind, first and foremost, and as such we must ensure all avenues are united in that ideal. You can send any future articles care of the chancellor for approval.

Sincerely,

The Graveyard

"This is *absurd*." Iris shoved the letter back into its envelope with the flowers. "I don't see how they can give Helena orders."

"Oath is changing, Iris," Attie said. "My mum says it's the same at university. The dean has given her a long list of things to avoid saying, for fear it will get back to the Graveyard."

"This bloody *Graveyard*," Iris murmured. "We leave the city for less than *two* weeks, and they take over. I don't understand why—"

"Excuse me, Winnow?"

Iris cut herself off and glanced to her left. One of the assistants had approached her and Attie's table, a pot of coffee in one hand, a notepad in the other.

"Is something wrong, Treanne?" Iris asked, but she bit her tongue. She needed to be careful. She shouldn't be spouting her irritation about the Graveyard in the office, or any public place. There was no telling who was a part of that group, as Sarah had explained.

"You have a phone call. It's waiting on you."

"Oh." Iris stood with a frown. She wasn't expecting a call, and she resisted the urge to glance at Attie before she walked to where the lone telephone sat on the wall.

Iris cleared her throat and took hold of the receiver, raising it to her ear.

"This is Iris Winnow speaking."

A crackle of static. Iris thought whoever it was must have hung up, but then she heard them breathing. A slow, deep exhale on the line.

"Hello?" she said. "Who is this?"

Another beat of stilted silence, and then a familiar voice said, "Iris E. Winnow?"

Iris felt the breath freeze in her lungs. Her eyes went wide as she stared at news clippings on the bulletin board, gripping the receiver until it felt like the blood had drained from her hand.

Kitt.

She made herself swallow his name until it sat like a stone in her throat. Something was wrong. She had sensed it last night, and she could hear it in the way he spoke now.

"Yes," she said, unable to hide the softness in her voice. "This is Iris."

"I have a message for you," Roman said. "It must be delivered in person. Are you familiar with Gould's Café?"

Iris was quiet, her mind reeling. She was trying to pick apart every word he was saying in hopes she could understand what was happening. She was trying to glean the words he wouldn't—or *couldn't*—say.

"Winnow?" he prompted.

He hadn't called her that in a long while. It took her back in time, as if they had flipped pages in a volume, returning to those *Gazette* chapters.

She said in a careful tone, "Yes, I know Gould's."

"When can you meet me there?"

"I can come now."

"Good," Roman said, but it sounded more like a sigh. Iris couldn't tell if it was spun from relief or longing. "I'll see you there in twenty."

He hung up the receiver.

It was so abrupt that Iris stood for a minute more, gazing at nothing.

But her heart was like thunder in her chest as she kept the receiver by her ear. As she listened to the empty waves of static.

The realization hit her with a gasp. Roman was in Oath. She was about to drink tea with him.

Iris set the receiver down on its hook with a clatter.

She rushed to the door and left the *Inkridden Tribune* without a backward glance.

33

Milk and Honey

Roman waited at a small table in the corner of the café, coat slung over the back of his chair. He had called Iris from one of the public phones just outside the train station, unwilling to risk using the one at his parents' house. It had taken all his wits to sneak out of the estate to begin with. He couldn't use the front gates without detection and so he had strayed deep in the gardens, where he knew there was a break in the property fence, far from sight of the back windows.

He drummed his fingers over his thighs, his gaze remaining on the café doors, watching people come and go. None of whom were Iris, but he had wanted to be the first one here, and by the ticking of the clock on the wall . . . she still had eight minutes to arrive on time.

The waiter delivered a tea tray but Roman didn't touch it. Fragrant steam danced from the pot, reminding him of those sulfur pools in the world below.

The bell chimed above the door. A young woman wearing a trench coat and a hat stepped into the café. Roman held his breath but it wasn't Iris.

He was fairly certain Val was trailing him. Roman hadn't caught sight of him on the brisk walk downtown, but he had felt a cold sensation creep down his neck. A prickle of warning that someone was observing him, keeping a tally of where he went and what he said.

Don't let your guard down, he told himself for the tenth time that morning. *Not even when you see her.*

Two more minutes passed before he finally caught sight of Iris through the café windows.

Roman froze like he was ensorcelled. He couldn't breathe as he watched her cross the street. Her trench coat was unbuttoned and flapping in the breeze, revealing a glimpse of her snug sweater and pleated skirt. He saw the flash of her pale knees as she hurried over the cobblestones, her hair tangling across her face as she glanced to the side, waiting for a vehicle to pass.

Make it feel like the Gazette *days,* Roman thought as Iris reached the door and pulled it open with an adorable scrunch of her nose. She stepped into the café, a gust billowing around her as if the very wind had brought her here, rosy-cheeked and bright-eyed. She paused by the counter and chewed her lip as she studied the crowd. As she looked for *him.*

Roman felt his pulse in his ears. Within those two beats, he tamed his longings and put a guard in place. His expression was cool, aloof. He could play this role well. It felt as familiar as an old, well-worn shirt. And yet when their gazes met over the bustle and noise, the entire world faded away.

It was only him and her.

It was only the ten steps between them, distance that felt both heady and crushing. It felt too far and dangerously close, and Roman stood, bumping the table. The cups rattled in their saucers; one of the scones toppled from the plate.

Iris smiled and began to weave her way to him.

Don't. Roman nearly panicked, feeling his blood pound hot and fast. *Don't smile at me like that.*

It made him want to collide with her, his lips on her neck, the curve of her ribs. Tasting her mouth. It made him want to draw out all those words he loved from her, but most of all the way she said his name.

By the time she reached their table, she sensed it. His cold exterior, the ice in his gaze. That cloud of reservation and politeness, building like a thunderhead.

Her smile faded but she didn't seem defeated. No, he only saw determination flare in her eyes, and Roman felt relieved. His shoulders relaxed a fraction.

"Hello, Kitt," Iris said in a careful tone.

"Winnow," he replied, clearing his throat. "Thank you for coming. Please, have a seat."

She removed her trench coat and sat. Roman lowered himself back down to his chair and reached for the pot. There was a slight tremor in his hands, as if he had drunk too much coffee on an empty stomach.

"When was the last time I saw you?" Iris said as he poured their tea.

Yes, perfect. Establish a timeline. He dared to glance up, meeting her stare as he handed her a cup.

"I believe it was your last day of work at the *Gazette,*" he replied. "When I won the columnist position."

"Ah, so it was." She sounded like the old Iris. The one who got under his skin with her perfect articles.

But he noticed how she rubbed the palm of her hand. How she studied the tea tray, a wrinkle in her brow, like she suddenly didn't know where to look. The blush was fading from her face as if she were speaking with a ghost.

"I must say you look well," he said. And then, because he was an utter fool for her, he bumped her foot beneath the table.

That brought her gaze back to him. Keen and full of light, warm as embers. "Are you implying that I looked ill before?"

He almost smiled, and he was pleased to see the color return to her skin. It could have been a bloom of indignation, or desire. They had played this game well at the *Gazette,* although if Roman could go back . . .

No. He shut the thought down. He wouldn't change a thing. Because if he could, would the two of them still be here, bound together by vow and trial and love that had crept up on him like ivy on stone?

"You look just as I remember you," he said.

Iris must have understood the hidden meaning. Her expression softened, just a fraction.

He wasn't acting this way—like they had stepped back in time—because his memories had faltered again. All those pieces were still there, aligned and restitched back together. He was acting reserved for another reason entirely, one he hoped to explain to her later, when it was safe.

"You said you have a message for me?" Iris reached for the pitcher of milk just as he reached for the honey dish.

Their knuckles brushed.

Roman almost froze again, his heart beating like wings against his ribs.

"Ah, I forgot," Iris continued seamlessly with a wave of her hand. "You only take honey in your tea, like all the poets did. The office was always running low because of you."

Roman was thankful for the lighthearted distraction. "And you like a little tea with your milk."

"Oh, come now," Iris said as she, indeed, poured far too much milk into her cup. "It makes it more substantial."

That sobered Roman. He remembered those office days, how he had never seen Iris eat or take a proper lunch break. He hadn't realized she had been keeping herself satiated as best as she could with tea until she was gone. It still made him feel like his lungs were full of water when he thought about it.

"Here," he said in a gruff voice, to hide how it wanted to shake at that memory. "I ordered some refreshments. Help yourself."

"I will, actually, take one of these *sandwiches.*" Iris reached for a triangle-cut cucumber sandwich but then covered her mouth. "Oh, gods!"

"What?" Roman was tense as he leaned forward, preparing to flee. Had she seen Val? Was this all about to crumble?

Iris sighed. "I forgot my purse at the *Tribune!* I left in such a hurry after you called, I—"

"Don't worry, this is on me," Roman gently interrupted. "I drew you away from work. The least I can do is feed you."

Iris quirked her lips to the side. Roman made himself look down into his tea, feeling an ache in his stomach. In his chest. In his bones.

He waited until Iris had eaten two sandwiches and a scone before he spoke.

"I was sent here to meet with you, by a specific request."

Iris frowned. "Whose?"

Roman could feel Dacre's name sitting on his tongue like a shard of glass. He didn't think it wise to utter it aloud, especially to Iris, who he knew wouldn't be able to hide how she felt about the god. Especially after everything Dacre had done. To her brother. To the land. To Avalon Bluff. To the army and innocent civilians. To both of them and the future they longed for.

Roman hesitated. This was the part he was most anxious about, but he reached into his coat pocket with confident ease, finding Dacre's letter as well as the one he had written that morning. He grabbed them both, keeping the elegant blue envelope on the top, his scrawled note concealed below.

"To read in private," he said, extending them to Iris.

Her frown only deepened when she saw her name, written in penmanship she didn't recognize. But she took the envelope and felt the folded paper hiding beneath. She kept the two together, gazing down at the blue one before tucking them away in her own coat pocket.

If Val was watching, he would never know two messages had been slipped to her.

"Very well." Iris drank the last of her tea before setting the cup aside. "Is there anything else you'd like to say to me?"

Roman stared at her. There were *hundreds* of things he wanted to say to her, and yet he couldn't voice a single one. Not here, in public. Not as he longed to do, as if it were just the two of them on an ordinary date, and after this they would take a stroll in the park, hand in hand.

Maybe one day.

"No," he said. "And I've kept you longer than I should." He rose and drew on his coat, putting the bill on his father's tab.

Iris also stood, although that worried gleam had returned to her eyes. She pressed her lips together as she donned her coat, buttoning it tight this time.

"I suppose that's it, then?" she asked.

It killed Roman to resist eye contact. To act like she was nothing more than a former colleague. He drew in a sharp breath, smelling a hint of lavender. He knew it was her skin, the soap she used.

"That's it," he said, hollow. "Good day to you, Winnow."

He turned and strode away, shoving the café door open so hard that the bell above almost rang itself loose.

He walked, hands clenched in his pockets, until the city had swallowed him whole.

Iris stared at Roman's retreating backside.

It felt like her heart had impaled itself on one of her ribs. That if she reached beneath her coat and sweater and touched her side, her fingers would come away bloodstained.

The dark spell was broken by the waiter, who began to gather up the dirty dishes.

"Excuse me, miss," he said.

"Oh, I'm sorry." Iris gave him a weak smile and stepped out of the way, but her mind was like a hive, humming with thoughts. She reached into her pocket and felt the sharp corner of the envelope again. Turning, she walked down the lopsided hallway to the lavatory.

It was empty, and Iris locked the door behind her.

She grimaced as she lowered the toilet lid and sat on it, bringing the notes out into the dim light. She stared at them both, as if caught between the starkness of the two. The blue one with her name in elegant ink—*Iris E. Winnow*—or the plain one, with Roman's endearing scrawl—*My Iris*—over the face of it.

She had always preferred bad news first, and she tore open the blue envelope.

Dear Iris E.Winnow,

I confess that I had never heard of you, or taken proper interest in your journalism, until your most recent article in the Inkridden Tribune, by which I was deeply moved. Forgive me, for overlooking you in the past. In all my years, I have discovered that the most precious of things are often taken for granted, and that we tend to let time wheel forward at such a pace that we cannot catch every detail that makes the whole. We miss a multitude of opportunities, and so we ask ourselves, decades later, what could have been.

I do not wish the same for you—it is a constant flame I see in mortal kind—and hope you learn from my wisdom. For I would offer you the world reforged if you would be brave enough to stretch out your hand and take it. A writer such as you, with words like iron and salt, could change the very course of time if you only had the right support.

Come write for me. Come write about the things that are most important. The things that are often overlooked, and what lurks just beneath the surface of what we see. Join me and my forces as we build a stronger realm above, one of healing and restoration. One of justice for old wounds. I would like to hear your thoughts, face-to-face. I would like to see what other words hide within that mind of yours, and how we may use them to sharpen the world around us and usher in a new and divine era.

Think on my offer. You will know when to give me your answer.

Dacre Underling

Lord Commander

Iris released a tremulous breath as she lowered the paper to her lap.

She sat numb for a moment, staring at a painting that hung crooked on the wall. Dacre's words spilled through her thoughts, permeating everything until it felt like she was about to sink into a bog.

"*Later,*" she whispered, tucking Dacre's letter back into the envelope. "I'll deal with this later."

A bad idea to delay something that would only grow to become a stronger monster. As if her indecision and terror would feed it.

But Iris still had Roman's note to read. She held it up, admiring his hand-writing before she unfolded it. Her palms were damp, her heart pounding so hard she thought it might tear its way free, through bone and muscle and veins.

She would always take bad news first, and Dacre's letter was one of the most sinister things she had ever read. But after her strange meeting with Roman, this could also be something terrible. Something she was not prepared for, just as she had not been prepared to hear his voice on the line, and Iris closed her eyes, afraid to read his words.

You look just as I remember you, he had said not half an hour ago.

She breathed deeply until her lungs burned. Only then did she open her eyes and read:

Dear Iris,

I know you're brimming with questions. You're wondering why I just met you for tea, why I am in Oath to begin with, and why I haven't written to you prior to this, letting you know I was coming for a visit. And I have the answers, but I can only give them to you in person, when we are not being watched. When we are in a safe and private place.

I will be here for one night only before I must return to my post. One night, and I would like to spend it with you.

I will have to sneak you into my house, of course. Be prepared for a climb. And I know this is not without its risks, to ask you to come by cover of night. But if you can . . . there is a break in my father's estate fence, toward the northeast side of the gardens. Approach from Derby Road—there is a footpath between homes 1345 and 1347—and you will see the weak point in the fence, just beneath an oak tree. It is nearly concealed by brambles, but if you look, you will find the path. I will be waiting for you there at half past ten, when the moon rises.

Love,

Kitt

P.S. A final note written by my future self, because I know I will be feeling this as I walk away from you: gods, you looked gorgeous at tea. I would like to take you to all the places you love most in the city, and then beyond. Think about them. Make me a list. We'll go anywhere you want to. We'll go together when the war is over.

Iris made it to the end. She couldn't quite read the words anymore, through the tears that stung her eyes.

Someone knocked loudly on the door. The sound brought her back to the present: she was sitting on a toilet lid, the sounds of a café muted through the walls. She pulled the lever to flush, alerting the person waiting that she was almost done, because her voice had rusted in her throat.

Rising, Iris tucked the letters back into her pocket and washed her hands at the sink, staring at her reflection in the speckled mirror.

She would not live in fear. She would not fulfill Dacre's silver-tongued omen for her.

It didn't matter how many years passed or what lay ahead for her. What the war would or would not bring.

Iris would never find herself lost to what *could have been*.

34

Twelve Past Eleven

Roman hadn't been aware that there was a new watch in Oath and curfew was now at dusk. Not until his parents told him about it over a very awkward dinner. He now waited for Iris in the darkness beneath the oak boughs, a few minutes shy of ten thirty, and his worry was gathering like moonlight on the ground, making monstrous shadows out of harmless shrubs.

It had been an odd day altogether, and it almost felt like Roman had seen Iris at the café *weeks* ago, not mere hours. A memory that had already turned sepia in his mind. But when he had left her at Gould's, he had walked the city until his emotions banked into coals and he could think clearly again.

He had remembered his hastily drawn map of the ley line, and the potential buildings that hosted magical doorways. Places that Dacre's army could potentially use to invade the city. The map was in his pocket—he planned to hand it over to Iris that night—and while he wanted to pull it out and compare it to the street, he didn't, sensing Val still trailing him. And so Roman had acted like he was casually walking, while in truth, he was studying the street and the buildings all the way back to his father's estate.

He had wanted to spend time with his nan and his mother, and he arrived through the front gate and knocked on the bright red door, as if he hadn't been there earlier. His mother had been thrilled, hugging him tightly in her thin arms, smoothing back his hair, pulling him into the sunroom, her favorite place in the house because it overlooked the gardens and Del's small grave. But most of all, Roman had been shocked that his father looked relieved to see him.

"How long are you here for?" Mr. Kitt had asked, puffing on his cigar.

The smoke tickled Roman's nose. He tried not to breathe too deeply, feeling his lungs wither in response. "I leave first thing tomorrow. I'll be staying here tonight, though. In my old room, if that's all right."

"Of course it is, Roman!" Mrs. Kitt had exclaimed, clasping her hands together. "We'll have a nice family dinner together. Just like old times, my darling."

It was not like old times. There was no going back to those days, as much as they might long to or fool themselves that time could be wound back like a clock. But Roman had only smiled, and when his mother called for tea and his favorite biscuits, he drank and ate again, as if he were empty.

At dinner, he had expected the questions he could not fully answer. *Where have you been, why haven't you contacted us, tell us more of what you're doing.* As instructed, Roman kept his replies vague, but two odd things happened while they were seated at the table.

The first had been his nan's whippet. The fact that the dog was allowed to sit in the dining room told Roman that his father had started to cave, because in the past his grandmother wasn't permitted to bring along any of her pets in this wing of the house. But the whippet sat, quiet and obedient, behind Nan's chair, until a sudden draft could be felt in the dining room.

The crystals on the chandelier above clinked together as they trembled. There was a creak in the hardwood beneath the rug. Roman watched as the wine in his glass rippled like an invisible stone had been dropped into it.

Nan's whippet barked.

"Hush that dog at once, Henrietta," Mr. Kitt had snapped, his face flushing red.

Nan rolled her eyes—only she could get away with such defiance in his father's presence—and set down her napkin. "Quiet, Theodore."

Theodore quit his barking, but Roman noticed the dog's nose was pointed to the eastern wall. The wall that the dining room shared with the parlor.

Roman returned his attention to his plate. Someone had just used the doorway. He wondered if it was Val, satisfied with Roman's behavior.

"This house is nothing but drafts these days," Nan had muttered, tossing a scrap of ham to the dog.

"Hmm" was how Mr. Kitt replied, but he met Roman's gaze over the candle tapers.

They shared a knowing look. Roman could only wonder if his father had dared to tread below, or if he was only being a genteel host for Dacre, letting Val come and go as he pleased.

Not ten minutes later, when the waitstaff were bringing out the third course, the second odd thing had occurred.

A man Roman had never seen before slipped into the dining room and approached his father, bending low to whisper something to Mr. Kitt. The man was short and stocky, wearing a dark coat with its collar flipped upward to shield his neck. His left ear looked permanently swollen, betraying his past as a boxer, and there was a scar on his jaw.

Roman said nothing as he watched the brief exchange, surprised that his father wasn't angry at the interruption. Whatever the man whispered to Mr. Kitt pleased him, because his scowl eased and he nodded.

Just as suddenly as the man had arrived, he left. He exited the manor out the front door, into the dusk, and Roman stared at his father until Mr. Kitt had no choice but to meet his gaze.

"Who was that?" Roman had asked tersely.

His father took his time in replying, taking a long sip of wine. "An associate of mine."

"An associate?"

"Yes. Is that acceptable to you, Roman?"

Roman bit his tongue. That man was something more than a mere associate, and it made gooseflesh rise on his arms.

"He helps your father handle the business side of matters, Roman," his mother said in her airy voice. "His name is Bruce. He sometimes joins us for afternoon tea."

"Some security," Nan murmured beneath her breath.

"Security?" Roman echoed. A chill touched his spine when he wondered if his father was in too deep with Dacre and felt like he needed a guard. But then he thought of Iris, sneaking in through the back garden to meet him that night. "He guards the property?"

Mr. Kitt chuckled. "No, although I don't see why it interests you, son. You never cared much for familial matters, or this house you'll inherit."

A jab. Roman's face flushed, and he decided to leave it at that until his mother mentioned the Graveyard and how thankful she was that these un-named citizens were striving to keep Oath safe. The Graveyard, who had en-forced a strict curfew. With Iris about to venture through the night-stained streets to meet him.

Roman's stomach churned as he had delivered the letter to his father after the final course, dismissing himself to his room.

He was halfway up the stairs when Mr. Kitt called up to him from the foyer.

"Do you know when you'll be visiting again, son?"

Roman paused on the stair. "No, sir."

Mr. Kitt nodded, but his eyes narrowed. "He must be quite pleased with you, letting you come home for a spell."

Roman ground his teeth together. Yes, he had done plenty for Dacre. All those words he had typed for him. All that propaganda.

It made him feel sick.

"Keep it that way." Mr. Kitt spoke in a hushed tone. "At least, for a little while longer."

That chilling phrase had followed Roman up the remainder of the stairs. His family was entangled with the dealings of a god, and he didn't know how they would be able to free themselves when the war was over. If Dacre won . . . they would be forever beholden to him. And if Enva won . . . the Kitts would be branded as traitors.

Roman slipped into his room and locked the door. He leaned against the wood, checking the time.

It was only half past nine.

He had one more hour until Iris arrived. He stripped off his clothes and stepped into the adjacent lavatory, turning on the shower.

He let the hot water hit his chest until his skin looked burned. He scrubbed with a bar of pine soap and washed his hair, his fingertips pruned by the time he shut off the valve and dried himself. After wiping fog from the mirror, he combed back his dark hair and shaved, then studied his reflection.

He looked hollow and far older than he should be.

He glanced away, heart quickening when he checked the time again. It was nearly ten o'clock.

Roman had padded from the lavatory and opened his wardrobe. He put on his best clothes, cuffing the button-down's sleeves to his elbows, leaving the neck open. Another pair of trousers, held in place with his leather braces. Well-worn shoes that would help him move quietly.

He sat on his bed and bounced on the balls of his feet, waiting.

When ten twenty finally hit, he rose and opened his window. He had done this a few times when he was younger, the thrill of defying his father's strict rules sweet as a piece of hard candy. But after Del had died, Roman had stopped doing things like this. Roman had stopped living in many ways, his guilt a smothering phantom.

But he eased his way out onto the roof, his muscles remembering the old motions. He moved to the edge, where the trellis was bolted to the side of the house, fragrant with blooming vines. Roman climbed down, relieved when his shoes hit the grass.

He had moved from shadow to shadow, keeping low and silent, pausing a few times to scan his surroundings. He sought any sign of Val. Any sign of his father's associate Bruce. But there was only a gentle breeze and the freshly bloomed flowers. The willows and the hawthorns and cherry trees. The perfectly manicured shrubs and the dance of a few sly weeds.

Roman continued on his way, reaching the appointed spot. He waited, pacing over the roots. He distracted himself with recounting the events of the day, over and over. But he checked his wristwatch in the moonlight, a knot of worry tightening his chest.

It was now ten forty-seven, and there was no sign of Iris.

Eventually, he was so anxious that he had to sit. He coughed until the pain sharpened and his eyes watered, and he closed them, focusing on his breathing. Slow and deep and meaningful.

He checked his watch again, unable to resist. It was ten fifty-eight.

How long until I give up?

The problem was that Roman didn't like to quit, and he would wait all night for Iris. Until the moon set and the sun broke the horizon, melting all the stars. Until he had no choice but to return to the parlor door.

It was twelve past eleven when he finally heard a branch snap.

Roman stood. He strained his eyes in the shadows, his worry dissolving when he recognized Iris's shape, moving through the brambles.

"Confound it all, Kitt!" she whispered. "You weren't kidding about the thorns."

Roman smiled into the darkness. He took her hand, drawing her from the brambles until she stood before him, so close he could feel her breathe. Moonlight spangled her face, catching in her eyes like stars.

"It's good to see you again too, Winnow," he said, watching a smirk spread across her lips. It evoked a pleasant pang in him, one that made him think of the old days, when he would stand at her desk and pester her. "And I'd give anything to know your thoughts at the moment, and what I've done to earn such a look from you."

"I'm here to call in the favor you owe me," Iris said. "A favor you granted me on a windowsill, far far away."

Roman had been waiting for this moment. How many times had he lain on his bed in the darkness, alone and sleepless, haunted by the longing?

He wove his fingers into Iris's hair and brought his mouth down to hers.

35

Forget Me Not

She tasted just as he remembered. Like sugar in strong black tea. Lavender. The first rays of dawn. Mist that has just burned away from a meadow.

Roman framed her face, his thumbs caressing the blush of her cheeks as his mouth opened to hers. He groaned when her tongue slid along his. She was everything familiar, everything beloved to him, and yet there was a hint of something new and unexpected when her teeth nipped his lower lip. A taunt, a challenge. A side of her that he was desperate to explore and memorize.

An ache spread through him when he felt Iris's hands grasp his shirt, tugging him closer. He eased them to the tree until her back was aligned with it, their feet lost among a tangle of roots.

Breathe, he commanded himself, and he forced his mouth to break from hers. There was no space between their bodies, and he bent lower, his lips tracing her neck, the hollow of her collarbone.

"*Roman,*" Iris whispered. Her voice was husky. Strained. Roman realized she couldn't draw a full breath, not with him pressing her against the tree as if the two of them were on the cusp of becoming immortalized, entwined amongst the branches like a myth.

"Am I hurting you?" he asked, his throat narrow as he eased away.

Iris's fingernails curled into his back, keeping him close. "No. Do you see that light? Over there, through the brambles?"

Roman glanced behind, rigid with dread. He had let himself forget, just for a moment, where they were. The world they lived in. And just as Iris had said, there was a torch beam, sweeping the neighboring property. He wondered if it was Bruce, but he didn't want to find out.

Roman's attention returned to Iris. Half of her face was dappled in darkness, but her eyes gleamed, soft and expectant, as she watched him.

We aren't safe here, he thought as he took her hand in his. The wildfire that had crackled through his blood dimmed, but he could still feel the heat in his bones. Embers waiting to rekindle.

"Come with me," he said, and led her away.

In another time, in another world where the gods had never woken, Roman would have walked Iris through the garden, showing her all his favorite places and stoking fond memories. But that world could only exist in a dream, and Roman held her hand, so warm in his cold one, and hurried her from shadow to shadow, back to the faithful lights of the estate.

They made it safely up the trellis and across the roof, slipping into his bedroom. Roman was short of breath, and he didn't want Iris to notice. He gave himself a moment to recover by closing the window and drawing the curtains. Only then, when the two of them felt tucked into a haven where no god could ever find them, did he watch Iris study his bedroom.

Unsurprisingly, she went to his bookshelves first, her mouth agape. She touched the gilded spines lovingly; it made him want to give them all to her.

"Quite the library," she said, casting him a wry glance. "How many thesauruses do you have on these shelves?"

"Only six."

"*Only?*"

"Half were inherited."

"Ah, I remember now. Some of these books belonged to your grandfather."

He nodded, his gaze following her as she walked to his wardrobe next.

"So *this* is where my letters first came to you," Iris said, opening the carved door.

"Mm. The paper made such a mess on my floor that I had no choice but to read what you wrote."

"All those sharp-edged words of mine. All those thoughts that felt too diffi-cult to speak aloud." She paused, studying his clothes hanging within, starched and arranged by color. "I'm surprised you didn't run from me then."

Perhaps it was her tone, or the words she didn't say but which he could still hear, hidden within the cadence of her breaths. Or the way her vulnerability flickered, like she was lowering a piece of steel.

"On the contrary," he said. "Your words only drew me to you."

She was quiet for a beat before saying, "I might need to borrow one."

"Borrow what?"

"One of your shirts to sleep in. Although your bed is quite narrow. A one-person bed, by the looks of it."

Roman took a step toward her. And then another, until he could count the freckles on her nose. "I thought you learned this about me during our *Gazette* days, Winnow."

"I learned many things that pertained to you in that office," Iris said, brow arched. "You'll have to be more specific."

He leaned down, his mouth angled close to hers. He watched her draw a deep inhale, her lips parting. But he only murmured, "I do love a good chal-lenge."

"Name it, then."

"My bed can fit the two of us."

"If you say so, Kitt."

Before Roman could reach out and touch her, she slipped past him. But he felt the sleeve of her trench coat brush his arm, leaving a trail of gooseflesh behind. He turned to watch her stride to his bed, where she sat on the edge of the mattress, judging its softness.

"I've always wanted to sleep on a cloud," Iris said. She proceeded to lie down, her hair spilling across his pillow.

"Does it meet with your approval?" he teased.

"It does. And you don't know this about me yet, but I steal blankets."

Roman smiled, following her to the bedside. "I do, in fact, know that from experience."

From the night I became yours.

He thought back to it now. The night before the world fell apart. They had been together but in utter darkness. There had only been their bare skin and their hands, their mouths and their names. Discovering each other slowly on a pallet of blankets.

Roman looked at Iris now, fully clothed in her sweater and skirt, trench coat belted at her waist. Stockings up to her knees. Boots coated in dust. She did not seem real in that moment, and he wondered if he was imagining her, like he had countless times before. Envisioning what she would look like in his bed.

"Join me," Iris whispered.

Roman eased down to the mattress, feeling it give beneath his weight. Iris turned on her side to fully look at him, one of her legs sliding between his own, her foot hooking around his ankle. He suddenly felt empty of words, as if the heat of her body had melted them all, but the silence was comfortable. He savored it, watching Iris intently.

She began to trace his face with her fingertips. The arch of his brows, the edge of his jaw, the corner of his lips.

"Do I look the same as you remember?" he asked. It was a foolish question; they had only been separated for a span of weeks. Not years. But he wondered if she could sense the changes that had evolved beneath his skin. The cracks and the wounds. He wondered if Iris would embrace those broken pieces or be wary of them.

"Yes." Iris touched the hollow of his throat, making him shiver. "Do I?"

He returned the caress, following the bridge of her nose, the bow of her lips. The waves of her hair. The dark curl of her eyelashes. And he knew that she had changed too. They weren't the same people that they had been when they first gave each other their vows. It only made him ache for her more, and his fingers drifted along her body, remembering the curve of her ribs.

"*Yes,*" he said.

His hand traveled farther, down to her hip, stopping only when his fingers hit something concealed in her coat.

Roman paused. "Is that a *book* in your pocket?"

"See for yourself," Iris replied.

He did, withdrawing a small green volume from her coat. There was a bird embossed on the cover, but Roman's attention was snagged by the blue envelope that was folded within the leaves. He recognized it with a wince. Reluctantly, he drew Dacre's letter from the pages, setting the book on the bed between them.

"What did he say to you?" Roman asked, his voice thick.

Iris sat forward. Their moment shattered, as if Dacre had crept into the room. Following them like a shadow to a place that had once felt safe.

"You can read it," she said softly.

Roman couldn't resist, his worry and anger getting the better of him.

As he pored over Dacre's words, Iris slipped from the bed. She had removed her boots and coat by the time Roman finished, his blood pounding hot in his veins.

"He thinks you are a bird to collect and keep in a cage," he said, rising from the bed. The paper crinkled in his fist. "A bird that should sing only for him. I hate that he's trying to draw you in."

"I confess that he has a way with words." Iris met Roman's gaze. Her expression was inscrutable. "And if I didn't know his true nature, he might have fooled me. But I have an answer for him. I've thought about it, most of the day."

"And what is your answer?"

She crossed the floor to stand before him, toe to toe and eye to eye, plucking Dacre's letter from his hand with a defiant tilt of her chin.

"He will *never* have me," she said.

Roman watched, spellbound, as Iris tore Dacre's letter into shreds.

She wasted no time, striding into the lavatory. A second later, Roman heard the toilet flush. He imagined Dacre's ink fading in the water. Disintegrating on its way down to the sewer.

"All right, Kitt," Iris said when she reemerged. She crossed her arms and leaned on the door frame. "We need to talk."

"About what?" he asked, surprised by how hoarse he sounded.

"How big this lavatory is!" she exclaimed. "In all my life, I've never seen a shower like yours."

"Would you like to test it as well?"

"I would, actually."

Roman smiled and walked past her into the chamber. The black and white tiles glistened as he opened the glass door and turned the lever. Water cascaded down from the ceiling, enveloping them in a sultry haze.

"There's soap and shampoo on that shelf there," he was saying, adjusting the temperature. "I'll get you a towel—"

Iris's hand on his arm brought him back around. Roman turned to look at her, mist shining in her hair. Slowly, she reached up to touch his leather braces, slipping them off his shoulders. He didn't breathe; his heart felt like it was tethered to a string, tugging deep in his chest. Like he was fastened to her every movement, her every word.

Iris began to unbutton his shirt but she paused halfway down, drawing her lower lip between her teeth.

He stiffened, wondering if the flash of his pale skin was making her hesitate. If she kept going, she would eventually see all his sharp angles. The concave curve of his stomach. The prominence of his ribs. The scars that marred his leg. There was never enough food among Dacre's forces, and hunger had become Roman's closest companion. His scars? A map that he traced, over and over, in his loneliness and solitude.

Shame welled in his throat. Another emotion he couldn't describe coaxed a flush across his skin. He was about to take her hand when Iris said, "I just realized something. You already showered tonight, didn't you?"

Roman let out a huff of air. Relief softened his bones, made him lean closer to her. "I did, but I can still join you, if you want."

She smiled. There was a gleam in her eyes as her deft fingers continued their path, down the buttons to his waist.

"I'd like that, Kitt."

Five minutes later, Roman's palms brimmed with shampoo. The air was warm, the shower close to scalding as the water rushed down their bodies in rivulets. But Iris continued to nudge the lever more and more to the left, as if she wanted her water to feel like fire.

Roman, skin splotched as if he were sunburned, would let her do anything, though.

"Close your eyes," he said.

Iris did, her nose scrunching as water beaded on her face. She gasped when Roman began to wash her hair, kneading the shampoo until it foamed. Again and again, he drew his fingers through her locks, admiring how long and dark they looked when wet. A deep brown with a touch of amber, like wildflower honey.

"This is why you smelled so good at the office," Iris sighed.

Roman began to rinse the shampoo, pleased when she groaned. "Did I?"

"The electricity could be out on the winter solstice, and I would know the moment you stepped into the *Gazette*. I hated you for it too."

He grinned as he drew circles on her back with the bar of soap. The scent of evergreen and meadow grass spread across the eaves of her shoulders. The curve of her spine. "And look where that disdain has brought you."

"I would have laughed if you had revealed my fate to me then."

"I know," he said.

Iris was quiet. The water continued to fall, filling the chamber with a mesmerizing drone, when she turned to face him. His gaze dropped, following the line of her body to her legs, where his attention stopped and held.

Roman had noticed when he had eased down her stockings. The bruises and scabs on her knees. And he hadn't told her, but he had watched her run through the meadow of Hawk Shire from the second-story window. He had seen with his own disbelieving eyes how she had dodged the gunshots. How a motorcar's headlights had cut through the darkness, carrying her away.

Run, Iris.

He had felt those kilometers like an illness, spreading through him. Blood to bone to organ. The distance that waxed like the moon. The wondering and the worries as to where she was going and if he would ever see her again.

Roman set down the soap.

He sank to his knees before her, his hands touching those tender marks on her skin. They told him she was strong and brave, but also that she was *his*. Their souls weren't mirrors but complements, constellations that burned side by side.

I want you to see me, he had once written to her. *I want you to know me.*

He pressed his face to her legs. He felt her bruises as if they were his own and he traced them with his lips, tasting the water on her skin. His blood was pounding, hot and fast. A summer thunderstorm in his veins, and yet the moment Iris touched his hair, Roman's mind stilled.

He looked up at her face, rosy and dark-eyed.

"I was so worried," Iris whispered.

"And what had you worried?"

"That you and I would never have another moment like this again."

Roman swallowed. He could have said a hundred things, but he realized she was shaking. He realized he was as well.

"You're trembling," he said. "Is the water too cold? Do you want me to stop?"

"Gods, no. I was only thinking how strange it is. To think how many people we cross paths with in our lives. How someone like me has found someone like you. And if I had never written that essay and sent it to the *Gazette* on a whim . . . would we still be here?"

"Are you getting philosophical on me, Iris?"

"I can't seem to help it. You bring out the very best and the very worst in me."

"I certainly bring out the best. But the worst?"

She only held his stare, water dripping from her jaw like tears. But then she caressed his hair again, a soft touch that he felt down to his toes. It wasn't power or fear or magic that cleaved his heart open but her hand, gentle with adoration.

"And the answer is yes, by the way," he said, kissing the curve of her knee. "I would have still found you, even if you had never written that essay."

The hot water went out three minutes later.

Roman grappled with the lever, shutting off the valve as frigid water sluiced over them. Iris gasped, but he didn't know if it was from the shock of cold or from the way he stood and took her in his arms, carrying her from the shower.

This wasn't what he had envisioned for the night, but when Iris wrapped her legs around his waist and kissed him, Roman decided that, for the first time in his life, he preferred to live in the moment.

He walked her to the bed and laid her down. His breaths were ragged; water dripped like rain down his back. But the sight of her chased away the lingering cold.

The way Iris gazed up at him, her eyes dark as new moons, drawing him in like the tides. The way she held to him, whispering his name against his throat. How she moved with him, in the light as well as in the darkness. The feel of her skin against his; the sensation of being bare and yet whole. Safe and complete.

She saw him as he saw her. With eyes open, with eyes shut.

As the stars faithfully burned beyond the window, Roman had never been more certain.

He could wake in the deepest region of Dacre's realm, as far from the moon and sun as divinity could shackle him. He could wake and not know his name, forgetting every word he had ever written. But he would never forget the scent of Iris's skin, the sound of her voice. The way she had looked at him. The confidence of her hands.

And he thought, *There is no magic above or below that will ever steal this from me again.*

36

Guests, Indefinitely

Iris dreamt of the Revel Diner. She sat at the bar with a book and a glass of lemonade before her, watching as her mother waited on tables. It felt like any other day, a page torn from her past, for she had often visited the diner before the war. Before Aster had started to drink heavily. That was how Iris knew she was dreaming. Her mother looked vibrant and whole again, quick to smile and laugh, her eyes bright as she moved around the café.

"Another lemonade, Iris?" Aster said as she returned behind the bar.

Before Iris could reply, a song crackled over the radio, filling the café with the melancholy tone of a violin. At once, the hair rose on her arms. There it was again. The melody that haunted her dreams when she saw her mother.

"Mum?" Iris whispered, leaning over the bar. "Why do I hear this song every time we meet in a dream?"

Aster set down a steaming coffeepot. "Do you know who Alzane was?"

Iris was startled by the abrupt change in topics, but said, "He was one of the last kings of Cambria, before the monarchy fell and chancellors were appointed."

"Yes, but there is far more to him than that. He was the monarch who oversaw the divine graves. He buried Dacre, Mir, Alva, Luz, and Enva centuries ago.

In a myth that has been cut away from our history, he inspired this lullaby to sing the gods to sleep. Since then, there have been many iterations of it, but the power of the notes remains, even if they have been forgotten by many."

Iris mulled that over. The world beyond the café windows was beginning to darken. A storm was brewing. Rain slid down the glass, and flickers of lightning illuminated distant buildings.

"I don't think Enva was ever buried," Iris dared to say, to which Aster quirked her red-stained lips to the side. "I think she struck a deal with the king, and she sang the other four to sleep while she remained hidden in Oath."

"A wild theory, sweetheart. But one that may have some truth within it."

Iris listened to the music, but her breath caught when the radio's static intensified and the dream began to break. Desperate, she reached out to take hold of Aster, but her mother had already faded into the shadows. The café began to spin, the glass windows cracking beneath the weight of the storm, until the pressure felt unbearable.

Iris startled awake.

A beat later, she realized a cough had woken her; the mattress beneath her shook as Roman rolled away, rising to his feet. With her eyes open to the darkness, she listened as he stifled another cough, then another. They sounded wet and painful, and she quickly sat forward and turned toward him.

A sliver of moonlight that snuck in through the curtains limned his body. His pale shoulders were hunched; she could count the ridges of his spine as he reached for his discarded shirt on the floor and coughed into the fabric, muffling the sound.

"Kitt," she whispered, moving to the edge of the bed. The floor was icy cold on her bare feet; her hair was still damp from the shower. "Are you all right?"

He straightened, but kept the shirt pressed to his mouth for a moment more. He cleared his throat and said, "I'm fine, Iris. Sorry, I didn't mean to wake you."

She stood and walked to him. "Can I get you anything?"

"You plan to sneak down to the kitchen and boil a pot of tea for me?"

He was teasing, but it only made Iris realize how impossible this was. How impossible *they* were. Mr. Kitt would be outraged to find her in his house, sharing a bed with his son. He would probably throw her out if he caught her wandering the corridors, or have his associate drag her off and drop her somewhere for the Graveyard to punish.

"If you want tea," Iris said, her voice husky and determined, "then I will sneak down to the kitchen and make it for you. Simply tell me what you'd like. And how to find the kitchen, of course."

Roman turned, a few tendrils of his black hair dangling over his right eye. Sometimes his beauty still struck her, made her knees feel weak. She realized that she loved the sight of him in the night just as much as she did in the day. How the darkness made him seem sharper in some ways and softer in others, like he was a starlit portrait in the process of being painted.

"I know you make a bloody good pot of tea, but I'm fine," he said. "Truly."

She didn't believe him. She was opening her mouth to protest when he continued.

"Sometimes I have a hard time breathing at night. My throat feels narrow. I've had a cough ever since my memories returned, but it's nothing that I can't handle."

"From the gas," Iris whispered.

Roman nodded. "When this is over, I'll seek proper treatment. See if a doctor in Oath can help me."

"Dacre doesn't know?"

"No. And I don't want him to. If he did, then he would realize his influence over me has broken. That I am no longer a captive to him. That I know he only healed me enough to make me pliable and confused."

He fell pensive, glancing down at the shirt in his hands. Iris was worried there would be blood on the fabric, and she could feel panic climbing her bones. But it was still the flawless white linen it had been before, save for a few wrinkles it had now garnered, from when she had tossed his shirt to the floor.

"You're cold," Roman said, studying her in the moonlight.

"A little," she confessed. "But I don't mind it."

"Give me a few moments, and I'll join you in the bed again. Since it does, in fact, fit two people."

She smiled and returned to the feather down mattress, still warm from their bodies. But her heart was heavy. She listened as Roman walked to the lavatory and turned on the sink faucet, drinking a cup of water. She was thinking about doctors and if it would be possible to find a way to sneak him medicine when Roman slipped under the covers.

"There's something I need to tell you, Iris."

"Then tell me, Kitt."

He sighed as he lay face-to-face with her.

Iris could feel herself grow stiff with unease. "Is it *that* terrible?"

"Yes. Dacre took me to Luz's grave."

The statement made Iris freeze. She listened as Roman told her about that stormy afternoon on the hill, not far from Hawk Shire.

"You think Dacre planned to kill Luz, then?" Iris surmised. "But it didn't happen because . . ."

"Someone already killed him," Roman concluded. "Which makes me suspect Alva and Mir are also dead in their graves. Or wouldn't they have woken by now, alongside Dacre?"

"Who would have killed them?"

Roman was quiet, but he reached out to trace the moonlight on Iris's face. "I think it was Enva."

They didn't drift off to sleep after that.

They continued talking, recounting the events that had led them each here. Roman told Iris of the keys, the doorways, the sulfur pools, the flute, and the ride on the eithral's back. She listened to every word, sharing pieces of her story as well. All the parts that Roman had been wondering about. Eventually, they shifted away from dire topics to more lighthearted ones, their arms and legs wound together, fingers carding through each other's hair as if they had all the time in the world to wake up slowly.

Roman could have listened to Iris for hours. When he noticed the darkness fading, he held to her tighter, as if his will could stop time. But sunrise was imminent, and they would have no choice but to let go as the light spilled into his bedroom.

It wasn't daybreak that drove him from the bed but the sounds of the servants on the floor below, moving furniture.

"Are there early risers in your family?" Iris asked as she took note of the predawn noise.

"Yes, but my father keeps to his study." Roman frowned. "We should probably go. I need to get you back through the garden before anyone notices. But first . . . I have something for you."

He forced himself up from the blankets, kneeling beside his desk. He removed the loose floorboard, the place where he had once hidden childhood treasures as well as Iris's many letters, and he brought out her wedding band and the map he had drawn.

"It kept me good company," Roman said, sliding the ring onto Iris's finger. "But I much prefer it on you."

Iris studied it, the silver winking in the morning light. "Are you sure you don't need it?"

"I'm certain. And this is a *very* poorly drawn map." He set it into her hands next, watching her brow furrow as she sought to make sense of it.

"A map of . . . ?"

"A ley line in Oath."

Iris's eyes widened. She listened as Roman explained to her what he had seen, the doors that might be enchanted should they be turned with a key.

"Kitt," she breathed, tracing his drawing with her finger. "This is brilliant."

"I hoped you would say that."

"Would it be too much trouble to ask for other ley lines, should you come across them?"

Roman shook his head. "I have access to the war table. I'll see what I can do."

Iris gazed up at him, her eyes shining. For a moment, he almost went to her, almost eased her back down to the warm tangle of the blankets, but a thud from the floor below brought him back to his senses.

There will be another time, he told himself as they rushed to don their clothes. *This is not the end.*

And yet, in some strange way, it *felt* like it was as Roman opened the window. He took Iris's hand, easing her over the sill.

He followed her across the slant of roof and down the trellis, and he took her back the way they had come. The light strengthened by the second, making the dew glitter on the grass and the flowers lift their heads and the trees look stark as the shadow melted.

When they reached the oak and the arbor of brambles, Roman hesitated, tightening his hold on Iris's hand.

"I'll see you soon," she whispered.

He nodded but drew her close, kissing her open-mouthed and ravenous, his tongue sliding along hers, until he forced himself to break away. He stepped back, but his gaze remained on her.

"Be safe, Iris," he said. "I'll write to you first, when I've returned to my station."

"I'll try to be patient," she replied.

That provoked a small smile from him. "I never scolded you for that, by the way. As you asked me to do in person."

Iris gave him a wicked grin. "Next time, then? Oh, and you were right, Kitt."

"About what, Winnow?"

She waited to answer until she had almost vanished among the brambles, her voice carrying through the vines. "Your bed fits the two of us perfectly."

He had to hurry back, coughing into his sleeve. Uneasy, Roman climbed the trellis, unable to take a full breath until he was safe in his room again, the window closed behind him.

He only had a few more minutes, and he straightened his room. He made the bed, smoothing all traces of him and Iris from the blankets, but his hand froze when he saw the small green book resting on the rug.

Iris's bird volume.

Roman picked it up, leafing through the old pages. He almost put it on the shelf with his other books, but he stopped himself at the last minute. This was such a tiny tome. Something he could easily carry with him. A tangible reminder of her.

He slipped it into his pocket.

He was opening his wardrobe door to find his jumpsuit when he felt the house shake. It was distinct enough to make him pause, a shudder crawling down his spine.

Roman walked from his room, listening to the sounds that echoed through the corridors. There were distant male voices, more shifting furniture, the sound of boots on hardwood floors.

He hurried down the hallway, stiff with trepidation.

His ankles popped as he descended the stairs, leaving the sleepy shadows of the upper story for the brightly lit ground floor, and he froze when he was five steps from the bottom, staring into the parlor.

The wardrobe door was wide open, chilling the air. But a fire was burning in the marble hearth. Officers and soldiers were milling about the chamber, moving the furniture so a table could be brought in. The war table, Roman recognized.

His hands curled into fists until he felt the bite of his nails, but the vision before him didn't waver or break. It only came into sharper focus when he saw the servants carry in trays of coffee and scones, setting them down for the officers and soldiers to serve themselves. When he saw his father, standing off to the side with his mug of brandy-laced coffee, watching the activity with approval. When he saw Lieutenant Shane emerge from the under realm, carrying the typewriter.

Roman's gaze fixed on that familiar black case, his distress surging on seeing the lieutenant handling it. He was devising a way to recover his typewriter when someone stepped into his view. Someone fair and tall with broad shoulders, flaxen hair, and eyes blue as the sky.

Dacre stood in the foyer, staring up at Roman on the stairs.

Their gazes met. Roman suddenly felt small and helpless. But his mind whirled, overcome with thoughts that only grew stronger the longer the silence stretched between them.

Has he come to wipe my memories again? Does he doubt me? Can he sense Iris's presence on my skin?

"Hello Roman," Dacre greeted him. "I see your father got my letter."

37

Those Hidden Strings

Iris took the tram but decided to exit at the university stop. She walked along the street beneath a line of sycamore trees whose gnarled roots were pushing up through the cobblestones. The sun was still making its ascent, spangling the pavement as Iris brushed shoulders with students hurrying to class.

She turned a corner and approached Attie's town house.

It was a three-story building, built of red brick, with navy shutters and an oakwood door embellished with carvings of the moon phases. Tendrils of ivy grew along its side, and flower boxes brightened the windows. Iris walked the stone path and up the porch stairs to ring the bell, noticing a few bicycles lying in the small grassy yard, as well as a kite with a knotted tail.

"I'll get it!" someone cried from within, and Iris could hear the pattering of feet and the lock turning.

She smiled when she saw one of Attie's younger sisters standing in the doorway. She wore a blue gingham dress and ribbons in her black hair.

"Hi," the girl said. "You're Thea's friend, aren't you?"

"Yes," Iris replied. "Is she home?"

"Thea! *Thea!* Your friend from the paper is here!"

There was the distant clink of dishes, a few more excited murmurs.

"Invite her in, Ainsley!" Attie hollered back.

Ainsley opened the door wider. "Come in."

"Thank you." Iris stepped over the threshold, but she waited until Ainsley had closed the door before she followed her down the hall.

Attie's family was gathered at the table, finishing breakfast. The dining room was painted a dark blue, with constellations dabbed in silver, all the way to the ceiling. Maps and photographs were framed on the walls, as were a few colorful drawings. Books were piled at the back of a china cabinet, which held teacups as well as multiple pairs of binoculars.

It was a welcoming room, and Iris soaked in in. She realized a beat later that Attie's five siblings and her parents were gazing up at her, expectant. Attie was the only one who continued eating, draining her tea and scraping the last of the butter off her plate with her toast.

"Would you like to join us, Iris?" Attie's mother asked. She was already dressed for the day in a plaid dress, her curly black hair brushing the tops of her shoulders.

"I'm so sorry, I didn't mean to interrupt," Iris said. "I was passing by the neighborhood and thought I'd stop by to see if Attie would like to walk to work together."

One of Attie's little brothers, who had an identical twin sitting beside him, laughed until Attie shot him a warning glance. It looked like he might have also been kicked beneath the table. Iris had no idea what that meant, and didn't have time to dwell on it, because Attie's father spoke.

"You're not interrupting, Iris!" Mr. Attwood shifted the glasses on his nose. He had a rich, deep voice and a gentle smile. He reached for the teapot and said, "We have more than enough if you're hungry."

"Thank you, Mr. Attwood. But, truly, I'm fine."

Attie stood from her chair with her empty plate in hand. "I'm glad you're here. I wanted to show you something before work. Follow me."

Iris waved to the family before following Attie into the kitchen.

Attie set down her dirty dishes. "Are you all right?" she whispered.

Iris blinked. "Yes. Why do you ask?"

"You're wearing the same clothes as yesterday."

Iris opened her mouth, but before she could say a word, Ainsley came bursting into the kitchen carrying her own dishes. She took her time at the sink, casting a surreptitious glance their way, as if she wanted to hear everything they said. Iris was thankful for the interruption, although Attie only cocked her brow at her little sister.

"You wanted to show me something?" Iris reminded her.

"Hmm." Attie led her down to the basement. It was cooler here, but just as cozy as the ground floor, with plush furniture, a purring cat—which Iris fondly recognized as Lilac, the feline Attie had saved from Avalon Bluff—on one of the cushions, and a host of paintings crowding the wall. A few paper stars hung from the ceiling, and Iris gazed up at them while Attie removed one of the hanging frames.

"Do you remember that story I told you, weeks ago on Marisol's roof?" Attie said, carefully setting the oil painting of the ocean to the side.

Iris remembered every word. "Yes. You told me about your violin."

"Would you like to see it?"

Wordless, Iris stepped closer to Attie, watching as she opened the door of a metal safe nestled into the wall. It was hard to believe that what they were doing was now illegal in Oath: being in the presence of a stringed instrument. It sent a shiver down Iris's back when she saw Attie hold her violin out in the space between them, its chestnut-colored wood gleaming in the lamplight.

"It's beautiful," Iris whispered, tracing the cold strings. "I'd love to hear you play it someday."

A nostalgic expression crossed Attie's face, but she gave her violin a soft caress before returning it to its case and closing the safe's door. Once the painting was back on the wall, Iris would have never known a violin was there, hiding behind the rolling waves of a painted sea.

"Only your parents know where it hides?" Iris said.

Attie nodded. "I used to play down here when the siblings were in class. When no one was home to hear me but Papa. Sometimes my mum. I honestly haven't played since I left for the front." Another flicker of sadness passed in her eyes until she met Iris's gaze, and something like steel flashed within her. "And I dreamt about 'Alzane's Lullaby' last night."

Iris's heart quickened. "As did I. How is this happening? Why are we dreaming about the same song?"

Attie gave her a wry smile. "Magic, obviously."

"You think a divine is trying to send us a message in dreams?"

"Yes. Which made me think about that myth you published in the paper. The one about Dacre being controlled by music in his realm." Attie gathered the purring Lilac into her arms, scratching behind her ears. "If Enva's harp could coax him to sleep with 'Alzane's Lullaby' . . . why not a violin? Why not a cello? Why not any stringed instrument? Maybe *that* is the true reason why the chancellor outlawed everything with strings. Not out of fear of Enva recruiting us to war, but because we ourselves could tame a god with our music if we only knew how to reach the realm below."

Iris was quiet, but her mind was racing. She knew where the active door was—in the Kitts' parlor. Her best friend had a violin. They knew the power of "Alzane's Lullaby." The only thing they lacked was knowledge of Dacre's exact location, or a way to coerce him underground. Roman could possibly help provide that information, though, and Iris suddenly felt shaky with apprehension.

"If we put Dacre to sleep . . ." Iris began.

"Then we could kill him," Attie concluded.

Lilac emitted a meow as if in agreement. Iris reached out to stroke the cat's fur.

"This lullaby we've dreamt of. Could you play it on your violin?"

"I can, but I need the full composition." Attie set the cat down on the couch. "I had a music professor a few years ago at university. I'm going to make an appointment with her, hopefully for tomorrow, and see if she can't help me obtain it. Apparently there have been many iterations of the song over the decades, and I need to make sure I'm playing the right one. The one we've been hearing in our dreams."

"Thea?" Her father suddenly called down to the basement. "Your ride is here."

"Coming, Papa!" Attie replied. She led Iris back up the stairs. "Perhaps we can meet up for dinner somewhere and talk more about this? You still owe me and Prindle a fancy meal, by the way."

Iris laughed as they reached the main floor. "You're right. For breaking and entering."

"Breaking and entering where?" Ainsley asked. She seemed to have come from thin air, her lunch pail in one hand, slate tablet in the other.

"Nothing," Attie replied quickly. "You ready for school, Ains?"

She nodded, her blue ribbons bobbing.

"Good. He's waiting for you on the curb." Attie guided Iris to the front door in Ainsley's wake, grabbing her purse and coat from the foyer rack. "Now listen. Don't get any grand ideas about this."

Iris gave her a bewildered look. "About what?"

Attie motioned to the open doorway. Iris looked to see none other than Tobias Bexley and his roadster, parked just outside the town house. Attie's siblings were gathered in the back seat, and Tobias was standing by the vehicle's dented door, laughing at something her brother was saying.

"He drives them to school, even though it's only five minutes away, and then me to work," said Attie.

"Since when?" Iris asked, smiling.

"Since yesterday." Attie began the walk to the curb, drawing Tobias's attention. "But we'll see how long he lasts with my siblings in tow."

"Are you sure I can't feed you three?" Marisol asked for the third time. Her black hair was wound into a low bun, and she was stirring a huge pot of porridge over a campfire. Lucy was beside her, stoic as usual and dressed in coveralls, pouring coffee for the soldiers who came by with their metal cups.

"I just ate, but thank you," Attie said.

Iris and Tobias also declined, although Iris could feel her stomach growl. After Tobias had driven around the block to drop Attie's siblings off at school, Iris had asked him if he could drive her to what had been dubbed the Drill Field—which in Iris's mind was better known as the-field-where-the-chancellor-barred-Enva's-army—just outside of Oath.

"How have things been here?" Iris asked.

"Good," Marisol replied in a cheerful tone. "The rain finally eased off and the ground has dried out, as you can see. Still a bit muddy in places, but much improved. And your article has been very helpful. So many people are now coming from the city to deliver food and other resources to us here. The support has been heartening. Thank you for writing it."

It was the article that had upset the Graveyard. The wounded had still been barred entrance to Oath, but support had trickled out from the city gates. Citizens had delivered food, clean water, blankets, medical supplies, laundry, and even things as simple as a pair of socks. Doctors and nurses from the hospital had brought medicine, cots, and relief to the field surgeons.

"Of course," Attie said, drawing out a small pad of paper from her back pocket. "Any further updates or needs I can write about today?"

While Marisol and Lucy both listed more requests for the soldiers, Keegan finally appeared, walking up a well-worn path between tents.

"Good morning, Brigadier," Iris greeted her. "Do you have a moment to speak with me?"

"Iris." Keegan nodded a hello. "Yes, come in." She ducked into one of the bigger tents, Iris close behind.

It was surprisingly homey inside, with rugs laid down over the ground, lamps hanging from above, and a few pieces of furniture. There was a table with a map of the city unrolled on it, the paper's edges held down by small stones. Iris stopped before it, her eyes racing over the intricate drawing of each street, until she found the Kitts' estate in the northern part of the city.

"How can I help you, Iris?" Keegan asked.

"I have something. From Roman." She produced the sketch, laying it down on the table.

Keegan leaned closer with a frown, not understanding until Iris explained it to her, pointing to the corresponding street on the map of the city.

"This is very helpful to know," Keegan said, placing coins over the buildings they suspected had the magical doorways. "But there's nothing I can do about this, Iris. My forces have been barred from the city. If an attack occurs, I can only provide support from the outside while the chancellor's law still holds. Lucy has also informed us of the existence of the Graveyard, who seem dedicated to seeing no one fight for either god. I can only imagine what might happen if we were to enter Oath under Enva's banner, even as protection for the people."

Iris bit her lip. There were many things she wanted to say, but she held them back, refolding Roman's drawing. "I understand, Brigadier."

Keegan must have sensed her disappointment. She leaned on the table, lowering her voice as she said, "Do you remember when Dacre bombed the Bluff? How some houses fell while others remained upright?"

Iris was quiet, but she remembered everything about that day. How she had stood on the hillside, dazed and overwhelmed by the suffering and destruction. How when she had looked back at the town, it had seemed like a web had been cast. Lines of protection amidst utter demolition.

"Yes," Iris whispered. "I remember seeing that." Marisol's B and B had been on one of those lines, its walls refusing to crumble even as its windows had shattered and the doorways had settled into strange angles.

Keegan pointed to the street of Oath that Roman had drawn. The street that they knew was also an under realm pathway. A ley line.

"I think houses that are built atop these passages can withstand Dacre's bombs. His own magic, working against him. They will be the safest places to take shelter, should another attack happen."

Chills swept down Iris's arms. "Safe places from the bombs, but what of the doorways that lead below?"

Keegan grimaced. "Yes, it's a dilemma. The safest place from one thing can be dangerous for another. But how are the doorways changed?"

"Roman mentioned keys being able to make the thresholds shift."

"Then find out more about these keys," Keegan said. "How do they work? How many exist? And if your Kitt can provide any further guidance on the ley lines . . . then we could build our own map. Of places to shelter in the city should it come to the worst."

Iris nodded, but her heart pounded at the thought.

It wasn't until she was walking back to the parked roadster with Attie and Tobias that she sensed it.

"Looks like we're going to be late to work," Attie was saying.

"I can still get you there on time," Tobias replied.

Iris stopped abruptly in the grass. There was a slight rumble in the ground; she could feel it through the soles of her boots.

"Wait . . ." Attie also sensed it, coming to a halt. "Is that what I think it is?"

Iris couldn't speak. Time suddenly felt like it was rushing along too quickly, as if a clock had lost a gear, losing minutes by the hour.

But it was exactly what Attie thought.

Dacre's forces had almost reached Oath from below.

It had been a long, surreal day. One that had seen Roman essentially under house arrest, with Dacre, his select officers, and his best soldiers milling through the rooms, invading all the spaces that had once felt safe to Roman.

His typewriter remained on the war table in the transformed parlor, as if Dacre had decided it was his. Everything in the estate, actually, seemed to be *his* now, and Roman's father had let him take that ownership without batting an eye. Even the books that had been on Roman's shelves, Dacre had confiscated to leaf through.

All morning, Roman had watched as Dacre tore some pages out, tossing them to burn in the fire. Pages of myths that could never be reclaimed. Pages that Dacre didn't like because their ink limned his true nature.

It made Roman's head ache. All those pages, lost to ash. His grandfather's books ruined.

Dacre had only been interrupted when a covered motorcar with black drapes shielding its windows pulled into the Kitts' drive. It was the chancellor, covertly arriving for a meeting, as Dacre's presence in Oath was still a heavily guarded secret. Roman was sent away from the room then, to sit with his mother and nan in the west wing of the estate. As far from the god and the war as his father could put the women.

But by sundown, Roman had still failed to come up with a clever way to get the typewriter back in his possession.

Exhausted, he retreated to his room.

It was dark, save for the moonlight that flooded in through the windows.

Roman stared at the very window he and Iris had crawled through—had it only been that morning?—before he sighed and stepped deeper into the chamber.

From the corner of his eye, he could see a patch of white on the floor, just before the wardrobe.

It caught his attention; his breath hissed through his teeth as he realized what it was. A letter, from Iris. He rushed to it, his knees hitting the hardwood as he gathered the paper into his hands.

"Light the lamp," he whispered hoarsely, and the house obeyed. His desk lamp flickered on, washing the room in golden light.

Roman trembled as he unfolded the paper. It looked creased, worn. There were smudges of dirt on it, but he was so relieved that he couldn't think straight. He didn't wonder how this impossibility had happened, since his typewriter was still in the parlor and not his room. He didn't wonder why this letter looked so tattered, and he read as if starved for the words:

I'll return most likely when the war is over.

I want to see you. I want to hear your voice.

P.S. I most certainly don't have wings.

Roman froze.

He knew these words, intimately. He had read them, over and over. He had carried them in his pocket; he had borne them in the trenches. Iris had both tossed these words at him in the infirmary, and then breathed life into them on their wedding night, giving the ink her voice.

This was an old letter. A letter she had written to him weeks ago, and one he had believed to be lost.

"How?" he marveled aloud, sitting back on his heels. His knees twinged in protest, but the pain turned into crackling static when he heard footsteps. When he saw a figure emerge from the lavatory.

Roman gazed up at Lieutenant Shane. Wide-eyed. Unable to breathe. Clutching Iris's letter to his chest like it was a shield.

Shane held up a stack of paper. Worn and crinkled and full of typed words. He threw the letters down; they spread across the rug. White as apple blossoms, as bone, as the first snowfall.

Shane's voice was pitched low, but his accusation burned through the air.

"I know you're the mole, correspondent."

38

By Invitation Only

W hat do you mean?" Roman asked.

He knew he sounded dense, but he was struggling to breathe. To think his way through this unforeseen encounter, one that could end either with him tortured and hung from his father's gate or with him coming through the night with the most unlikely of allies.

Shane stepped closer, his boots crinkling the letters on the rug. Roman winced but didn't break their stare. He didn't move or cower when the lieutenant reached into his pocket, but it was only to procure another folded sheet of paper.

He held it out to Roman, daring him to take it.

Swallowing, Roman accepted.

This paper was crisp, fresh. But he could see the inked words within, and he unfolded it to read:

This is a test to see if the strike bars **E & R** are in working condition.

EREEERRRRR

E

"You find this incriminating?" Roman asked, but it felt like ice had lodged in his stomach. "I type these messages out occasionally before I start work, because the strike bars E and R often get stuck, and I don't want to—"

"Don't lie to me, correspondent," Shane said in a clipped voice. "And don't take me for a fool. I know you've been exchanging letters by way of enchanted typewriters and wardrobe doors. With someone you call E., who looks to be, in fact, Iris *Elizabeth* Winnow. A journalist championing Enva's cause."

The sound of Iris's name broke through Roman's fear like an axe in a frozen pond. Anger stirred his blood, making his skin flush hot. If Shane had all the old letters as well as the newer ones, then he had a good deal of knowledge that Roman would prefer he didn't have. The main piece being that he had identified Iris, which meant Roman needed to play a different game.

He dropped his clueless guise.

"What do you want?" Roman asked.

"I want your confession, in writing."

"What confession? That I fell in love with someone before Dacre found me?"

"I want to know everything you typed to Elizabeth . . . no wait, sorry. To *Iris E. Winnow* about the Hawk Shire assault."

"You have no proof that I was the one who tipped them off."

"So certain, are we?"

Roman was silent, wondering why Shane sounded so confident. He only had half of the puzzle. He only had Iris's letters, and the one that Roman had typed with all the information on Hawk Shire? He had asked Iris to burn it.

Shane withdrew another letter from his pocket.

Roman braced himself as the lieutenant read, "'I do agree to what you ask, but only because you seem to have stolen the words from my mouth. *You* are in a precarious position—far more than me—and giving up Dacre's movements and tactics is something I dread to ask you to do, even as it feels inevitable.'" Shane paused, glancing at Roman with a cruel smile. "Is that enough to jog your memory?"

Cold sweat began to seep through Roman's shirt.

It was his own fault that Shane had found such an incriminating letter. Roman was supposed to destroy them after reading, leaving no trace of his and Iris's correspondence. He had tried, *gods* how he had tried. He had lit a match and held it to the edge of one of the letters, but he hadn't been able to watch it catch flame. And so he had hidden them beneath a loose floorboard.

"You, correspondent," Shane began with a shake of his head, "are admirably bold but remarkably foolish. You should have destroyed her letters, like she told you to do."

"*If* I write this confession," Roman said, ragged. "What then? You turn me over to Dacre?"

Shane was quiet, as if weighing his options. In that span of silence, the night seemed to tilt toward balance again, for reasons that Roman didn't quite understand. But he waited, Iris's letters still in his hands.

"No," Shane replied. "Unless you do something that would warrant it."

"Such as?"

"Betray me first."

"And why would I betray you, Lieutenant?"

Shane reached into his pocket a third time. He took out another letter, but this one was unfamiliar to Roman. It was a proper envelope, sealed with wax. There was no name scrawled over the face of it, and it was light as a feather when Roman reluctantly accepted it.

"Tomorrow morning, the chancellor is going to announce an impromptu press conference," Shane said in a low voice. "It will take place in the Green Quarter, a little courtyard in the Promontory Building. It will be by invitation only, and this is when the chancellor plans to give the stage to Dacre, to allow him to make a plea to the most influential people of Oath. To see if bloodshed can be averted in his plans to take the city. Dacre will ask you to accompany him, as you are his correspondent. *Before* he takes the stage, I need you to deliver this message to someone very important."

"What is this message?" Roman asked.

"That isn't your concern," Shane countered. "But you will need to be quick about it, without Dacre or his other officers noticing. There will be a man wearing a red anemone pinned to his lapel in the crowd. This envelope needs to be handed directly to him. Once you do that . . . leave the court-yard immediately."

"Why?"

"Trust me. You won't want to be there."

Roman was quiet. He didn't trust Shane, but the warning sat like smoke in the air.

"Do you agree to do this?" the lieutenant asked, impatient. "Or should I present Iris's letters to Dacre now?"

Roman studied the envelope in his hand. He didn't know what to think of this situation; he could be delivering a message far worse than the ones he had been dutifully typing up for Dacre. But after so many weeks living in fear and ignorance, the truth was coming to light. Shane was not devoted to Dacre any more than Roman was. And Roman was not the mole; Shane truly was, if he had worked his way up in rank with the sole purpose of betraying the god he claimed to serve.

What does he want? Roman wondered, but then realized Shane might be involved with the Graveyard.

"I'll do it," Roman said. "But I would like Iris's letters back."

"You can keep the letters on the floor."

The old letters. The ones she wrote before Roman was torn away from her. The ones that Shane couldn't use as leverage over him.

"Where did you find them?" he couldn't resist asking.

"At the B and B, just after we took Avalon Bluff. I was clearing the space for Dacre's arrival and found them in an upstairs room. I read them and thought they were . . . quite moving, you could say. So I decided to keep them for a rainy day."

Roman couldn't tell if Shane was being honest or mocking him.

In the end, it didn't really matter. They were both holding something over the other, and Roman needed to adapt. He needed to learn the steps to this new waltz.

"My typewriter," he said, slowly rising. His feet throbbed with pins and needles. "I need it to type the confession."

"You can write with a pen," Shane said. "And I'd avoid making a claim on that typewriter. He's growing more suspicious by the hour. Don't make him doubt you. Don't give him any reason to start you at square one again."

Roman had no reply to that. He walked to sit at his desk, a motion he had done a hundred times before, but this time it felt different. His hands felt weathered as he found a sheet of paper and a fountain pen from the drawer.

His heart was pounding. Worry and disgust shot through his veins, made his mouth dry.

Soon, he had promised Iris. This would all be over soon, and he would take her to the places she longed to go, as if life had never been interrupted.

Soon.

That promise was beginning to feel fragile, unattainable. A ship that was gliding farther and farther out to open sea.

But Roman wrote his confession.

Silent and grim, he surrendered it to Shane.

Iris stared at her typewriter through the curling drift of cigarette smoke. It was half past nine in the morning, and she was at the *Inkridden Tribune,* trying to write her next article.

But the words wouldn't come.

She was thinking of the fact that she still hadn't heard from Roman when Helena arrived at the table.

"Attie gone for the day?" Helena asked, noticing Attie's chair was empty.

"She's meeting with a former professor," Iris replied. "But she'll be back before lunch. Why? Did you need something?"

"No," Helena said. There was an unlit cigarette in her mouth, but her eyes looked brighter, as if she had been finally getting some good rest. "A letter came for you in today's post."

Iris accepted it, surprised by how the envelope felt like velvet. Her name was written in bold handwriting, and there was purple wax on the back, pressed with the city seal.

"What is this?" she asked, hesitant.

"Not sure," Helena said. "But I'd like to see for myself, since it was delivered to the office."

Iris opened it, wincing when the edge of the envelope cut her fingertip. She withdrew a deckle-edged piece of paper and read:

Miss Iris Winnow,

You are cordially invited by the chancellor himself to a press conference, to take place today, at half past five in the evening in the Green Quarter, located in the prestigious Promontory Building. As this is an exclusive invitation, it also serves as your pass for entrance. Please come dressed in your finest, for this will be a cause for celebration. As always, thank you for your devotion to the good of this city, and for being one of Oath's leading minds and innovators.

Sincerely,

Edward L. Verlice

Chancellor Fifty-Three of Eastern Borough and Protector of Oath

Iris handed the invite to Helena, who scowled the entire time she read it.

"Do you want to go, kid?" Helena asked.

"Shouldn't I?" Iris pressed against the sting of her paper cut. "It sounds important, although I don't know why they invited *me*, of all people."

"Because you're writing about the war. And this"—Helena stabbed the invitation—"most likely will have something to do with Dacre's imminent approach."

Iris bit her lip and reread the chancellor's letter. But then she thought of another string of words that had been written to her. Ones she still mulled over when she had a quiet, dark moment.

Think on my offer. You will know when to give me your answer.

Was this it, then? Was this the moment she was to give Dacre her reply?

"Iris?" Helena said.

"I'm going," Iris replied. "But I don't have anything *fancy* to wear."

"Then take the rest of the day off to prepare." Helena began to walk away, then turned back around, removing the cigarette from her mouth. "But be careful, Iris. The meeting is at half past five. Almost dark, and a vulnerable time these days. Don't forget curfew, and call me here at the *Tribune* if you need anything."

Iris nodded, watching Helena return to her office.

She flicked off her desk lamp and picked up the invitation again, ignoring the inquisitive glances from the other editors and assistants.

It's time, she thought with a shiver.

She was ready to give Dacre her answer.

39

Silver on the Green

R oman rode with Dacre and two officers in a vehicle to the Promontory. The back windows were covered with dark velvet drapes,
holding the light and all views of the city at bay. As tempted as he was
to part the curtains and watch Oath roll past, Roman didn't dare move. The
letter Shane had given him was tucked into the inner pocket of his suit jacket,
and every time Dacre looked his way, Roman could feel his heart falter a beat.

Once he had believed Dacre could read minds. He had since learned that it
wasn't true, but it didn't dispel the fact that Dacre had uncanny abilities when
it came to interpreting people.

Thankfully, the ride through downtown was a quiet one. But there was a
perceptible chill in the air, as if hints of the under realm clung to Dacre's fine
raiment of gold, red, and black.

Something was going to happen tonight. Something that would crack the
world in two.

Roman exhaled. He could almost see his breath.

They reached the Promontory, an old building that had once been a castle
in a different era. It had been updated and redesigned over the past decade,

turning it into a structure that seemed caught between nostalgia and modernity. A place that didn't seem to quite know where it belonged.

Roman quietly climbed down from the motorcar, walking in Dacre's shadow as they entered through a private back door of the building. No one was supposed to know Dacre was in the city, and that he was speaking to the upper echelons and most influential of Oath's denizens after the chancellor tonight. His officers, one of whom was Captain Landis, walked close behind while four of Dacre's elite soldiers also followed, two dressed in uniform and two dressed in black coats and trousers, starched white button-downs, and jeweled cuff links for the event. Shane, of course, was not among them; he was still at the estate. As Dacre was guided into a room to rest before the event, Roman took a quick inventory.

The chamber was spacious but only had one door, no windows. Flames crackled in the hearth, and a massive tapestry hung from the wall. There was a table of refreshments, although no one touched the chilled wine, fruit, and cheese. Only those Dacre trusted most were in the room, but no one relaxed save for the god himself, who sat in a chair before the fire.

Roman stood awkwardly off to the side, trying to make himself as unnoticeable as possible. But his hands were trembling, shot through with nerves. He needed to get out of this room. He needed to be in the courtyard, to deliver the message, but when he moved toward the door Dacre saw him.

"Come, Roman," he said, inviting him closer. "Have a seat."

The last thing Roman wanted to do was sit. But he did as Dacre bid, sitting in a high-backed leather chair beside him.

"What do you make of tonight?" Dacre asked, studying his face.

"I think it's going to be an important one, sir. A turning point for us."

"Do you think I will be able to convince them to join me?"

Roman paused. *Them* being the people the chancellor thought were powerful in society. But the problem with that notion was that there was far more to Oath than the noble, wealthy, and influential residents. There were the working and the middle class. The artists and writers and teachers and dreamers. The stonemasons and plumbers and tailors and bakers and construction workers. People who were made of mettle and drive and courage, who kept the city alight and moving forward. Some of them might support Dacre, but Roman knew that most of the people who had volunteered to fight for Enva had come from classes of society who could see the world as it truly was. Who could see injustice and who were willing to take a stand against it.

Dacre's desire for surrender—a "peaceful" overtaking—would not be possible without their support. Oath would sunder in two before it happened.

"I hope so, sir," Roman replied.

"You never told me about your meeting with Iris E. Winnow," Dacre said, changing the topic so fast that Roman's posture went rigid. "How was it?"

"It went well, sir."

"Do you think she will be open-minded?"

"Maybe. It's hard to tell with her, sometimes."

"And why is that?"

"She's quite stubborn, sir."

Dacre only chuckled, as if he liked the thought. It made Roman's blood feel clotted with ice, and he wished he hadn't said such a thing.

But then Roman couldn't stop himself. He asked, "When you do expect an answer from her?"

Dacre was quiet, gazing at the fire. "Soon."

The door suddenly opened. Chancellor Verlice swept into the room.

Roman rose when Dacre did, moving out of the way as the chancellor offered a greeting. The leaders were soon preoccupied, conversing in low voices. But the air was heavy with anticipation as the clock ticked closer to half past five. The event was about to start.

When Roman noticed the two soldiers dressed for the event slipping out the door, he was not far behind them.

The Green Quarter was an inner courtyard in the heart of the Promontory, which once, long ago, had been the gathering place for medieval life. But the only trace of the past was the forge, located on the right-hand side, which had since been converted into an open café. Even then, it had changed so drastically that Roman would have never known it had once been a place where weapons were crafted, save for the blacksmith's anvil that remained behind.

He watched from the edge of the courtyard as servers carried out flutes of champagne and trays laden with small bites, weaving through the gathering crowd. Hanging chandeliers burned against the encroaching dusk. Soon, it would be dark, stars and swollen moon shining overhead. And what of the curfew, Roman wondered, his eyes seeking the person with the red anemone. All the guests would be stranded here or would have to risk traveling home through mercurial streets.

The envelope was heavy as a stone in his pocket. He forced himself to mingle with the crowd, feeling checkerboard grass and stone beneath his shoes. Shane's words continued to echo through him: *There will be a man wearing a red anemone pinned to his lapel in the crowd. This envelope needs to be handed directly to him. Once you do that . . . leave the courtyard immediately.*

Roman bumped shoulders with someone and quickly apologized. Sweat began to trickle down his face as his desperation grew. He could hear a wheeze, catching the end of each breath, his cough flaring. He accepted a flute of champagne, downing the fizz, feeling it trickle through him like fire.

He recognized some of the guests here. Most of them were older, hailing from rich and noble families. People his father had been desperate to win approval from, and it made Roman feel like spiders were crawling over his skin as he continued to weave his way through the throng. He reminded himself to be mindful of Dacre's two soldiers who were also pretending to be guests, milling around in their fine clothes. If they saw Roman hand off a message, then they would know he was a traitor.

Roman sighed and came to a halt at the edge of the courtyard again. He looked for the two soldiers in disguise, finding the tall, handsome one talking to a woman in a silver dress.

The soldier shifted, granting Roman a view of the woman's face.

It was Iris.

Roman was frozen to the ground as he stared, taking in her every detail. Her red lips, the dress that shimmered when she breathed, the way her skin looked in the candlelight. She had cut her hair shorter; it was crimped in a wavy bob, the ends touching her bare shoulders.

A pang went through him when she granted the soldier a small smile. She was politely listening to him talk, but she angled away when he leaned in closer to her.

Roman took two steps and then halted. He couldn't approach them. He couldn't walk up to her and slide his hand around her waist like he yearned to. He couldn't lace his fingers with hers and whisper words into her ear to make her smile and then blush. He couldn't acknowledge her as his wife. Not now, and maybe never, if Dacre's plans took root tonight.

And yet Roman couldn't help but feel like his insides were twisting the longer he gazed at her.

Look at me, Iris.

Look at me.

The soldier was still talking, but then Iris's attention shifted to the stage that was set up at the front of the courtyard. Everyone in the crowd looked that way as the chancellor began to speak, his voice commanding the dusky air. Everyone but Roman, who could not draw his eyes away from Iris.

One breath.

Two.

Three.

He felt his composure crack.

He didn't make out what the chancellor said—the words melted together—but Roman finally dragged his attention away from Iris when the atmosphere turned cold and quiet. When a smattering of applause covered up a few gasps of alarm, and Roman saw that Dacre had now taken the stage.

Roman had missed the handoff.

He had failed to do what Shane had ordered, and it took another minute for the truth of his current predicament to scrape down his ribs.

Leave the courtyard immediately.

Roman needed to know why. He needed to know what was imminent because Iris was here, her face blanched and her lips parted as she listened to Dacre and his honeyed words.

The air shuddered through him as Roman retrieved the envelope from his inner pocket. No one around him noticed. They were all either transfixed or horrified by the sight of Dacre in the courtyard. A god here in Oath, in plain sight.

Roman broke the seal and slipped out a small square of paper.

A blast alone won't do. You must sever the head.

The words swam before him as he read them a second time. A third. He slipped the paper back into the envelope and calmly tucked it into his pocket. But his gaze cut through the crowd. He found Iris again as if she were the only one in the courtyard. A glimmer of light in the growing shadows.

He began to walk to her, nudging people out of the way. He didn't care if he caused a scene. He didn't care if Dacre saw him striding to her. To Iris E. Winnow, a woman Roman was only supposed to have an acquaintance with.

Something terrible was about to happen, and neither Roman nor Iris would be here to witness it. He was going to take her hand and flee with her, far away from this place. From this city, from the war. It had bruised and wounded them enough, and he simply *did not care*—

Someone grasped his arm, their grip like iron. It stopped him in his tracks.

"Come with me," an unfamiliar voice said in his ear. "Don't draw attention to us."

Roman swallowed, his eyes remaining on Iris. "I'm not going anywhere with you." But he felt the prod of a revolver in his ribs, and his shoulders curved with submission.

"Yes, you are," the man said. "*Now.*"

Roman allowed himself to be propelled through the crowd, a gun jammed discreetly into his side. When they stepped into the empty corridors of the Promontory, he jerked away and spun, glaring at the person who had come between him and Iris.

To his shock, Roman recognized him.

Even wearing a nice suit and hat, his father's associate couldn't fully disguise his rough edges. *Bruce,* Mrs. Kitt had called him, boasting of how he kept their family safe.

"What are you doing here?" Roman asked tersely.

Bruce kept the gun trained on him, but Roman sensed it was only to make him comply. This man had no intention of shooting his boss's son.

"I'll tell you on the way back to the house." Bruce took hold of his arm again, twisting Roman around, forcing him to step forward. "Your father wants you home. And this is not a safe place."

"You don't understand." Roman dug his heels into the floor. His shoes squeaked as he slid over the polished marble. "I need to return to the courtyard."

"You'll thank me later."

"My *wife*!" Roman hissed. "My wife is in that crowd!"

That revelation made Bruce pause. But whatever he planned to do— whether it be to go back for Iris or to propel Roman onward—Roman would never know.

There was a flash through the windows, followed by an ear-splitting boom that Roman felt in his chest like his heart had torn free.

The explosion rocked him from his feet.

PART FOUR

A Crescendo for Dreams

40

Come Up for Air

Dazed, Roman let Bruce haul him up to his feet. Smoke drifted in through the shattered windows. Glass glittered like constellations on the floor.

"Get up and *walk*," Bruce ordered, dragging Roman down the corridor, farther and farther away from the cries that were rising from the courtyard.

Roman coughed, light-headed.

"Iris," he whispered, remembering the red slant of her mouth, the silver of her dress. The way she had stood in the middle of the crowd.

Roman struggled to pull free, glancing over his shoulder. The smoke and screams continued to intertwine. Gunshots rang out. His heart lodged in his throat.

"*Iris!*"

It was the last thing he said before the side of Bruce's revolver came down hard on his temple. Roman saw stars glide across his vision. But Iris bloomed in his mind's eye, her pale hand reaching for him.

He watched her dissolve into mist, just as everything went dark.

. . .

When he woke, he found himself sprawled across the back seat of a vehicle. They were taking a hard turn, the tires screeching over the cobblestones. Roman slid across the leather bench and vomited, all over himself and onto the floorboard of the motorcar.

The world felt as if it had turned inside out.

He gagged and heaved again, his vision blurring. Or perhaps it was only the streetlamps, which flashed as they sped by, their golden auras smudged through the window.

The car took another sharp curve. Roman scrambled for purchase. He could feel vomit smear across his shirt.

"We're almost there," said a gruff voice.

Bruce.

Roman squinted, his head throbbing. Something was tickling his face. When he reached out to touch his temple, his fingertips came away sticky with blood.

"Last turn," Bruce said. "Try to hold your guts in this time."

The vehicle jerked.

Roman closed his eyes. He counted the seconds that ticked by, tasting acid in his mouth. But at last, the car came to a skidding halt.

He panted, still sprawled on the seat, until Bruce opened the door.

"Get up. We need to move quickly," he said.

"Where are we?" Roman rasped.

Bruce didn't reply. He took hold of Roman and dragged him out of the car.

It was dark, the hour just after sunset, when only a vestige of pink light could be seen fading from the western horizon. But the moon was full, and the stars teemed in a clear night sky. Roman swiftly recognized where they were: Derby Road, on the footpath between estate numbers 1345 and 1347.

"What happened?" he asked when he saw the fence line come into view. "How are you involved in all of this?"

"You'll have to get those answers from your father," Bruce said, finding the oak tree and the broken fence, buried beneath the brambles. "Quickly, now."

Roman hissed through his teeth, irritated by the lack of answers. By the fact that he wasn't strong enough to break away from this man and return to the Promontory for Iris.

As he pushed through the brambles, feeling the thorns grasp his hair and his suit jacket, he asked, "Was the plan to kill everyone in the courtyard?"

"I told you to ask your *father*," Bruce grunted from behind, pushing Roman to go faster, as if a spell would break at midnight, turning them into stone. "But because your wife was there, I'll say this . . . no. Only him."

Him as in Dacre.

Roman couldn't hide how he shuddered. How his hands were freezing but his chest was burning. He felt caught up in a strange medley of relief and shock, indignation and hope, and he pulled a string of brambles from his hair when he emerged on the other side.

He paused, his breath ragged. Bruce must have sensed he needed a moment because the man finally didn't urge him onward.

"A bomb alone won't kill him," Roman eventually said, remembering the message he still held in his coat pocket.

Bruce frowned. "What do you mean? It was directly beneath the stage."

Roman winced as he envisioned all that wood splintering in the blast, flying through the crowd. Impaling innocent people. He swallowed hard and said, "It takes more than that to kill a god."

"I pray you're wrong. Because if you're right . . ." Bruce didn't finish the thought.

Not even Roman knew how to complete that sentence.

They hurried through the back half of the property, where even now it felt like a different world. One far removed from Oath and the war. But before the estate came into view, Bruce stopped in the shadow of a hawthorn.

"This is as far as I can go without the soldiers seeing me," he said. "Go directly to your father."

"Are you part of the Graveyard?"

Bruce didn't reply to the blunt question. Roman took it as affirmation.

"Will you go back for her?" he asked next, unable to hide the way his voice shook. "Will you go back for my wife?"

"Don't worry about Miss Winnow. She's a smart girl."

"Does that mean you'll do as I ask? I—" Roman cut himself off, narrowing his eyes. "I never told you her last name was Winnow. How did you know that?"

Again, Bruce was silent, but he held Roman's stare with a clenched jaw.

Pieces began to fall into place. Roman stepped closer, using his height to loom over Bruce.

"You've seen her before. When?"

"There's no time for this."

"*When?*"

"Before she left for the front, a few weeks ago. Your father asked me to deliver a message to her. Now don't lose your head. It's not the time for—"

"What was the message?" Roman's voice was cold and smooth.

"It was money."

"Money?"

"Enough for her to live comfortably if she annulled your marriage. Which by the looks of it she didn't, so get out of my face and do what I told you to do, before all hell breaks loose."

Roman's hand curled into a fist.

But he had gained the answers he wanted.

He turned and strode away.

His blood was still boiling when he approached the back doors of the mansion.

He noticed two things through his haze of anger: there was a massive stack of crates beneath the pavilion, brightly labeled with CAUTION, and Dacre's soldiers were patrolling the backyard as if they were no longer afraid of being spotted by the neighbors. Roman walked directly through their line and realized he held more power than he had once believed. They yelled at him to halt, to lift his hands, and yet they did *nothing* when he refused to comply. He acted like they didn't exist as he stepped through the back doors of his house.

His shoes clicked on the polished floors. He headed to his father's study, drowning in his thoughts.

He hadn't been able to reach Iris. He hadn't been able to protect her when she needed him most—from his father or from Dacre. Roman had no idea if she was alive, if she was wounded, if she was dead.

She's not, he told himself, even as he ground his teeth. *I would know if she was dead.*

The door to his father's study was cracked. Roman kicked it wide open, startling Mr. Kitt, who had been pacing with a cigar in hand.

"Shut the door," his father said in an urgent tone. His blue eyes widened when he saw how disheveled Roman was. The vomit, the trickle of blood. The scrape of brambles. "What happened?"

Roman was silent as he stared at Mr. Kitt. He felt like he was indeed hewn from stone, worn down from years of guilt and fear and longings he could never pursue. And yet he was finished being ruled by such things. The past weeks had chipped and cracked him; he had crawled from that husk of a shell, cut away old strings, and now he held the stare until his father submitted, extinguishing the cigar on the desk.

"Why are there crates stacked beneath the pavilion?" Roman asked in a sharp tone. "Don't tell me it's more of that damn gas you had the chemist professor make."

Mr. Kitt blinked, taken aback by Roman's abruptness. But he recovered quickly, drawing closer to whisper, "No, in fact. But has it been taken care of?"

"What do you speak of, Father?"

Mr. Kitt glanced beyond Roman, to the door that still sat open. It was the first time that Roman had ever seen his father appear frightened.

Mr. Kitt lowered his voice even further, murmuring, "Is he *dead?*"

Roman had suspected his father was playing both sides of the field—with Dacre, and with the Graveyard. Of course he would, because he wanted to emerge on the winning side, no matter the outcome. But now Roman knew for certain.

Mr. Kitt was in too deep. He knew nothing of gods from below, nothing of life at the front or the claws of war and the wounds they inflicted. And the Graveyard, while passionate, appeared highly unorganized and disorderly. They had bungled an assassination attempt, and now the entire city would pay for it.

"I don't know," Roman replied.

"What do you mean you *don't know*? Did the bomb go off or not?"

"It did, but your man dragged me away before I could see any further."

Mr. Kitt began to pace again. But he looked confident, as if knowing the blast had happened meant he could move on to the next step.

"We should——"

He was interrupted by a cold draft. The walls shuddered. The chandelier above clinked. The hardwood groaned beneath a pair of heavy feet.

Roman knew that sound, that *feeling*. He watched his father freeze as he recognized it too. They listened, horror-struck, as the parlor door slammed.

"Get behind the desk," Mr. Kitt whispered, grasping hold of his arm in a painful grip. "Hide there. Don't come out until I tell you to."

Roman yanked free, but his father's terror was contagious. He could feel it tickle the back of his throat. "I can't hide here. It's too late for that."

"Do as I tell you, son. I won't lose you to this." Mr. Kitt strode from the study, shutting the doors in his wake and leaving Roman behind in a smoky, oppressive room.

He breathed through his mouth, but he didn't move. He stood in the center of the chamber, listening . . .

"My lord!" his father exclaimed. "What has happened?"

An uncomfortable pause. But when Dacre spoke at last, the house seemed to magnify his voice.

"I want all my officers and soldiers who remained behind to line up in the hall. Now."

Roman could hear the sudden rush of bootsteps as Dacre's order was heeded. One of those officers would be Lieutenant Shane, who held Roman's confession like a grenade. Lieutenant Shane, who no doubt believed he'd been betrayed, since Dacre's head was still fastened to his body.

Roman bared his teeth, heart thrashing. But he hurried to his father's desk, stifling a cough as he struck a match. Quickly, he pulled the incriminating letter from his pocket, and he held it by the corner as it caught fire.

He watched the paper curl into smoke before he dropped the last of it on the rug, stamping out the hungry flames. His head continued to ache, but he took the time to set the blackened match in the ashtray, lined up with all the others his father had used.

Only then did he leave the study and step out into the hall.

Breathe, slow and deep.

The soldiers and officers were in the corridor, lined up and standing at attention. Their focus was set firmly ahead, even as Dacre walked before them, his eyes scrutinizing each of their faces as he passed.

Roman stopped. He could only see Dacre's back, but the god's clothes were ripped and bloodied. His long blond hair was tangled.

"Someone here has betrayed me," said Dacre. His voice was smooth, thick, like oil on water. "This is your chance to come forward and confess."

No one moved or spoke.

Roman found Lieutenant Shane in the lineup. By all appearances, Shane was perfect. His face was well guarded, his uniform was pristine as if he took great pride in it. He didn't quake in fear or take shallow breaths. He seemed completely in control, as if the idea of betrayal had never crossed his mind.

"You," Dacre said, pointing to one of the privates. "Step forward and kneel."

The soldier obeyed.

"Hold out your right arm."

Again, the soldier did as Dacre commanded, although Roman could see the man's hand was shaking.

"I will break your arm, unless you confess or give up the names of your comrades who have betrayed me," Dacre said, taking hold of the soldier's forearm.

"M-my lord commander," the man stammered. "I truly don't know. I'm wholly devoted to you."

"I will give you one more chance to reply. Confess, or give me a name."

The soldier was silent, but urine dampened the front of his trousers.

Roman had seen enough. He was full of quiet fury, and he was tired of bending to a god who thrived on mortals' fear and subservience. Who took delight in making wounds and then healing them halfway when it suited him.

Roman resumed his walk down the hall. But his hand drifted into his pocket; his finger traced the edge of Iris's small book, which he had carried ever since she had left it in his room.

"Lord Commander?" he called.

Dacre's head snapped up. His eyes gleamed as he took in Roman's appearance, and Roman was suddenly thankful for the vomit and the blood on his clothes. The dirt and the wrinkles and the brambles. Simultaneously, he was shocked to see how unscathed Dacre was. The blood that marred his raiment was not his, as there was not a single scratch on his face or his hands.

"Roman," Dacre said, releasing the private's arm. "I thought you were dead."

"No, sir." Roman passed Shane. He could feel the cool gaze of the lieutenant, brief but chilling, as he came to a stop before Dacre.

"Why are you here?" the god asked. "How did you survive?"

"I was on the outer edges of the courtyard. When the blast happened . . . I didn't know what to do, so I came home, knowing you would return here, sir."

Dacre was silent, mulling over Roman's reply.

In that strained moment of waiting to see how Dacre would respond, Roman realized that the other officers—Captain Landis included—and soldiers who had been with him in the Green Quarter must have died in the blast. It was their blood on the god's face and clothes. And one of those men had been standing beside Iris.

Roman felt a prick of grief. His distress began to devour his bones, making him quiver from the weight. He almost bowed over. He almost melted to the floor.

Hold it together.

He repeated those words, a framework on which to hang his mind and his body, and bit the inside of his cheek. He laced his fingers behind his back. But there was a scream building in his chest, tearing through his lungs.

If she were dead, I would know.

"Hold out your right arm, Roman," said Dacre.

If this was a test, then Roman couldn't afford to fail it. And if it wasn't, then Roman would know true breaking at the hands of a god.

He held out his arm without hesitation. But within, his mind was a dark, deep current. Spinning around and around. *You will regret breaking my bones. You will regret ever taking Iris from my mind. You will release something from my marrow that you will wish you had never touched.*

Dacre took hold of Roman's arm. He drew him closer, until their breaths mingled.

"Do you know who betrayed me?" Dacre asked.

"No, sir."

Dacre's grip tightened. Roman could feel his hand begin to tingle; he could see his father at the corner of his eye, stepping closer, grimacing in horror.

"No, I don't have a name," Roman said, stronger this time. "And I don't think anyone here is a traitor."

"Convince me of your reasoning."

"We have been with you, lord. We have served you below as well as above. We know your true nature, your power, your magic. If one of us attempted to kill you, do you think we would be foolish enough to use a bomb?"

Dacre released Roman's arm. But he raked his hand through his snarled hair, and it was so human-like that it almost made Roman laugh.

A god could be killed. But they would have to be smart about it the next time.

Emboldened by Dacre's hesitation, Roman pressed on. "Sir, this is a very precarious time. Instead of doubting us, let us strategize on the next step."

Dacre studied him again. He sighed as if bored. "Go and change your clothes. Meet me in the war room in ten minutes." To his officers and soldiers, he said, "To your posts."

Roman stood in the hallway, surrounded by a sudden stream of life. Soldiers returning to their patrols or to the dining room for a meal. To the library-turned-barracks. Whatever they had been doing before Dacre had returned and marred the night.

Shane brushed Roman's shoulder.

A sign of comradery or a warning, Roman couldn't tell, and he was too weary to attempt to parse it. He climbed the stairs and retreated to his room. Alone at last, he ripped off his jacket. He fell to his knees, clawing at his throat.

He gasped as if he had just broken the surface of the sea.

· · ·

Nine minutes later, Roman returned to the parlor dressed in clean clothes. The blood and vomit had been washed away and his dark hair had been slicked back. His posture was straight, a bit rigid, but he had always been like that, hadn't he?

By all outward appearances, he seemed normal. He looked fine. Groomed and put together, even after narrowly escaping a bomb.

But within? He felt splintered.

Dacre was too preoccupied to notice. He stood in front of the parlor hearth, full of vitality, as if he had never felt the sting of an explosion. He too had changed and washed away all trace of mortal blood, the firelight illuminating his angular face. But for all his inward distance, he heard Roman enter the room. Without turning, he said, "There's an important letter I need you to type for me."

Roman took a seat before his typewriter, waiting to feel a rush of relief to be near it again. The Third Alouette. His connection to Iris. He felt empty as he studied the strike bars E and R.

But then he noticed something else, lying on the table. A bloodstained iron key, strung on a chain.

The key that had been around Captain Landis's neck.

"Tell me when you're ready," Dacre said.

Roman returned his attention to the task, feeding a sheet of paper into the typewriter. He couldn't help but study the iron key again, only an arm's length away. The power to unlock thresholds, just beyond his reach.

"I'm ready, sir," he said.

And yet he was not prepared for the words that came from Dacre's mouth. For the person this letter was addressed to. Roman listened but was unable to type the name.

Dacre noticed the silence. He stopped speaking and glanced at him with a frown.

"Is something wrong, Roman?"

"No, lord."

"Then why aren't you typing?"

"Sorry, sir." Roman flexed his fingers, two of his knuckles popping. "Please continue."

I would know if she were dead.

Dacre repeated himself, and this time Roman turned his words into ink, even as his eyes remained on that first line:

Dear Iris E. Winnow

{ 41 }

Conversations with a Figment

Iris ran down the dark side street.

Somewhere along the way she had lost one of her high heels, and her bare foot stung with every lopsided step. Her dress was torn; her knees were skinned. She couldn't tell how badly she was hurt because her body was numb.

All she could feel was her heart, pounding an erratic song in her ears, down the twisted lines of her veins.

Don't stop! It's not safe yet.

Exhaustion crept over her, making her slow and clumsy. Her muscles were tight and hot beneath her sweaty skin. She couldn't seem to push herself to run any faster and yet she worried she would collapse if she stopped moving.

Where am I?

She felt completely turned around, lost in a shadowy maze. Swallowed whole by a nightmare she was desperate to wake from. She shivered as she limped to a reluctant stop at the next intersection.

A few motorcars sped past, tires splashing through rain puddles. The streetlamps began to flicker to life, their amber light drawing a host of moths. A newspaper was disintegrating on the cobblestones.

It was evening, and curfew was imminent. Oath was eerie in the solemn darkness, as if the city grew teeth and claws when the sun set. She needed to find a safe place to rest for the night, and she didn't know where that haven was until she realized what street she had arrived at.

She took a tentative step forward.

There in the distance loomed the museum, with its white columns and flickering lanterns and bloodred doors. Those doors would lock after nightfall; no one would be able to follow her inside. They would shelter her from the Graveyard.

As if sensing her thoughts, gunshots rang in the nearby distance, followed by shouts and a blood-chilling scream.

Iris winced and crouched. But she didn't stop moving. She hurried along the sidewalk until she was almost at the museum's stairs. Then she sprinted, kicking loose from her other shoe until it was just her bare feet slapping on the marble.

She opened the heavy door and slipped into the museum just moments before the locks magically bolted for the night. Iris shuddered—*you're safe, you're safe*—and took five steps across the foyer before her legs gave out.

"You're safe," Iris whispered to herself, as if speaking the words aloud would make them real. But she didn't believe her own voice.

She didn't believe her words anymore.

In the moments leading up to the explosion, Iris had thought Dacre's speech conceited, overwrought, and silver-tongued. She didn't trust a single word he spoke—she saw through him like he was glass—but when she had glanced at the people around her . . . their expressions were awed and intent. She saw that they were being drawn in by his appeal for Oath.

There will be no bloodshed. There will be no need for death.

I am here to heal your old wounds and restore this city to glory.

She wondered if this was the beginning of the end. If Oath was about to bow in feverish surrender. She wondered what her life would be like beneath Dacre's rule.

That was when she heard the strange clicking.

Iris didn't know what it was initially, but her body went rigid when she remembered being in the trenches with Roman. How the grenade had made a similar sound before it exploded. The tall man at her side also seemed to know what the clicks meant. He drew a sharp breath and stepped forward, directly in front of her, like he was about to storm the stage.

There was no time as an explosion rocked the courtyard.

A blinding light, the crack of wood, the weight of thunder. The sting of hail and the whistle of metal in the air. The melting of gravity and the splinter of bones. The taste of blood and smoke and the ring of death.

Iris didn't remember being blown off her feet. But when she could blink the grit from her eyes, she realized the man in front of her had taken the brunt of the blast. The man whose *name she didn't even know* had died as a shield for her, whether he had intended to or not. He was now draped across her legs, punctured by pieces of wood, bleeding onto her dress. He was dead, and she had to wrench herself free from his weight, her lungs heaving as she realized what had just happened.

She rose on shaky legs.

Through the smoke, she could see some people coughing and crawling along the ground, but most of those around her were dead. Gripping the front of her dress, Iris looked up.

She met Dacre's fiery stare. He stood hale and whole amid the wreckage, blood dripping from his face, his clothes hanging from his powerful body in tatters.

When he stepped forward, she scrambled backward, tripping over bodies and hitting the ground with a jar.

Run.

It was the only crystal-clear thought she had.

Run.

As gunshots broke through the haze, Iris lunged to her feet and ran.

It was strange how she couldn't get herself to rise now.

Iris lay on the floor of the museum's foyer, her cheek pressed to the marble. The last time she had been here, she had been stealing the First Alouette with Attie and Sarah. A night that felt like centuries ago.

She retraced that memory, hoping it would calm her heart. But it reminded Iris that the museum always had a guard patrolling at night. She wasn't alone here, and she didn't want to be caught.

With a groan, she pushed herself to her knees, then to her feet. Now that her adrenaline had ebbed, she could feel a hot pulse in the arch of her right foot. She examined it to see a few shards of glass embedded in her skin.

She had bled onto the floor but had nothing to wipe it clean.

"Later," she told herself, hobbling down the hallway.

Only a few bulbs were on, emitting faint light. Most of the museum was draped in shadows, quiet and cold as if underwater, and Iris was almost to the room where the Alouette had once been displayed when she heard the echo of a door closing.

She froze, listening.

Someone was walking down the other corridor, in the direction of the foyer.

It had to be the night guard, and Iris darted into the one of the back rooms, falling on her hands and knees to crawl behind a statue. She pulled her legs tight against her chest. Her breaths were labored, her foot throbbing in tandem with her frantic heartbeat.

She closed her eyes as the bootsteps drew closer.

She was so *tired*; she had no more strength to dodge another foe. To run from room to room like quarry, seeking a place to hide.

Iris closed her eyes and swallowed.

After a few more beats, she could see a beam of light seeping through her eyelids. Tense, she waited. And when the light finally spilled over her, she knew there was no more pretense. No more hiding.

She opened her eyes, squinting up at the guard who stood before her. A middle-aged woman with long hair, dark as night with a few streaks of silver. Her skin was pale but radiant, and her face could have been one that Iris had seen many times before and forgotten save for her eyes. They were a startling shade of green. She was tall and slender beneath her navy guard's uniform, but she carried no weapon. No gun or baton, only a metal torch, which she politely pointed downward.

Iris trembled as she waited for the woman to make her demands. She waited for what she expected—*Who are you? You're trespassing. You need to leave at once. Get out.*

But those words never came.

"You're hurt," the woman said. "Let me help you."

And when she extended her hand, Iris didn't hesitate.

She accepted the help, and the woman drew her up off the floor.

"I'm sorry," Iris said. She was sitting in a worn leather chair in the museum office, and the woman—who had no name badge—was kneeling before her, preparing to draw the glass from her foot with a pair of tweezers.

"Sorry for what?"

"For trespassing after hours."

The woman was quiet as she examined Iris's foot. Her hands were cool and soft, but her knuckles were swollen. Iris wondered if she was in pain of her own until she said, "The museum is more than just a home for artifacts. In many ways, it's a refuge. And you were right to come here if you were in need."

Iris nodded. She was beginning to feel faint, looking at those tweezers.

The woman sensed it. "Close your eyes and lean your head back. This will be over before you know it."

Iris did as the woman instructed, taking a deep breath. But the silence fueled her worries, and she found herself saying, "How long have you worked at the museum?"

"Not very long."

"Are you from Oath?"

There was a plink of glass in a metal tin. Iris hadn't even felt her pull it free.

"Not originally, no. But it's my home now. I haven't left in a long time."

"Do you have any family here?" Iris asked next.

"No, it's just me. I keep company with music."

"You play any instruments?"

A long pause, followed by a slight tug. Iris winced as she felt a shard of glass pull free.

"I did once," the woman replied. "But no longer."

"Because of the chancellor's decree?"

"Yes, and no. A man such as him couldn't keep me from playing if I wanted to."

That brought a smile to Iris's face. It reminded her of Attie, drawing a bow across her violin in the basement. Refusing to give it up to the authorities when they came to confiscate all the other stringed instruments.

Another piece of glass was dislodged. This time it burned, and Iris hissed through her teeth.

"I'm almost finished," the woman said. "Just a few more shards."

Iris remained quiet this time, her eyes clenched shut and her head angled back. But she soaked in the sounds of the museum at night: there was a kettle boiling on the small cooker in the back room, another clink of glass pulling free, the woman's steady breaths as she worked, and a reverent silence, woven through it all.

"Finished," the woman said. "Let me bandage it for you."

Iris opened her eyes. She had bled on the woman's pants, but she didn't seem to mind as she wrapped Iris's foot in a swath of linen.

"And now for some tea." She was up and moving to the cooker before Iris could blink, setting aside the tweezers and the tray full of shards.

Iris listened as she washed her hands in the sink, and soon the room was fragrant with the scent of lavender black tea and warm honey.

"Here you are." The woman set a cup of tea in her hands. "Drink. It'll help you sleep."

"Thank you," Iris replied. "But I should stay awake."

"Have you never wondered what your dreams would be like if you fell asleep in a museum?"

Iris smiled. "No, I haven't."

"Then wonder. You're safe here. Let yourself dream, if only to see where your mind will take you."

Iris took a sip. Her mind was foggy now, and a sense of comfort and bliss began to steal over her, as if she was lying in the grass with summer sunshine on her face. She wondered if it was the tea, or if she was truly that weary.

The woman draped a blanket over her legs.

Iris drifted off into sleep before she knew it.

"Iris."

She startled at the sound of her name. A sound like reeds in the wind. A rush of magic beneath a wardrobe door.

Iris opened her eyes. She was in the museum.

She took a step deeper into the foyer only to see she wasn't alone. The night guard from before was with her, only she now wore a simple homespun dress and her feet were bare.

"Come with me," she said, beckoning Iris to follow her into one of the rooms. "There is something I want to show you."

Iris trailed her, surprised when the woman stopped in front of a glass display holding a sword.

"I've seen this before," Iris said, admiring the shine of tempered steel and the inlay of small gemstones in the golden hilt. "I think I looked at this sword the last time I was at the museum."

"Indeed," the woman replied mirthfully. "When you broke into the museum to steal the First Alouette."

Iris should have been afraid that the guard knew of her crime. But this woman didn't inspire fear, and Iris only smiled. "Yes. You're right. Why did you want to show it to me now?"

The woman directed her attention back to the sword. "This is an enchanted weapon. It was forged by an Underling divine and given to King Draven centuries ago when this land was ruled by one man, and he carried it with him in a battle against the gods. This blade has killed many divines in a time nearly forgotten."

"But the plaque says it was only used for—"

"That is a lie." The woman's voice was firm, but not unkind. She met Iris's gaze, and her bewitching green eyes were both angry and sad. "Many pieces of the past have been rewritten or lost. Forgotten. Think of all the books in the library with pages torn free."

Iris was silent, but she could feel the weight of those words. She considered the sword again and asked, "What is it enchanted to do?"

"It cuts through bone and flesh like a knife does butter, if only its wielder offers the blade and the hilt a taste of their blood first. A sacrifice, to weaken yourself and wound your own hand before striking." The woman turned and resumed her walking. "Come, there is more to see."

Iris followed her through the museum, surprised when the walls suddenly became narrow and rocky. The air turned dank and cold, tasting like moss and rot. Firelight danced from iron sconces.

"I didn't realize the museum had a place like this," Iris said, ducking beneath a cobweb.

"It doesn't," the woman answered. "This is my husband's domain."

"Are we going to meet him?"

"No. I want to show you a door. But first, pay attention to the floor. The way it slopes. It will guide you through the many passages, taking you deeper into the realm."

"Deeper?" Iris's pace slowed.

The walls began to waver. One color was bleeding into the next.

"Don't think too hard about it, Iris," the woman said, her raven hair shining blue in the strange light. "Or else this will break."

Iris nodded, trying to relax. They finally reached the door. It was tall and arched, its lintel carved with runes.

The woman touched the iron knob and paused, as if lost to memory. "When I dwelled here, there were no locks. I could come and go anywhere in the realm, as long as I didn't return to my life above. My husband thought he was granting me freedom, but it was a cage."

Iris felt a flare of dismay. "Who was your husband?"

The woman looked at Iris, but she only said, "Beyond this door is the heart of the realm. A wild yet vulnerable place. It is here that my music was strongest, perhaps because of the risk. But you will need a key to unlock the door."

"Where do I get a key?" Iris asked, her head beginning to throb.

The woman didn't reply, but when she pushed, the door opened. Iris followed her, surprised when the dank air of the tunnel became warm and bright again.

They stood on a grassy hillside. Around them was a landscape of flower-speckled vales and bluffs that rolled into distant mountains. Clusters of pines and a river that flowed along a valley bed.

"It has been a very long time since I could stand here and soak in this view." The woman's voice was soft with nostalgia. The wind touched her with a sigh, gathering her long hair like a loving hand. "You asked me if I was from Oath. I am not, and I once roamed these hills with my family. Anywhere I could see the sky, any horizon I could chase. The freshly churned ground of graveyards. That was my domain, and yet I surrendered it when I exchanged a vow with Alzane, all because he feared my growing power. Since then, I have been beholden to Oath. I cannot leave the city, or else I would have met him in the west when he woke."

"Met who?" Iris whispered.

"Dacre," the woman said. "He can mend what he breaks but I am music and knowledge, rain and harvest. I am nightmares and dreams and illusions. And if he were to kill me as he longs to do, then he would take all my magic into himself. There would be no end to his power, and he would feast on mortal fear and service. He wants to conquer this realm. He wants you to worship him and him alone."

"But if you have such vast magic," Iris began, "then shouldn't you be able to conquer him? If you are illusions and nightmares and—"

"Oh, but that is the cost of it," the woman gently interrupted, a wistful expression on her face. "I took the other three's powers not because I was hungry for them, but because I didn't want *him* to harvest such magic when he woke. But little did I know that doing so would weaken what was mine to begin with." She lifted one of her hands, and Iris could see her swollen knuckles. "I can still play my harp, but not without agony."

The sky overhead had turned overcast and dour. Thunder rumbled in the distance, and the wind howled with a hint of rain.

"Please help us defeat him," Iris whispered.

A look of compassion stole over the woman's face. She reached out to trace Iris's cheek, her fingertips cold as river water in winter.

"I have given you all the pieces that you need to vanquish him," she said. "I confess that if I am the one to face him, my hand will be stayed. I won't be able to plunge the sword into his neck, even after all the enmity that has grown between us. He will tear me to pieces and glean my powers. Then he will be the only divine remaining in the realm and, at some point in time, whether it is within your generation or another, a mortal will be brave enough to end him, burying him headless in a grave. When that happens, magic will also die, because there will be no more gods walking among you or sleeping beneath the loam. Once we are dead, it will all fade away."

A knot pulled tight in Iris's chest. It almost hurt to draw air, to think of what the woman described. A world in a cage. A world culled of freedom and magic, a memory of what had been.

It made her think of her typewriter. The enchantment in small, ordinary things. She thought of the letters she had passed beneath her wardrobe door to Roman. Words that had spanned kilometers and distance, grief and joy, pain and love. Words that had made her drop her armor after years of clutching it close.

Kitt.

Iris gasped. Her mind was sharpening as she remembered who she was, and the world around her started to melt. The mountains and the sky, the valleys and the wildflowers. Stars she had not even known existed. All of it was draining away like water in a bathtub, but the woman held firm before her, flowers blooming in her dark hair.

Not a woman, but a goddess.

"I don't want you to die. I don't want magic to fade, but I am not as strong as you," Iris said. "He will surely defeat me."

"You are capable of far more than you know. Why do you think I look at you now and marvel? Why do you think I draw close to your kind? I have sung many of you to eternal rest after death, and I have found that the music of a mortal life burns brighter than any magic my songs could stoke."

She leaned forward to kiss Iris's brow. For a split second, she looked like Aster—long chestnut hair, a quirk to her lips, a dusting of freckles on her nose. Tears burned Iris's eyes when she realized that all this time, she hadn't been dreaming of her mother but of this goddess.

Before she was ready for the dream to break, Iris startled awake.

She was sitting in a leather chair, the museum office limned in predawn light. A cup of cold tea was beside her, a warm blanket draped over her legs. Her right foot was bandaged, and she took a moment to catch her breath, still tender from the dream.

She noticed there was a set of boots on the ground before her, unlaced and polished. A clean outfit, of a knee-length skirt and a forest green blouse with pearl buttons, folded on the chair beside her. A pot of tea, steaming in wait for her to pour.

Iris threw off the blanket and rose, minding her foot although there was only a whisper of pain when she stood on it.

"Enva?" she called.

There was no answer. The air was heavy and quiet.

"*Enva!*"

She was wondering if it had all been a fever-struck imagining, a way for her mind to make sense of the world after surviving the bomb, when a flash of gold caught her eye. Iris turned to see a sword with a jeweled hilt leaning against the wall, its steel hidden within a scabbard. It was the very blade Enva had shown to her in the dream. Draven's sword. The one that had killed many divines in the past.

Iris walked to it. She hesitated, replaying everything Enva had said and shown her. The sword, the door, the words.

Why didn't I realize who you were you the moment I saw you? Iris wondered, aching at the thought of a goddess kneeling before her, drawing glass from her foot. Wrapping her wounds. A goddess making her tea and walking a dream with her.

You are capable of far more than you know.

Once, not long ago, Iris wouldn't have believed those words. But she felt the tides pull beneath her, as if she stood beneath a bloodred moon.

She took the hilt in her hand.

42

Surrender My Hands

Iris set the sword down on her desk. In the mellow lamplight, the blade *almost* looked like it belonged next to the typewriter. But as she gazed at them, she felt as if two worlds and two vastly different times were colliding. Her mind was distant as she retraced her dream.

The *Inkridden Tribune* was quiet and empty. Only a few desk lamps were on, making it feel like the dead of night when it was just after sunrise. Iris, sword in hand and wearing the clothes Enva had left behind for her, had gone directly to the *Tribune* as soon as the museum doors had unlocked. It was only a block away, and she didn't want to try to fight the morning rush to her flat with a sword in tow that was most likely worth more than all the gold in Oath's vault.

"Who's there?" Helena's voice rang from the office. She sounded haggard and irritable.

"It's only me," Iris replied. "Early for once."

A beat later, Helena appeared in the doorway, wreathed in smoke. She took a long draw from her cigarette as she strode around the desks.

"You all right, kid? I heard there was a bomb last night in the Green Quarter."

Iris's mouth went dry as she pushed down the memories. Memories that made it seem like she still had glass trapped beneath her skin. "I'm not hurt."

Helena came to a stop, intently studying her. "You certain? I can take you to the hospital now, if—"

"I'm okay." Iris smiled, even though her face felt stiff. "Truly."

"Well, I smoked an entire pack last night, thinking you were dead and despising myself for letting you go alone to that jamboree." She extinguished the cigarette in a nearby ashtray. "Do you know what happened?"

Iris released a deep breath. "Dacre was there. I assume it was an assassination attempt?"

"That's what my informant told me. Fifty-three people killed, twenty more injured. Eleven still unaccounted for. The chancellor is in critical condition at the hospital. They don't expect him to make it. Dacre, on the other hand, vanished. No one knows where he is, but a survivor said he looked completely unscathed from the blast. Not even gunfire could touch him." Helena paused, reading Iris's expression. "Here, sit down, kid. You look pale. Let me make you some coffee." That was when she finally noticed the sword on Iris's desk. "And *that* is King Draven's sword. What in all the gods' names is it doing here in my newsroom?"

"It was given to me," Iris said. "And I need to hide it in your office. Just for a little while."

"*Hide?* Iris, have you—" Helena cut herself off when they both heard footsteps, descending the stairs above. Someone was approaching the *Tribune,* even though it was only a quarter after six and work didn't commence until eight.

"Please, Helena," Iris whispered.

Helena sighed. "Fine. Quickly now, before someone sees it. I don't want word to get around that I stole a priceless relic from the people of Oath."

Iris took the hilt and hurried after Helena into her office. It wasn't a large room, and they had no choice but to hide the sword beneath Helena's desk.

"Ms. Hammond?"

Iris froze at the sound of Tobias's voice. She turned to see him weaving around the desks, approaching the office door. He also seemed shocked to find Iris there so early, his brows rising as he came to a stop.

"Tobias," Helena greeted him. "Something wrong?"

"I was given an urgent post."

"For the *Tribune*?"

"For Iris, to be delivered here at first light," he said, holding out an envelope.

Iris stared at it. She went cold with dread when she recognized the spider-like handwriting. But she accepted the post from Tobias. Her nail bent as she broke the seal and read a succinctly typed request:

Dear Iris E. Winnow,

I would like to invite you to my estate for tea at half past four this afternoon. There are some important matters we need to finish discussing. Please come alone. You will be safe here.

Sincerely,

Mr. Ronald M. Kitt

"What is it, Iris?" Helena's anxious voice broke the silence.

Iris folded the letter. It hadn't occurred to her until then, and she almost felt foolish for it. But she should have known the moment she watched Dacre take the stage at the Green Quarter. She should have realized where the god had been hiding. What door he had used to reach Oath from the inside.

"Only an invitation for tea, from my father-in-law," Iris said.

"Do you want me to send someone with you?" Helena asked. "Perhaps Attie?"

Iris knew Attie had asked for the day off. Her meeting with the music professor had been successful, and Attie planned to practice "Alzane's Lullaby" in her basement, again and again until she could play the notes perfectly no matter her surroundings. In the dark, in the light, standing still, constantly moving.

But even if Attie had been available, Iris wouldn't have asked her to go to the Kitt estate. Not with so much danger lurking in the corners.

"I can drive you there if you'd like," Tobias offered. "I'll wait for you at the curb, and then drive you back, when you're done."

Iris nodded, shoulders relaxing. "I'd be very thankful for that, Tobias. And no, Helena. I should go alone. There's no need to worry."

Helena didn't seem convinced. Neither did Tobias.

Please come alone. You will be safe here.

Iris felt Mr. Kitt's—*Dacre's*—letter crinkle in her fist.

No place in the city was safe anymore.

At four twenty-eight in the afternoon, Iris stared at the iron gates of the Kitt mansion. They didn't open for the roadster, which had led Iris to presume Dacre wanted her to approach the front doors on foot.

"I'll be waiting right here if you need me," Tobias said, parking at the curb.

Iris nodded and slipped from the vehicle. Just as she thought, the gates creaked open when she approached them.

She walked the long driveway alone, carrying nothing but her frayed tapestry purse, and she was struck by how quiet and still the yard was. No birds flittered amongst the perfectly trimmed shrubs. No damselflies or bees glided from one flower to the next. No wind touched the trees, no sunlight flickered through the clouds. It seemed a shadow had fallen over the estate, and Iris shivered as she ascended the stairs to the front door.

Her palms were damp as she lifted her hand to ring the bell.

She never had the chance. The door opened, revealing Mr. Kitt. He looked so disheveled that she was taken aback. His black hair looked greasy, his eyes were rimmed in red, and he reeked of cigar smoke.

Iris didn't have a greeting prepared. She was stunned that he was receiving his own visitor. Where was his butler? The servants he no doubt had running this place? A breath later, she understood.

"Come in, Miss Winnow." He welcomed her inside.

"Thank you," Iris said, but her voice sounded small, easily swallowed by the grand foyer. As soon as the door latched behind her, she saw the soldiers, standing in the shadows. There were seven at this entrance alone, armed with rifles, and as she followed Mr. Kitt, she counted five more in the hallway.

The mansion had turned into a secret military compound.

"Tea will be served in the parlor," said Mr. Kitt.

Iris opened her mouth. She was about to ask where Roman was but caught the words. She had assumed he'd returned to his post, just as he told her, but that notion no longer made sense if Dacre was here.

Perhaps that was why he still hadn't written to her.

Perhaps something had happened to him.

Her pulse was thick in her throat as they reached the parlor doors. She couldn't believe how shaky she felt, as if the ground were uneven. But she reached for the golden locket hiding beneath her blouse. The gold was an anchor, reminding her of Forest and her mother. The difficult things she had already come through.

The parlor doors opened.

Iris saw Dacre sitting at a long table set for tea, directly in her line of sight. Their gazes met and held like a spell had been cast. He was ageless, timeless, cut from sharp and terrible beauty. His appearance was difficult to look away from, both pleasing and deadly, as if one had stared too long at the sun. Iris could still see him when she closed her eyes, like his impression had been burned there.

"Iris Winnow," he said with a friendly smile. It almost made him appear human. "Come, join me for tea."

Iris stepped forward. She startled when Mr. Kitt closed the doors, leaving her alone with Dacre in the parlor.

"Sit," the god insisted, pouring the first cup.

Iris eased herself down to the chair, tense. She watched the steam rise, wondering if the tea would be safe to drink, when Dacre interrupted her thoughts.

"You remember your former colleague?"

Iris frowned, but she sensed someone staring at her—she could feel it like starlight on the darkest of nights. Eyes that had traced her many times before.

Her breath hitched as she glanced over her shoulder.

Roman stood against the wall, gazing at her. His face was pale and lean, even more so than it had been the other night when she had slept in his bed. She wondered if he was eating, if he was sleeping. His expression was impassive, his eyes cold as the winter sea. He looked just like he had in the *Gazette* days, professionally stitched together on the outside in his freshly starched clothes and slicked-back hair. But she could see a muscle tic in his jaw. She noticed his hands were bunched in his pockets, hiding his fists.

"Yes," she breathed, returning her attention to Dacre. "I remember Kitt."

"He gave you my letter at the café, did he not?"

Iris accepted the teacup and saucer from Dacre. She was mortified by how her hand trembled. How small and weak she seemed, compared to the divine.

"He did," she said, resisting the urge to look at Roman.

Act like you hate him again. Despise him. Like he isn't the other half of you.

Dacre studied her as she poured milk and honey into her cup, taking her time as if it would delay the inevitable.

"I saw you last night at the Green Quarter," he said.

Iris set down her spoon. "Yes, I was there."

"I was the one who put your name on the invitation list. I wanted to meet you." Dacre leaned closer, dropping his voice to a deep rumble. "Why did you run from me, Iris?"

"Sir?"

"I saw you through the smoke. I was coming to heal you, to help you. And you ran."

"I didn't feel safe there."

"Are you afraid of me?"

Yes, she wanted to say. She was afraid of him. But she held his stare, her tongue pressed against her teeth.

"What did you think of my speech?" Dacre asked. "Before it was . . . interrupted?"

"Truthfully? You said everything those people wanted to hear. You were selling them a dream, not a reality."

"You disapprove, then?"

"It simply doesn't align with what I've heard of you."

"And what, Iris Winnow, have you heard? And from where?"

Iris hesitated. She wasn't sure how to answer. She felt like she was playing a game of chess with him, and there was no chance of her winning.

"I've heard plenty of stories," she said, tracing the porcelain handle of her teacup. "From my time reporting on the front lines."

Dacre was pensive, but it seemed he knew exactly what she implied. Had she not seen his destruction with her own eyes? Sometimes she still couldn't sleep at night, for fear of seeing those memories again. The panic and blood of trenches under fire. The Bluff, broken after the bombings.

The silence stretched thin, uncomfortable. Iris forced herself to take a sip of tea, now lukewarm and far too sweet. She could hear the faint draw of Roman's breath behind her.

We are trapped here, she thought, her stomach aching. *We are trapped within his web, and I don't know how to free us, Kitt.*

"Why have you summoned me?" Iris asked.

"You know why, Iris." Dacre's lackadaisical demeanor was infuriating. And yet the tension was brewing between them, pulling taut as a rope that had almost reached its limit.

"If you want my answer from your previous query," Iris said, "it's no."

"No . . . ?"

"I will not write for you."

"But you'll write for Enva? That's quite the, oh, what do you mortals call it? Roman, what word am I searching for?"

Roman was quiet, a beat too long. When he spoke, his voice was a rasp. "Hypocrisy, sir."

"Hypocrisy," Dacre repeated with a sharp-edged smile.

"I don't see how that's so," Iris said. "We mortals have the freedom to choose who or what we worship, if we worship at all."

"So you worship *her?*" His eyes narrowed, taking in Iris's garments. The dark green shirt, the pearl buttons. Clothes that Enva had left behind for her.

Iris didn't move. Could he sense it? That she had been with Enva through the night?

"What do you know of the divines?" Dacre said, his gaze returning to hers. Even then, Iris could hardly breathe. "Do you know that all of us, even the Skywards—Enva's self-righteous kin—seek our own gains? We are selfish by nature. We will do anything, even kill our own children, our siblings, our spouses to survive. Why do you think so few of us remain after there had once been hundreds of us, above and below?"

Dacre continued, oblivious to the thoughts cascading through Iris's mind.

"We care not for you and your kind other than to see what you may do for us, whether that is serving as a ward or dying glorious deaths. Or entertaining us with your silly songs and your craft, or even warming our beds if we desire it. And as the war has shown me . . . you long to worship something greater than yourselves, and you'll die for it if you must. You are fragile yet you are resilient. You hope even when there should be none."

He paused, watching Iris's face. Her mind was whirling, and he seemed to enjoy the bewildered gleam in her eyes.

"But most of all, you are fighting for a goddess who is a coward. She hides in plain sight. If war broke out in the streets of Oath, she would remain in the shadows. She will never offer you her aid, and she will gladly let you and your people die in her stead. Would you rather write for her, a goddess who has used her magic to lure me here, destroying your land in the process, or would you rather write for me, who walks shoulder to shoulder with you? Who has shown you that yes, a god can be cruel, but he can also be merciful?"

Iris broke their gaze. Her bones were humming, her doubt swarmed like a flood.

She thought back on the night before. Enva had been kind and gentle to Iris. She had aided her, sheltered her, given her knowledge like breadcrumbs to sustain her in the coming days. But Enva was still a divine. She wasn't human and she didn't understand the full breadth of mortality.

"I've never been devout," Iris said, meeting Dacre's stare. "And I write for no one but myself."

"A lonely mountain to claim," Dacre responded with a hint of derision.

"Is it? You say that I know nothing of your kind, but even after all this time walking among us, I don't think you truly understand us either, sir."

"Do not challenge me, Iris," he said. "Unless you think you will win."

His warning chilled her.

"Roman?" Dacre glanced at him. "Will you bring the typewriter to Iris?"

Iris swallowed as she felt Roman step closer. She could smell his cologne; it made her want to weep, to think of those old days when they had sparred with words and assignments. To remember how young they had seemed then, and to acknowledge where they both were now.

He moved her teacup aside, his hand pale, elegant. A hand that had touched her, explored her every line and bend. Fingertips that had once traced her lips when she gasped. Then he brought the typewriter over. He set it down carefully before her. The Third Alouette.

She studied it, blinking away the sting in her eyes. How many words had she written on this typewriter, a loyal companion through lonely nights? How many ideas had it taken of hers, turning them into eternal ink on paper? How many poems and letters had her nan typed upon it, years before Iris was born? How many hours had it comforted Roman, an anchor for him in the darkest days of his captivity?

It was immeasurable. Infinite. The magic still gathered, and it called to her.

And yet Iris refused to touch the keys.

Dacre stared at her, waiting. His patience was like ice in spring, breaking swiftly. A dark expression flickered across his face.

"Paper, Roman?"

Iris bit her lip as Roman obediently reached for a fresh page. He had to stand behind her, leaning over her shoulders, to roll the paper into the typewriter. She could feel the heat of him. She could feel his breath in her hair. He was careful not to touch her, even as his hands fell away and he straightened. He was mindful, like he knew his own limits, as well as hers.

If they touched now, it would shatter the story they had written to survive.

"Now can we discuss what I called you here to write?" Dacre asked. "I have an important article that I would——"

"I will not write for you," Iris cut him off.

Dacre arched a brow. He appeared surprised at first, as if her defiance was a burst of unexpected rain. But then his annoyance was evident as he pressed his lips into a thin line.

"You answer without even knowing the words I would ask you to type?" Dacre asked. "What sort of journalist are you, refusing to listen when knowledge is offered up to you? Knowledge that would save thousands of your own kind?"

Iris gritted her teeth, but she was shaking now. It felt like she had been set out in the snow and the wind, and no fire or sunlight could ever thaw her bones again. She was terrified, and her stomach was churning, threatening to heave up the meager toast and soup she had eaten that day.

Dacre snapped his fingers. "Roman? Set her hands upon the keys since Iris has forgotten how to type."

"Lord Commander," Roman said, but his voice was hoarse, like it hurt to speak. "I—"

"Or have you lost all your sense as well?"

"No, sir." He dutifully stepped forward again. Iris could feel him gazing at the fingers she had laced tightly on her lap. The shine of her wedding ring.

Roman hesitated.

If he touches me, I will sunder in two, she thought, fire in her blood. *If he touches me, I will come undone.*

Iris set her hands on the keys before Roman could reach down. But she still felt him, his presence close behind her. She could hear the sigh that unspooled from him.

"There now," Dacre said. "That wasn't so hard, was it, Iris?"

She couldn't answer. Her head ached when she realized how he had coerced her. How she had acquiesced to writing for him. Something she never wanted to do.

"Tell me when you're ready," he said, triumph gleaming in his eyes.

She sat there for a few more minutes, her hands frozen on the keys, her gaze on the strike bars. She wrestled with her vast disappointment, the slippery ghost of her fear, the anger, the longing, the words that had gathered and formed a painful dam in her chest.

But was she truly surrendering if she was staying alive? If she only gave him her hands?

Iris lifted her eyes. She looked at Dacre's neck, the cords of his throat that moved when he drank the last of the tea.

"I'm ready," she said.

43

Courtesy of Inkridden Iris

The afternoon air had cooled into evening by the time Tobias drove Iris away from the Kitt estate. But the city felt unnaturally quiet for what was normally its busiest hour.

Iris noticed most of the streets were empty, litter gathering at the curbs like flotsam in a river. Stores had already closed for the day. Flowers had been set in windowsills for the chancellor, who was still fighting for his life at the hospital. No children played in the yards or in the park, and people strode along the sidewalks with their coats belted tight and their eyes wide with worry. Doors were locked against the world, as if the war couldn't cross a threshold uninvited.

Iris knew better. She also knew Oath was shaken over Dacre's arrival and the fallout from the assassination attempt. Innocent people had died, and fresh graves were being dug in the cemetery. They wouldn't be the last, and the city felt like it was balancing on the edge of a knife, waiting to see which way it would fall.

Come tomorrow at noon, they would have their answer. She reached for the paper tucked into her pocket. A page inked with Dacre's words.

The sun was sinking behind the buildings, casting the clouds overhead in gold, when Tobias parked in front of the print factory. This was a place that never slept, printing newspapers through the midnight hour so they were ready to be picked up by newsboys at dawn. Iris could only hope that she wasn't too late to catch the *Inkridden Tribune.*

She slipped from the back seat, her legs shaky. "Thank you, Tobias. I can't tell you how much your help meant to me today."

He nodded, his arm hooked over the back of the seat. "Do you want me to wait here for you?"

Iris hesitated. Curfew was fast approaching, but this day was far from over. "Can you do one more thing for me?"

"Of course."

"Could you drive to the *Inkridden Tribune* and bring Helena here? Tell her it's extremely important."

"I'm on it." Tobias was already shifting the roadster into first gear. "I'll be back in a minute."

Iris watched him speed away, tasting the exhaust from the car.

She hurried up the stairs to the factory entrance, feeling the sting in her right foot. She wondered if her wounds were bleeding, but didn't have time to worry about it as she slipped through the heavy front doors.

"Excuse me?" Iris approached an older lady who sat behind a desk in the lobby. "I need to speak with Mr. Lawrence, the head printer."

The lady scrutinized Iris through her thick spectacles. Her gray-blond hair was wound in a tight bun. She looked like she never broke rules.

"He's busy in the composing room, overseeing the linotypes. But I can schedule you for an appointment tomorrow. He's open from noon to one, and then from——"

"I'm afraid this is incredibly urgent," Iris said with a forced smile. *Try to be pleasant,* she told herself, even as she felt like screaming. "I'm a reporter with the *Inkridden Tribune,* and I have an edit for tomorrow's paper."

"Edits aren't accepted this late."

"I *know,* ma'am. But this is an unusual exception. Please, I need to speak with him."

"You'll have to have an *appointment,* miss."

Iris didn't know what to do. She sighed in defeat, glancing at the glass wall to her left, where she could see into the composing room of the factory. Countless linotypes were at work; she could feel their steady humming in the floor. Iris walked closer to the window, watching as employees typed on the keypads before each machine. There was constant clicking and rattling as the linotypes created hot lead slugs to be used by the printing press on the second floor. It was fascinating to watch, even from a distance, and Iris wondered if one of the workers was currently typing out lines for the *Inkridden Tribune*'s paper. If so, Iris would have to convince Mr. Lawrence to scrap those lines of type and redo them.

She felt a wave of uncertainty until she glanced down at her hands, where she continued to hold Dacre's words. The god had been insistent on her publishing his article on the front page of tomorrow's *Tribune*. And Iris, who had clenched her jaw the entire time she had typed for him, knew she had no choice but to see such a command through. He hadn't cared when she said the paper might have already gone to print.

Then you had better hurry, Iris E.Winnow, had been his smug reply. Like he had had known she would have to run from one side of town to the other, rattled and worried. Like he had known she would have to fight tooth and nail to get this edit done for him.

Iris unfolded the paper, skipping over Dacre's introduction—all his flowery words that he used to reel people in—and she read the meat of the matter again. It was strange how much it still felt like a knife in her side, making her shoulders curve inward. She had typed these very words not an hour ago, and yet they still struck the breath from her.

As I am merciful, I will give you each a choice. Those of you who would join me in this new era of restoration and justice, come to safety. Come to my side of the city before the clock strikes noon today. Cross over the river to the northern side of Oath, where my soldiers will be waiting to welcome and shield you. No harm will come to you and your own should you make the crossing before midday. For those of you who refuse my offer and remain behind, south of the river, I cannot offer you protection. And as I am a

god who upholds justice, given what was done to me in the Green Quarter, you must prepare to face the consequences of your actions.

The lobby doors swung open.

Iris turned to see Helena and Tobias, both striding toward her.

"What's happened?" Helena panted.

Iris sagged in relief. "I need this to be the headline for tomorrow's edition." She handed over Dacre's speech.

Helena frowned as she skimmed the sentences. But then she realized whose words she was reading, and her face went deathly pale.

"Gods," she whispered, meeting Iris's stare. "He plans to bomb the southern side of Oath tomorrow?"

Iris nodded, stomach clenching. "I know that you were determined to never publish a word of his, Helena, but—"

"No, this is an exception. He's given us no choice." Helena looked at the glass wall, where the linotypes continued to work. "Where's Lawrence?"

"Mr. Lawrence is *busy*," the woman behind the desk said loudly. "I can schedule you for tomorrow at—"

"Yes, and there's a good chance this building won't be standing after tomorrow, Greta," Helena snapped. "Call Lawrence to the lobby. *Now.*"

Greta's face went red, and she huffed in indignation. But she picked up a telephone receiver and rang a call to the composing room. Five minutes later, Digby Lawrence arrived, his steel-gray hair smoothed back, his sleeves rolled up to his elbows. His fingertips were stained with ink, and there was a hearty scowl on his face, although Iris had never seen him *not* frowning in the rare times when she came by the printer.

"You know I don't take last-minute edits, Hammond," he said.

Helena ignored that comment. "Have you printed the *Tribune*?"

He must have heard the urgency, the fear that tinged her voice. "No," Lawrence said, softer. "It's on schedule to have its line of type created in an hour. Why?"

"I need to make an edit to the first page. I'm sorry, Lawrence, but I've no choice in the matter." She held the paper out to him.

Iris cracked her knuckles as Lawrence skimmed it. But she knew when he reached the threat, because the furrow in his brow deepened.

"All right," he said. "Let me halt production. Then you can come help me at one of the linotypes, and we'll make the edit."

"Wait," Iris breathed. "Has the *Gazette* gone to print?"

"Not yet. I always print it after the *Tribune*."

"Then will you also hold it alongside ours?"

"Iris," Helena said in a warning tone. "I can't interfere with another paper's production."

"I know," Iris replied. "But I have an idea. And I'm going to need the *Gazette* in order to pull it off."

Helena hesitated, as did Lawrence. It was Tobias who stepped forward, standing next to Iris.

"What does it matter?" he said, raising his hand. "Come tomorrow, this won't even be something we worry about."

"You're right." Helena reached for a cigarette in her pocket, twirling it in her fingers. "Lawrence?"

He stood there silent, far longer than Iris liked. But then he nodded.

"Fine. I'll hold both. Which means we'll be printing papers just before dawn." Lawrence glanced at Iris, eyes narrowing. "Whatever you have planned for the *Gazette* better be worth it, Miss Winnow."

Iris crossed her arms. It had been a long while since her words had been published in the *Gazette*. She didn't miss it most days, but every now and then, she would let herself fall back to the nostalgia, when she had been bright-eyed and eager, thinking she would become a columnist at Oath's prestigious newspaper.

It seemed rather fitting that she would commandeer the *Gazette* and write for it one final time.

She said, "Of course, Mr. Lawrence. I'm going to use it to tell people how they can find shelter during the bombing."

While Helena accompanied Lawrence to the composing room, preparing new slugs for the front page of the *Inkridden Tribune,* Iris and Tobias sat in the lobby with sheets of paper and pencils, writing down all the magical streets and buildings south of the river they could think of.

It wasn't as easy as Iris had originally anticipated because she knew the ley lines below didn't match the streets above perfectly. And while one half of an apartment complex or a building might be safe, there was the chance that the other side wouldn't be.

Iris rolled the pencil in her hand, staring at the addresses and street names she and Tobias had scribbled down. Some places she was certain of, recalling the map Roman had drawn for her. Other places she knew from experience, like that corner grocery she had often stopped at on her walks home from the *Gazette*. There was no denying it was an enchanted building with roots on a ley line, whose walls and roof would withstand a bomb. A safe place for people to shelter during the attack. But sometimes magic was softer. More discreet. Sometimes a structure wasn't as forthright about it, and Iris sighed.

"I don't want to misguide people," she said, rubbing her temples. "Claiming a building is safe to shelter in when it might not be."

Tobias was quiet, studying their list. "I know. But this is going to save more people than you realize, Iris."

She studied their list again, aching when she thought of how many people lived in the southern half of the city. The university was there, as were both the *Gazette* and the *Tribune*. Most of downtown. The Riverside Park. The opera house. The museum.

Iris lived south of the river, as did Attie and Tobias. The places they had grown up, the places they loved. All of it would be broken by Dacre tomorrow.

Iris glanced at the lobby doors. Night was fast approaching.

"You should head home, Tobias," she said. "I don't want you to get caught after curfew."

"What about you and Helena?"

"We'll be safe here. Thank you for all your help today."

"Anytime." He smiled, but he seemed sad. Worried. "I'm going to stop by Attie's on the way home, to let her and her family know what's happening, since they're south of the river."

Iris nodded. "I was going to walk there first thing tomorrow morning."

Tobias embraced her in farewell, and Iris felt his words rumble in his chest as he said, "Don't worry. We've gotten through quite a bit, and the last lap of a race is one of the hardest. But we'll make it through this time."

If Iris had said the words, she might have struggled to believe them. But Tobias had made the impossible bend like heated metal before, and she found comfort in the thought.

After he left, she gathered up their papers. Greta gave her a pointed look but didn't stop her when she slipped past her desk to find Lawrence and Helena working at one of the linotypes in the loud composing room.

"All right," Iris said, straining her voice to speak over the constant clicking. "I—"

Before she could continue, Helena took hold of her arm and guided her out into the quieter hallway.

"What do you have for me, kid?" Helena asked.

"This is what I'm thinking." Iris took a deep breath before continuing. "Dacre will be reading the *Inkridden Tribune* tomorrow, to see if I complied and got his announcement on the front page. I don't think he'll peruse the *Gazette* as well, but just in case, I think we should list a few addresses on the front page, like it's a mere advertisement, and then have it continue on the second or third, ending with the statement that these are presumed buildings on ley lines, and can provide the best shelter during the bombing."

Helena, unlit cigarette in her mouth, smiled. "I think that's brilliant, kid."

"Until Zeb Autry calls me in the morning and threatens to sue me," Lawrence said gruffly. Iris hadn't realized he had followed them into the hallway. "I know it won't matter after noon, but how am I to answer for his paper getting an 'advertisement' he never agreed to?"

"It's quite simple, actually." Iris laced her fingers behind her back. "Tell him it's courtesy of Inkridden Iris."

{ 44 }

Iron and Salt

It was almost dark when Iris walked to the closest tram stop to wait beneath the glow of a streetlamp. Helena had decided to stay at the printer through the night to assist Lawrence, dismissing Iris shortly after they had agreed what to do about the *Gazette*.

"Get home before nightfall, kid," Helena had said, lighting her cigarette at last. "Your brother, I'm sure, is keen to see you."

Iris hadn't protested. She felt exhausted and battered now that the article was out of her hands. And she did need to get home—she wanted to see Forest—but then she remembered the sword, still hiding under Helena's desk.

With a sigh, Iris began the brisk walk to the *Inkridden Tribune*. It wasn't far from the print factory, and she thankfully made it to the office before the last editor left.

"Lock up behind you, will you, Winnow?" he asked, shrugging on his coat.

Iris sat at her desk as if she planned to work through the night, but she nodded. "Yes, of course. Goodnight, Frank."

She waited until his footsteps faded away on the stairs before she rose and snatched a spare jacket from the rack. She hurried into Helena's office, worried that the sword would be gone. But it was still there, just as they had left it.

Iris knelt and wrapped the scabbard and hilt in the jacket. It was the best way she could think of transporting the sword home without revealing what it was—gods, what would she do if the Graveyard caught her with it?—and she was about to rise to her feet, sword awkwardly in tow, when she heard footsteps again. They were growing louder. Someone was descending the stairs, approaching the *Tribune*.

Iris remained behind Helena's desk. She hadn't locked the door when Frank strode out, thinking no one would swing by since curfew had almost struck. But now she was stranded in Helena's office, unsure who was coming.

She heard the main door open and close. Footsteps walking around the desks, almost hesitant, as if they were lost, or looking for something.

Iris held her breath as they drew closer to Helena's office. *Go away,* she thought, thinking whoever it was couldn't be here for anything good. But then she heard a muffled cough. Someone cleared their throat.

"Iris?"

The voice was familiar.

She shot to her feet, sword in her arms, and stared wide-eyed at the last person she had expected to see.

"Kitt?"

He nudged the office door open, the lamplight washing over her face.

"You hide under desks often, Winnow?" he drawled.

The mirth in his voice, the slight smile tugging on his lips, the way her last name sounded in his mouth. It was like they had fallen back in time, and it made Iris's chest ache. She had to swallow a sob, and she couldn't resist glaring at him.

"It suits me from time to time," she countered, but then her voice dropped low. "What are you doing here?"

"I was making sure you were all right when you left my house. And that you made it home safely. I've been waiting outside the printer and was surprised when you made a detour." Roman's eyes fixated on the bundle she carried. "Do I want to know what that is?"

"I'm sure you will. But let me bring it out to the light. Here, to my desk, actually." She walked past him, just shy of grazing his chest. But she heard his sharp inhale, and it made her pulse quicken.

Roman followed to her—lamentably—disorganized desk because who had time for keeping things neat these days? Her work typewriter sat with a half-typed sentence in its clutches, a few books sat open, and there was a messy pile of paper. She discreetly shoved the plate of old toast out of the way.

Roman watched as she threw off the jacket and exposed the sheathed sword.

He gave a low whistle. "You steal that from the museum, wife?"

"Do I look like a thief?" Iris grimaced. "Maybe don't answer that."

"Well, now that I get a better look at you . . ." Roman smiled, his eyes moving down her body, and then slowly up again. "I like your new haircut, by the way."

Iris snorted, but her cheeks flushed as she traced her hair. It was still crimped from the stylist, the shorter ends now brushing her collarbone. "Thank you. And this sword was actually *given* to me."

"By whom?"

"By Enva."

Roman froze. He listened, hung upon her every word, as Iris told him of last night: the bomb, finding refuge in the museum. The dream. The things Enva had revealed to her.

"You were right, Kitt," Iris said in conclusion. "She did kill Alva, Mir, and Luz, taking their power for her own but only as a preventative measure, so Dacre wouldn't steal their magic when he woke. The cost of it, though, has weakened her own gift of music and has kept her here, beholden to Oath."

"And why didn't she just go ahead and slay Dacre in his grave while she was at it?" Roman asked sharply. "It would have saved us endless trouble if she had done that *one* thing."

Iris hesitated, chewing on her lip. "I'm not sure. I didn't realize it was her until the dream was about to break. I wish I could have spoken to her longer."

Roman was quiet, his gaze drifting to the sword. "And she now wants *you* to kill Dacre."

"Yes."

"She has all that power at her disposal, and she still commands you to go."

"She didn't *command* me," Iris said, but then wondered why she was feeling defensive. In some ways, she could see the draw of the Graveyard and their beliefs. Meddling with gods never seemed to benefit humans. There was always a catch.

"I don't know how to get Dacre below where he'll be enchanted by music," she confessed.

Roman began to pace, raking his hands through his hair. Iris carefully set the sword aside and sat on the edge of her desk, legs dangling, as Roman sorted through his wild ideas. But then he stopped and turned, staring at Iris with dark, glittering eyes.

"Do you remember when we were in the trenches? How Lieutenant Lark told us that the eithrals never appeared at the front but were reserved for civilian towns, kilometers from the actual fighting?"

Iris nodded.

"I think it's because Dacre is the one who commands the eithrals when they drop bombs, and to do that, he must be underground," Roman continued. "During any bombardments in the trenches, he wants to be above, overseeing the assault. But during the stalemates, when nothing happened for days, he would descend into his realm and send out the eithrals to terrorize civilians. And he was always in complete control of the beasts."

Iris traced the bow of her lips. "If that's true, then Dacre will be . . ."

"Below tomorrow, when the city is bombed," he finished. "There's over a hundred crates in my backyard. The bombs he plans to use. He'll be sending his eithrals there to pick them up, one by one, to then carry them southward to drop. That is when we need to make our move."

"We?"

"Did you think I would let you go alone?"

"Attie will be with me."

"And what door do the two of you plan to use?"

"Your parlor door?"

"It's heavily guarded. I don't think I'll be able to sneak you in."

"What about the keys?"

Roman rubbed his jaw. "I might be able to find a key. One was on the war table yesterday, unclaimed."

The idea of Roman stealing one of Dacre's beloved keys made Iris's blood go cold. She was quiet, desperate to think of another way, but there was none. It would need to be the parlor door, which was surrounded by Dacre's soldiers, or a key to unlock their own threshold.

"I wish it didn't have to come to this," she said.

Roman's expression softened, like her words had struck a bruise. He stepped closer until he stood between her legs. Leaning on the desk, his hands on either side of her, he bracketed her in.

Iris didn't move, spell cast as Roman's gaze aligned with hers.

"If you had touched me today, Kitt," she whispered. "I don't think I could've hidden it anymore. Who you are to me. Who I am to you."

"Like this?" He brushed her knee with his thumb, just beneath her skirt. His touch was soft but possessive, and Iris closed her eyes. "Or this, Iris?" She could feel his fingers caress up her arm and across her shoulder, stopping at the buttons of her blouse.

"Yes." She tilted her head back when she felt his mouth on her throat.

"Did you think I would let him tell me when and how to touch you?" Roman's voice was hoarse as he traced her jaw with his lips. "Did you think that I would let him steal this last moment from me? When I would surrender only to you, take you in my hands, and burn with you before the end comes?"

"This is not our last moment," she said, holding his stare. But she felt the weight of his statement as if it were fate.

She wrapped her legs around his waist, her skirt pooling on the desk. Over the papers and the books, the typewriter glinting as the table shuddered beneath them.

"Write me a story, Kitt," she whispered, kissing his brow, the hollow of his cheeks. His lips and his throat, until she felt like love was an axe that had cleaved her chest open. Her very heart beating in the air. "Write me a story where you keep me up late every night with your typing, and I hide messages in your pockets for you to find when you're at work. Write me a story where we first met on a street corner, and I spilled coffee on your expensive trench coat, or when we crossed paths at our favorite bookshop, and I recommended poetry, and you recommended myths. Or that time when the deli got our sandwich orders wrong, or when we ended up sitting next to each other at the ball game, or I dared to take the train west just to see how far I could go, and you just so happened to be there too."

She swallowed the ache in her throat, leaning back to meet his gaze. Gently, as if he were a dream, she touched his hair. She smoothed the dark tendrils from his brow.

"Write me a story where there is no ending, Kitt. Write to me and fill my empty spaces."

Roman held her gaze, desperation gleaming in his eyes. An expression flickered over his face, one she had never seen before. It looked like both pleasure and pain, like he was drowning in her and her words. They were iron and salt, a blade and a remedy, and he was taking a final gasp of air.

Please, Iris prayed, drawing him closer. *Don't let this be the end.*

But it made their joining all the sweeter, all the sharper, with skin glistening like dew, with breaths ebbing and flowing, their names turned into ragged whispers.

To write the story they both wanted that night.

To think it could be their last.

45

A Hundredfold, a Thousandfold

Roman knew he had stayed out too late. He tried not to dwell on the consequences as he walked Iris home, one hand woven with hers, the other holding her jacket-wrapped sword. The streets were emptier than he had anticipated—even the Graveyard kept to their dens that night, as if they sensed the end was near. A slight rumble in the ground coaxed people to draw the curtains, lock the door, and curl up close to the ones they loved.

Iris's flat came into view just as it began to mist. The lights glimmered like fallen stars, and Roman stopped between streetlamps, in a velvet patch of shadow. But he could still see Iris, faintly. The way the mist gathered, iridescent in her hair. How her eyes shined, and her lips parted as she gazed up at him.

"Do you want to come inside?" she asked. "Forest is there. I'm sure he'd like to say hello."

Roman shifted, uncomfortable. He had conflicted feelings about Forest, but he didn't want Iris to know that. The main issue being how he had watched Forest drag her along unknowingly during the bluff attack. How Forest had intentionally run *from* Roman, separating him from Iris.

And yet after living among Dacre's forces, disoriented and lonely, carrying wounds that still ached . . . Roman understood things better. He felt like he had only been looking at life through a periscope before. And now he saw how vast the horizon was. There was also the fact that Roman, in a strange way, felt like he knew Forest, from all of Iris's letters in the beginning.

"I'm afraid I need to get back," he said, which was the truth. "But I'd like to see Forest soon. Perhaps we can go to the Riverside Park together?"

The park, which might be demolished by tomorrow evening.

Iris nodded, but Roman could see her swallow. He couldn't tell if there were tears in her eyes, but he could feel his own sting in warning.

He kissed her goodbye. And he wanted to be gentle, but it was a clash of their mouths, nips with their teeth and gasps that made a shiver trace his bones. He felt Iris cling to him, and he knew if he didn't pull away from her that instant, he never would. He would follow her into her flat. He would peel away their damp clothes and lie beside her in bed. He would hold her to his heart and pray the morning never came.

"Goodnight, Winnow," he whispered, setting the sword in her hands. He took a step back, surprised how the distance made it feel like a rib had cracked. "I'll see you tomorrow."

"All right," Iris said.

Neither of them moved. They had forged a plan to meet up in the north side of town, Iris and Attie using Dacre's invitation for safety as a cover. Roman would hopefully have the key the girls needed to hand off to them at half past eleven. If he failed to snag it, then they would fall back to the only option they had: Roman would sneak them into the mansion and clear the way to the parlor door.

"I'll wait here," Roman said. "Until you make it safely inside."

Iris took a step away, still facing him.

He watched as the lamplight gilded her, then she turned and hurried up the stairs to the apartment. He watched, hands in his pockets, heart in his throat, until he made sure Iris had entered her flat and closed the door behind her.

Only then did he surrender to the shadowed streets, heading north of the river.

To the place that he called home but felt like the furthest thing from it.

All right.

That empty phrase had been the last words she said to him.

Iris felt numb as she stepped inside the flat, locking the door behind her.

All right, as if they were meeting up for tea tomorrow. As if the world wasn't about to collapse and burn.

"Iris? Is that you?"

She snapped out of her daze when she heard Forest's voice drifting from the kitchen.

"Yes." She set the sword on the sideboard and hurried to meet him in the center of the room, letting him sweep her up off her feet in a bear hug. The air was squeezed out of her; Iris almost laughed. It reminded her of the embraces he used to give her in the old days, when their mother was still with them. Before things had fallen apart.

"Gods, Iris." Forest set her back down, cradling her face in his calloused hands. "I was worried about you."

"I know, but I'm *fine.*" She smiled to reassure him. "Just a few scratches on my knees."

She had called the mechanic shop that morning from the *Tribune* telephone, knowing news of the Green Quarter bombing was going to spread. She had never heard Forest's voice shake like it had on the line, and she felt guilty that she was getting home so late.

"Is Prindle here?" she asked.

"No, she's with her family tonight. And you should have been home *hours* ago."

"I had something urgent to deliver to the printer. It took longer than I expected." She walked to her room, thoughts tangling together. "And there's something I need to tell you, but let me change my clothes first."

"Funny you say that," Forest said. "Because I have news for you as well."

Why did Iris's heart twist? Why did she assume it was something bad?

"I'll make us some tea," her brother offered, as if sensing her trepidation.

When Iris reemerged into the living room, Forest was sitting on the couch. A pot of black tea with two chipped cups was waiting on the table, and she accepted one gratefully, wrapping her cold fingers around the porcelain.

"You go first, Forest," Iris said, settling beside him on the cushion.

"Well," he began, but hesitated, scratching his jaw. It looked like he was trying to grow out a beard, but it was still too sparse. "You know I went to the doctor last week? He gave me medicine to ease my symptoms, which have been helping, but he also wanted to take an X-ray. So he did and . . . I had another visit with him yesterday about the results."

Iris braced herself for anything. She felt light-headed as she said, "What were they, Forest?"

He sighed, staring into his tea. "They found bullet fragments still in me. I think when Dacre healed me, he left them behind intentionally. To serve as a punishment if I ever broke away from him. Maybe he even thought the pain would eventually drive me back to his side. But now I realize it's been gradually making me feel sick, a little more each day."

Tears welled in Iris's eyes. She set her teacup aside and turned to face Forest on the couch, reaching out to take his hand.

"I'm so sorry," she whispered. "I can't even imagine what that feels like, Forest."

He chuckled. A way to deflect, but there was a tremor in his hands as he also set down his tea. "The bad news is I need more surgery. But the good news is the doctor believes he can remove all the fragments, and while I'll probably still have symptoms, they won't be as bad as they were. The medicine will help me manage them."

"And I'll be here to help you," Iris said. "When do they want to do the surgery?"

"Next Mir's Day."

Now Iris was the one to hesitate. The hospital was south of the river, and she wouldn't put it beyond Dacre to bomb it.

"What is it?" Forest whispered, reading the lines on her face.

Iris told him about Dacre's ultimatum. How she'd had to rush to the printer to force the edits, and how she believed certain streets and houses would be safe despite the imminent bombing. She hated how the words burned through her like smoke. How the hope in Forest's eyes, kindled by his recovery and his hope for the future, swiftly dimmed.

He leaned back against the couch, staring up at the water-stained ceiling. "We won't be safe here, will we?"

Iris wasn't sure. Sometimes their flat had strange quirks, but she didn't know if it was due to a ley line or the fact this building was old. She glanced around and tried to imagine what it would feel like if their home turned to rubble, but she still felt numb.

"I think we'll need to shelter elsewhere. I know a few good places that aren't too far from here." She almost told Forest that she wouldn't be with him the entire time, that while Oath was weeping, she would be in the realm below. But the words tasted like rust; she kept them to herself, and instead reached for a thick book on the table. "One of Prindle's?"

Forest seemed glad for the distraction. "Yes. I've been reading to her in the evenings. She's trying to convince me that I do, in fact, like fiction. I just need to find the right story."

"Will you read it to me?"

Her brother gave a shy smile but accepted the book, opening it to where he and Sarah had left off. "I might put you to sleep."

"That's all right," Iris said, pulling a blanket over her legs.

All right. Those two words again. They didn't fit the night, or maybe they did, and she just couldn't realize it until now.

Iris let herself rest, listening to Forest read, his deep voice a comforting burr. She didn't tell him that she was afraid to sleep alone, worried about what she would meet her in dreams. Explosions and broken bodies and blood and Dacre following her through the smoke. She didn't tell him that she was afraid, but the more he read, the more her fears gave way. They lurked in the corners, but were weak compared to Forest's steady, luminous presence.

Iris fell asleep with her head on his shoulder.

. . .

There was no need for Roman to sneak back into the estate. After he had watched Iris leave the parlor that afternoon, he'd decided to approach Dacre directly, his heart smoldering. He had looked the god in the eye and calmly asked if he could trail her.

"Why?" Dacre had said. He didn't sound suspicious, but he wanted to be convinced.

"So I can ensure she does what you ask," Roman had replied.

"You think she won't?"

"Did you not see how stubborn she is, sir?"

Dacre was pensive. But then, for some wild reason, he had agreed to it.

Roman had walked out the front gates of his own volition, and now he was returning, hours later. He knew his time of freedom was overspent and Dacre would be wondering what had delayed him. He also knew he needed to snatch the key from the war table where it had sat on a pile of papers, the iron darkened from Captain Landis's blood.

Roman was thinking about that as he approached the front doors, clicking his fingernails together. The mist had beaded on his trench coat, soaked through his hair. He coughed into his hands, again and again, clearing his lungs despite the razor-sharp pain in his chest.

It tasted awful, but he swallowed it down, his stomach nauseous from the walk home.

His mind was far away as the doors groaned open. Two soldiers met him, stone-faced and silent as Roman started to walk past them, his wet shoes squeaking on the foyer floor.

"The Lord Commander is waiting for you at the war table," one of the soldiers said.

It was never good to keep Dacre waiting, but Roman was prepared. He nodded and made his way to the parlor, but with each step, his confidence waned, until he felt like a husk of who he had been just hours ago when he was with Iris.

The parlor doors were open. Light spilled out into the corridor, and Roman stepped inside, surprised to see a group had gathered within the room.

Dacre was sitting at the table in his favorite chair, with the fire crackling at his back and shadows dancing over his face. Four of his officers stood beside him, one of them being Lieutenant Shane. Mr. Kitt was also present, but he looked the most haggard Roman had ever seen him, his clothes rumpled, his body slumped in a chair like he had lost all hope.

It was the red-eyed despair of his father that made Roman's heart falter.

Something was wrong.

"Lord?" Roman said, his gaze returning to Dacre. "She delivered the article to the printer. It should be on the front page of the *Inkridden Tribune* tomorrow, as you desired."

"You are quite late, Roman," Dacre replied, as if he hadn't heard a word Roman had said. "How come?"

"It took her a while at the print factory. To make an edit like that . . . the head printer gave her some resistance."

"Hmm." Dacre smiled, but it didn't reach his eyes. He traced his lower lip with the edges of his teeth. "Why did you steal from me?"

Roman's breath wavered. "Sir?"

"Have I not been good to you? Have I not given you more freedoms than most?" Dacre stared at him for a long, torturous beat. "Search him."

The two soldiers who had greeted Roman at the door stepped forward. They roughly tore his coat away and began to pat him down.

Don't resist it, Roman told himself, even as he bristled.

"Sir?" he said. "I don't understand."

Dacre didn't reply. The soldiers came up empty save for the green bird volume. They tossed it onto the table, and Roman watched as Dacre sifted through the brittle pages. His brow arched when he realized there were no hidden messages to find within it. There was nothing to cast guilt upon Roman. It was simply a book about birds, and Dacre snorted, hurling it into the fire.

Roman flinched as Iris's book flared into a bright flame. Slowly, it melted into smoke, leaving behind curls of ash. But the words and illustrations remained, seared into his mind.

He thought about the owls, the herons, the albatrosses, the nightingales. The pages that had been worn down the most. Dog-eared and smudged, as if they had been touched by countless hands, read over and over again.

He thought about the birds that had broken their wings, refusing to remain captive.

"Where is the key, Roman?" Dacre asked.

"What key?"

"Don't play coy. I know you saw it, sitting on this table. It was here this morning before Iris Winnow visited, and now it is gone. What have you done with it?"

Roman's mind raced. Sweat broke out on his palms. "Sensitive information was removed from the table before Iris visited, to be stored in a back room. So she wouldn't see anything of note. It was your own orders, sir, and the key must have been misplaced—"

"How many other lies have you told me?" Dacre interrupted.

Roman froze. *This is a test.* And yet he didn't know how to answer.

Footsteps sounded in the corridor. A lazy, confident pace. A second later, Roman felt the rain-soaked presence of someone tall and intimidating standing behind him.

Roman turned to see Val, jaded eyes boring through him.

"Report," Dacre said.

Val's gaze shifted to meet Dacre's. "He followed her to the printer, as he told you. He waited outside for hours, until Iris Winnow emerged. She walked down the street; he trailed her. When she made a stop at the *Tribune,* he did as well. They were together for an hour or so before he walked her to her flat. They had . . . quite the romantic exchange."

The blood drained from Roman's face. Up until that moment—when he realized Dacre had sent Val to follow and observe him—Roman had believed he could salvage this situation. Even with Dacre's paranoia about the missing key. But now he knew his time had come to an end. There was nothing he could say, no lie he could spin, that would free him from the web.

"I take it Iris *E.* Winnow is Iris *Elizabeth* Winnow," Dacre said in a smooth, dark tone.

Roman's attention snapped back to the god. He finally noticed the papers spread before Dacre on the table. Roman's handwriting, sprawled across the pages. His confession, which Shane had been holding.

It's over.

You don't have to pretend anymore.

Roman glanced at the lieutenant.

Shane appeared bored, his hands laced behind his back, his eyes heavy-lidded. But his nostrils flared when their gazes clashed.

Roman wanted to ask him *why*. Why betray him now? Why expose him now? His fingers curled into fists, nails biting crescents into his palms, and he wondered if he should likewise expose Shane for who he was.

You have no proof!

The truth rang through him like he was hollow. He had burned the missive Shane had given him, because he had been afraid to have it on his person. A mistake now, although maybe it wouldn't have mattered in the end.

Shane had the upper hand, throwing Roman to the wolves to save himself.

And Roman would not do the same to him. Even now, in the moment before his disgrace took root, Roman wouldn't see another man brought low and wounded by a devious god.

I've played my part, and I've been outsmarted.

But his chest stung when he thought of Iris. She was depending on him tomorrow.

Roman's silence had gone too long. Dacre rose, his full height menacing. Every wall, every person in the room seemed to lean toward him, like he was a whirlpool. A collapsed star. The center of gravity.

"I will ask you four final questions, Roman," Dacre said. "Four questions, which you may answer. Choose your words wisely because I will not tolerate any further lies from you."

Roman gave a slight nod, waiting.

"Why did you betray me?" Dacre asked. "Why did you give Iris *Elizabeth* Winnow the information about Hawk Shire? Was I not good to you? Did I not save you?"

Roman exhaled. He was thinking about his reply, what he wanted to say and how to articulate it, when his father stood abruptly from his chair.

"Lord Commander," Mr. Kitt pleaded. "Please, my son is unwell, as you can see, and—"

Dacre held up his hand. "Be quiet. Let Roman speak."

Mr. Kitt bowed his head.

Roman didn't look directly at his father, but from the corner of his eye, he saw how he was quaking. A strange thing to witness, one's formidable father brought low.

"I betrayed you," Roman began, "because I love her."

Dacre wasn't expecting that response. He appeared baffled, and then he laughed, a rich but scathing sound. "And that is grounds to destroy yourself? My, you mortals think with your hearts when you should give power to your minds."

"I betrayed you because I love Iris Elizabeth Winnow," Roman continued smoothly, as if he hadn't heard Dacre's taunt. "She represents all that is good in this realm, and your attack on Hawk Shire, simply put, threatened her.

"I couldn't bear to live in a world where she was slain by your selfishness, and so I warned her. I couldn't bear to live in a world where you killed countless of my people or wounded them, only to heal them in part so that they would feel confused, indebted, and beholden to you. You, sir, never healed me as you should have. You are the author of my wounds to begin with. I would have never breathed the gas that has scarred my lungs if not for you. I would have never felt the bite of shrapnel in my leg if not for you.

"And what a cruel and terrible thing it is, to be a divine with such power and magic, and yet find yourself so small-minded and afraid that you decide to live out your endless days harming others. Instead of letting us *choose* to love you for the good you could be, you have forced us to serve you by way of pain and terror. That is unforgivable, and a lesson you will have learned too late, when you lose this war against us.

"You never saved me, like you claim. In the field of Avalon Bluff. You didn't save me, but Iris did."

Dacre slammed his fist on the table. His lips curled back in a sneer. All his immortal beauty morphed into something so ugly that Roman winced to see the true bones beneath the skin. The rotten heart of Dacre, a divine who only cared for himself.

"You betrayed me for a woman?" Dacre said. "You are the greatest fool in my forces, as well as my greatest shame."

The words rolled off Roman. He smiled, feeling like he had swallowed a flame. It was lighting up his marrow. Illuminating his veins.

"Oh, I would betray you a hundredfold," he said, his voice rising. "I would betray you a *thousandfold* for her."

"*Enough!*" Dacre's outburst cut through the air. Tension crackled in the room like lightning; Roman waited to be struck.

He wasn't afraid. Even as his knees shook, he knew the trembling was forged from courage. He had spoken the words he wanted—the words that he *felt*—and he had no further regrets.

"Take him below and shackle him on traitor's row," Dacre said to Val.

Roman didn't resist as he felt Val grip his arms from behind, twisting them to make Roman acquiesce.

"Then, once he is secured below," Dacre continued, and his voice took on a delighted edge, "go and fetch Iris. Bring her to me. I'd like to speak with her again."

"No," Roman whispered. The full force of Dacre's command hit him like a sword, splitting him open. He began to flail. He fought Val's iron-tight hold. "*No!*"

He screamed until his voice felt ripped clean from his throat. Val was dragging him to the parlor door, which waited open like a maw, shadowed from the realm below. But Roman made it difficult. He almost slipped away, his skin tingling with bruises, when Dacre loomed over him.

The god lifted his hand and curled his fingers.

Roman gasped as his lungs tightened in response.

The strength drained from his limbs as he began to slump. Stars speckled his vision. But he whispered her name in his mind. He clung to it as the darkness devoured him.

Iris.

46

Your Soul Sworn to Mine

Iris opened her eyes, uncertain what had woken her. Her head was propped on Forest's shoulder, his breathing heavy with sleep.

They were sitting on the couch, and it was dark beyond the window curtains. The tea was still on the table, and the book was open on Forest's lap. Only one lamp was lit, and its light was a hazy amber, casting streaks on the walls.

It was quiet until Iris heard the water running in the kitchen. There was the unmistakable clink of a kettle being set on the cooker. Someone was in the flat with them, and Iris rose to her feet, gooseflesh rippling over her skin.

She walked toward the kitchen, rounding the corner to see the intruder.

Long dark hair. A homespun dress. A belt made of woven flowers.

"Enva?" Iris said, unable to hide her shock.

Enva turned to regard her. "Hello, Iris."

"Are you truly here, or am I dreaming?"

The goddess didn't reply in words, but when she reached for the steaming kettle, the pot melted in her hands.

A dream, then, Iris thought. "Why have you come to visit me again?"

Enva straightened, as if she suddenly felt uncomfortable in a kitchen, seeking to do mortal tasks. "I wanted to see you again. Before you made the descent below."

Iris studied her a long moment. "How many other dreams have you walked?"

"More than I could count."

"You've visited Attie."

"Yes," Enva replied carefully. "I wanted you both to hear the lullaby."

"What about Forest?"

"A few times."

"And Kitt?" Iris asked. "Have you visited his dreams?"

"Not in the way you think."

"How, then?"

Enva waved her hand over the cooker. The kettle reappeared and remained solid as she gripped it, pouring hot water into a teacup. "I helped him remember who he was."

Iris was silent, recalling the words Roman had typed to her. *Every night when I dreamt, I was trying to bring all the pieces back together. I was trying to find my way back to you.*

"By which you undermined Dacre," said Iris.

Enva kept her gaze on her teacup as she doled out a spoonful of honey. "There were a number of soldiers from Oath who I inspired to fight. Your brother was one of them. I hoped they would give enough aid to the west so that Dacre could be killed by a mortal's hand. But many of these soldiers died in graves I have yet to sing over, and some my husband healed and used for his forces in a twisted way. I could not leave the city in my corporeal form, but I could use Alva's magic to reach these soldiers in dreams. To help them remember who they were."

"Why didn't you kill him when you had the chance?" Iris asked quietly. "If you killed Mir, Alva, and Luz in their graves, why not Dacre?"

At this, Enva turned away. Her posture was rigid as she breathed, and Iris wondered if she was about to dissolve from the dream, choosing to wane rather than answer.

"Have you ever given someone a vow, Iris?"

Enva's question was so unexpected that Iris merely blinked. But when she closed her eyes, she could still hear an echo of herself, speaking vows to Roman in a twilit garden.

Even then, may I find your soul still sworn to mine.

"Yes," Iris said.

"When I went below to rule beside him, I gave him my vow as he gave me his. But I didn't realize that Skyward promises are vastly different from those of Underlings. With my words, I vowed to never end his immortality, but he didn't grant the same to me. I didn't fear that he would kill me in those honeymoon days, even as I wandered deep in his domain. I knew that he was charmed by my presence, but one day he would grow weary of me. One day, I would find him holding a blade to my throat, hungry to steal my magic and be rid of me." Enva drank the tea and set the cup on the counter. She looked over her shoulder and held Iris's gaze. "I could wound him, though. Humiliate him. Leave his realm if I could outsmart him. But I could not break my vows and kill him."

Iris let the words sink in. She wondered if upholding immortality was woven into Skyward vows to prevent spouses from marrying and then killing each other. To prevent gods from stealing more power from the ones they were closest to. The ones they were supposed to love.

"I lied to my husband many times," Enva continued. "And I lied to Alzane, your mortal king, when he asked me to kill the other four divines. We had an agreement that I could be the last goddess in the realm——the last vessel of magic——but I needed to give another vow and stay in Oath so the king could keep me within his clutches. The song I sang over Mir, Alva, and Luz was like a blade to their sleeping throats. They were trouble, and it was good to see them gone. But Dacre? I could not kill him, and so I sang for as long as I could, to hold him in a grave for centuries. Alzane never knew it; he thought all the gods dead save for me, and he spun a story that we were all sleeping, so his people could continue to worship and live in blissful magic and peace."

Iris studied Enva's face. She wondered what it would be like to hold a lie for so long. To be sworn to a husband who yearned for bloodshed. To be immeasurably powerful but trapped in a city. To find only anguish in magic that had once been incandescent with joy.

"He's in Oath," Iris said. "At the Kitt estate."

"I know." Enva glanced away. "I found him in a dream. It was then I knew he would stop at nothing until he held my severed head in his hands."

"*Iris.*"

It was Forest's voice, distant but laced with urgency. Iris could feel his hand on her knee, shaking her.

The dream began to waver, threatening to break. Iris gritted her teeth, striving to keep it intact for a moment longer, even as the floor began to vanish in patches beneath her.

"Why did you come to me as my mother?" she dared to ask. "Why not show me who you were to begin with?"

Enva smiled. It was a sad crescent of a moon, and her hair began to whip around her as if she were being drawn into a storm.

"You mortals are slow to trust. And I needed you to trust me, Iris."

The dream collapsed without warning.

Iris startled awake, light-headed and cold with sweat. Forest was shaking her knee again, and she straightened, feeling a crick pull in her neck. "What is it?"

"Do you hear that?" His voice was so low she almost couldn't catch the words.

They both listened, unmoving, their breaths shallow. *There,* she heard it that time. It sounded like someone was picking the lock on the front door.

"Get up quietly," said Forest. "Hide in the kitchen. If things turn bad, I want you to run. Go straight to Attie's, all right?"

Iris couldn't speak, her eyes flaring in fear.

"*Go,*" Forest urged, drawing her with him as he stood.

She did as he wanted, rushing into the shadows of the kitchen and crouching behind the row of cabinets. She didn't have a vantage point of the living room from here, and that made her anxious. She couldn't see Forest, and she didn't understand why this was happening. Why would someone break into their flat in the dead of night?

The door creaked open.

For a moment, there was nothing but utter silence, so keen that Iris was afraid to draw breath. Then came the footsteps. The air suddenly smelled like mist, dank stone, and worn leather. The lamplight flickered.

Iris bit the palm of her hand, smothering a surge of terror.

The stranger came to a stop.

A beat later, there was a loud crash and a grunt. It sounded like a table had cracked, bodies rolling into furniture and bumping the wall so hard it made the lone picture frame rattle. The amber light flickered again as the lamp was overturned. The flat was overcome with darkness, and Iris panted, her muscles burning as she continued to crouch.

Someone cried out in pain. It went through Iris like a shock of electricity, and she knew it was Forest. She knew it like she had been struck herself.

He wanted her to run and leave him behind. But she gritted her teeth and rose, remembering the sword she had left on the sideboard.

She knew this flat intimately. She could walk it in utter darkness, and she moved without a sound. But as she entered the common room, a thread of light from the streetlamp bled inside. Iris saw the broken table, the teapot shattered across the floor. Forest's medicine bottles were cracked, revealing a trail of pills. She could see two shadows wrestling each other up against the couch, the one on top punching the other relentlessly.

Forest cried out again, caught below the intruder.

"Where is she?" the unfamiliar voice asked. "Where is your sister?"

He wanted *her,* and Iris reached for the sword.

The jacket fell away as she unsheathed the blade. She was shaking as she eased forward. She wondered if her bones would come out of their sockets as she lifted the sword, belatedly remembering what Enva had told her about it.

It cuts through bone and flesh like a knife does butter, if only its wielder offers the blade and the hilt a taste of their blood first. A sacrifice, to weaken yourself and wound your own hand before striking.

Iris hesitated before she reached for the sword's edge. She winced as the steel stung her palm, her blood beginning to flow and drip, hot and swift. It hurt to hold the hilt with both hands; the metal became slick, and she had never felt more awkward wielding something in her life.

But she stepped forward again, a piece of the broken pot crunching beneath her foot.

The intruder stopped striking her brother and turned to look at her, a sliver of light cutting across his face.

Iris recognized him. It was one of Dacre's men. Val. The one who had been transporting Roman's articles to the *Gazette*. The one who commanded ei-thrals and rode on their backs.

"Put the sword down, Iris," he said as he stood and faced her. He held out his gloved hand. There were metal spikes on the backs of the knuckles. "Come with me, and I'll let your brother live."

Forest groaned on the floor. It distracted Iris, and she glanced at her brother. His face was bloodied; his nose looked broken.

Val darted forward, taking advantage of her split attention.

He intended to knock the sword away from her, no doubt believing it would be an easy feat. But Iris lowered her hands so that the pommel was braced against her waist, the point of the sword angled up. Val walked directly into it, the steel sinking into his chest.

He let out a strangled gasp, staring at Iris in shock. She saw the recognition flash though him, a moment too late. Which blade she held.

As he fell, the sword continued to slice upward, catching on two silver necklaces that hung beneath his clothes. A flute and an iron key. The chains broke beneath the steel's enchantment, clinking to the floor like chimes as the blade continued to cut until it had divided his heart, his sternum, the branch of his ribs.

I just killed him.

Iris whimpered, but she didn't let go of the hilt. She watched as Val collapsed on the floor, blood pooling beneath him. She stared at the key and the small flute, islands in a growing red lake. Her skin prickled as her gorge rose, a bitter taste haunting her mouth.

I just killed a man.

"Iris."

She dropped the blade and stepped over Val to reach her brother.

"Are you hurt?" he rasped.

"No," Iris said, even as her palm burned. "But you are." Focusing on him gave her a distraction. She reached for the blanket on the couch and gently wiped his face.

"It's not as bad as it looks," Forest said. "But who was that? What did he want with you?"

"He's one of Dacre's men," she replied, helping Forest to his feet.

The two of them stared down at Val, uncertain what to do. Should they leave him here? Bury him somewhere? Burn him?

Iris bent to take the flute and the key, amidst Forest's protests.

"Don't, Iris!"

She didn't answer, her fingers closing over the key. She reached for the sword next, and before Forest could demand any further answers from her, she spoke first.

"We can't stay here tonight. We need to leave."

I killed someone, Iris thought, clenching her eyes shut.

And she shivered when she acknowledged that he wouldn't be the last.

Attie's father didn't appear shocked to find Iris and Forest on the front porch, quietly knocking on the door in the dead of night. The town house's lights were on, illumination seeping through the shutters, and it had made Iris feel a little better about disturbing her friend's family at such a late hour.

Mr. Attwood took one look at Iris, with her snarled hair and the sword sheathed at her back, and Forest, whose face was battered, and he opened the door wide.

"I'm so sorry," Iris said, breathless from their harried trek over. "I . . . we didn't know where else to go."

The scent of treacle and sugar biscuits drifted from the house. It almost made Iris sink to her knees.

"Come in, *come in,*" said Mr. Attwood, reaching out to welcome them. "You look like you've had a rough night, and we just brewed some tea."

. . .

"Sometimes I bake when I can't sleep," Attie said, setting the plate of warm biscuits on the dining room table. "A few nights in the Bluff, I baked with Marisol. She taught me a thing or two about scones, which I can never get right."

Iris smiled, reaching for one of the sugar biscuits. She didn't feel hungry, but there was something about the sweetness, melting on her tongue, that made her feel as if she had returned to her body. It cut through the numbness.

Forest sat beside her, thankful for Mrs. Attwood's ministrations as she took a needle and thread and sutured his split eyebrow. Tobias sat on the other side of the table, next to Attie. Iris wasn't surprised to see him there, or that Attie's family had insisted he stay the night when the curfew had hit during his visit.

The Attwoods were all aware of what was coming. It was why they were still awake; sleep seemed impossible that night. Only Attie's younger siblings were tucked away in their beds on the upper floor, oblivious to what would happen in the morning. Their parents had wanted it to feel like any normal night, so the children wouldn't worry.

"We'll go to the McNeils' tomorrow," Mrs. Attwood said, setting down a freshly brewed pot of tea. "I know their house is on a ley line. We'll be safe there."

Mr. Attwood nodded, although he seemed troubled.

Tobias had hardly spoken a word, lost in his thoughts as he munched on his fourth sugar biscuit. But Attie met Iris's gaze over the table. Neither of them had mentioned their mission below, and they didn't know how to break the news either.

By three in the morning, all the tea had been drained and the biscuits eaten. The group shifted to the living room, to sit in a more comfortable space. While Mr. Attwood stoked a fire in the hearth, Iris helped Attie carry the dishes to the sink in the kitchen.

"Does it even matter if we wash them?" Attie sighed. "This place might not be standing tomorrow. Although if anything of this house survives, watch it be the kitchen sink."

Iris turned on the faucet and began to scrub anyway. "I need to tell you something."

Attie's attention sharpened. "What? You used the sword tonight, didn't you? I saw that your hand is bandaged."

Iris grimaced. "Yes, but there's something else." She paused, handing Attie one of the cups to dry. "I found a key."

"To the realm below?" Attie whispered.

Iris nodded. "And I made plans with Kitt earlier tonight, that the two of us would meet him north of the river, so he could pass off a key to us or, at the very worst, smuggle us to his parlor door. He wants to accompany us below. But now that I have a key . . . I think we should just go to the closest door we can find tomorrow, after we have our families in a safe place. Because if we crossed the river and met up with Kitt with me carrying a sword and you a violin, it would be too risky."

Attie was quiet, weighing Iris's words.

"You're sure, Iris?" she said, hanging the clean teacups on the rack hooks. "I can only imagine how much you'd like to see Kitt before everything happens. For him to go with us."

For a moment, Iris couldn't speak. The bandage around her hand was now damp, and the cut on her palm began to throb.

"Yes, I'm certain," she finally said, handing Attie another cup. She forced a smile, to ease the sadness in Attie's expression. "I'm sure I'll see him tomorrow. When all of this is over and done with."

47

Where All the Traitors Lay
Their Heads

Roman stirred, his face pressed against warm stone. He felt heavy, weighed down. His head was aching, his mouth parched. The air tasted of sulfur and rot, and he could hear the hiss of steam, the boil of liquid.

He opened his eyes and saw that he was in the heart of the under realm. Yellow bubbling pools, cloying shadows, scattered skeletons, dancing steam. How odd that it felt familiar to him. But when he tried to move his hands, he felt resistance, followed by a clang of iron on rock.

Roman studied his body like it wasn't his. He was too numb to acknowledge what he saw at first, but then the past came rushing back over him like a cold, sobering tide.

He remembered Iris sitting on the desk at the *Tribune*, her legs wrapped around him, her hands in his hair as they came together. He remembered Dacre's accusations and questions in the parlor. He remembered how he had answered, regrets peeling away like calloused skin, and the agony that had followed.

This was the fate of Dacre's traitors. To slowly die, shackled amongst steam and shadows.

No, Roman thought, yanking on the chains. They were fastened to both his wrists, their rusted edges cutting into his skin. He tried to stand but they weren't long enough to permit him to, and old, brittle bones crunched beneath his boots.

He yanked on the chains again, feeling blood begin to drip down his forearms.

There was a whoosh of icy air above him.

He froze, but he could see the shadow of wings rippling over the sulfur pools. The eithral screeched, a sound that made the hair rise on Roman's arms.

Don't move, Kitt. Don't speak, don't move.

Iris's voice whispered through him. A memory of a golden field, her body against his as she held him to the earth. Breathing with him. Commanding him, desperate to keep him alive.

Roman eased himself back down to the stone floor and sat among the bones. But he could see the eithral circling back, as if the creature sensed he was near and was intent on finding him.

Don't move.

Roman closed his eyes, sweat trickling down his temples.

This was the fate of Dacre's traitors. The people who defied him or disagreed with him. The ones who broke away from his hold.

Dacre didn't heal their lingering wounds. He didn't mask their pain and wipe their memories again, forcing them to start anew.

He fed them to his monsters.

48

A Door You've Passed
Through Before

The *Inkridden Tribune*'s headline broke the morning in two. Into a *before* and an *after*. Blissful ignorance and terrible realization.

Iris stood at the Attwoods' front window and watched as Dacre's ultimatum spun up a fury in the street. People were leaving their homes, carrying valises and precious belongings, anxious expressions on their faces. Some were heading north; others were rushing southward, toward, Iris hoped, a safe building.

She watched the panicked exodus, her stomach roiling.

She hated how familiar this felt. She hated how she saw Avalon Bluff every time she closed her eyes.

Tobias had left at first light, to drive the roadster home and pick up his parents. Attie had given him the address of the McNeils', their prearranged meetup and shelter for the rest of the day. And he was right to leave before the newsboys flung papers onto door stoops, because after eight o'clock, the streets were so clogged and chaotic that Iris didn't think a vehicle would be able to pass through.

"I need to go get Sarah," Forest said as he came to stand beside Iris at the window. "Do you think she's at the *Gazette,* or should I run to her father's first?"

"I bet she's already in the office. She was always one of the first to arrive at work." Iris wondered what was currently unfolding at the *Gazette.* How Zeb would be bewildered and envious that the *Inkridden Tribune* had stirred up a frenzy, and then furious to see his front page had been altered.

Although Iris wouldn't believe it until she saw the paper with her own eyes.

She followed Forest to the street, taking hold of his sleeve. His face looked bruised this morning, and a bit swollen around his right eye, but his gaze was clear and focused. Iris could tell he was already kilometers away in his mind, imagining which route he would take to reach Sarah.

"Bring her to 2928 Thornberry Circle," Iris said. "The McNeils' house. We'll be waiting there for you."

Forest nodded. "We might be late, if she's at the *Gazette* and we need to go back for her father."

Iris bit her lip, wanting to protest. But then a breeze sighed through the street, and a newspaper fluttered against the curb. Just from the headline font, Iris knew it was the *Gazette.* She reached down and picked it up, smoothing the front page.

She couldn't explain the feeling that bloomed in her chest to see her sneaky article right there, front and center, on the first page. To an unsuspecting reader, the block of text would seem to only be a strange list of addresses, with *continued on page three* at the bottom. She thumbed to the third page, Forest frowning as he leaned closer to see what she was doing. And there, another block of addresses. Another, and another, with an explanation of what they were.

THESE ADDRESSES ARE KNOWN OR SUSPECTED TO BE ROOTED ON MAGICAL LEY LINES, AND CAN PROVIDE SHELTER DURING THE BOMBING.

"If you and Sarah and Mr. Prindle can't reach the McNeils' in time," Iris began, setting the *Gazette* in Forest's hands, "go to one of the addresses listed here, or a building you know has magical tendencies. It should keep you safe."

Forest finally understood. A light sparked in his eyes as he threaded his fingers through Iris's hair and kissed her brow.

"Did I ever tell you how proud I am of you?" he said.

"Yes, but I'll never grow tired of hearing it," Iris wryly countered.

"And also . . . I like your new haircut. It suits you."

"Did you *just* now notice it, Forest?"

He only smiled as he stepped into the street. Newspaper tucked beneath his arm, he turned and melted into the crowd.

Iris stood there awhile longer, trying to tame her worries. Worries about Forest and Sarah, Tobias and his parents. Marisol and Lucy and Keegan, still on the city outskirts. About Roman, and what he would think when Iris and Attie failed to show at their appointed meet-up.

She traced the iron key, hidden in her trouser pocket.

"Are you about ready to go?"

Iris glanced behind to see Attie walking down the front steps to join her at the curb.

"I think so."

"There's porridge and eggs on the table if you want any. Papa insisted on everyone eating a good meal before we set off."

"I'm not sure I can eat at the moment."

"Same." Attie grew quiet, shielding her eyes against the morning rays. "It's strange to say this out loud, but I didn't know what I would think."

"About what?"

"About how many of our neighbors packed all their valuables in a valise and went *north*."

Iris was quiet, watching people pass by. Families arriving from the northern side of the river, families fleeing from the south side. Some people who were simply spinning in circles, confused and weeping. Some people who acted like everything was normal, attempting to carry out their daily routines.

She had overheard a few panicked individuals say all southern gates and waypoints out of the city had also been barricaded and blocked by Dacre's army. No one could leave Oath; they could only choose which side of the river to shelter on.

"I thought more people I knew would refuse to kneel to Dacre, but I suppose I was wrong." Attie shrugged, but Iris could tell how hurt and sad she was.

"Sometimes," Iris began, "I don't think we know what we're made of until the worst moment possible happens. Then we must decide who we truly are and what is most important to us. I think we're often surprised by what we become."

They stood shoulder to shoulder for a while longer, silently lost to thought.

Attie finally broke the quiet. "Here. This is for you." She pressed a smooth and sticky ball into Iris's hands.

"What's this?"

"Wax for your ears," Attie explained. "As much as I want you to hear me play, it'll be best if you don't. I don't want you falling asleep on me."

Iris hadn't even thought of that, but she shivered in relief. Of course she also would be vulnerable to the spell of Attie's music if she heard it below, and she tucked the wax away into her pocket for later.

"Will you play 'Alzane's Lullaby' for me when this is over?" Iris asked. "Aboveground, that is."

Attie smiled. "I promise."

A ten-minute walk took nearly half an hour.

Iris held Ainsley's hand as they followed the path Mr. Attwood forged for them through the teeming streets. He carried a small caddy with Lilac, who emitted a steady stream of plaintive meows, inside. Attie was close behind, her youngest brother perched on her back, her violin case strapped to her chest. Mrs. Attwood's fingers were woven with those of both twins, one on each side. But it was still a difficult feat to stay together as they jostled shoulders with strangers and tripped over abandoned items in the streets. As they went with the flow as well as fought against it.

Iris's knees felt like water, her clothes damp with perspiration, when they finally reached the McNeils' front door.

Mrs. Attwood rang the bell, but Attie was already shaking her head.

"It doesn't look like they're here, Mum."

"Let me knock, then. I don't think they would go north . . ."

Iris studied the house. The shutters were bolted shut. No lights were on. The door was locked.

Mrs. Attwood slumped as the truth sank in, her face creasing with worry.

"We can find another place," Attie said confidently. "What about the museum?"

The museum was as enchanted as it was spacious. A building with hardly any windows. It would also provide some distraction as the hours passed.

"A good choice," Mr. Attwood said. Lilac mewed in agreement. "But we need to hurry. It's going to be a long walk in this traffic."

"We need to leave a note for Tobias and Forest first." Attie opened her violin case to pull out a sheet of music.

Iris found a tube of lipstick in a discarded purse, handing it to Attie. She wrote in big red letters over the musical score: *TOBIAS & FOREST, WE ARE AT THE MUSEUM!!* before she pressed the sheet to the McNeils' front door with a piece of the wax she had given Iris.

From there, they headed farther south to downtown, painstakingly weaving their way through the crowd.

It was nearing eleven o'clock—only one hour until impact—by the time the museum came into view.

To Iris's shock, there was a crowd at the doors, as if every nook and cranny within were already taken by people who had read the *Gazette,* desperate to find safety. There was no chance of the Attwoods finding room, and Iris began to feel panic tingling at her fingertips.

"Mum, where are we going?" Ainsley asked, exhausted from the walk. "I'm thirsty."

Mrs. Attwood didn't reply, her eyes scanning the impossibility before them.

"What other enchanted buildings are close?" Attie whispered to Iris. "I'm trying to think but my mind feels scrambled . . ."

Iris stood up on her toes to study the tall structures around them. The sheathed sword was heavy, and she rolled her aching shoulders. She thought of the list she and Tobias had made, and the one place they had forgotten about.

"What about Gould's?"

"The café?" Mr. Attwood said, overhearing.

"Where the tea never grows cold, and the scones are always warm. It's not far from here." Attie shifted her brother on her back. "I think we should at least walk by and see if it's full."

They pressed on through the crowd. Iris felt the tension dissolve from her bones when she saw there was plenty of space inside the café. A few waiters were even serving tea and cake to customers, as if the bombs weren't coming.

"Here, my loves. Let's sit in that booth on the far wall," said Mrs. Attwood, her relief nearly tangible.

The siblings slipped into the big booth, as far away from the windows as possible, with Lilac in tow, and while Mr. Attwood went to the counter for a pitcher of lemonade and some sandwiches, Attie pulled Iris to the side.

"I'm going to go back to the museum," she said. "To tell Tobias and Forest where we are when they arrive."

Iris licked her chapped lips, tasting salt from her sweat. She couldn't ignore the sinking feeling in her heart, like her chest had caved in. It had taken them so long to get from one point to the other, she didn't know if Tobias and Forest would be able to catch up to them.

"Okay," she said, ignoring that twinge of dread. "I'll figure out if there's a door here we can use."

Attie nodded. "Good. I'll be back at ten till."

"Be safe," Iris said.

She watched as Attie slipped back into the street, where the crowd was thinning as noon approached. Uneasy, Iris walked around the café, her eyes searching for a door that might shift its threshold. She passed by the table where she had once met Sarah on a rainy morning, then the table she had sat at with Roman, sharing tea and sandwiches, not so long ago. She traced the back of the chair as she passed, tears in her eyes.

Stay sharp, stay strong, she told herself. *Focus for just a little while longer. This will be over soon.*

Roman had mentioned that Dacre's doors preferred to be close to hearths. But there was no fireplace in the café, and Iris was beginning to think she would need to scout for another door in a different building when a waiter approached her.

"Lovely sword you have there. Would you like a cup of tea?" he asked, extending a dainty cup set in a saucer. "Compliments of the goddess."

Iris startled. "*Enva* was here?"

"No," he said with a smile. "This is simply our way of saying *Dacre can return to the hell he came from.*"

"Oh." Iris gave a shaky laugh. "I'll drink to that. Thank you."

She sipped the tea, surprised by how it settled her stomach, and continued to walk around the café. Or perhaps it wasn't the tea but the bravery, the unexpected comradery. She looked at the people who had gathered, some of them with their valises and bags brimming with valuables, others with nothing but the complimentary tea and cake the café was doling out. There were people in their older years, others who looked quite young. Some were dressed in suits and heels, others in uniforms or grease-stained jumpsuits. One woman sat with a shawl wrapped around her shoulders, a poetry book cradled in her slender hands.

And yet they were all connected by their decision to *stay.*

Iris watched as the café owner and some of the waitstaff began to carry out large panels of wood, to nail over the windows outside. Mr. Attwood and Attie's brothers rushed to help, and the light inside gradually waned as the sunshine was blocked out.

Iris continued to meander around the café, down its crooked corridor, where the kitchen was brilliant at the end of the hallway, beckoning her with its light and the aroma of fresh blueberry scones. She passed the lavatory, the very one she had read Roman's and Dacre's letters in, and the key in her pocket warmed.

She paused, gazing at the door.

This was it, then. A threshold that would shift.

She drained the rest of the tea and rejoined Attie's family at the booth, a lantern set on the table to provide better light.

But the minutes continued to tick away. Soon, the clock on the wall read eleven forty-five, and Attie had yet to return. The air in the café was beginning to feel anxious and grim, and Iris couldn't stay still.

She walked to the front door and gazed out into the street of Oath.

It was empty now.

It looked eerie, abandoned, even under the full brunt of the midday sun.

At five till noon, Iris's fear had fully hooked her heart. She crossed her arms to hide how her hands were shaking.

"I'll go after her," said Mr. Attwood.

Iris turned to see he was standing behind her, also gazing beyond the door, waiting for Attie's return. If he left now, he wouldn't make it back to the café before noon.

"Let me go instead, Mr. Attwood," Iris offered. "We're planning to—"

"*Wait,* there they are!"

Iris whirled back around. She opened the door, the bell above ringing as the heat of the day washed over her. Tobias and his parents were rushing behind Attie as she led the way into the café.

There was no sign of Forest and Sarah.

Iris swallowed that realization like it was a jagged piece of ice. It scraped down her throat. She felt irrevocably cold.

"We're back," Attie announced, for her father's sake. Then she turned to Iris and whispered, "I'm sorry. I stayed as long as we could, but Forest and Prindle never showed."

"I'm sure they sheltered elsewhere," Iris said. She glanced at the clock again. Two more minutes.

Attie drew Tobias and her father off to a private corner. Iris knew she was breaking the news to them, and she led the Bexleys back to the booth. She formally met Tobias's parents, shaking their hands and offering a smile.

"We've heard so much about you, Iris," Mrs. Bexley said warmly. "It's nice to finally meet you. Tobias told me to bring my deck of cards so we could hopefully pass the time faster. Would you like to join us?"

"I would love to, Mrs. Bexley," Iris said, fighting tears. "There's something I must tend to first, but maybe after that?"

"Of course. We'll save you a spot."

Iris nodded, her feet leaden as she moved aside for the waiter. He brought out the last of the complimentary tea, the last of the cake. It felt like the dying gasp of normalcy, a final vestige of life as they had once known it to be.

It occurred to Iris, then, that she would need something to leave a trail below. She asked for a few biscuits, and the same waiter who had given her the cup of tea handed her three blueberry scones, still warm from the oven.

"I'm not sure what you have planned," he said, eyeing the hilt of her sword again, "but I do hope you're successful."

Iris didn't have a chance to reply to him; Attie called for her over the murmur of conversations, violin and bow in her left hand. Iris walked across the café to meet her friend.

Tobias appeared stricken. His lips were pursed, his eyes downcast. But he stood close behind Attie, his fingers woven with hers. Mr. Attwood looked stunned as well, but there was also a sheen of pride in his eyes as he gazed at his daughter, holding her instrument in a public space.

"I told them everything," Attie said. "Did you locate the door?"

"Yes. It's over here."

Iris wove around the tables. Attie's violin drew more stares and whispers than Iris's sword, and she was thankful when they reached the cover of the corridor.

The key grew warm in her pocket again. Iris brought it out into the dim light, let it lie flat on her palm. For a moment, no one spoke or moved. They merely stared at the under realm key until a distant boom rattled the walls.

The first bomb, and it didn't feel far off.

"One of Dacre's tactics is to bomb and devastate, and then bring his forces in to scavenge and plunder," Iris said, glancing up at Mr. Attwood. "I'm going to unlock this door so we can pass through it, and then I'm going to lock it behind me. So this threshold won't remain active, but it's still something to keep in mind."

Something to keep in mind if we fail, Iris finished inwardly. But she didn't want to speak that possibility aloud.

"How long will you be gone?" Tobias asked.

Iris and Attie exchanged an uncertain look. There was no way for them to know.

"We're not certain," Attie replied. "But we hope it won't be too long."

Another bomb rattled the walls. A few waiters rushed by, disappearing into the kitchen. The electricity flickered.

"Ready, Iris?" Attie said, and while she appeared confident, Iris saw how she still held Tobias's hand, as if leaving him was the last thing she wanted to do.

Iris nodded and faced the door. She held the key up to the knob, amazed when she saw a keyhole form. She slipped the key into it and turned, the door popping open.

She smelled it first, the scent of the under realm. Damp rock and cold musty air. Carefully, she drew the door open and stared down the passageway. It was a steep stairwell hewn in the pale rock, and it descended into thick, cobwebbed darkness.

"Tobias?" Mr. Attwood said. "Will you bring us the lantern that's at the booth?"

Tobias quickly obliged, his fingers slipping from Attie's. Within seconds, he returned with the lantern in hand, passing it to Iris.

"Thank you," she said, unable to hide the warble in her voice. But she was grateful for the light, and she took her first step down, and then another.

Iris paused when she realized Attie wasn't behind her.

"Do you remember everything I taught you, Thea?" Mr. Attwood was saying.

"How could I forget, Papa?" Attie countered mirthfully, but it sounded like she was about to cry. "I used to think I would play in the symphony one day."

"Yes, and all those hours you devoted to that dream, playing in secret." Her father paused, caressing her cheek with his knuckles. "Now I see all those moments prepared you for this one. I'm proud of you, sweetheart. Be careful."

He kissed her brow. Attie rapidly blinked back tears.

Tobias stepped forward next to embrace her. She rose on her toes to whisper something in his ear, and he listened, his fingers splayed over her back. Whatever the words were, he relinquished her, but his eyes burned through the shadows, following her as Attie took her first step down.

"Return to me, Thea Attwood," he said.

Attie spun to look back at him. "In case you didn't know, I have nine lives too, Tobias Bexley."

That drew a small smile from him, but it faded as Attie took another step down into the musty under realm. Tobias flinched, like he wanted to follow her into the darkness.

Iris could hardly breathe as she reached for the door handle. "I'll bring her back safely," she promised.

"We'll be waiting here for you both," Mr. Attwood said, setting his hand on Tobias's shoulder.

It took everything within Iris to close the door, to watch the light fade with the motion. But she did, sealing off one realm for another. She slipped the key into the hole and locked the door behind herself and Attie.

49

The Weight of Fifty Wings

Tobias stared at the lavatory door, his heart pounding as Iris turned the lock from within. He took two deep breaths before reaching for the knob, unable to help himself.

He opened the door to see it was just the lavatory. Black-and-white-tiled floor, a commode, a sink with a speckled mirror, floral wallpaper.

Attie and Iris were gone. Vanished, as if they had never been.

"Let's return to the table," said Mr. Attwood.

Tobias nodded, despite the fact that he could have stood there for hours and stared at this door, waiting for them to return. He would wait for however long it took, even if the walls collapsed.

But he couldn't forget the words Attie had whispered in his ear, just before she had left.

Please watch over my family while I'm gone.

He walked with her father to the booth, where his parents were speaking with Mrs. Attwood. Attie's siblings were huddled close together, the sweetness of the lemonade and cake long since forgotten as another bomb dropped, splitting the air like thunder.

Tobias sat on the bench beside Garrett, one of the twins. The boy's eyes were wide with fear, his shoulders hunched. Another bomb dropped, closer this time. The dishes rattled; the paintings shivered on the walls. In the kitchen, it sounded like a stack of plates had overturned and shattered.

Tobias reached into the small leather pack he had brought with him from home. His mum had thought he was going to take his trophies, his ribbons. All the objects that embodied his success on the racetrack. But he had reached for his old car collection. His wooden toys from childhood.

He set one on the table and nudged it to Henry. Then one to Ainsley. Hilary. Laven. And last, to Garrett at his side.

"I used to race these all the time when I was your age," he told them.

Another bomb fell. The ground shuddered and Ainsley cried out, but she clutched the wooden car to her chest.

"Which one of you thinks they can beat me?" Tobias asked.

"I can!" Garrett was swift to reply.

"No, me!" Laven insisted.

As the siblings began to talk about who thought they could win, admiring the different details of their assigned cars, Tobias glanced up and met his mother's gaze. There was a smile on her face, a glimmer of tears in her eyes. He had never seen her wear such an expression, and he had to distract himself before the emotion snared him.

"All right," he said, setting the last car on the table. "Let's race."

Helena sat at her desk in the *Inkridden Tribune*, smoking her ninth cigarette of the day. Her feet were propped up beside her typewriter, whiskey sparkled in a glass by her elbow, and she was gazing up at the ceiling tiles when the bombs began to drop.

She was alone in the office, but that was how she wanted it to be.

She drew in air, the scent of the *Tribune*. She breathed out smoke.

The bombs shook the earth and split the afternoon, one after the next after the next. Cracks crept across the ceiling. Dust rained down in streams. The pipes groaned and the electricity finally flickered off.

Helena let her feet drop to the floor. She drank a sip of whiskey and reached for the paper on her desk, feeding it into the typewriter.

It was so dark she could hardly see, but a stream of sunshine still found its way through the small window in the wall behind her. The light spilled across her desk, cut through the paper like a fiery blade.

She hadn't written for herself in a very long time.

And as Oath crumbled around her, she did the only thing she could manage. She lit another cigarette, and she began to type.

Marisol stood beside Keegan on the hill, gazing at Oath in the distance.

They had marched the army kilometers back to take shelter in a valley, and a breeze was blowing from the west. The sun was at its zenith, and Marisol shielded her eyes, watching the eithrals swoop through clouds and glide between the skyscrapers, their wings iridescent in the light as they dropped the bombs.

Marisol had counted twenty-five eithrals. The most she had ever beheld at one time.

Smoke and dust soon rose, making it hard to see as the southern half of Oath began to collapse.

"Keegan," Marisol said, a sob breaking her voice. She covered her mouth with her hand, but the name slipped between her fingers again. "*Keegan.*"

It was the only word she could say. Her wife's name, for within it was everything Marisol loved and dreamt of. It was strength and comfort, safety and wildness. A past and the present and the future.

Keegan pulled her close. Marisol pressed her face to her chest, where Keegan's heart pounded. She felt the stars pinned on her uniform bite into her cheek, but Marisol welcomed the pain as she closed her eyes.

Once, months ago, Marisol had dreamt of life returning to normal after the war ended. How life had been *before* the war. She had thought their days could eventually return to such an era, as if they had never been touched by this storm. But as she felt the ground tremble, Keegan's arm tightening around her, she knew how naïve she had been.

Some scars might fade in time, but others never would.

Marisol would never forget that day in the Bluff. How it had changed her. Left a mark on her soul.

And she would never forget the day Oath fell.

Forest held Sarah's hand, crouched behind a parked motorcar in the street. He had found her at the *Gazette* and she had wanted to return home for her father before they met up with the others, as he had predicted.

But Forest hadn't expected the streets to be overflowing, chaotic. The trams had shut down, and Sarah lived a good distance from Broad Street, toward the southernmost part of the city.

The bombs had started before they could reach her neighborhood.

"We're almost there," Sarah whispered, but he could feel her trembling. "Just a few more blocks."

Forest swallowed. His adrenaline was like fire in his blood, but he could also feel the nausea and fatigue settling into his bones. He hadn't taken his medicine that morning, and his side was aching.

He needed to get them to shelter, but he wasn't familiar with this part of the city. He had also given away the *Gazette* he had been carrying to a hysterical father with three daughters.

Forest dared to look over the hood of the motorcar. "We need to—"

A bomb exploded on the next street over. Bricks and shingles arced through the air. Splintered wood and fragments of glass and pieces of furniture spilled onto the road. Sarah cowered and screamed, but Forest never closed his eyes. He never let go of her hand, and through the smoke, he saw a clear path to a house with an open door.

He didn't care if it was ordinary or enchanted. They needed cover.

Forest drew Sarah up and began to run, keeping her as close to his side as he could.

He glanced down at his shadow, spilling across the broken cobblestones and debris as he sprinted. He watched as his shadow grew two long wings, until it was not his shadow at all but that of something else, blocking the sun as if the moon had eclipsed it.

A cold shiver rattled his spine. He quickened their pace, looking up again, his eyes on that open door.

"Forest," Sarah panted. "*Forest,* my dad!"

"We're almost there. Keep running, Sarah."

They were three strides away from the door when there was a startling bright light, as if a star had fallen. A pressure in his ears, a boom that he felt in his chest.

Even then, Forest never let go of her hand.

50

A Lullaby for Doomed Lovers

R oman had been sitting quiet as a statue for some time now, his eyes closed as the eithrals' wings beat the air overhead, when he heard the distant note of a flute.

It startled him. He couldn't keep his arms from jerking, the chains clanging in response.

One of the eithrals spotted the movement.

It swung down and landed directly before him with a screech, the ground shuddering beneath its clawed feet. The sulfur pools on either side of Roman began to rise, threatening to bubble over and burn him.

He couldn't breathe past the fear, but he stared at the eithral. The creature opened its mouth, revealing bloodstained teeth and rotten breath, and let out another screech that made Roman's heart falter. He winced, clapping his hands over his ears.

The eithral was lunging for him, ready to snap his body in two, and all Roman could think was *I'm not ready for this.* But the impact never came. More notes claimed the air, shimmering like rain in the sun. A spell had been cast. A command given by flute.

The creature stopped suddenly, flinging its head up in resistance. Roman fell backward, sprawling on the stone, trembling. He watched as the eithral spread its sinewy wings and took flight, following the sound of the flute as more notes were given.

Roman lay like that for a while, feeling like his bones had melted. He stared up into the drifting steam, and he listened as the notes continued to ring through the under realm. Eventually, he sat forward with a groan, and he saw something strange in the distance. A pillar of sunlight, breaking through the shadows.

It was the steam vent, he realized. It had opened, and the eithrals were flying out.

The bombing had commenced, and a surge of scalding anger overtook Roman.

He screamed, hoarse and desperate, yanking on his chains. He pulled until the shackles cut deeper wounds at his wrists and he bled again. He screamed until his strength dwindled and his lungs felt small and tight, his heart broken by anguish.

Roman slid to his knees, kneeling among the skeletons.

He stared at that pillar of light. A chill spread through him, like frost creeping over his skin, when he realized it would be the last time he saw the sun.

It was quiet as a tomb in the under realm.

Iris led the way down the stairs, remembering the words Enva had told her in the dream. *Pay attention to the floor. The way it slopes. It will guide you through the many passages, taking you deeper into the realm.* She also remembered what Roman had told her about the lowest level of this place, where the eithrals dwelled and could be commanded by a flute.

She still had Val's flute in her pocket, alongside the key, the ball of wax, and now three blueberry scones. All important items to carry on a death mission below.

When the stairs at last fed into a corridor, Iris chose to take them to the right, because the floor angled downward. She left a crumb of scone on the ground every time she and Attie made a turn, so they could find their way back. But she also paid attention to the clusters of malachite, which were so beautiful they made her pause to admire them.

"What do you think these crystals are for?" Attie mused aloud, tracing their green facets.

"I wonder if they're supposed to be a map, or road signs," Iris said. "A way for people to know where they are?" Roman had described seeing amethyst clusters on his walk beneath Oath.

"A lovely thought." Attie wiped the dust from her fingers. "But why have they overgrown into the passages?"

"Maybe when Dacre slept, wild things took over?"

Thoughts teeming, the girls continued onward.

"Do you think there are rats here?" Attie asked as Iris set another crumb down.

"I hope not." If rats came along and ate her trail of scones, then they would never find their way back to the café door. But so far they had only passed thick curtains of gossamer and spiders with eyes that winked like rubies in the lantern light.

Soon, they came to an intersection, and Iris was surprised to see the fire-light that burned in iron sconces on the walls. She hid her lantern behind a cluster of malachite and studied the different routes they could take.

"Wait," Attie said when Iris began to step forward. "Do you hear that?"

Iris froze, straining her ears. Two breaths later, she heard what Attie did. It sounded like boots marching on the stone, drawing closer.

"Quick," Iris said, moving back the way they had come. "Hide."

The girls ducked behind an outcropping of rock and mineral. Iris held her breath as the footsteps drew closer. She dared to peer around their hiding place to see a stream of Dacre's soldiers, marching through the intersection. Rifles were propped on their shoulders, packs fastened to their backs.

It was as Iris suspected. Dacre would wait until he had pummeled the south side and then call back the eithrals. His soldiers would then emerge through select doors to round up anyone who had survived.

It was Avalon Bluff, repeated on a larger scale.

Which meant Iris and Attie were running out of time; they couldn't afford to have an interruption like this. Just when Iris was thinking they might need to double back and return above to find another doorway to pass through, the end of the soldiers' line came in sight.

The girls waited a few beats before they rose and hurried to the intersection. Iris chose the passage with the steeper angle again, even though it was darker than the others.

She could hear her breath, feel her heart pound in her ears by the time they reached a door. It looked similar to the one Enva had shown her, with runes carved into the lintel. Like in the dream, it was locked.

"Is this it?" Attie whispered.

"Yes," Iris replied, although she didn't know for certain. But she brought out the key and watched as it fit, unlocking the door.

This time, the passage they walked was overgrown with vines and thorns. Iris had to break her way through, feeling the briars catch in her hair, drag like talons across her face. She might have stopped in discouragement had she not seen the light in the distance. A hazy yellow beacon, woven with the sharp scent of sulfur.

"We're almost there," she panted to Attie, hope warming her blood.

Twenty-one thorn-infested steps later, the girls arrived at the boiling heart of the under realm. Iris gazed into the steam, amazed by how vast this place felt. She noticed that the vines ran along the treacherous floor but soon faded, as if they were only there to mark where this passage was located. She turned and looked behind, to see the lintel was thick with thorns, and also noticed the malachite that had grown along it, nearly hidden.

We need to find the doorway marked by thorns and malachite when we return, she told herself before easing forward.

Iris and Attie walked around the pools, stepping over skeletons and iron chains. The sight made Iris shudder, but she continued to break up pieces of scone and leave a trail, her skin shining with perspiration.

All too soon, the melodic notes of a flute hung in the air. One second, they sounded distant, the next, close enough to touch. Iris tried to follow them, and it was impossible until she saw a pillar of light in the distance. That should be their marker, she realized, and she began to lead them toward it, using the last of her scone crumbs. That was where Dacre would be, playing the flute to command the eithrals as they flew above.

It felt like they had walked for an hour, chasing those notes and that beam of sun, although it was most likely only ten minutes, when Iris heard someone screaming in the distance. She froze, Attie halting close at her back.

"Do you think that's real?" Iris asked, her voice thick. "Or is it just an illusion?"

"I don't know," Attie said.

They didn't have time to investigate and help. Iris moved forward, ignoring the nagging guilt in her stomach. The sour taste in her mouth. The way her heart lurched when the screaming finally fell silent.

They drew closer to the light, the place where the world above touched the realm below. She finally saw Dacre, standing in the sun as he blew notes on the flute, his face and hair gilded as if he were a myth from an old tome. He was beautiful, mesmerizing. The sight made Iris both furious and sad, to see such divinity and what it could be, and to know it was nothing more than ruthless ambition.

"Ready, Attie?" Iris whispered, her fingers wrapping around the sword's hilt.

"Yes," Attie replied. "Don't forget the wax!"

Iris *had* forgotten it amidst the wonder and terror of the under realm. She reached into her pocket and found the wax ball, quickly dividing it and then stuffing some into each ear.

It was like sinking underwater.

She could no longer hear the hiss of the pools, the ringing magic of Dacre's flute. She could no longer hear Attie's voice or her footsteps, or the first note her friend coaxed from the violin strings. Iris could only hear her own breath and her heart, pounding a steady rhythm in her ears.

She unsheathed the sword. It glimmered, like the steel was laughing, amused to find itself reflecting the under realm.

Iris let it bite her palm. Her blood flowed like a bright red promise, and she took the hilt again.

She felt Attie nudging her.

Iris glanced behind her, only to see Attie's eyes were wide with terror, her fingers slowing on the strings as she backed away.

"Iris!" Attie's mouth shaped her name.

Iris whirled just in time to see Dacre loom over them, his eyes glowing like embers, his blond hair shimmering. He reached out his hand to strike them; the girls scattered, Iris going left, Attie going right.

Iris ran a few steps along the winding stone path, minding the pools. But she turned, watching Dacre's shadow fade through the steam. He was chasing Attie, which meant Attie had to stop playing to evade him.

Iris pursued him, sneaking up from behind. Dacre was crouched forward, preparing to lunge for Attie, who was gripping her violin by its neck, unable to play as she dodged and ducked.

With a grunt, Iris swung the tip of the sword out in a wide arc.

She knew that her cut would come up short. It only grazed Dacre's long hair. The strands instantly broke, drifting down as a thousand golden threads.

He paused, as if he felt the sting of every broken strand. Slowly, he turned, looking at Iris with such malice that it made her heart stutter.

She stepped back. He crept forward.

He smiled, revealing the flash of his teeth, and he licked them, like he was imagining how her death would taste. And then he raised the flute to his lips and blew.

Iris didn't know if Attie was playing again. She didn't know how long her friend would have to play before the magic snared him, but she was rattled by the fact that Dacre wasn't slowing. The violin didn't seem to have any effect on him, and Iris was beginning to believe that Enva had fooled her.

All you divines do is lie, Iris's mind cried as she ran from one bone-and-chain-littered path to the next, feeling Dacre gain on her. *You care only for yourselves.*

She thought he was on her heels until he emerged from the steam before her. She slid to a halt and flinched as Dacre struck her hard across the face.

She felt one of her back molars dislodge as she spun and hit the ground, only a handbreadth from a sulfur pool. She coughed up blood and her tooth. Her heart was frantic, its rhythm throbbing in her ears.

But she still held the sword in her bleeding right hand. And she was too slow as Dacre set his boot on that wrist, threatening to press hard. As he did, Iris winced, knowing he would grind every tendon to dust.

The only thing that stopped him was a sudden windstorm. Iris panted, her eyes stinging. Hair whipped across her face as she lifted her chin and saw the eithrals hovering above them, flying in circles. Dacre had called them back to aid him, and Iris didn't know if she should weep or laugh, to realize the bombing had halted, but only because the eithrals would now pick her bones clean after Dacre was finished with her.

The sight of the beasts made her incendiary. She fought and flailed, teeth grinding as she worked to slip her way free.

Dacre pressed his foot harder on her wrist. She cried out in pain as his long, cold fingers slid into her hair, moving down to her throat.

This was the end, she realized, freezing as Dacre prepared to snap her neck.

Iris swallowed, tasting the copper of her blood. The salt of her sweat.

She closed her eyes and exhaled a shaky breath, but it was strange how fear seemed to wane, leaving behind nothing but brilliant stars in her mind. And in that lacuna of darkened time, she found herself waiting for the impossible.

For the magic to still gather.

Roman held his breath, straining to hear over the gurgle of the pools around him.

To his utter shock, a violin was playing in the distance. Its wistful lullaby claimed the underworld like myrrh-hearted perfume on the wind. He had never given much thought to how music tasted or smelled, but this song was reminiscent of the brine of the winter sea, strawberry cake on the first day of spring, the fragrance of moss-covered woods just after the rain.

It cut through the rotten air that haunted this place.

Roman inhaled, drawing the music deeper into his lungs. The song was calming. It coaxed his focus inward until he was braced by yearnings so fierce it felt like his bones had turned to iron.

He wasn't aware of his strength fading until his limbs tingled with pins and needles. His mind turned foggy like a greenhouse window, but it was too late. Roman fought it before realizing it was better if he simply embraced the strange dream that beckoned to him.

He lay down and drifted off to that smoke-laden sleep.

Dacre's fingers slid from Iris's throat, his clawlike nails scoring her skin. She didn't know what had stayed his hands until her eyes flew open.

It was Enva, standing eight paces away, a creek of sulfur bubbling between them. But through the curls of steam, Iris saw her vividly.

The goddess was radiant, dressed in a blue sleeveless dress with constellations sewn along the hem. Ruby-spun brooches gleamed at her shoulders, and a golden belt was cinched at her waist. A crown made of bloodred flowers and berries graced her brow, and her hair was long and loose, dark as midnight.

Iris was so stunned by the sight of her that she could only shiver, knowing this was how Enva had looked the night she had joined Dacre below, giving him her vows. The night they had married each other, beneath striations of minerals, far from the shine of the moon and the veil of clouds. A night that had planted the seeds for this war, centuries to come.

Dacre took a step closer to Enva. He paused, transfixed by her; she held her ground as he continued his approach, his strides becoming urgent.

Iris, heart pounding in her throat, pushed herself up to her knees. *No,* she wanted to shout, but it felt like she had swallowed sand. All she could hear was the roar of her pulse in her ears, making her light-headed, but she was certain Dacre was saying something to Enva. He was almost face-to-face with her, his body taking a violent stance, and Iris lurched up to her feet, grasping the sword.

The words Enva had shared with her in the museum dream burned through Iris again, propelling her forward.

If he were to kill me as he longs to do, then he would take all my magic unto himself. There would be no end to his power.

"No!" Iris felt the word rumble through her chest. *We can't let him win this battle. We've come too far for this.*

She was about to jump over the sulfur creek when she felt someone grasp her arm, holding her back. She turned to see Attie, violin tucked under her chin and bow clenched in her right hand. Attie's curly hair whipped in the windstorm, and her eyes were wide but keen.

"*Wait*," she mouthed to Iris, resuming her playing with a seamless motion.

Iris wanted to protest, but Attie had noticed something that she hadn't. She spun around, looking at the divines again.

The eithrals continued to circle overhead, their wings churning cold, moldering air around them. Dacre's shorn hair tangled in the breeze, as did Iris's and Attie's, but the gale didn't touch Enva. Her hair remained sleek and still, her raiment like the water of a quiet pond.

Dacre raised his hand to strike her. All the tension gathered in Iris's bones; she couldn't breathe as she stared at Enva. Enva, who didn't move or speak but only beheld Dacre with a dark gleam in her eyes.

His fist never touched her.

His legs failed him first as he dropped to his knees before her. He wavered for a beat, as if fighting the spell that was pervading his bones, but even Dacre couldn't resist the siren call to sleep. His hand dropped limp at his side as he sank to the stone, sprawling on his back.

After him, the eithrals began to fall, one by one, from above.

Iris and Attie crouched down and huddled close to each other, the rotten air stinging their noses. But Iris kept her eyes open, watching as the wyverns crashed into the pools and the stone pathways. Their bellies split open on the impact; their scales melted in the sulfurous water. The ground shook as their wings splintered.

And then the world became quiet and tranquil.

Iris pulled the wax from her ears and rose, drawing Attie with her.

The girls stared at Dacre's supine body, Enva standing before him. The goddess gazed down at her sleeping husband before she lifted her eyes and looked at Iris and Attie.

It felt like a welcome, and the girls walked carefully along the slick stone to reach the divines.

"Enva," Iris said, full of wonder. How had she reached them here? Why hadn't she fallen to Attie's enchanted lullaby? But then it occurred to Iris, standing close enough to notice the translucence on Enva's skin. The faint shimmer of her wedding dress.

Iris stretched out her hand. Her fingers passed through Enva's arm.

It was one of her stolen powers at work. The magic of illusions and deceptions. She was here but not truly, as if she had known her presence was a fated thread in the tapestry of Dacre's demise.

Enva didn't seem to be able to speak, but she indicated Dacre with a tilt of her head.

Iris stared down at him, sensing his coldness. He looked younger and softer in sleep, and Iris thought of what could have been, and what could still be now that he would be gone from the world. Extinguished like a flame. His soul and magic turned into smoke, dissolving as it rose skyward.

Teeth bared, she brought the sword down on his neck.

It was easier and harder than she had expected. Easy, because the sword cut through bone and sinew as if Dacre were nothing more than a cobweb. And hard, because another bruise formed on her heart, marked by the killing.

Dacre's blood began to flow, a glittering gold on the stone. A sickly-sweet smell enveloped the air as Iris found herself dropping to her knees, the sword clattering from her hand. But she felt the pressure change, making her heart skip a beat.

From the corner of her eye, Iris watched as Enva's illusion evanesced into the shadows.

51

Spilled Ichor

Roman was still dreaming when he felt the ground slide beneath him. There was the clink of iron, a hiss of steam. A painful throb around his wrists. A man's voice, cursing through the static.

"Wake up!"

A hand shook him and, when that failed to rouse him, slapped his cheek. Roman stirred, his eyes heavy-lidded and full of grit. It took a moment for the colors to return to his sight, for all the blurred edges to turn crisp and defined.

To his immense shock, he was staring up at Lieutenant Shane.

"What are you doing?" Roman asked.

"What does it look like? I'm getting you out of here." Shane took hold of his arms, dragging him up. "Can you stand?"

Roman found his feet but wobbled. "Give me a moment."

Shane supported Roman's weight but huffed in impatience. "We don't have a moment. We need to hurry. Things are evolving in ways I didn't expect, and we need to return above."

"What do you mean?" Roman took a step forward. With each passing moment, he felt steadier, although his head viciously throbbed. He flexed his hands, realizing they were free from the chains. "How did you . . . ?"

Shane withdrew a key from his inner pocket. It was still stained with Captain Landis's blood. The key that had gone missing, or, Roman realized, that Dacre had set out as bait on the table, to see which of his soldiers would swipe it.

"Why did you steal it?" Roman asked. "Are you part of the Graveyard?"

"Yes. And we need its power," Shane said, hurrying him along the path. He kicked a small skull out of the way. "We can lock or unlock any of Dacre's doorways. We can glean the resources from the under realm now."

"What about the other four keys?"

"Val is presumed dead. He never fetched Iris, if you were worried about that. We don't know where he is, but he failed to return after he brought you here. His key is unaccounted for, although I can imagine who has it."

Roman drew in a slow, shaky breath. But his bones ached when he wondered where Iris was.

"Dacre is also dead," Shane said simply. As if he were announcing a weather forecast, and not the end of a god. "But I haven't heard where his key is."

Roman tripped. "*Dead?*"

"Your girl Iris cut off his head. Brought it up to a café not long ago. Or so the rumors are spreading. Here, we need to hurry."

Roman didn't have time to process it, although when he blinked, he saw a flash of Iris, dragging Dacre's severed head by his golden hair.

He shivered at the vision.

"You left Oath to enlist for Dacre," Roman said next, slowly piecing together Shane's past. "But you never had the intention to serve him. You've been fooling him this entire time, gathering information for the Graveyard. How to kill a god. Finding a key for the underworld. Memorizing the ley lines."

"Does that shock you, Roman? Were you not doing the same?"

"He wounded me and then took me into his service against my own volition. I didn't choose him."

The men's conversation stalled when they reached the door, lined with citrine crystals and vines. Roman tried to keep pace with Shane, but his breath began to heave. His throat felt constricted, his lungs small. He paused to cough into his sleeve, numb when he saw a constellation of blood spotting the fabric.

Shane noticed through the gloom.

"You'll need to see a doctor soon," he said. "In fact, there are about to be many sick soldiers, now that his spell has broken."

Roman said nothing. He dropped his arm and continued onward with Shane, even as the incline made his chest burn. He didn't recognize the passages they wove through, but when they reached the foot of a stairwell, he stopped Shane.

"Why did you give me up to him?" Roman asked. "Why did you betray me?"

"Why didn't you deliver the message as I asked you to? Dacre would have been dead days ago, and the bombing would have never happened," Shane countered. But then he sighed, his posture softening. "Listen. When I stole the key, Dacre began to search us all, hell-bent on discovering which one of us was the mole. I gave him your account to save myself, as selfish as that may sound. And I wouldn't have cared what happened to you, save for the fact that you refused to give me up in turn. So here I am now, risking myself to pay back my debt."

"There are no debts," Roman rasped.

"In war," Shane said, "there are always debts. Now come on. We're almost to the safe house."

Iris stood on Broad Street, staring at the *Oath Gazette.* The building had been struck and torn open. Bricks, glass, twisted pieces of metal, and personal possessions sat in heaps, glittering in the afternoon light. She could see a few typewriters, half-buried in the rubble.

The *Gazette* was gone.

The fifth floor had been blown away, its remnants scattered like chaff. She knew she should be feeling something, but her chest was numb.

Forest had come here first, for Sarah. Chances were, they had gone to her place, to be with her father.

Iris turned, her eyes sweeping the street and the jagged new skyline of buildings that had collapsed or had disintegrating walls. It was unrecognizable; it felt like she had never stood in this spot before, where the tram tracks cut grooves into the cobblestones.

Where did Sarah live? Iris didn't know for certain, although she'd heard Sarah mention a neighborhood in the southern reaches of Oath. Remembering, Iris had to bite down her panic.

I'll find them. They're safe. They're fine.

She began to walk, climbing over debris. The slices on her palms began to bleed again. She could hardly feel their sting as she picked a path through the rubble.

Should I head north, to the Kitt estate?

She paused, torn between venturing farther south for Forest and Sarah, or pressing north for Roman. A few young men ran past her, wielding guns, their excited voices carrying on the warm breeze. The sight should have scared her, but Iris could only blink in their wake. She was overwhelmed by the wreckage. How would they ever rebuild this? It would never be the same, feel the same.

More people were beginning to venture out into the streets. In the distance—the way she had come from—voices were cheering and shouting. She knew it was at Gould's Café, which had stood unscathed during the bombing, suffering only two cracked windows, ceiling tiles that had been knocked loose, and multiple broken dishes. That was where she had left Dacre's head. Champagne was popped and passed around, as well as more biscuits and cake in celebration, but Iris had slipped away through the crowd after she had ensured Attie was safely reunited with her family and Tobias.

Iris began to wander, hardly knowing where she was going.

She didn't know why she felt so hollow. Why she didn't feel like celebrating Dacre's death. Surely, the war had now come to an end. But then why did she sense that something else was brewing? Like another shoe was bound to drop.

"Stop it, Iris," she scolded herself, shaking away her pessimism. "Where are you going?"

She finally realized where she was. She walked through more wreckage, only stopping when three young men approached her. They bore guns, but they looked at her in awe.

"Are you the woman who cut off Dacre's head?" one asked.

Iris was silent. But she couldn't hide the ichor that was splattered over her trousers, staining her clothes. Dacre had bled and bled after his head had rolled away. It had made her gag, retch.

She walked past the men, felt them stare at her as she kept walking. Soon, she reached the place she both longed and dreaded to see, uncertain if it had survived.

The building with the *Inkridden Tribune*.

It still stood, although most of the windows had blown out, and a portion of the walls from the uppermost floor had crumbled. Iris was gazing up at it when she heard a familiar voice.

"What are you doing here, kid? I thought I gave you the day off."

Iris turned to see Helena on the other side of the street, smoking a cigarette. Her heart leapt to see her boss, hale and alive albeit rumpled and bleary-eyed, and she hurried to embrace her.

"Don't worry, I'm fine," Helena said, awkwardly patting her back. "And before you ask . . . the *Tribune* pulled through, also. What about Attie?"

Iris nodded, tears welling in her throat. "She's okay."

"Good. Now what in Enva's name are you doing out here, alone and—" Helena was interrupted by a sudden peal of gunfire.

Iris jumped, pulse quickening as she crouched down. Helena took hold of her arm, rushing her toward a pile of rubble for cover.

"Listen, kid," Helena said, stomping on her cigarette. "You need to get home or stay with people you trust. The streets aren't safe, and they won't be that way for a while. Not with the Graveyard emerging from their dens."

"The Graveyard?" Iris repeated. "Why would they be coming out and firing at people? At a time like *this,* after what we just survived?"

Helena raked her fingers through her hair. "Because the chancellor's dead. A god is also dead, if the rumors are true." She noticed the ichor stains on Iris's clothes. "They're rounding up Dacre's soldiers. To execute them."

Roman and Shane passed over the threshold to the realm above.

The light was dim, but as Shane locked the door behind them, Roman could see they were standing in a decadent bedroom. Floor-to-ceiling curtains were drawn over the windows, but a slice of sunlight limned a four-poster bed and a massive mirror, ornately trimmed in gold. The carpet beneath Roman's grimy boots was plush and soft.

It was the sort of bedroom his parents would have, which meant they must have emerged somewhere north of the river, in one of the wealthier neighborhoods.

"Where are we?" Roman asked, his voice hoarse.

Shane didn't reply. He moved to the bedroom door and opened it, slipping out into the corridor.

Roman followed, but when they reached the foyer, Shane came to a startled halt.

Soldiers rushed back and forth from one room to the next, overturning parlor tables and chairs, taking shelter behind anything they could find, including a grand piano. Their guns were ready, their faces tense, like they were about to engage in a skirmish.

"We need to get out of here," Shane murmured as he spun, taking hold of Roman's upper arm. "Quickly. Back to the bedroom door. This place isn't safe."

Roman didn't understand what was happening, but he could sense the pressure that was building, like he had swum down to the darkest, coldest depths of a pond.

It reminded him of the trenches. The moment before the barrage.

A line of Dacre's soldiers jostled past him, hissing orders at each other. Confusion, bewilderment, and desperation hung in the air, and Roman was as eager as Shane to get away from it when he saw a soldier slumped against the wall, coughing into his sleeve.

Blood dripped from his chin. Pain glazed his eyes. His face was remarkably pale.

Roman stopped.

He knew the sound of that wet cough. He could taste it at the back of his mouth, and he knelt before the soldier.

This wasn't someone who had willingly fought for Dacre, despite the uniform he wore and the forces he was among. This was someone who had been wounded and nearly killed by the gas, and then healed just enough to serve, his mind scrambled by Dacre's magic. Someone just like Roman.

"Leave him," Shane said, panic clipping the words. "We don't have time!"

Roman was not about to abandon this person. He eased the man's arm over his shoulders and helped him rise.

"Can you walk?" he asked.

"You should . . . leave me," the soldier said, coughing up more blood. "The Graveyard . . . is coming to kill us . . ."

"We need to get you to a doctor." Roman glanced down the hallway, but Shane had vanished. Shane had left him behind, and while Roman was grateful he had saved him from the prison below, he couldn't help but think how cowardly the lieutenant was now. To run and hide when the end was nearing. "Let's try to leave out the back."

The two of them limped down the corridor, arriving at a sunroom. Through the glass walls Roman could see figures crouched low, running through the gardens. Individuals who wore masks to hide their faces, rifles in hand, coming closer.

Before Roman could turn around, a rock sailed through the glass wall. No, not a rock, but something round and metal, ticking as it came to a stop on the floor.

His eyes widened.

"*Run*," he whispered. He turned and dragged the soldier with him, back down the corridor. *Run*, and yet he felt like his legs were knee-deep in honey. Like he was in a nightmare, and everything was slow and resistant.

He counted five pulses, five beats in his ears, before the grenade exploded.

It blew out the walls.

Roman and the soldier went down, where they both remained dazed, sprawled over the floor. Pieces of the house were scattered around them. Dust coated their clothes, snuck down their throats, making them both cough.

Roman lay on his back, stunned. He stared up at the crystal chandelier that dangled crooked on the ceiling above him. Glittering through the smoke.

His ears were ringing, but he could hear the crack of gunshots.

We need to get out.

A shadow rippled over him, blocking the view of the chandelier. Roman wheezed as he felt someone take hold of his shirt, pulling him up from the rubble.

"Round up any survivors," the stranger said, tightening his grip. There was a bright red anemone pinned to his waistcoat. "It's time the people of Oath witness justice."

Iris was almost to her flat when she heard footsteps echoing off the piles of rubble. It sounded like someone was running *after* her. She stiffened, glancing over her shoulder to scan the growing shadows.

The sun was setting, and Iris had decided to return home, hoping to find it still standing and her brother safe within its walls. After parting ways with Helena, she had witnessed firsthand the unpredictability of the streets. She had seen valiant recovery efforts as people drew survivors from collapsed buildings as well as chaos as the Graveyard ran rampant with their guns.

"Forest?" she called.

The footsteps grew louder. She could see someone sprinting down a side street, heading in her direction. When they finally emerged into the clearing, the light spilled over them.

Iris's breath snagged.

The person was wearing a mask. A member of the Graveyard. They had a broad set of shoulders beneath their dark clothes, betraying a strong build. And they were running directly at her.

Iris spun and dashed toward the closest rubble pile. She could feel the distance closing between them, and her heart was frantic as she ripped a piece of pipe from the debris, pivoting to face her attacker.

"Miss Winnow!" the man cried in a rough voice as she threatened to strike him with the pipe. He held up his hands and came to a stop. "*Miss Winnow,* it's me."

She gaped at the stranger. She had no idea who he was, and she kept the pipe between them.

He relented to pull off his mask.

It was Mr. Kitt's associate. The man who had once followed and threatened her. Handed her money to null her vows to Roman.

"Get away from me!" She swung the pipe again.

He easily dodged it. "Listen!" he shouted. "We don't have time. I need your help."

Iris didn't trust him. She began to bolt again, slipping past him, until his words chased after her.

"It's Roman! They're about to kill him on the firing line."

Iris halted. Her blood went cold as she turned on her heel. "*Who* is about to kill him?"

The associate stepped closer. "The Graveyard. He was captured among Dacre's soldiers, and they are taking no prisoners. I couldn't convince my comrades to let him go. They want *proof* of his innocence. Do you have anything? Anything at all that could keep him alive?"

Iris's thoughts reeled at this revelation, but she bit her tongue, focusing. She had all his letters that he had written to her from Dacre's side. She still had the Hawk Shire letter, even though Roman had once beseeched her to *burn my words.*

"*Yes,*" she whispered. "I have a letter. In my flat, if it survived."

Mr. Kitt's associate broke into motion, taking her hand and pulling her through the rubble. He was strong, kicking debris out of their way, cutting through the remains of a collapsed house to get them to their destination faster. Iris didn't know if she should be thankful or afraid that this man knew exactly where she lived, but when they finally reached her street, every thought and feeling melted away.

Her apartment building still stood.

She dashed tears from her eyes as she raced up the stairs. The front door hung open; it was dark inside, the electricity still out.

"Forest?" she cried, ragged. But there was no sign of her brother. Only Val's dead body lay on the living room floor, and she leapt over the corpse to rush into her room.

Mr. Kitt's associate lingered just outside the door, but she could hear his labored breaths.

"Hurry, Miss Winnow," he said.

She fell to her knees and reached beneath her bed, yanking the hat box out from the shadows. She threw off the lid and began to sort through all the letters, her hands shaking. But there it was, creased and smudged, but very much legible.

Burn my words.

"I have it," she said.

Roman thought he was dreaming when he saw Iris in the crowd.

His hands were bound, and he stood against a brick wall. He was in a line with fifty-one other soldiers; prisoners of war who the Graveyard was about to execute without trial.

Beyond the firing line, a group of onlookers had gathered. Some were cheering, others looked troubled. Roman felt dizzy, overcome by the jeers, the noise, the sight of people pleased to see his death.

His knees trembled.

He thought he was about to faint until he saw her. Iris was pushing her way to the front. Her face was scratched and smeared with dirt, speckled with luminous gold. She was holding up a piece of paper and shouting but her voice was lost amongst the roar.

That was when her eyes locked with Roman's.

"Ready?" a voice called.

The line of rifles lowered.

Roman couldn't stop it. He couldn't stop Iris from moving forward. He couldn't stop her from coming between him and the bullet.

"Iris," he pleaded, but only he could hear her name. A whisper in the chaos. *"Iris, no."*

She moved through the crowd like the world would bend to her. Her gaze remained fastened to his as if nothing could come between them. No gods or war. Not even the sting of a mortal wound.

"Aim!"

Let our breaths twine and our blood become one, until our bones return to dust.

A sob broke his breath.

Even then, may I find your soul still sworn to mine.

Iris passed the firing line, hair tangling across her face, her boots pounding over the blood-soaked cobblestones.

"Fire!"

She came between Roman and the rifle just as gunshots cracked through the air.

52

What Could Have Been

I ris froze.

    She was aware of only three things.

    The high-pitched whine of bullets.

The way the soldiers in the lineup jerked and fell forward, crumpling face down on the bloody cobblestones.

And the way Roman stood and breathed, untouched by the gunfire. How he looked at her.

His eyes were wide, frantic. They burned with horror as he waited to see the blood bloom across her shirt and spill down her chest. For her to collapse with the others.

But Iris remained standing. Her lungs continued to fill with air; her heart continued to pump furiously within her.

She turned to stare at the man who had been prepared to shoot Roman. His face was concealed by a mask, and he still held the rifle, pointing it at her. But he had never shot.

"Get out of the way, miss!" he shouted.

"Put the gun down," she said. Her legs were shaking from the run; sweat trickled through her hair. She was so relieved she had made it in time that she had to swallow down the acid in her throat. "You are about to shoot an innocent man."

"These soldiers are not innocent."

"I have proof." Iris held up the letter. "Roman Kitt is the only reason why so many of Enva's forces survived. He was secretly giving away Dacre's plans and movements for weeks now. If not for him, none of us would be standing here, breathing, so I will tell you one more time. You have committed a terrible war crime by shooting these soldiers without a trial. And you need to lower your gun."

The silence that followed was uncomfortable, weighed by shock. A tall man in a mask stepped forward to meet her. Only then was the last rifle lowered, and she sensed he must be important in some way to the Graveyard. Perhaps their leader.

He extended a gloved hand. Two flowers were pinned to his dark jacket—a white and red anemone. They struck a strange contrast with his arrogance, and Iris gritted her teeth. But she gave him the letter.

She watched as his eyes sped over the lines. When he was done reading, he met her gaze. He took in her ichor-stained clothes, which she was now very thankful for. The scratches on her face, the stray thorns in her hair. The bruises on her arms and the nail marks on her neck. All testaments of her journey below.

"Part of what she claims is true," the man said to the crowd. "This letter is a warning about the Hawk Shire attack. Although I require more proof. How do I know the enigma of R. is *this* man? How do I know you didn't type up this letter yourself to save him?"

Iris's skin flushed with ire. She was opening her mouth to reply, but another voice beat her to the moment.

"I can speak on her behalf."

The crowd parted to reveal Keegan. The stars pinned on her uniform shone in the fading light, and her face was stern. Her voice was powerful, and her stance was one that didn't threaten but commanded respect. She carried no gun and held up her hands when the Graveyard swung their rifles toward her.

"I am unarmed," she called. "I want a peaceful discussion, as do the soldiers in my brigade, some of whom call Oath home and are your fellow *citizens* who have been fighting in this war for *months*. People who have bled and gone hungry and have given up time with their families. They deserve to have a say in what happens to their home in the coming days, as well as to lend their voices to what happens to the soldiers who fought for Dacre, who— given the *laws* of the realm and the mere *decency* of humankind—should be taken as prisoners and treated humanely. So do as Iris Winnow politely asked of you. Lower your guns and let us engage in an intellectual, democratic discussion about what is moral as it is just, and how we are to move forward to begin healing from this."

The Graveyard leader was displeased, but he handed the letter back to Iris before motioning for his followers to drop their weapons. As Enva's soldiers moved forward through the crowd, breaking up the executions, Iris hurried to Roman.

He was on his knees, gasping.

She knelt before him, touching his pale face with her hand. He felt so cold, like he was carved from marble. Fear struck her heart when she saw the bloodstains on his sleeves, the wounds on his wrists. She didn't know what had happened since the last time she had seen him, but she sensed that his story would tear through her like rusted steel.

"You're safe, Kitt," she whispered, drawing him into her embrace. She wanted to weep, feeling how he shook and wheezed for air. She caressed his hair. "You're safe with me."

He pressed his face to her neck. When he wept, she felt empty of words, like they had been scraped clean from her bones. There were only her hands, her arms, and her mouth, pressed to his hair.

And she wept with him.

If Roman was being honest, he didn't remember much after that moment when Iris had come between him and death. The hours that followed were strange ones, slipping by like he was in a fever. He felt lost in a swirl of storm clouds and smoke, and while he could hear and see, he couldn't take those moments into his memory.

But when he fully came to again, he found himself lying in a hospital bed, an intravenous needle in his hand.

He stared up at the ceiling, listening to the quiet bustle of nurses and doctors, the click of wheels, a whimper from two beds down. He was afraid to fully acknowledge where he was until a svelte older woman with short gray hair and brown eyes stopped at his bedside.

"How are we feeling, Mr. Kitt?"

"I'm *not* Mr. *Kitt,*" Roman ground out. But then he realized how rude he sounded, and he sighed. "I'm sorry."

"There's no need to apologize," the doctor said with a hint of a sad smile. "Do you want to tell me the history of your symptoms, starting when they began?"

Roman hesitated, his chest tightening when he remembered Avalon Bluff. But he let his hands relax at his sides, realizing that he was safe here. And he needed to open those old scars so they could heal.

He told the doctor everything. How long he had been feeling his symptoms, and what made them worse. How he had breathed in the gas at Avalon Bluff.

The doctor listened and recorded it all down on her clipboard, but then she placed her stethoscope on his bare chest and asked him to breathe. Roman did as she requested, anxious to look at her face. When she drew back, her expression was inscrutable, but there was a hint of sorrow in her voice.

"I would like to take an X-ray of your chest," she began, "but I can tell you what I believe it is, due to the dozens of patients I've already seen and treated today for conditions identical to yours."

"Tell me honestly, Doctor," Roman said.

"Your lungs have scar tissue, which was created by the gas you were exposed to. The scarring makes it difficult for you to breathe, as you described, and it has also created stress on your heart. There's no surgery or medicine that will fully treat this condition, but there are things you can do to help ease your symptoms when they worsen. Most of all, you will need to make adjustments in the days ahead, to ensure you are taking care of both your lungs and heart. Otherwise, this condition can be fatal, leading to cardiac arrest or making you susceptible to consumption."

Roman was silent.

"Do you have any other questions?" she asked gently. "If not, I'll send one of the nurses over to start your first breathing treatment and to administer some medicine."

"Yes," Roman said as he stared into the distance, at the white walls and faint blue curtains, dividing patients from each other. "When can I leave?"

"When you've been cleared, both by me and by the new chancellor."

"The new chancellor?"

"Yes. She's requested that all of Dacre's soldiers be held either in the prison, or in the hospital if they need medical attention."

Roman swallowed his panic. "I'm not a soldier."

"I know." The doctor squeezed his shoulder. "Don't let this worry you. Focus on your recovery, so that I can discharge you soon. Your family is also keen to see you. We can't admit visitors due to the circumstances, but your mum and Iris are both thinking of you and are eager to have you back."

The doctor moved on to the next patient.

But Roman's heart quickened, pounding until his breath wheezed. He wanted to go home; he wanted to be with Iris. And yet how long would he be here, cloistered in the hospital?

Chilled, he laid his palm over his breast. Over the hollow ache of his heart.

It was noon and humid, like summer had devoured the last weeks of spring. Iris paused to wipe the sweat from her face. The muscles in her arms and back were sore from all the hours she had spent moving rubble aside, but she wouldn't stop. Not until they had recovered all the people who had died and were still buried beneath stone and brick. Not until they had rescued all the survivors, although as the days continued to progress, the chance of finding people still alive was greatly diminished.

Iris didn't dwell on this fact, though, for one simple reason. It had been three days since the bombing, and she still hadn't found Forest.

He's fine, she thought as she pushed herself to work harder, scraping through piles of crushed rock until her fingernails broke.

But it wasn't just the fact that her brother hadn't appeared yet. Two days ago, the hospital had refused to let her visit Roman. The last time she had seen him, he had been lying on a gurney, surrounded by nurses who were rushing him into the infirmary. She had held his hand until she was forced to relinquish him, uncertain whether he had felt her touch or heard her voice.

Iris raked her fingers through her damp hair. She let her anger fuel her as she continued carrying bricks and twisted pipes and broken window frames to the wagon bed. Again and again, until Helena brought a canteen of water.

"You need to take a break, kid," she said, looking Iris over with a worried gleam in her eyes. "Why don't you collect names for a little while?"

Iris drank the water. She wiped her mouth and said, "No, I'm fine. Thank you, though."

She left Helena gazing after her, and worked for another hour. Then another. Any time someone called for assistance, she lunged to join them, wondering if they had located Forest and Sarah, trapped beneath the debris, waiting to be drawn up to freedom.

Whenever a body was found, it was gently carried to an appointed spot in the street, to be identified. Helena would record the names of the deceased to print in the next day's paper, for while many buildings in downtown had been demolished, both the *Tribune* and the print factory had survived. And the paper was the best way to circulate news as Oath sought to find balance again. The city was struggling for many things it had taken for granted, like electricity and clean water, hot meals, and making sure the hospitals had everything they needed to treat the wounded.

The *Inkridden Tribune* was helping people who had been separated find each other. Or at the very worst, have closure for their losses.

Dusk had fallen when Iris chose to finish the day on a southern street she had never seen before. It had been badly bombed; only a few of the houses were still standing. She was carefully picking through the rubble when she heard one of the men, farther down the street, shout for assistance.

Iris couldn't explain why it chilled her. Why her dust-streaked hands, raw and scored with a hundred scratches, began to quiver.

But she ran to where the man was kneeling on a small hill of debris. She was careful as she knelt beside him, peering down at what he had found.

It was Forest and Sarah.

Iris stared at them as if they were strangers, unable to fathom what she was seeing. Her brother, bruised almost beyond recognition. He had shielded Sarah with his body, but it hadn't been enough. The heap of rubble had killed them both, hands entwined.

They would never breathe again. They would never laugh and argue and grow old together.

Little Flower.

Iris turned away and slid down the pile.

She took two steps and then fell to her knees.

It felt like she was drowning. Like she was swallowing mouthfuls of water, and everything was burning. She gasped before she doubled over, holding her hands to her sides because if she didn't, her ribs would splinter.

Iris was vaguely aware of the people around her, holding her up. Helping her stand. Helena and Attie and Tobias, coming into focus.

But in her mind, she was far away.

She was broken by what could have been. By what now would never be.

53

A *Tribune* That Bleeds

When Roman realized the *Inkridden Tribune* was the only newspaper being printed in Oath, he began to request it every morning from his hospital bed. The first thing he did was read through the list of names on the front page. Names of all the people who had been killed and people who were still unaccounted for. He then read news on the war trials, which had started under the new chancellor and a panel of judges.

It was within the *Inkridden Tribune* that Roman read the fate of his father, who was one of the first citizens to be put on trial.

Mr. Ronald M. Kitt has been found guilty on three charges: First, for being a willing accomplice in the transportation of hazardous gas. Second, for conspiring with the enemy and harboring them without proper counsel or boundaries. Third, for knowing of the plan for mass destruction, and for doing nothing. His sentence is seventy years in prison, with no chance of parole.

Roman shivered when he realized his father would die in prison. He also read the fate of two other people of interest:

Dr. Herman O. Little, Professor of Chemistry at Oath University, and his daughter, Elinor A. Little, are hereby proclaimed guilty of war crimes and sentenced to life in prison, for the creation and production of hazardous gas and bombs that were used as a weapon against civilians and soldiers.

Roman turned the page. He could almost see his former fiancée again, how guarded her demeanor had been on the one lunch date they had been forced to share.

On his fourth morning waking in the hospital, the patient beside him succumbed to his wounds, unable to breathe through the scarring of his lungs. Everyone on the third floor was a victim of the gas, and Roman stared at the empty bed for a while before fresh sheets were spread and a new patient was admitted.

The nurse brought him the *Inkridden Tribune* along with his watered-down coffee and breakfast, and he went through the routine he had created, hungrier for words and knowledge than for food. First he read the names of the deceased and the missing, then the trial reports.

He wasn't expecting to see a name he recognized among the dead, and he froze. Not one name but two, close together as if linked by invisible threads.

Sarah L. Prindle
Forest M. Winnow

Roman stared at them until the words blurred. He could taste pond water; he could feel his sister's limp weight in his arms. The way his stomach had ached like it had been sliced open. How his heart had beat itself numb as he carried her home.

The grief tore through him, just as sharp as it had been that day four years ago.

Roman hurled the blankets off his legs, the newspaper scattering. He overturned his breakfast tray. Coffee and eggs spilled across the bedsheets, but he hardly noticed. His bare feet hit the floor as he yanked the intravenous needle from the back of his hand.

He was leaving this place. These walls couldn't hold him any longer, and he strode to the doors, halting only when a security guard intercepted him.

"Get back in bed."

"I need to see my wife," Roman said.

"You can see her when the doctor clears you."

Be rational to convince him, Roman thought, but his next breath was a string of curses. His voice rose until the doctor appeared. She firmly took hold of Roman's arm, escorting him back to bed.

"Take a deep breath," she said, securing the needle to his hand again. "Have you forgotten what I told you? It's not just your lungs you need to worry about."

"I don't care anymore," he said through his teeth.

"Is that so?"

"You need to let me out. My wife . . . she lost her brother. I need to see her."

The doctor sighed. "I'm sorry to hear that, but we've all lost someone in this war."

"Will you at least let me call her?"

"I can't make any exceptions now that the trials are in progress."

Roman let out a scathing laugh. "And how long do you plan to hold me here?"

The doctor merely stared at him until he flushed and glanced away. He could only imagine how wild he seemed, screaming obscenities at the guard, insisting on being released.

"That," the doctor said, "depends on you."

Roman sat back. If there was one thing he was good at, it was accepting a challenge.

Two days later, the doctor discharged Roman with a list of prescriptions and strict instructions to rest. A soft rain was falling when he emerged from the hospital in borrowed clothes. He walked over broken cobblestones and piles of rubble, passing only a few people who darted past with umbrellas or newspapers tented over their heads. But Roman didn't mind the rain, and he began to head east, toward Iris's flat.

When he came to an intersection, he paused. He wondered if Enva was close by, coaxing the storm clouds with her magic, and a shiver raced over his skin. It was odd to be standing in a place that only days ago had been vibrant and full of life. Motorcars and buggies and wagons and bicycles. Now he seemed to be the only one breathing its air, remembering how it had once been.

"Roman!"

He turned and saw Iris farther up the street. She was drenched through, her dress nearly translucent, hair plastered to her face. But he knew then that she had been waiting for him to emerge from the hospital.

He ran to her.

They collided in the center of the bomb-torn street. Roman stumbled backward, clinging to her. He would have lost his balance if she hadn't used her strength to hold him upright.

"I believe I'm quite good at this," Iris said. She pressed her face to his neck, chuckling to hide the sob in her words.

Roman held her close, feeling her chest rise and fall with her breath. He remembered the golden field of Avalon Bluff. The way she had sprinted to him, pressing him down to the earth. Covering his body with her own to protect him.

"And what's that, Winnow?" he said. "I have an entire laundry list of things you're good at doing."

Iris laughed again. A beat later, she leaned back to meet his gaze, rain gleaming on her face.

"At taking you by surprise, Kitt."

54

Dear Iris

THREE MONTHS LATER

Iris stood before her flat, holding an empty box. She had been delaying this for weeks, preoccupied by far too many other important things that needed her attention. But she knew it was finally time. She needed to go through her things, deciding what to keep and what to leave behind before she sold the flat. It was time to sort through her mother's belongings, as well as Forest's.

"We don't have to do this today," Roman said. He stood close beside her, their arms touching. The wedding ring shone on his left hand, a silver band to match her own. He also carried an empty box, although Iris knew she wouldn't be able to fit her entire life into two crates.

"I know," she said, gazing up at the sky as storm clouds rolled in. The first few drops of summer rain began to fall, sizzling on the hot pavement beneath her boots. "But I don't want to put it off any longer."

She smiled at Roman, to ease the crease of worry in his brow.

"Together, then?" he said.

"Yes, together," Iris agreed.

They headed into the shadows of the flat just as the storm broke.

Iris went through her belongings in her room first because it would be easiest. She thought she would struggle to leave things behind, like she was surrendering ghost after ghost. But it was more liberating than she had anticipated.

She kept a few of her favorite skirts and sweaters. Her boots from the trenches. A pearl bracelet that had been her nan's. All her books, and the horse figurine that had once graced her desk at the *Gazette*. Her typewriter was already in the new flat she and Roman were leasing, as well as most of her essentials.

In many ways, it felt like she had finally outgrown the skin that had been her childhood. With every object she left behind, it split a little more, until she suddenly felt like she could take a full breath. It was okay for her to leave behind the sofa and the old teacup her mother had used as an ashtray. The sideboard with all the melted candles from powerless nights. The painting on the wall that Iris had always hated because it made her sad every time she looked at it.

When she stepped into Forest's room, which had belonged to their mother before him, the two crates were full.

"Let me find another box," Roman said.

He left the front door open, so Iris could hear the rain. The flat soon smelled like petrichor, and the fragrance steadied her heart and her hands as she began to go through her brother's belongings.

He didn't have much. Growing up sleeping on the sofa and sharing a wardrobe with his sister had given him no choice but to be content with little. But he did have a leather messenger bag at the foot of the bed.

With a sigh, Iris opened it.

She let the contents spill out over the mattress. She hated how it felt like she was snooping until a letter drifted from the bag, settling on the mattress. It was folded, written on yellow work paper. *Little Flower,* the outside read, in Forest's messy handwriting.

Iris stared at the letter, thunder rumbling in the distance. When her heart finally quieted, she picked up the paper and sat on the floor to read it.

Dear Iris,

I have a confession: your friend Sarah has been visiting me. Or, I have been inviting her to stay for dinner. At first, I thought you had put her up to it, to check on me while you're away. But then I realized that she is just as lonely as me. We both miss you, so, in a sense, you have brought us together.

I have another confession: I went to the doctor, like you asked me to. I realize now that I had no need to be afraid of my scars. There was no need for me to be afraid to tell the doctor the true story of what happened to me. I don't know why it fills me with shame, but it still does. I'm hoping it fades in time.

Maybe one day I will write it all down. I think I'd like to tell you everything. But for now, I am content just to share these words with you. I hope you know how proud I am of you, and how I think you are brave, returning to the front. I want to tell everyone I pass on the street that you're my sister. That Iris E. Winnow of the Inkridden Tribune *is my sister.*

Come home soon, Little Flower. I can't wait to see you again.

Love, your brother,
Forest

She hadn't understood why she had waited so long to spread Forest's ashes, but now she did. She had been waiting for his words. For his letter to find its way into her hands.

Iris had given their mother's ashes to the field of Avalon Bluff. And she decided somewhere in the east would be more fitting for her brother. A place that was green and promising, with hills that never seemed to end.

Tobias drove her, Attie, and Roman kilometers north of Oath. There was a hill, he told her, that made it seem like you were the only one in the world when you stood upon it.

Iris climbed it alone, carrying the urn with Forest's ashes.

It wasn't a steep hill, but the grass was long and verdant from summer storms, and wildflowers bloomed, thick and dusted with pollen. When Iris reached the crest, she was awed by the sight that unrolled before her. Valleys and sparkling creeks. Patches of evergreens and birch trees.

"I think I've been here before," she whispered to the wind, remembering the place Enva had showed her in the dream. A goddess she might never see again, but who Iris knew still walked the streets of Oath in disguise.

Iris opened the urn.

She held it for a breath before turning it over. Eyes burning, she watched Forest's ashes spill into the breeze, becoming part of the land. The pines and the grass, the vales and the streams. Iris would have been content for a while, standing in ankle-deep wildflowers, but then she felt the first drop of rain on her face, mingling with her tears.

Another summer storm was billowing in, and Iris hurried back down the path to the road, where Tobias, Attie, and Roman waited. The roadster shone bright as a newly minted coin, even with all its dents and marks and flecks of mud from the road.

Iris slid into the back seat with Roman, while Attie sat up front with Tobias.

"Where to next?" Tobias asked, cranking the motor.

"Where to?" Attie echoed. "It's about to *rain,* Tobias."

"This car has outlasted more storms and flat tires than I can count." He met Iris's gaze in the rearview mirror. "What do you say, Iris?"

Iris smiled. "To home."

Tobias turned the motorcar around, shifting into second gear. They sped along the road, leaving thunder and swells of rain behind. Iris was tempted to glance back at the hill she had given to Forest, but a break in the clouds stopped her. A ray of sunlight pierced the gloam up ahead, promising a blue-skied afternoon.

Roman reached for her hand, weaving their fingers together.

Iris closed her eyes, savoring the warmth of his palm against hers. The way the wind blew through her hair. The sunlight on her face. And for a moment, it almost felt like she had wings.

55

The Last Word

ONE YEAR LATER

Iris knelt in the garden.

Her flower beds were coming to life as the days grew warmer and longer, and the first green unfurling of vegetables was breaking the soil. She smiled as she plucked weeds from the aster and daisy patches, and then she shifted to the rows of dirt, feeling how dry the soil was.

She was just about to rise and fetch her water pail when a triangular folded piece of paper crashed into the loam, right at her knees.

Iris glanced up, not at all surprised to see Roman regarding her from the second story window. His elbow was propped on the open sill, his chin on his palm, and he only smiled as he waited for her to read his message.

"Are they ready for me?" she called up.

"You'll have to read the note to find out."

She scowled up at him, but it was playful, and she enjoyed their games as much as he did. She took the paper in her dirt-stained hands and unfolded it, reading:

Dear Iris,

I'm sure they're an absolute waste, but pages 81–104 are waiting for you on the kitchen table. If you hurry, the perfectly˙ brewed pot of tea will still be warm.

Love,

Your Favorite

Kitt

˙always up for debate

P.S. If I hand over too many pages at one time, I have an inkling my dense prose will put you to sleep, Winnow.

Iris smiled, but when she looked back to the window, Roman was gone. If she listened, though, she could hear the metallic clink of his typewriter as he returned to his manuscript. She could hear the birds flit through the shrubs and sing from the willow tree in the neighbors' yard. She could hear the distant rapids of the river, which was a short walk from their tiny town house, a stone, ivy-laden structure that had withstood the bombings, located on the edge of the park.

Iris tucked the page into her pocket and rose.

She knocked the dirt from her coveralls and left her boots at the back stoop, stepping inside the very cramped but cozy kitchen.

On the table, she found pages 81–104 tucked beneath the corner of her typewriter, just as Roman had promised, and a pot of tea that still steamed. Iris poured herself a cup, stirred in far too much milk and honey, and then sat in her favorite chair and read Roman's pages.

They were beautiful, transportive. Every time Iris read a new chapter of his, she felt as if she belonged within the story. It was about a boy who sailed a ship in the clouds, and the adventures and challenges and friends he met along the way. It was not always a happy story, although it was an honest one, and hope never faded for the boy and his friends, even in their moments of loss and grief.

She also found two typos and had three questions about a side character's motivations, and so she took up the fountain pen Roman had left beside the teapot, and she wrote them down on the page margins. Sometimes she thought he intentionally left typos behind, just to see if she would catch them.

She always did.

Tea drained to the dregs, Iris gathered up the pages and climbed the stairs to Roman's favorite place to write, which was a small nook of a bedroom at the back of the house, with a view of the river and Iris's garden. The door was cracked and she nudged it open farther; he was sitting at his desk, his fingers flying over the keys of the First Alouette.

"They're rubbish, aren't they?" He turned in the chair to gaze at her, a tendril of black hair cutting across his brow. "I need to start over entirely."

"On the contrary," Iris said, walking to him. She set the pages down on the table, next to his medicine. Bottles of pills, tins of salves, and the oil that he mixed in the steam kettle to inhale when his throat constricted or his cough worsened. Treatments that helped calm and soothe his lungs and airways but couldn't heal the damage that had been done to them.

Iris leaned down to brush her lips against his cheekbone, following it up to his ear. She whispered, "They might be my favorite yet."

"Don't tease me," he replied, but there was yearning in his voice. He lifted his hand and wove his fingers in her hair, to keep her close.

"I'm not. You'll find my notes in the margins."

She kissed his palm as he reluctantly let her go. But she knew he preferred to read her feedback in private, so she moved toward the door, picking up two empty teacups on her way out.

"And don't forget, we're having dinner with your mum and nan at six tonight, and then Attie's concert is at eight. Tobias is picking us up."

"I haven't forgotten," Roman said, but he often lost track of time when he wrote.

"Oh, and one last thing, Kitt?"

"What's that, Winnow?"

Just before she shut the door, Iris said, "Check your left pocket."

· · ·

Roman shouldn't have been surprised. Iris was always one step ahead of him. But he laughed as she shut the door, and then he faced the dilemma of reading her feedback first or checking his left pocket for whatever she had craftily slipped in there that morning.

He decided to read her feedback first, thankful she caught his typos and then mulling over her other notes. He scrawled down a few other questions to ask her later, and then he reached into his pocket.

His fingers met a crinkle of paper, folded so tiny he would have never found it until laundry day.

Roman drew it out to the light. A note with typed words that said:

This is not the true message but a prequel. You'll find the other in our wardrobe, hidden in the pocket of your red coat jacket.

—I.W.K.

P.S. This only applies if you gave me new chapters today. If not, expect me to beg for them tonight... in bed.

Roman smiled. He decided he was done for the day and rose, following Iris's intriguing message down the stairs and into their bedroom. They only had one wardrobe in this house, and they shared it, their clothes packed tightly together. But Roman found his dark red jacket, and the letter Iris had just typed, tucked within the pocket.

He carried the folded page into the kitchen, so he could see her though the open doorway. She was weeding the garden, her braid falling over her shoulder, nearly touching the ground as she bent.

Sometimes, she distracted him when he was trying to write, but most of the time, he felt a deep sense of peace and comfort when he was in her presence. When he looked at her, watching her go about simple but lovely everyday tasks. When she sat in her favorite chair by the hearth and read to him in the evenings. When she woke in the mornings—always after him—and when she stole most of the blankets at night. When she came home from the *Inkridden Tribune,* smelling of newspapers and spilled coffee, full of brilliant ideas.

And that, he had come to realize, was when his best words emerged. When he was with her.

Roman unfolded the paper. He, of course, would always let her have the last word, and he read:

Dear Roman,

Books are difficult things to write, or so I hear. As the author, you will love the words one day, and despise them the next. But I'm going to echo what a very smart, very handsome, and very infuri- ating former rival once said to me:

"Keep writing. You will find the words you need to share. They are already within you, even in the shadows, hiding like jewels. —C."

I look forward to the next chapter. The one you will write in your story, as well as the one we write together.

Love,

Iris

P.S. Impossible, Kitt.

Coda

She ordered the same tea and cake every Dacre's Day when she visited the café. The same blue-eyed waiter served her each time, and while he knew her favorite order by heart, he tended to forget the exact features of her face by the time she paid and left.

To him, she was like all the other customers he encountered. A polite but reserved individual who enjoyed a table for one on the patio, so she could watch the bustle of Oath pass her by while drinking a pot of tea that never went cold.

On this particular Dacre's Day, Enva spent longer than usual at Gould's. It was springtime, and the first afternoon of the year that was warm enough to sit outside without a coat. She didn't truly need one—she had been born in the coldest reaches of the sky—but she wore one regardless when it seemed useful, to blend in among the mortals as she walked the streets and visited certain shops.

Enva closed her eyes when she felt the sunlight warm her hair. Reflexively, she reached for the iron key she wore about her neck.

Iris had surrendered it, leaving it hidden on the altar of Enva's cathedral.

And if she wanted, Enva could open thresholds and reawaken the under realm. It slept again, dwindling down to embers with Dacre's death. But as long as there was a divine breathing, it wouldn't collapse. Once, it had been home to her, even if she hadn't been able to root her windblown heart to the rocks.

The blue-eyed waiter approached her table, a round tray tucked beneath his arm.

"Another pot of tea, madam?" he asked.

Enva knew he must have noticed how long she was lingering that day. A break in her usual pattern. She smiled and said, "No. I'll take the check."

He set it beside her teacup with a bow of his head before hurrying to tend to another table. Enva overpaid, as was the norm for her, before rising and studying the tall buildings on the other side of the street. Oath had been rebuilding over the years, but there were still scars from the war, if one knew where to look.

Rather than continue on her typical route to watch the opera rehearsal, Enva stepped inside Gould's. She stood for a moment, soaking in the fluster of movement and the tart air of freshly baked scones. Slowly, she began to weave through the café. She passed by the table she had sat at during the bombing, a blue shawl around her shoulders and a poetry volume in hand. Iris and Attie hadn't realized it had been her, but Enva had watched as the girls descended below.

She stepped into the dim hallway, approaching the lavatory door.

Enva paused, staring at the chipped paint on the wood. The key around her neck warmed, and it occurred to her then. She had been captive to Oath ever since she had struck the bargain with Alzane. She couldn't break her vow and tread beyond the city gates or let the wind gather her up and carry her elsewhere. But would she have the power to travel the realm if she went below? Not just in dreams and in illusions, but with her flesh and blood?

It had been a cage to her once, but now it taunted her with freedom.

She had not seen the west with her own eyes in a long time. Or the north, the south. Beyond the borders of Cambria, where the horizon melted into the ocean. But she could sense the graves of soldiers, the loam dry and cracked without her music. Souls waiting for her to sing them onward to rest.

Enva slipped the key into the door. It unlocked with a slight shudder, swinging open to reveal the stairs leading to the under realm. Quiet, dusty, and dim.

She took a step. Then another. Her hands ached as she brought out her harp from beneath her coat, hidden and weightless in the charmed pocket she had woven for it.

Down she went, deeper into the shadows. But this place felt familiar to her, as if she had caught a glimpse of her reflection in midnight waters. It made her reminisce about the last time she had played her instrument.

It had been to sing mortals to war. On street corners and in smoky pubs. In the university yard and by the mossy riverside. But that would not be her last verse, even if she was the only divine remaining.

With her harp in hand and magic gathering at her fingertips, Enva vanished into the dark.

Acknowledgments

Dear Reader,

If you are the type of soul who likes to read acknowledgments such as these, then you know very well that behind every book is a group of people who have given their time, love, and expertise to the author and their writing. I'm always humbled and thankful when I have the chance to look back over a book's creation and recognize the many extraordinary people who have invested hours into me and my novels. It's also bittersweet to be closing the final chapter on Iris and Roman's story in *Ruthless Vows,* while it's simultaneously very exciting (because that means you now get to read and enjoy this sequel). What a journey the Letters of Enchantment duology has been for me, and I want to acknowledge the people who have made it so:

First, to my Heavenly Father. You remain the portion and the strength of my heart.

To Benjamin, my better half. There is no one else I'd want to walk through life with, hand in hand. Our words for this year: garden, growth, courage, and those honeybees.

To Sierra, always. You're twelve years old now and I savor every day I get to spend with you, even if for most of them you're sleeping while I write.

To my parents—Mom and Dad—and my siblings—Caleb, Gabriel, Rome, Mary, and Luke—for sharing in my excitement, bravely keeping up with all the books I churn out, and being a foundation and support I can always depend on. To my in-laws—Ted and Joy—and my grandparents, whose love has been a guiding light to me.

To Isabel Ibañez, one of my dearest friends and my fearless critique partner who, quite literally, saved a particular chapter or two (or three!) of this book.

To my agent, Suzie Townsend. We've been working together for eight years now, and every single one has been wonderful. Thank you for being the best publishing spouse.

To Sophia Ramos, who is a ray of light and encouragement and whose emails I always look forward to. To Olivia Coleman, for always being there for me and helping me keep up with all the important things behind the scenes. To the New Leaf team, who are a dream to work with: Joanna Volpe, Kate Sullivan, Tracy Williams, Keifer Ludwig, Pouya Shahbazian, Katherine Curtis, Hilary Pecheone, and Eileen Lalley.

To my editor, Eileen Rothschild. I will never get over that Wednesday afternoon on July 26 at 5:17 PM when you called me (but I didn't answer the phone because I thought it was a spam number from NY!), and then the email you proceeded to send me (subject line *Rebeccccaaaa!!!!*) and the incredible news you shared of *Divine Rivals* hitting #1 on the *New York Times* bestseller list, sixteen weeks after it published. It's an email I should frame on the wall (I'm sure Kitt would approve). But what a joy and an honor to share that moment with you. Thank you for loving and championing this duology.

To my incredible team at Wednesday Books, who have poured so much love and time into this duology to truly make it shine and have supported me every step of the way: Meghan Harrington, Alexis Neuville, Lisa Bonvissuto, Brant Janeway, and Sara Goodman. I could not have dreamt of a more perfect team of people to work with. To Olga Grlic, who continues to work magic on my book covers. To my production editor, Melanie Sanders, and to Angus Johnston for copy editing and ensuring I used the word "vestige" correctly (every author has those problem words they frequently switch and misuse and "visage/vestige" were mine for this book).

To my amazing Macmillan Audio team, who ensured the audiobooks for *Divine Rivals* and *Ruthless Vows* were perfect: Katy Robitzski, Amber Cortes, Chrissy Farrell, and Claire Beyette. To the incredibly talented narrators who brought Iris and Roman to life: Rebecca Norfolk and Alex Wingfield.

To my wonderful UK team, who have given this duology a loving home across the pond: Natasha Bardon, Vicky Leech, Elizabeth Vaziri, Chloe Gough, Fleur Clarke, Kate Fogg, Rachel Winterbottom, Ajebowale Roberts, Robyn Watts, and Kim Young.

To Kelley McMorris, whose illustrations of Iris and Roman are simply stunning and made such beautiful covers for the UK editions.

To the authors who joined me on the *Divine Rivals* tour and celebrated with me: Margaret Rogerson, Rena Barron, Emily Bain Murphy, and Gina Chen. Thank you for giving me your time and friendship and sharing a meal with me before each event.

To the bookstores and book-loving companies that have been a tremendous support to this series: Little Shop of Stories, Barnes & Noble, Books-A-Million, Book of the Month, OwlCrate, and FairyLoot.

There may be a few names I missed or wasn't able to mention here, simply due to the nature of deadlines and when I had to turn in these acknowledgments, and I just want to say thank you for all the love and hard work you've given to this book. It wouldn't be what it is today without you.

And lastly, to you. My readers. It is my deepest honor to share my stories with you, and I will be forever thankful for all the love, reviews, beautifuls posts, fan art, and word-of-mouth recommendations. Your support for my books has given them wings. It has been (and will continue to be) one of the greatest wonders and joys of my life to watch my stories take flight and find a home on your shelves.

Yours always in words & magic,
RJR